To Stev
Thanks for your help
Geof

The Oosterbeek Affair

– GEOF WILLIS –

An environmentally friendly book printed and bound in England by
www.printondemand-worldwide.com

This book is made entirely of chain-of-custody materials

www.fast-print.net/store.php

The Oosterbeek Affair
Copyright © Geof Willis 2014

All rights reserved

No part of this book may be reproduced in any form by photocopying or any electronic or mechanical means, including information storage or retrieval systems, without permission in writing from both the copyright owner and the publisher of the book.

All characters are fictional.
Any similarity to any actual person is purely coincidental.

The right of Geof Willis to be identified as the author of this work has been asserted by him in accordance with the Copyright, Designs and Patents Act 1988 and any subsequent amendments thereto.

A catalogue record for this book is available from the British Library

ISBN 978-178456-083-6

First published 2014 by
FASTPRINT PUBLISHING
Peterborough, England.

Dedication

This book is dedicated with respect, affection and memory of my dear grandfather, George Crawley.

From a loving grandson and close family.

Acknowledgment

I would like to thank John Crawley for his help and sponsorship with the publishing of this novel 'The Oosterbeek Affair'

Thank you to both Trevor Hing and Evonne Morton for their valued opinions

Chapter 1
The Funeral

The interminable time approached ten-thirty in the morning. Warm summer rain, on a windless grey day, steadily poured misery down upon an already depressed funeral cortege, which had gathered outside the black wrought iron gates of the church in Colerne village. Incessant rain drops shaped ringlets of water on the surfaces of evergrowing puddles. Many of the small community had made an effort to attend the inhumation, regardless of the weather. Absent were the sick, immobile, elderly or very young, all of whom were being tended at home by a future up and coming generation of young house wives or keepers. Also in attendance, from the beautifully sculpted Georgian city of Bath, was a small entourage of close family friends. Others, from various surrounding villages, had made their way in the awful weather to pay their respects. Fellow farmers and gentry, along with their wives, remained aloof from the labouring classes, the men folk discussed agriculture in general whilst the women debated the virtues of pickling vegetables and fruit, or chicken and pig husbandry. Whispering respectfully, the whole assembly solemnly awaited the hearse which would contain the cadaver of Mrs. Helen O'Dell, their lowly mutterings reflecting the melancholy mood of the occasion.

George, Mrs. O'Dell's grieving husband, was naturally unapproachable. He stood determinedly, but with great difficulty, due to his aged and arthritic body, hill farming having taken its toll. Behind his shoulder at close quarter his grandson Daniel watched silently, on hand should the old man stumble whenever any painful steps were taken. Two simple hazel stools cut from the hedgerows around the farm gave George extended stability. The inseparable pair had left the old farm cottage earlier, and had supported each other subjectively in silence whilst surveying the farmland in the valley below, recalling sweet tales of a much loved wife and grandmother.

Both now anticipated the arrival of Andrew, George's eldest son, with his wife and two children. Andrew, a brilliant surgeon, had earned his ribbons during the 'Great War', working tirelessly amongst emaciated soldiers and amputees brought back from Northern France on over crowded hospital ships. His current position, consultant surgeon at St. Mary Abbot's hospital in Kensington, kept him fully occupied, a much admired and dedicated physician.

Also missing, thus far, was Elizabeth, George's eldest daughter, who for some time has held a very high position at the Royal College of Nursing office in Birmingham.

Joy, the last of George's children, was born as a late entry into the family and considerably younger than her siblings. She married James and are *young* Daniel's parents. Daniel had been born illegitimately and within Colerne village his conception and subsequent birth was one of intrigue. Six weeks before the end of the 'Great War', during action, *young* Daniel's father, James had been involved in an incident which led to the death of Joy's other brother, also called Daniel, after whom *young* Daniel had been named. Having returned from France, after the war had ended, James soon absconded from the army without formal demobilisation. His initial intention was to find the family of his immediate superior officer, the deceased Captain Daniel O'Dell, and deliver some personal belongings and explain the unfortunate circumstances of his untimely death.

At the battle front Captain O'Dell had discovered that Private James Godwin was an under-age soldier, who at that time during the 'Great War' were classed as political 'hot potatoes'. Captain O'Dell refused him permission to follow an attack out of an entrenched position near the village of Epehy, but James ignored him and proceeded to join the assault. Captain O'Dell turned and shot James in the leg to prevent him going any further with the intent of saving his life. Simultaneously Captain O'Dell took a bullet in the back and died shortly afterwards in the bottom of the trench, cradled in the arms of the headstrong, stricken James.

James eventually turned up at Captain O'Dell's home village, Colerne, but soon became smitten with Captain O'Dell's young sister

Joy. He began an affair with her and so never initially explained the original reasons why he had appeared at the obscure Cotswold village. After the affair was uncovered he was harassed into leaving the area and spent a long time being pursued by the military police. He eventually gave himself up and told his story at a court martial and was completely exonerated, perhaps due to the British militaries low public image at the time. During James' months on the run he was completely unaware of Joy's pregnancy and eventual birth of Daniel. Joy's father, George O'Dell, had a change of heart and blessing, allowing James to marry his young daughter Joy.

Naturally George found difficulty controlling his emotions as he continually reminisced the past years, contemplating his long marriage with a dear wife whom he already deeply missed. There had been favourable periods, strenuous times brought about by seasonal farming, but also distressing occasions. One such occasion, oddly enough the incident of his son Daniel's death, eventually led to a reversal of fortunes at their farm and they managed to maintain the business in the family name. After all the mixed fortunes they had suffered during a lifetime together George and Helen never once allowed their relationship to deteriorate or affect those closest to them.

Very soon the attention of everyone was taken, and all deliberations amongst the throng ceased immediately. A car could be heard struggling up from behind the village primary school in Watergates. The noise from the engine was exacerbated by the confinement of stone wall housing and damp atmosphere in the narrow lane, especially when the driver changed gear to negotiate the bends and gradual upward slope from the valley below. The car appeared, turning the final corner, and began the short incline up Vicarage lane towards where the followers had gathered in the corner of the Market Square. Everyone stood back and allowed the "New" Ruby Austin Seven pass by. The Austin was James' pride and joy. With him was his wife and sister-in-law, Elizabeth. Following soon afterwards came Andrew and his family. They parked behind the 'Richard Walmsley' memorial and the immediate family stepped out. Simultaneously a sombre black hearse arrived with the coffin of Mrs. O'Dell, bedecked in flowers and coloured ribbons. They had to make an effort not to be seen to be disrespectfully late, and hurriedly approached the old patriarch. Each family member quickly acknowledged the beginnings of the proceedings with devotional ceremonial handshakes and pecks on cheeks. With nodding of their heads and tipping of hats they recognised and appreciated everyone who had made an effort to attend.

As the procession ambled along the flagstone path towards the west door, swifts screamed as they sped around the lower half of the church tower. Doves perched, unconcerned, on a nearby roof, whilst a black and white cat stalked the ancient gravestones unaware of the family histories lying below its stealthy paws. The noise from the rookery at Martin's Croft could plainly be heard as if the entire black dynasty was mocking Mrs. O'Dell's demise.

Inside the pallbearers placed the coffin on the catafalque in front of the altar as the verger ushered everyone into their hard wooden pews. From the pulpit the vicar began the service with a short eulogy suggesting Mrs O'Dell would be able to meet her brave beloved son Daniel who had lost his life in the 'Great War'. He then asked everyone to take up their hymn books and sing 'Abide with me'. The organist struck his first note and the congregation stood and began its morbid rendition.

After the funeral, the celebration of Helen O'Dell's life took place in the Fox and Hounds. A lavish amount of food was laid on in the back room and the bar itself was very congested. The long stone shed at the rear of the building served to take the overspill of mourners, or the odd hanger-on there solely for free drinks and food. In the alcove George was found a comfortable seat alongside his old friend doctor West and amongst the farming community whom he knew well. Both sat drinking their favourite tipple, Macallan's whisky, debating the looming menace of foreign politics and were far from being the only ones who had the German threat of invasion on their minds.

In nineteen-twenty Herbie had taken over 'The Edinburgh Castle' public house in Bath after the death of 'Jock', a much loved landlord. Herbie was now married to Sarah a very sympathetic lawyer who, along with her then colleague Alfie, and the indomitable Rob Goode, had saved James from the wrath of the military police, and subsequently a possibly biased British army court martial. After the war the brewery had offered up 'The Edinburgh Castle' for a peppercorn rent on the proviso that the building next door be kept as a hostel for wounded ex-soldiers. Stothert and Pitt, the largest private employer in the city, financed the project.

Herbie was explaining to James the current situation. "Eighteen years have passed since the war finished and everyone has left. The less severely wounded and the shell shocked victims have long been reintegrated back into society whilst most of the worst cases, who are still alive, have been settled in special needs homes in the countryside. Except for a couple of homeless people the hostel is now empty and falling into disrepair. The building is a waste really but no-one wants to do anything about using the place for anything else."

Rob stepped in. "Ironically from what I can gather we're going to need that institution again and not in the too distant future. Reports have come back from Europe that Hitler has rearmed the Rhineland and already his Luftwaffe is immense compared with our paltry air force." Rob held his right arm up in resignation of Hitler's intentions. His experiences of war were all too apparent. He'd lost his left arm and the same side of his face during the last major conflict, as well as continuing to live with pieces of shrapnel which were still lodged inside his fragile body.

Young Daniel was now standing by his father. He had his own opinions on what would happen and butted in. "We have a German teacher at school and he is adamant there will be another significant war. In Parliament and along the corridors of power, rumour has already suggested that the Royal Navy should expand. Britain needs to upgrade all of its ground force equipment within the army in preparation for a serious conflict. He is convinced a war is imminent."

Other people overheard his comments. One in particular, Ed Moses, now a friend of them all and retired from the military police. Ed was one of two men who had pursued James across the south west of England before bringing him to a military court martial. He asked the young man why he thought another war would happen.

"A new conflict has been talked about for several years but no one has done anything about Hitler and his up and coming henchmen. Baldwin, the prime minister, is indecisive. He is too old and thinks that Hitler will abide by the 'Treaty of Versailles'. No chance! Hitler is an expansionist! First of all he will gain full military control of Germany, if he has not already achieved that aim. This issue is complicated because their constitution was altered, possibly in nineteen thirty two. When Hindenberg died in nineteen thirty four the role of President and Chancellor were amalgamated and Hitler became outright leader of the

German state, which included the Supreme Commander of the armed forces. He now has the final word, and is in the ultimate position to control the invasion of his border countries. He is almost sure to sack the generals who do not agree with him and install pro-Nazi sympathisers instead. Not only that, Mussolini conquered Abyssinia last year and the League of Nations did nothing about the situation but talk around the table. Hitler and Mussolini are now hand in hand, gun by gun. Effectively they are in cahoots with each other." The subject excited Daniel. He understood the geographical-politics of what he had said but would his diminutive audience believe him. Someone tapped him on the back. He glanced over his shoulder and was told his grandfather needed him. He nodded in acknowledgment. "I'm afraid I have to go now, I have to take George home," he told them and went immediately to his grandfather's aid.

Rob stole a glance at his old friend Herbie and tried to smile. His injuries to his face had eased over the years but still looked ghastly, especially to young children. Few of his friends took any notice anymore. He often joked that he was just a part of the 'broken furniture' but in the same breath hoped he had never let his wife hear him. Rob would laugh as best he could.

James felt a little sheepish having listened to his young son's short oratory but did not realise his brother-in-law had been listening. Andrew O'Dell shuffled himself towards the group of old friends as James turned and ordered a round of beers. Before Andrew could say anything farewells were being sounded out to George. Naturally the old man was visibly upset but nevertheless took off his cap and thanked everyone for coming. Young Daniel, forever his guardian when not at school, helped him over the threshold. Slowly he ushered the old fellow onto the back of their brand new Ferguson tractor, one of the first production machines produced from Huddersfield. Joy went outside and spoke to them both if only to reassure herself that her father would be quite safe as long as Daniel stayed with him. She explained she wouldn't be long herself. Once Daniel had settled his grandfather onto an improvised backboard he climbed into the driver's seat, started the engine, and they set off slowly and carefully back to Eastrip Farm.

The conversation inside the Fox and Hounds resumed. "Do you know what he intends to do with his life James?" Andrew asked Daniel's father as if he already knew the outcome.

"Continue on at school, I hope, for the moment. After that, I am not sure if he's made his mind up. Staying at the farm and helping out would be a good idea for me and Joy. Why do you ask?" James pondered his brother-in-law's question.

Before he answered, Andrew gazed at the expressions of both Rob and Herbie who were waiting in anticipation for some kind of explanation. He stared hard at James and then said, "he intends to join the armed services," Andrew watched them all and then added, "no matter what anyone says, Daniel has the impression there will be a lot of misgivings when his intentions are revealed."

They all looked at James. His face remained dead-pan. He thought for a while and then asked, "does his mother know about this?" He visually searched the room for her among the many mourners to make sure she could not hear. She was safely out of earshot sitting talking to Sarah and Judith, Herbie and Rob's wives.

Andrew shook his head slowly. "I am more than sure Joy doesn't know anything," he went quiet, but then briefly supplemented, "so far."

"What about your father, George, does he know? Why did Daniel tell you first and not me?" The implications were beginning to sink into James what Andrew had just revealed.

Rob studied James' face with a barely discernible wry smile. He wondered what he could possibly say to Daniel, knowing his father's own past. 'He'd run off to the last war underage'.

"I'm sure someone has influenced him. Probably not my father, but whether Daniel has told George of his intentions I don't know because they are very close to each other." Andrew shrugged his shoulders. "He gave me the impression he told me so I would be the one to break the news to you."

"Which service is he wanting to join?" Herbie asked, inquisitively.

"I had quite a long chat with him and I'm sure you will not be able to dissuade him from enlisting. The general idea he gave me was he seemed to be open to suggestions as to what line his service career should take. I offered him some advice but now it's out in the open perhaps we can all make some recommendations. James I'm afraid you will have to sit him down and have a serious talk with him." Andrew looked at Rob. "Rob with your experience you should have a chat with him as well, and you Ed."

"When you think about the possible circumstances, if another European war does start, he'll almost certainly be called up anyway, and so he'd just as well enlist now and get his feet under the table." Herbie was being logical. "He'll then probably be able to pull rank over most conscripted soldiers from experience alone."

"He is learning German?" Rob intervened.

"Yes. Apparently he's quite good at the language. When I think back, now you mention his intentions, I am sure that perhaps his German teacher at King Edwards school has had an influence over him, a Mr. Hayman. Prior to him attending the school, myself and Joy went to a pre-school seminar and met the headmaster and several other teachers. At the end I had a conversation with Mr. Hayman about the 'Great War' and he told us his own story. He was living in Germany when the war broke out and all British civilians were interred at a special prisoner of war camp just outside Berlin. I can't remember what he called the place now."

Rob stopped him. "Ruhbelen. Does that ring a bell?" he suggested.

"Yes that sounds like the place, Ruhbelen, now you've reminded me. Anyhow this teacher also sounded politically minded and spoke passionately about the causes of war. In fact if another conflict does start, with Germany being the aggressor, the outcome will be exactly what Mr. Hayman predicted." The conversation was coming back to James. Daniel's interest in politics and the fact that he was also learning the German language all added up in his mind. His son seemed to have had a hidden agenda of his own.

"If Daniel does learn to speak the language fluently he would perhaps be better off with a good job in one of the war ministries. Maybe that's his objective." Herbie was impressed by the youngster's astute way of thinking but could only offer some paltry advice. Daniel, if he ever did listen to Herbie's opinions, had possibly already made his mind up.

"Look! let's not broach this to anyone please until I can talk with him. Maybe tomorrow. I'll have to see. I can't imagine what his mother will say if and when she finds out. Hopefully he might change his mind." James was optimistic that he knew his son well enough, or so he thought. Andrew on the other hand was extremely doubtful.

The wake petered out at the Fox and Hounds and after many sentimental drunken commiserations, appreciations and goodbyes, the clientele emptied out onto the streets in the mid-afternoon.

After a few drinks in Bath and returning back to the Fox, James subsequently ended up quite late staggering around the farm in his best clothes trying to make sure everything was safe and secure. He then stood, uncertain of himself, in the centre of the yard with his hands in his trouser pockets staring at nothing in particular. The yard was dark anyway, fortunately though the rain had swept through and the sky was clear. He mulled over in his head what Andrew had told him earlier in the day. He stepped through the barn door, fumbled whilst finding and turning on the solitary lamp which hung just inside, and watched the cockroaches scurry for cover. He then sat down on a sack of old musty grain, ruined by rain during the previous harvest. He could not think straight and held his head in his hands. All sorts of notions were passing through his mind. The funeral, perhaps an up and coming war, his eldest son wanting to leave and enlist into what might again become terrible circumstances, and then above all he had to be up milking the cows at four o'clock the next morning, although that now seemed quite trivial considering the days conversations. He ran his fingers through his thinning hair and shook his head at the same time.

"You know don't you?" The words startled James and his befuddled mind wondered where the voice had come from. Just inside the door stood Daniel, his young face barely illuminated by the paltry light.

"Yes. Sit down. Please, sit down." James asked him quietly, invitingly patting the sack of grain next to him.

"Dad you're in no fit state to talk sensibly tonight. Come on. Let's go down to the cottage and have a nightcap and then you can go to sleep." Daniel waited for him to reply. His father's face painted a grim picture under the kerosene lamp. 'Bloodshot eyes and wrinkles exacerbated by shadows would put fear into any susceptible mind', thought Daniel.

After some thinking James asked his son, "does your grandfather know about your intentions?"

"Dad I do know of the circumstances when you and uncle Daniel both left home. Two different reasons I suspect, two entirely different situations, but if you don't want me to just disappear out of the door like you both did then you are going to have to listen. Come on. Let's go and have some sleep and we'll talk about my future tomorrow." Daniel was sober and fully in control. He walked over to his father, took his arm and lifted him to his feet. Initially they stumbled but soon regained their balance, and after stuffing out the lamp, made their way down to the cottage.

Between them they finished off a quarter bottle of George's whisky as he slept in his armchair by the refectory table. Neither spoke for fear of waking the old man, and then they both retired to bed.

Chapter 02
The Confession

Another band of rain blew in harder still buffeted by a south westerly wind as Daniel helped his father with the milking. Daniel's relative sobriety following the funeral the day before helped considerably that morning. A half an hour only seemed to have passed since they had lay down their weary heads. Both started as they had left off from the night previous, neither speaking a word as they prepared the bovine beasts prior to attaching them to the vacuum pumps. Everything seemed to take a long time to James as he tried to shake off the excesses of alcohol consumption. Slowly he began to feel better but his stomach could still reject a fried breakfast which would almost certainly be awaiting him when he returned to the cottage. One matter bothered him, the revelations about his eldest son, which would soon come to a head like a festering boil when Daniel's mother unexpectedly discovered her son's notions.

Together the pair eventually ushered the last of the herd out of the sheds and coaxed them through the yard and into the fields below, closing the gate behind them. They watched them amble slowly away down the slope as if they hadn't a care in the world, never looking back, relieved of their creamy load only to begin again another twice daily production.

The rain was still incessant, and Daniel and his father turned back to finalise their morning's work, which entailed cleaning the old Cotswold parlours and yard that were mired in green watery excrement, brought about from the ingestion of wet grass and the herd's digestive system.

Eventually the impasse between the two was broken. "We need to speak," James told his son, "and *before* we go back down to the cottage."

Daniel said nothing and went about hosing everything down and pushing the muck into the slurry pit at the bottom of the yard where the spreader was parked. His father systematically cleaned all the milking equipment with detergents and scalding water.

Joy appeared with two mugs of tea unaware of any tension between father and son. She would inevitably be pivotal in the eventual outcome of Daniel's revelations. Joy told them there was to be a family breakfast before Andrew and his family left to return to London. Elizabeth, she added, would leave a little later, back to Birmingham. Both acknowledged that they would be down at the cottage in about half an hour.

Again they sat in the barn together, sipping tea, out of the rain. Daniel spoke first. "Do you remember anything about last night?" he asked his father.

"Not everything but I understand you intend to join the army. Why didn't you speak to me first? instead of your uncle Andrew." James was slightly peeved.

"Apparently uncle Daniel went to see Andrew before he joined up, or so I was told. During the unfortunate circumstances of grandma's funeral I had a rare opportunity to speak to him yesterday and we did so for some time." James went to intervene but Daniel insisted he should carry on. "Uncle Andrew is a brilliant surgeon who I think doesn't take sides in political arguments. He is only interested in keeping the nearly dead alive and repairing the other unfortunates, a dedication for which we can only admire him. He told me of his war time role and where he learnt his gruesome trade but you already know that from your own experiences. Whatever he told you yesterday won't change anything James. I *am* going to enlist into the services, no matter what. My mind will not deviate from that ambition until my dream is fulfilled." Daniel was emphatic.

James looked up from his lukewarm tea surprised that Daniel had referred to him by his first name. "Why did you call me James?" he asked.

"If me and you were on a battlefield together and you were the officer in charge would you expect me to salute you and say 'yes dad' whilst all the others say sir." Daniel waited for his response but never received one.

James smiled inwardly without visibly moving a facial muscle, they were sitting on the bags of old grain not on the battlefield. One thought loomed in his mind about his son only ever calling his grandfather George. Odd, but as long as there was mutual respect between them nothing would matter using Christian names. After further discussion James ascertained that Daniel was not going to change his mind. "Come on! Let's go and have some breakfast and get this over and done with before Elizabeth and Andrew leave."

The senior family sat around the refectory table but George remained in his armchair. Except Daniel the younger members were settled in the small sitting room. George had had a piece of toast, a cup of tea and now a small tot of scotch rested on the arm of the worn out furniture. The clinking of cutlery against the porcelain somehow annoyed Andrew but he knew he would soon be on his way, back to a world far from his austere upbringing. Joy offered some more bacon which was taken up with gastronomic fervour and she sat back down from the stove. James then detonated the bombshell.

"I don't know if any of you have heard but Daniel plans to enlist in the armed services." James carried on eating as if nobody would care, but he was deluding himself.

There were a few seconds before Joy understood the statement which her husband had made. Andrew's eyes almost turned up into his head, 'why couldn't James have waited until they were half way back to London,' he thought.

Elizabeth politely placed her knife and fork either side of her plate and asked James to repeat his last words. George for the second time that day struggled to his feet and replenished the spittle stained glass at the Welsh dresser. He was well aware of what was coming next and needed to be sat comfortably before Joy fully percieved the gist of what James had revealed.

James nodded in Daniel's direction. "In layman terms Daniel has decided to have a career in the armed services. There's nothing more simple than that," he tried to explain with a pathetic smile on his face.

The squirming cat was out of the bag. George seemed to have known all along and only the women had been kept in the dark over the issue. The problem was for the men to sort out, or so they thought. Andrew's wife stared hard into the side of her husband's face but he resolutely faced forward with one elbow on the table and stroked his chin. The women kept looking across to Daniel and then amongst themselves. Why on earth hadn't they been told, appeared to have crossed their minds?

George sensibly and calmly began a discussion. "He's been talking about the army for ages. No-one has taken any notice. Enlisting is what he wants to do." George stopped and gazed across to James and smiled. "Like father, like son perhaps," he remarked, then swigged his whisky and closed his eyes.

Daniel was agitated. The conversation was developing as if he wasn't even at the kitchen table. In his mind he was preparing to leave for the solitude of the barn, leaving his family arguing foolishly about his future.

Joy turned her attention first of all to James. "You knew about this! Why did you deliberately not say anything to me?" Her own assumptions were that 'she had been kept in the dark'.

"Believe me Joy I only found out yesterday," he nodded towards George, "given the circumstances of your mother's funeral, saying little was the correct option at the time," he told her quietly.

George, still with his eyes closed, smiled, 'blame poor Helen', he thought.

"Daniel!" Joy turned her wrath onto her son. "Why didn't you tell me? You're still at school for Christ's sake! Another two years and you can enter university!" She demanded an answer, a proper and immediate response.

"Mum. Do yourself a favour. Buy a decent newspaper every now and again and at least read what is going on in the world. There will be another war. A European war. If not another world war. I want to join one of the services anyway. Which one I haven't decided," he looked around the kitchen, "just look on the bright side, maybe this war won't happen at all," the room was silent and then he added sullenly, "but I am convinced there will be some form of conflict." Daniel stood up from the table and excused himself. "James I'll go and feed the pigs. I'll see you later." He left them all in silence. None knew what to say.

"Father! father!" Andrew tried to wake George. The old man opened his eyes and muttered indiscernible words. "Tell us please what you know about Daniel's aims."

George tried to pull himself up in his chair and sit more comfortably. He grimaced with the pain. First of all he asked to have his whisky glass topped up again. He'd had a bad night and so desperately wanted to go to sleep but all eyes now turned on the old patriarch. Comfortably sat with a drink in hand he began. "Daniel mentioned to me months ago, or rather, asked me for some advice. He was probing, but I didn't realise at first for what he was angling. Have any of you noticed he always reads the more intellectual papers and keeps up as best he can with any current news from the European scene, especially Germany and Italy. He is convinced there is going to be another war. Two of his favourite subjects at school are modern history and German."

Joy stopped her father. "What's all this to do with him joining the army?"

George looked hard at his daughter. "I appreciate your involvement with running the farm and having to look after the other two children, myself included of course, but I think you have failed to recognise that Daniel is entering an important phase in his life. You're not the only one Joy, all of us have failed to realise that he is approaching full maturity and has his own opinions," he glanced over to James, "Daniel's not stupid. He knows what he wants. Think yourselves lucky he's not out drinking every night and fornicating with all the girls from miles around. The boy has a sensible head on his shoulders but now is the time to begin treating him as a young adult and not an adolescent."

James nodded his head guiltily. Himself and Joy were not actually angelic in their behaviour as young people. Indeed, even though they were now married, Daniel was born out of wedlock, and still the butt of some crude jibes. "You're probably right George so please now tell us what you think he intends to do."

"He's going to stay on at school," there was a sigh of relief from Joy, "but only for one more year."

Joy couldn't believe what she heard. "Why? He needs to do another two academic years and he can apply for a university place."

"He's sixteen but he thinks he'll have a better chance next year to enlist, besides he wants to intensify his German course at school by which time he hopes he'll be almost fluent." George shrugged his shoulders. There was little more he could say, especially to appease his daughter.

Andrew smiled. "I can see his point. A German speaking British soldier would be a precious commodity if a war did break out."

Joy was not impressed. "Maybe, but not a dead one," she retorted sarcastically.

"Can you let me finish because I need some sleep?" George asked. They all agreed. "This September he is joining the army cadets or, as Daniel describes them, the British National Cadet Association. If he can prove his worth there he will have a good chance to progress into the army. I'm afraid, that unknown to you all, he has his own future mapped out." George took a swig of whisky and hoped there would be no more questions.

"Do you know which regiment he wants to join?" James asked George, ignorant of his own son's feelings.

"He keeps talking about the Wiltshire regiment but I have suggested he should wait and see what happens when he joins the cadets. They will assess him and point him in the right direction. I have explained they might find him to be adept at engineering, electrical or some other trade. Just remember he is still relatively young and at that age people are normally fit and naturally exuberant. Young people don't imagine problems which we have experienced in later life. Daniel wants to see action. Whatever happens, he doesn't want a desk job." George studied the expression on Joy's face.

Elizabeth put her arm around Joy. Having lost their younger brother in the last war she knew exactly what her sister was thinking. After a couple of minutes silence George was gently snoring. His mouth was slightly open and he dribbled from the side of his hanging jaw.

All the arguments were spent and Andrew and his wife decided to make their way back to London. In the early afternoon, later than anticipated, he and his family climbed into their car and waved goodbye. Daniel had thanked Andrew for listening to what he had to say the day before and subsequently mooting the subject with his father. He had felt much better that most of the family were present at breakfast when they all found out, as the chances were that not everyone would take a negative view. Now the general mandate appeared to be that there was no obvious objection to his wishes, except perhaps from his mother. He would have to wait and see what she thought. Every move he made he felt his mother's glare, whichever way he faced. He would bide his time and confront her vitriolic stance when she was off her guard.

Joy barely slept that night. James felt her restlessness but needed to be up at four to milk the cows. Her mind kept reverting back to her own brother Daniel, who her son was named after, and how he had died, as told by the man lying by her side, her husband. Joy's life was going around in a circle, and now an even greater danger was losing the son which she had doted on for years but had failed to understand his needs or desires. He was entering adulthood, something which she herself was thrust into by adolescent impetuosity, Daniel himself being the result. She lay on her back and wondered what had been going through James' mind all those years ago when he had originally left home. Joy needed her husband on her side. She turned towards him and slid her hand across his abdomen and down into his groin. Shortly afterwards they made love and then both fell asleep.

Daniel had difficulty sleeping. He kept mulling over in his mind 'The Battle of Eastrip Farm'. He rose early and went to fetch in the cows. James brought two mugs of tea from the cottage and before beginning work they sat and drank them.

"You realise your mother is depressed about your decision to enlist," his father told him.

"Of course I know, her mood is plainly obvious," Daniel smiled at his father, "only this time she isn't going to have own her way."

They proceeded to alleviate the cows of their frothy white foam.

Joy rose early. She desperately wanted to speak to Daniel. Both he and his father had more or less finished clearing up at the yard but her mindset was for a confrontation.

At the breakfast table she screamed at Daniel. "You are going to stay on at school! You are going to study and earn the right qualifications to go to university! We've paid for that and now you are going to pursue your education for the next two years. You don't understand what a privilege you have."

Daniel sat listening impassively. James realised his son probably had his reply firmly supplanted in his mind and was waiting to unleash his own opinion onto his mother. James had learnt more about his eldest son in the last two or three days than since he was born.

"Daniel you *are* going to stay at King Edward's until the end of your school life. Your education we paid for and that's the way the money will be spent!" His mother repeated herself. She was livid.

Daniel stood up. Calmly he looked at his mother straight in the eyes and spoke in German. "Mother I *am* going to enlist in the army to fight against the European Fascists. Nothing will deter me from my intentions. Not you, or father, or anybody. I know what grandfather has told you so please believe me, I will be leaving. I could stay here but I am not. I want to follow in uncle Daniel's footsteps and join the army." He brushed past his mother and went back up to the farm.

Joy was dumfounded. She looked at James in shock. "What did he say?

James shrugged his shoulders and shook his head. "How do I know. He was speaking in German. Judging by his mannerisms I don't think you are going to dissuade him too easily."

Chapter 03

The Highlander

"So how did your first evening progress, satisfactorily?" As James drove back through Bath along the London road to Colerne in his Austin Seven with Daniel he felt bound to ask his son the ultimate question.

Daniel sounded pleased with his initial evening at the army cadets. "We had a drill sergeant who was immediately onto us regarding health and hygiene. 'An army marches on a healthy stomach' he told us, and referred to when Napolean went to Moscow and the disaster which followed because they had hardly any supplies. I know I'm lucky living on the farm where obtaining food is easier. Some of the lads come from poor areas of Bath but are determined to break from their dour life styles. Whoever the sergeant was he showed us how to wash in one bowl of water from head to foot. The evening was quite comical really. Where would you start?"

"Clean my teeth first then wash my bollocks and arse last. Do you think I don't know?" They both laughed. "Was your sergeant a local man or didn't you have the chance to speak to him?" James asked his son.

"I am more than sure he is a Scotsman but from where I don't know, possibly the Highlands because he mentioned a particular regiment who I've never heard of, the Seaforths. He doesn't seem that old, middle to late twenties perhaps. He was relatively strict with us but came over as a genuinely decent bloke." Daniel was obviously content that his initial interaction amongst the cadets that evening had gone well.

James glanced at his son knowing his mother was hoping the first night would be a disaster. "Nothing went wrong then?"

"Not for the initiation evening, no. We did exercises which some of the lads really struggled with, but us fitter boys helped them through. Then we did drill. Marching up and down turning here and there. Overall we had some good fun." Daniel looked towards his father who was concentrating climbing the notorious Bannerdown hill.

In his mind James could only picture his pessimistic wife looming over the horizon as they reached the very top and he trundled onward to Colerne deep in thought. A drink in the pub came to mind, but he decided to refrain.

When they arrived home Daniel immediately went upstairs to soak in the bath. Joy glared at her husband. "Well! What did he say?"

"Joy! I'm going to say or tell you this once and once only. He appeared to enjoy himself and I think you had better alter you mindset and accept what he does. Support him, do not criticise him. If you really think you can dissuade him from joining the army then I think you are living in a 'fool's paradise'. If you want to lose him sooner rather than later then maintain your current attitude. Don't forget one thing." James paused expecting some kind of scathing retort but she remained quiet. "Don't forget he's my son as well as yours." James kissed her softly on the forehead as he went out of the door.

Joy heard the car start up and leave. She sat down at the table and held her head in her hands. Daniel came down the stairs and held her tightly. Joy wrapped her arms around his young slim waist and heard the words she dreaded.

"I'm sorry mum, but my mind is made up, I want to join the army."

Chapter 4
Misguided Governance

Winston Churchill leaned awkwardly forward perched on the edge of his stool in the conservatory painting a water colour of the view across the 'Weald'. Clementine, but for the occasional rustle of paper, sat silently nearby browsing through a copy of the Times. Winston stretched his aching arm and chose briefly to break his concentration before speaking to his dear wife. "Ralph and Ava are coming to visit us tomorrow evening my dear. I think you'd probably better give everyone a day off and put your hand to the cook pot." He never had eye contact with his wife, and in between brushstrokes continually drew on his cigar or sipped his whisky. Clementine immediately realised there was an underlying meaning for the visit and stopped reading, then placed the folded paper on the table. She went to inform their butler.

Ralph Wigram and his wife Ava arrived promptly at seven thirty with the intention of leaving within three hours of their arrival. They each inquired after their families, talked of old friendships and colleagues from the past and eventually settled down to dinner, not once indicating the real purpose of Ralph's visit. Afterwards, whilst mellow from imbibing fine French wine, Winston and Ralph left the two women and retired to the drawing room for some serious discussions.

"How is Sir Robert," asked Winston of Ralph Wigram's immediate boss, Sir Robert Vansittart.

"Sir Robert is fine but very concerned about the political developments in Europe." Ralph Wigram sounded very nervous. His information he was about to divulge was informal but if found out about his visit to Winston the press could have a field day, possibly ending his civil service career.

Winston reassured him he had nothing to be afraid of. He reiterated that the house was secure. No-one else was listening.

Ralph took a deep breath and lay back in his chair with a glass of fine port. "Our intelligence boys are more than sure Hitler will begin an expansionist attack on Europe. Our members of parliament are not taking heed. Although we eventually won the last disastrous war this lot are lacking aggression, Conservatives included, but Germany's armaments factories are in full production. You wouldn't believe how the Luftwaffe now out number our own air force. German air power goes beyond anybody's imagination. The current estimation is that they have eight hundred bombers, whereby we don't even possess fifty. We are so far behind numerically with military machinery the statistics don't bear thinking about. Hitler's navy is now equal to ours although his biggest problem is access to open waters. Something needs to be done but not soon. Now! If he decides to take out Britain initially and we capitulate then all the European countries will be doomed. France will not be able to last long. Within a generation twenty-five percent of the population will be speaking the German language. Our information is relatively reliable. Germany will expand her borders but at whose expense first of all remains to be seen. War is, I am afraid to say, inevitable."

Winston puffed a cloud of bluish nicotine smoke into the air. He visually perused the lightbeams dissipating from the chandelier which hung from the ceiling. A cobweb caught his eye. "France has the strongest and largest army in Europe but I am afraid she has done nothing but sit on her hands as their neighbour threatens."

"Baldwin has told the French foreign secretary that he couldn't commit Britain to a war and that we are in no financial position for such a conflict. If you think our government is divided so are the French, half of them will not confront Hitler unless we back them up." Mr. Wigram was adamant.

"What do you think we should do?" Winston eventually asked him.

Ralph Wigram paused. He was an experienced civil servant with an intellectual mind and many 'here today, gone tomorrow' members of parliament had passed through his office. "The Prime Minister and his slow acting cabinet have to be removed from power, although I'm not sure that *power* is the right word to use. If something isn't done soon we could be in deep trouble. We have to first of all put our armaments manufacturers onto a war footing without raising public fears. The timing has to be crucial but the press have to be curtailed."

"I will begin sending official letters to the necessary leaders. We need a separate ministry run simply on the assumption that Germany is going to war but who should be its minister in charge remains to be seen. For now he would have to be seen as non-aggressive so as not to push Hitler too far and over the brink. A very shrewd diplomat at the least." Winston again puffed on his cigar and sipped his whisky. His astute brain added up the new information and formulated the intelligence with everything of which he was already aware.

Winston and Ralph unintentionally debated deep into the early hours and the guests were offered accommodation but both emphatically refused. After Ralph and his wife had left and Clementine had retired to bed Winston, quite alone, strode up and down the drawing room for at least two hours, smoking cigars, drinking his whisky and mulling over in his mind the looming possibility of another European war. What concerned him most was the apparent inaction of the prime minister, Stanley Baldwin, and his cabinet. His good friend and confidante Ralph Wigram had now convinced himself a war was inevitable. His next immediate move was to persuade all others in parliament that unless action was taken soon, all could well be lost.

For hundred of years or more British foreign policy had been based on neutralising the main and largest aggressor. The low countries and smaller nations were to be protected so they could retain their own identities. Over the years Britain had fought against the Spanish, the French and the Germans but now history could well be repeating itself. Letter writing was now his paramount concern in an attempt to motivate the 'powers that be' and persuade them to understand the evil which was being created not five hundred miles away from Britain's shores.

Winston sat down in his chair and studied his half finished painting. His mind was far off in the distance and soon he drifted off to sleep. His arm hung precariously over the side with his cigar about to drop from finger and thumb to the floor. His glass, almost drained, sat obliquely on his lap.

His forever present butler quietly crept into the drawing room and removed the offending articles from his weakened grasp and then left noiselessly. There was always someone awake at Chartwell, contrary to what Winston had told Sir Ralph.

Winston Churchill regularly slept well, although this night he was not in his own bed.

Chapter 05
The Altercation

Under the command of Company Sergeant Stuart Sinclair and Corporal Waite the Bath army cadet force set off for Salisbury Plain in three canvass backed wagons, supplied for the weekend, courtesy of the Somerset Light Infantry Regiment. After school or work on a late Friday afternoon the youths, or young men as they now wished to be known, had all been warned that on arrival they would have to pitch their tents and make themselves at home before nightfall. They had practised tent erection several times but, should they be too slow, in the dark canvass assembly would be a different kettle of fish.

The two day exercise would comprise of drill training, physical fitness, marching and above all, which everyone looked forward to the most, shooting on the firing range. Using military guns would be their first experience with live ammunition.

When the troop arrived just outside Tidworth barracks there was approximately one hour before sun-down, but to make matters worse the clouds were overcast. The force were divided into three sections blue, red and yellow. Each had a section leader chosen on merit. Daniel Godwin had his first chance to prove himself and he was the leader of yellow section. He had eight men under him. The three young corporals, as they were now known, had chosen their comrades one by one at an earlier cadet meeting in the week. Each had taken turns to choose fellow soldiers to make up his small unit. Being under canvass was to be a competitive weekend for them all. Surprisingly Daniel's first choice had been Mark Campbell a little known young African-American. He had only been in their cadet force for little over a week.

Previously a member with the Bristol force, for some non-divulged reason he had switched over and joined the Bath force.

Each section quickly chose a level spot to bivouac and set about creating their temporary weekend home. After a lot of initial banter they finally achieved their aim as the light faded away completely. Not long afterwards and basically settled, they were all marching down to the barracks and into the mess hall where they were fed ample food to last until daybreak. At the tables the conversations were lively. They all chattered excitedly about the forthcoming events. Sergeant Sinclair soon brought them back down to earth and marched them around the entire barracks, stopping occasionally in the dim light to explain what buildings served what purpose and to whose regiments they belonged. He explained that the red brick structures were all named after British army battles in India and Afghanistan. The army had bought the land for military training at the very end of the nineteenth century and the barracks eventually grew to its current size. The exercise was more to do with tiring his young force out rather than a history lesson and afterwards, having returned to their tents, he made them perform routine physical fitness training for an hour before retiring them to bed. One young soldier was designated from each section to keep watch for two hours and then hand over the responsibility to a reluctant colleague, and so the shifts would continue during the night. The others excitement dwindled quickly having had a long day and soon they slept quietly.

Sergeant Sinclair had borrowed the use of a bugler from the Hussars, and at five thirty prompt in the morning they were all woken with the sound of the 'Reveille'. The new day was about to begin.

After a few stretching exercises they were each reminded how to wash from head to toe with a meagre bucket of cold water. 'Clean your teeth first', he smiled at them 'and wash your arse last'. The sun hadn't risen, dark prevailed and the recruits struggled by the light of the camp fire. Sinclair reminded them that in a war zone their options would be severely hampered but cleanliness was of paramount importance. As the sun rose from behind a low dense bank of cloud each section had cookery utensils to cope with and uncooked food laid on by the Hussar's independent catering corps. They had to make their own breakfast and were given occasional advice by the members of the corps. Little did they know every cadet was being assessed to find out who possessed the necessary skills for each and every task. The evaluation would be operating all weekend.

Soon they were up on Wiltshire's treeless rolling uplands route marching along meaningless tracks and pathways. They each carried a weighted backpack. Occasionally a tank could be seen on the horizon on trial. Unknown to the young observers they were Mark 1 Infantry tanks, the 'Matildas' as they were nicknamed. Several other different types of turreted vehicles passed them by, or some were merely transporters. Others were parked up, incapacitated by engine failure or track displacement, their crews stood around smoking and talking, awaiting the arrival of the engineers.

The day went well. They were shown every aspect of real army life that was possible in a short space of time. Each one was being weeded out or examined for their possible strengths. Again they were made to cook their own food, lunchtime and evening, but only on the camp fire. Disappointedly there was no sign yet of a visit to the rifle range.

That evening, a surprise to them all, they were taken down to the corporal's mess and given their freedom. There was live music playing and the place was relatively busy. The section leaders were allocated beer tokens to be shared amongst them, but more than enough for them to become intoxicated.

Local girls began to enter the dance room and the mess became busier. A bus arrived from Salisbury and more lasses disembarked. The inexperienced Bath cadet force looked on forlornly as the beer took hold. Some girls came over and tempted them to get up and dance. A couple of them did but they were soon rebuffed by regular soldiers who stood between them and commandeered the excited women. Daniel stayed with his band of men talking about what might happen the next day. The evening grew into a fine atmosphere and the dance floor was alive with soldiers hugging female figures. Drinks and cigarettes were in hand everywhere. With the loud banter and music, hearing any conversation almost became impossible. People began to shout at each other only to create a bigger din. Excessive drinking began to affect the soldiers minds and the dancing became wild. The ladies from Salisbury became excessively flirtatious. If they were not being chatted up or asked to dance they made the first move. One such woman approached the table of the Bath cadet force and bee-lined for Mark Campbell.

"Hello darling," she rubbed her hand across his broad shoulders and back, "do you fancy a dance?" she asked provocatively.

The boy was embarrassed and initially declined but she insisted. Daniel watched him carefully, unnoticed, and took into account the surrounding frivolities. Servicemen standing at the bar were watching their table. Daniel gained the attention of two other of his counterparts, and after gesturing with his eyes they then realised the girl might cause them problems. Mark spoke to her trying to avoid an incident but then conceded. He was the only dark skinned man in the mess and possibly in the whole barracks. The pair placed their drinks on the table and went to the dance floor.

Being near the end of the evening, the music was slow. First of all they kept at arms length but after a while they became closer. "Where are you from?" the girl asked.

"I was born in Bristol. My parents are from America. They moved to England because of the racial segregation," he told her with a slightly pitiful look.

She pulled him towards her and spoke into his ear. "Do you know they don't like you being in here?"

As they smooched around he watched over her shoulder. "I guess that's because I'm the lucky one."

Temporarily the music stopped and they parted but she had become infatuated with the tall handsome youth and went back to ask him to dance again. They became closer and most eyes in the mess were on them. Daniel was watching, weighing up Mark's situation. The end of the evening was nigh, with the last dance playing, but there were drunk servicemen who needed women and one such girl happened to be cavorting with a black man, who also happened to be a mere cadet. Daniel and his fellow cadets could feel the tensions rising.

The last slow piece of music was finally played out and the whole place became surreal. Amongst a few others, Mark and the girl carried on talking in the centre of the dance floor. Groups of soldiers hung around together, gossiping, their gestures obviously referred to the unlikely pair. One soldier, entirely drunk, staggered over to them and pulled Mark away from the young woman. "Hey nigger boy, fucking leave our women alone! You go and fuck your own black bitches!" His eyes were glazed over but he meant what he said and he appeared to be backed up from a certain corner.

"I beg your pardon." Mark's reply was well mannered, he also looked his assailant up and down. He fancied his chances should the drunk square up against him.

"You fucking heard what I said! Go and fuck your own black bitches!" He turned to gain support from his regimental colleagues who then began laughing and clapping.

"I think you owe this young lady an apology." There was silence. "Did you not hear me. I'll speak louder! I think you owe this lady an apology!" Mark slanted his head and raised his eyebrows slightly. He was far from being afraid of the drunken soldier.

The girl tugged on Mark's shoulder. "Leave him. He's drunk. Nothing matters because I have to go now. Our bus is going back to Salisbury."

Daniel watched carefully and was waiting for the next move. He had the whole cadet force readied for a fight, albeit some of them were inebriated.

As she went to leave Mark held her back. He stared at the soldier. "She's not leaving until you apologise to her."

Daniel rose from his seat and went over to them and spoke something into Mark's ear. He then looked at the girl and asked her not to move. He proceeded over to the corner where the foul mouthed soldier's regimental colleagues were gathered and faced up to one particular character. The mess hall suddenly went completely quiet. "I've been watching you. You're the ringleader. I haven't a clue which regiment or corps you belong to but I'll give you two options."

The soldier turned to his friends rallying support for himself. He turned back. "So what do you have to offer then boy?" he asked with a confident smarmy grin.

"First of all you leave my man and the girl alone and call your 'white monkey' off. If you don't my men, all between the ages of fourteen and seventeen, will embark on an all out assault on anyone who attempts to threaten them both. Try to imagine that in the papers. 'Professional soldiers attack army cadets'. Even better if you lose. I've taken the situation into account. There are twenty five of us but only thirteen of you." Daniel was self assured. Everyone in the hall were now listening. What he didn't know was the military police had surrounded the place and were watching from various doorways, which was normal at weekends because of inter-regimental rivalries. "Your other option is that me and your 'white monkey', who seems to be full of fighting spirit, finish off the argument here and now. Better still I'll take you and him on at the same time. What do you say to that?" Daniel was up for a serious altercation.

There were cheers from all corners and chanting to tempt them into a fight. The military police were about to step in but Sergeant Sinclair, also watching with interest, pulled their captain back.

Daniel stood face to face with his adversary.

"Daniel! You don't have to fight over me. I can handle myself alone." Mark Campbell called across to Daniel. "He's only jealous because I might have something bigger in my trousers than he has. Besides he's drunk."

Laughter filled the room except from the one particular corner, and the squaddies were now banging on the tables hoping to see a live fight, especially with the cadets involved.

Daniel turned back to his adversary. "Well what are you going to do! Fight? Me and you. Me and both of you, or a general punch up?" he surveyed the room.

The soldier had been put on the spot. Whichever way he chose, Daniel had him beaten. With much cheering from other regimental supporters the loser reluctantly, but more so embarrassingly, had to pull his so-called 'white monkey' from the dance floor.

Before the girl left she slipped a piece of paper into Mark's hand. Daniel called the entire force together and they marched proudly out of the mess, although some needed help. As they left most of the supporting soldiers clapped and cheered them but a few were not so happy.

Outside the climate changed. Sergeant Sinclair gave an order. "Corporal Godwin take your most reliable men and dismantle the tents lock, stock and barrel. We have to move as quickly as possible. A wagon will be over there soon." Daniel went to ask why, but Sergeant Sinclair was adamant. "Shut up! Just do as I say!"

Daniel asked no more questions. Within three quarters of an hour they were parked up in front of Lucknow barracks and unloading everything they owned. Soon they were sound asleep and safe in the empty barrack block. Late in the night Sergeant Sinclair and his second in command Corporal Waite walked quietly past their sleeping cadet force. Both had been impressed with their behaviour especially that of Daniel's and the way he had handled the situation earlier. Neither knew what he had said but there would be a lot of embarrassment among the Royal Fusiliers that morning.

"Where the fuck have they gone? They were only here this afternoon. I saw them." The drunken soldier was more than irate. He wanted his revenge from being ridiculed by an army cadet that evening.

"They can't surely have gone home," another remarked.

"I'll beat seven bales of shit out of them when I find them. Especially the black bastard."

Alcohol had misconstrued their minds.

Chapter 06

In the Firing Range

"The barrack commander wants to see you Stuart." His corporal, Mick Waite, told him informally.

"Do you know what he wants Waitey?" he asked him, with a surprised look on his face.

"His messenger didn't have a clue but I'm sure something to do with last night will be on his desk," he answered smiling.

As Sergeant Sinclair left the Lucknow barrack block he asked him to prepare the boys for a four mile hike, with packs, to the firing range.

Stuart Sinclair was led to the office of Colonel Peter McIntyre by the headquarters clerk who tapped lightly on his door. The voice of a rather official sounding military man from behind the door, invited him to enter. Having done so, the clerk then introduced Sergeant Sinclair, and promptly left.

With the Colonel was a Provost Sergeant, John Miles. After formalities they sat down around a large oak desk and the Colonel began an informal interrogation.

"How are your lads this morning?" was his first polite inquiry.

"Fine. Some of them are a little hung over but other than that they are all eager to go to the rifle range." He elaborated no further and waited for the next question.

"Do you know exactly what happened in the mess last night involving your boys and some fusiliers. I understand from the military police report, which I have in front of me, that there was a near miss situation which could have led to a lot of broken bones and bloodshed." He flipped some pages and then sat back and watched Sinclair's reaction.

"I was called out from the Sergeant's mess. By the time I arrived at the corporal's mess hall the military police had surrounded the place. Their captain allowed me through and followed me to the door. By the time I had arrived, in a corner, one of our young corporals was having some sort of verbal diatribe with some soldiers, as you correctly say sir, fusiliers. A relatively sober squaddy told us the situation arose about some racist remarks which a complete drunk had made, or in fact was still making, to one of my lads who had been cavorting with one of the local girls."

The Colonel stopped him. "Why would he be making racist comments?"

"The lad with the girl is black, or half black, and I suppose the fusilier took umbrage to the fact that he was with a white girl. I'm not really sure because I was going to question them all this morning but you summoned me here and I came over straight away."

"I am sorry about interfering with your weekend assignment, but please do carry on Sinclair. Do carry on."

"Whatever our young corporal said to the soldiers certainly stopped them in their tracks. Squaddies nearby could hear what had been said and began clapping and cheering. They were obviously from different regiments and were pleased to see another put down in such a manner, especially by one so young. The only words I caught was when Godwin, the lad in question, told him to pull his 'white monkey' off, adding insult to injury I suppose." Sinclair held his hands out as if to say that was all he knew.

The Colonel looked at his Provost sergeant and gestured for him to elaborate. "When I arrived at work this morning I had three soldiers to contend with. They were caught late last night trying to break into Lucknow barracks. You obviously never heard anything." Sinclair shook his head. "Who gave you permission to stay there last night?"

"When we left the mess the military police captain firmly recommended we stayed there in view of what had happened. I am sorry but I didn't catch his name. He envisaged there would be more trouble and now, knowing what you've just said, has obviously proven to be right. He arranged to let us in the block and we moved camp. We took less than an hour." Sinclair wasn't sure where the incident or interrogation was leading.

The sergeant continued. "The three have been charged with attempt to break into and enter the barrack block with the notion of taking out revenge on your cadet force. However, there are several witnesses who have come forward and made statements as to what was said to your young black or half caste cadet, however you describe him, on the dance floor."

Sinclair looked at the Colonel. "Let's be fair sir nothing really happened in the end so why not forget about everything?"

The Colonel told him to listen to the Provost Sergeant who went on to explain. "The Military Police have insisted that the soldier who made the remarks to your cadet should be charged."

Sinclair was quick to ask. "Charge him with what?"

"Inciting racial hatred." The Provost Sergeant raised his eyebrows not knowing what reply to expect.

"So are we going have a law about 'inciting regimental hatred' as well." Sinclair asked him with an air of sarcasm, knowing how rife was the extent of regimental infighting within the British army.

Colonel McIntyre was smiling. "Gentlemen please let me inform you." He stood up with hands firmly clasped behind his back and strolled briefly around the large room. He turned back to them both. "Often I have to go to London for various briefings. I cannot divulge most things but one is important to us all." He returned to the table and leant with his knuckles down and glared at them both. "We are now late in nineteen thirty six but the belief is Hitler is going to drag us into another war. Another European war. When? No-one knows. The government, however weak on foreign matters, will try to avert such a scenario diplomatically. None of us within military circles believe they can achieve a peaceful result. We have a standing army but are undersized, and unlikely to be anywhere near large enough to compete against the Germans. We also need re-arming. I cannot speak on behalf of the Royal Air Force or our Navy. There is one vociferous supporter on our side but he is out of governmental office at the moment." The Colonel cocked his head to one side wondering if either knew who he was talking about.

"According to young Corporal Godwin that can only be Winston Churchill." Sinclair implied.

"Corporal Godwin?" The Colonel asked raising his eyebrows. "Is he the one who prevented the melee last night?"

"Yes sir. He has an incredibly astute mind for politics and is an excellent young soldier and leader." Sinclair was actually proud to have him under his command, albeit only in a cadet force.

"He might go far then, if we can point him in the right direction." The Colonel looked at Sinclair knowingly. "Godwin you say. What is the other one called?"

Surprised, Sinclair told him Campbell's name. He didn't understand why he had asked. The Colonel glanced at the written brief he had before him and then picked up the phone. He told the clerk on the other end to go and collect them both and while he was doing so, arrange an escort to take the rest of the cadets to the firing range. He then poured attention over the Provost Sergeant and told him to round up his witnesses and reprobates and bring them all to his office. The procedure was unprecedented in army circles.

The Colonel was left alone with Sergeant Sinclair. "You are a Highlander I assume?" His dossier on Sinclair was on his desk which he had already read. As a security precaution Sinclair's references had been sent some time prior to the cadets arriving at Tidworth.

"Yes sir." Sinclair knew there would be more than an informal chat.

"Why did you leave the army having such a good service record?" The Colonel was prying.

"I had an injury and was declared unfit for physical duties. I could have stayed in with a desk job but hated the thought of sitting down all day, besides that, my six years enlistment was almost up. I was given the options to stay but chose to leave instead." Sinclair was wary.

"So what do you do now?" he was asked.

"Work for a plumbing company in Bath." He gave him no other information.

"And the boys?" The Colonel wanted to know about his involvement with the cadets.

"For me they are just a part time voluntary job. We try to get them off to a good start, teaching them from our own experiences." Sinclair hoped that there would be a knock at the door. "We run the cadet force voluntarily with a small grant from the British National Cadet Force. The government are blind because they don't see a war looming or, if they do, they are burying their heads in the sand. We're going to need these boys thoroughly trained at an early age."

"If a war does begin what would be your intentions? Remain on civvy street or help towards the war effort?" The Colonel was genuinely interested in the man sat before him.

"I would attempt to rejoin the army and my old regiment where I feel I am more useful. Indeed I know I am. My old injury has now basically healed." A knock at the door came. Sergeant Sinclair was relieved as he didn't enjoy being interviewed or, as he believed, interrogated.

"Come in!" Colonel McIntyre called out with his university accent.

The Provost sergeant had found three of the 'would be' witnesses. Also with him, under guard, were the attempted assailants and the verbal abuser. They were asked to take a seat as they were waiting for the two young cadets. Shortly afterwards after being briefed on protocol Daniel and Mark were escorted into the office and stood before the Colonel's desk and saluted. He returned the gestures. Two more chairs were brought in and they were invited to sit down.

Colonel McIntyre looked them both up and down and smiled to himself. He wished he was their age again. "You two have made quite a name for yourselves at the barracks and in just two days as well." He glanced down at the paperwork in front of him. "Campbell, Mark Campbell. I am afraid we have little information about you but as you were the centrepiece of the whole episode would you mind explaining to us, in your eyes, what happened."

Mark told them about the approach by the girl and how they danced together. Afterwards as they were chatting a very inebriated soldier came over who began shouting obscenities. He went on to say that was when Daniel intervened and went over and confronted the drunk's regimental colleagues.

The Colonel stopped him. "What did the soldier actually say?"

Mark thought for a while. He looked up. "I am sorry sir I cannot repeat the words. That sir would be beyond my conscience to say what he said to me."

Daniel turned to him. He fully understood what Mark was thinking. Colonel McIntrye watched their interaction.

"Sir?" Daniel asked to speak.

The Colonel turned his attention to Daniel. He was the one man he alluded to and wanted to know more about his character. From what he had been told that early morning, Daniel had impressed quite a few people the evening before. "Carry on Godwin what do you have to say?"

Daniel leaned towards the Colonel. He went to explain what had happened in basic terms but Mark grabbed him by the wrist. "No! Please don't say anything. What happened last night is over."

Daniel shrugged him off. "Now is the time someone told the truth." He reverted his gaze back to the Colonel. "Sir." The Colonel waited in anticipation with raised eyebrows. "Sir! You are white. If I was a black skinned man and approached you and your dark skinned woman on a dance floor and then began telling you to fuck off and go and fuck your own white bitches what would you say to that?"

Sergeant Sinclair searched for answers as he stared down at the floor. Daniel was digging himself into a large hole. Any witnesses present resolutely said nothing, sitting twiddling their thumbs.

Colonel MacIntyre spread his fingertips as if they were a spider on a mirror. He now understood the gist of what had been said. "What did you actually say to the abusive soldier's colleague?"

Daniel was annoyed but tried to show no emotion. "I took a chance with their ringleader and threatened him. First of all I told him to call off his 'White Monkey'. I then asked them that they either apologised or I would fight against him to resolve the situation. In fact I offered to fight him and his 'White Monkey', the drunk. He was caught. He had a choice of beating up cadets or backing down. The whole dance hall knew what was happening." Daniel contemptibly shrugged his shoulders.

"Did you fancy your chances?" The Colonel asked, quietly amused.

"One punch and the drunk would have been down. As for his back up? I might have taken a bit of pain but I believed I could win. That's probably why he stood off. He was unsure. That's the difference between winning and losing battles," Daniel said nothing for a few seconds, "as you probably know sir," he added with an air of sarcasm.

Colonel McIntyre stood up and began to pace around the room. He was contemplative. After a while he decided to speak.

"You witnesses. Do you believe that was basically what happened?" They agreed entirely. He stared back at the two young up and coming soldiers. "I shouldn't really be telling you this but you're all going to find out sooner or later." He sat back down into his chair. "Once or twice a week I am summoned to London for discussions about the state of the British army. Sometimes the meetings are held with some very important ministers present, Anthony Eden the Foreign Secretary, Neville Chamberlain the Chancellor to name just two. Perhaps the Prime Minister is sometimes in attendance. Lately the discussions have become more intense. As you have probably read, the mood in Europe is becoming more threatening. We now know for a fact that Hitler has re-armed and is still re-arming. War is inevitable but when and where he makes his first move no-one is sure." As the Colonel spoke he nervously rolled an ink pen between his fingers. "Short of raising some sort of taxation we will not be able to compete against the German menace. That is the major stumbling block which the government cannot decide on and which Winston Churchill, in no uncertain terms, persistently tells them if they don't do something soon everything will be too late." He paused and wondered if he was telling them too much." The point I was going to make concerns manpower. These young men here are now only sixteen or perhaps seventeen years old and will inevitably become the backbone of the forces in four or five years time. After we have these meetings in London the top brass from all services convene their own unofficial get-togethers discussing most matters within the forces. Often we talk about the levels of enlistment within all the services. We have to maintain a standing army at all times, although there are many other areas of conflict throughout the world within the British Empire which keeps most servicemen occupied. We all want to attract young men and even women into the forces but we can only do so by making the army an attractive, worthwhile and enjoyable career choice." Colonel Mcintyre stood up and again paced the room.

Stuart Sinclair guessed what he was about to say next.

"We have a growing ethnic minority in this country and we have agreed that they should have the same opportunities and rights as everyone else. We want to attract them into the services and so we all agreed to come down hard on any racist prejudice and bullying. If we can prevent racism happening in the very beginning then we might prevent problems for all time in the future. In view of the events which have not yet happened in Europe, but seriously might eventually occur, I can envisage we will be needing as many soldiers as we can muster from whichever race or creed. Whether they are white, brown or black of skin, English, Scottish, Welsh or Irish, they may come from Canada, Australia, New Zealand or wherever from across the world, but you will be all fighting alongside each other." Colonel McIntyre watched his sheepish audience and then went to the door. He called out for some refreshments and turned back. With his hands clasped behind his back Colonel McIntyre stood in front of the man who had caused all the problems on the dance floor. "Name and rank?" he asked.

The hung over soldier sheepishly replied. "Private Howard, Sir!"

"Do you recognise either of those two lads sat there?" he asked him.

Howard looked over. "Yes sir."

"From where then? In a war zone?" McIntyre wanted to speed up the proceedings. He turned and asked Mark and Daniel to stand up in front of the private. "Which one do you recognise?" He pulled Daniel to the front. "Him!"

"No sir." Howard knew he was in a lot of trouble.

McIntyre pushed Daniel away and presented Mark. "What about this fellow do you recognise him?"

Howard looked up. He'd made a mistake, knowing if he denied ever seeing him he would be a laughing stock. He also knew that because he hadn't recognised Daniel but admitted to knowing Mark his prejudices would be found out. Howard took his time and stared at Mark trying to appear to recollect his thoughts.

"Of course he fucking remembers!" A fellow from his regiment spoke out. "We're all to blame sir. We're down here for the annual football tournament and that is how the night panned out. Too much beer. A different environment. What happens? A stupid confrontation with two lads in the cadets. I was no better. We went looking for them after the lad there humiliated us. Howwie knows he was out of order but we were still on his side. We've had time to think about what we did and agree we were all out of order."

The refreshments turned up and they were all asked to relax and eat and drink the sobering Kenyan tea. There was still a tension in the room.

McIntyre stood with the Provost Sergeant suggesting what should happen to the itinerant fusiliers. Sinclair stayed on the side of his two young cadets. The witnesses debated loudly the shenanigans of the night before and the impact on the army as a whole. The fusiliers were concerned about the outcome.

Colonel McIntyre reconvened the meeting. "Sunday lunch is due and I am about to say my last thoughts about this unfortunate incident. Stand up please Godwin and Campbell!"

They did so with an air of trepidation.

"If our future army is built on your attitudes and reliabilities we will have nothing to fear. Thank you." He told them simply and gestured for them to sit back down.

"Howard! Have you anything to say before I leave you in the hands of the Provost Sergeant." Colonel McIntyre had been called out for this unseemly debacle and desperately wanted to go home for dinner.

Howard stood and bowed his head slightly. He marched towards Mark and stood before him. Mark rose from his chair. "I am profoundly sorry for what I said last night and after listening to Colonel McIntyre I will sincerely change my attitude. I am sorry. Please send an apology to the young lady. Your friend was right. I was completely out of order and let down my regiment." He offered his hand and the pair shook. His face was a picture of embarrassment. He turned around and went and sat back down in his seat.

"Sinclair!" Sergeant Sinclair stood up surprised. "Why did you allow your young cadets to enter a senior soldiers mess and drink alcohol knowing that they could be endangered?"

Sinclair thought he had some form of trust with the Colonel. "I was testing them out sir! Like you said we are going to need them. The ones who react well under the influence of alcohol are important components in our war machine, it is a part of their basic training let's say. These two young men were exemplary last evening and those, he pointed to the culprits, were found out."

Colonel McIntyre stepped away and then turned to face them all. "This issue is an example to us all. We must all believe in companionship no matter what colour or creed. The foreseeable future, I believe, is going to be dire. Please, become more tolerable to each other." He went over to the window and stared across the barrack square. For a while he said nothing, as if he was reflecting on his life. He picked up a tiny carved ivory souvenir acquired during his travels and then stared down at a waste paper basket made, strangely, from an elephant's foot. As before, time and time again in his mind the great grey pachyderm, which he couldn't miss, keeled over as one simple shot to its head took the beast's life away as the animal had attempted to protect his harem. The target was so large, and the act of killing the elephant, cowardly. There at his feet on the floor was the useless, empty, unused basket. In his hand was the intrinsically carved bear on ski's. The two souvenirs were all that remained of that magnificent beast he had put to death so many years before.

He finally faced the men in front of him. "Howard! I will tell you a short story but nothing goes beyond this room." He gazed slowly at them all and each one nodded in appreciation. "As a young officer I was fortunate to be posted to Kenya just after the last war. At the time Kenya was a difficult place to govern. However, whilst I was there I met a young woman with whom I fell in love. She wasn't the most attractive woman in the world but she was slim, intelligent, but above all, good company. We began a sexual relationship and for me she was everything a young man wanted. Her sultry eyes, her soft lips and sensuous body I will never forget. She still haunts me to this day." He walked back to the window and gazed out with a sad expression. When he turned he looked at Howard and told him. "I wanted to marry her. I honestly wanted to marry her." The Colonel's face appeared forlorn. He was in deep thought. No-one spoke as he caught eyes with them. None knew where his story was leading. He continued. "Rumour was rife about me and her and soon I was summoned in front of my commanding officer. I had to give my account of the innuendoes which were circulating within the camp. I had to admit to the relationship or my career was dead in the water." The Colonel was affected by what he wanted to say. "I let her down by telling the commanding officer the rumours were true. I rue that day. Within twenty four hours I was on a ship being posted back to England. I didn't have a chance to say goodbye to her and I have never heard from her since and probably never will." Colonel McIntyre sat down. He had told his story.

No-one wanted to speak out of turn. Daniel stared at him. He smiled. "She was as black as the 'Ace of Spades' wasn't she sir?"

Colonel McIntyre thought deeply about what he had been asked and smiled back. "Yes, she was, but she was also a beautiful woman. I want you all to understand what the future might hold for you or more probably your children and grandchildren. The British Empire is slowly becoming unaffordable and the notions are that each country under their own individual flag will have their independence. There will be many displaced people from countries across the world who will have fought for the British flag but needing a new home. What began one hundred years ago will come to an end and those people who worked so diligently for the empire will have only one place to go, here in Britain. We will become a mixed race nation. The possibilities are unending. Indians, Africans, Jamaicans, let alone the people of religious or political diversity. Our very own civilisation will be affected by their cultures and we will have to be very tolerant for years to come." Colonel McIntyre viewed everyone in the room one by one and wondered what was passing through their minds. Would they take heed or simply carry on and take one day at a time. "When you leave this room think about what I have told you, make your own minds up, but whatever happens I can only ask you to tolerate others, no matter, from where in the world they arise."

Having dismissed them all after asking the Provost Sergeant to sentence the reprobates leniently, Colonel McIntyre sat reminiscing about his past. The Great War came to mind but most nostalgically his woman in Kenya. A knock at the door came and the clerk told him his car had arrived. His wife and family were waiting and his Sunday lunch would soon be on the table.

Chapter 07
Hitler 1938

One particular Monday evening as the family ate their evening meal little was being said. Normally there was a conversation about current affairs, or at least the state of the farm. Joy thought the atmosphere was unusual. Daniel often talked about his day at school but he was quiet. She occasionally glanced at him but he hardly looked up and when he did move his gaze he stared at the ornaments on the wall above and behind his younger brother and sister. He eventually finished and politely laid his knife and fork down and waited for the others. He refused the offer of apple pie and cream but remained seated until the very end. Whilst his siblings went up to change clothing he finally spoke.

He looked inquiringly at his father, "have you heard?" Daniel asked him.

"Heard what?" Nothing out of the ordinary came to James' mind.

"The Germans have invaded Austria and have declared the country a part of their own," his well informed son told him.

James glanced towards Joy and then back to his apple pie. "Who told you that?" James was not totally surprised because the move had been talked about in political circles and posted in the papers for a long time. After all, Hitler was an Austrian.

"My German teacher, he said there was a short report in 'The Times' this morning and the border crossing happened some time very early on Saturday morning. The details haven't filtered back yet." Daniel leant back awaiting the thoughts of his parents.

Joy's mind seethed. Two years before she had confronted his German teacher about indoctrinating her son. He had defended his actions, telling her that Daniel was the best student he had ever encountered and when the pair of them were in conversation they would only naturally talk about German affairs. One thing he had done though, which pleased her no end, was to persuade Daniel to stay on at school until the final year. However July was approaching fast, less than four months away, and her son still had his heart set on joining the army.

"So how does that affect us?" she asked her son suspiciously.

Daniel was matter of fact. "Hitler won't stop there. What's the point of completely rebuilding the German armed services and then sitting at home polishing the hardware. He is mind bent on invading elsewhere."

His father butted in. "I'm afraid Daniel's right Joy but where Hitler spreads his lurid tentacles again is anybody's guess."

"We members of the debating club at school have come to a conclusion regarding his next move," Daniel paused, "Czechoslovakia! There are many German speaking people living there, especially in the north, who would enjoy an alliance with their mother country. They are known as the Sudentese and now Austria has been taken, the area is practically cut off economically and would have few options but to sign a treaty with Germany." Daniel was more than sure that Czechoslovakia would be Hitler's second objective.

Joy held her head in her hands. She had a vision of her son marching off to war, similar to her brother, and never coming back. Daniel junior was resolute with his intentions and the despairing mother was more than aware of them, but there was nothing she could do to deter him. Joy never considered what James was thinking. If only her powers of persuasion could influence her son to take an easier option, especially with his ability to speak the German language so well. Another option was that he could remain working at the farm and claim agricultural indemnity from enlisting in the army, if war should occur.

James could see the sadness in her face and asked Daniel a question which both of them wanted to know the answer. "When you do finally leave here who are you actually going to join up with? More importantly, what as? Although I say so as your father but you are an intelligent young man and there are many options in the armed forces."

Daniel thought for some time before answering his father but when he did there were no certainties about his intentions. "In the cadets Sergeant Sinclair takes into consideration all of our abilities and then makes basic assumptions as to where we would fit into the armed services. He isn't actually bias towards the army and he considers us for the navy and air force as well. We have had conversations on the subject, but myself personally, I haven't made my mind up yet." Daniel watched his mother carefully as she held her forehead in the palm of her hand with her elbow firmly planted on the table.

She suddenly looked up to say something only to be stopped by the children descending the stairs. They were laughing. In turn they woke George. Joy looked at them scornfully as if everything was their fault. Their father insisted they went outside and make sure the pigs and chickens were secure.

George could see from his armchair he was missing something and looked at them all quizzically.

"Sergeant Sinclair says I have an enormous chance to join the officer cadets but where I do not know. When we go out on a Friday night we all meet up, have a few drinks and talk seriously about the future. When I don't come home it's generally because some of us go back to his and his wife's house and drink and talk into the early morning. Mark comes with us sometimes, and often a couple of other lads. Nothing more than companionship really, but nonetheless relaxing. All of us have something in common. Give me some time and I will tell you who I want to join up with in the armed services. I'll warn you though it will probably be an infantry regiment," he rose from his chair, "I'll go and make sure Robert and Helen are alright." He touched his grandfather on the shoulder, an acknowledgement, and went out of the door.

George indicated to his daughter to put some whisky into his glass. James moved first and poured one himself. The old man eyed them both, smiled then told them what he thought. "Joy! You lost a dear brother. Me and your mother lost an irreplaceable son. You gained a husband, we gained a son-in-law who has filled our Daniel's boots. Probably the way Daniel would have wanted." George went quiet. James and Joy knew not to say anything. George looked mournfully at his daughter. "Your brother didn't need to go to war and indeed he decided to enlist late on but our Daniel junior intends to make his career in the army." George scratched his head. He sipped some more whisky and wiped his mouth as some dribbled down his chin. "Don't go against him. Help the boy. If that is what he wants to do, then let him go."

James was watching his wife from the corner of his eye. He hoped George would persuade her to relax more on the issue of their son.

"Doctor West and I have no illusions that there will be another European war. Therefore, choosing which direction to take now would be far better if Daniel establishes himself early on rather than be conscripted into a unit later, one in which he isn't suited. Far better the choice is his and his alone. He is intelligent, speaks the enemy language, that is if we do go to war against the Germans, but above all he is a leader." George was adamant.

"How do you know he's a leader?" Joy looked at her father puzzled.

"When you were both at the market in Bath his sergeant in the cadets paid us a visit. He came to see you both but I was the only one here. The man had nothing but praise for him." George contemplated them both with no expression of his own, letting them muse over Stuart Sinclair's visit. The old farmer knew James accepted his son's wishes but he had to win over his daughter's views if only to prevent a rift in his family. He was more than aware of what a family feud might cause. "Joy. Joy! Please! We lost Daniel. There were hundreds of thousands of others who lost their relatives. Fathers, mothers, uncles and aunts, brothers and sisters, cousins, the list goes on and on. One fact is we didn't lose our lives, they lost their own. Unless we stand up to Hitler's crazy ideology and a possible invasion then we are all doomed. My grandson is right. Take Hitler by the throat now or have your own throat slit." The sound of a car horn was heard from some way up the lane. George raised his eyebrows knowing full well his old friend doctor West was only two minutes away.

James and Joy slid their chairs from beneath them and went out to find their children. As they walked up to the yard James spoke. "Your father is right Joy. We're going to have to put up with what Daniel wants to do. He has chosen his career. We have to help and not hinder him. That way we'll at least find out what is going on in his mind."

Joy never answered him. They found the children playing in the barn. Daniel wasn't with them.

Chapter 08
The Double Celebration

Daniel was rapidly maturing both mentally and physically. He was now eighteen but not quite six foot tall and commanded much respect from those around him, senior or junior. His reward for staying the last year at school had been selection as head boy and captain of the rugby team. A disrupted summer term due to poor weather and examinations thwarted his membership of the cricket team. Well known in the city Daniel was continually sought after by the young women of his own age, attracted by his strikingly good looks, intelligence and charm. Aside of the ladies, other ideas were on his mind more crucial to his future. His time in the cadets had come to an end but more importantly to him he had finalised his education at 'King Edward's' school.

Daniel had two good excuses to celebrate and with some of his colleagues from school, fellow cadets and friends of friends decided to take the train into Bristol and visit the numerous bars in the Old Market district of the city. They arranged to meet first of all in the Station Hotel in Bath. James gave Daniel a lift into the city and remained initially, but only to meet Rob and Herbie whose 'time on earth' had persuaded the aging three not to continue the revelry into Bristol.

Stuart Sinclair had brought his wife along, Stella. She was an attractive woman and most of the cadets knew her on speaking terms. Daniel introduced her to the others from his school. The evening was informal and everyone was on first name terms. They all put money into an imaginary pot. Stella, having drawn the short straw, had the dubious task of taking charge of the funds and buying the drinks all evening, an idea callously contrived earlier. The poor woman, with a handbag abound with money, would have to remain relatively sober. She resolved herself, for the time being, with one glass of red wine. When everyone had arrived and had had a couple of drinks they went to board the train.

Within the hour they were laughing and joking in the Palace Hotel or, as all Bristolians called the bar, the 'Gin Palace'. Their fun was short-lived. Mark Campbell appeared through the glass swing doors and except for Daniel's entourage from Bath celebrating, the rest of the bar went quiet. Stella quite deliberately went over to him and acknowledged the young man with a peck on the cheek.

"What would you like to drink?" she asked knowing full well the staff wouldn't want to serve him because of his colour.

"Just a beer please, Mrs. Sinclair thank you."

Several regulars silently moved out of her way as she went to the bar and made his request. "A pint of 'Courage Best' please."

"Is that for him?" asked the barman nodding in Mark's direction.

She glanced over her shoulder back at Mark. "Yes. Why do you ask?" then stared at the barman bemused.

"I'm afraid we don't serve people like him here," he told her nervously.

From those few utterances the whole clientele had now been reduced to complete silence.

"What do you mean by people like him?" Stella again looked towards Mark and turned back, glaring defiantly at the barman, "what has he done wrong?" she asked, becoming irate by the ignorant attitude of, how she ascertained, the pompous idiot.

Daniel was angry and went to move towards the bar and express his own opinion but Stuart held him back. "Leave her, and just listen," he told him.

"Do I assume the colour of his skin is a problem. If that is the case, I will tell you something. He was in the Bristol army cadets but was forced out because of the attitude against him. Two years ago he came to us in Bath and was made welcome. Now I don't know if you're able to read the papers, and I can only assume you can't, but when I read the stories or journalistic reports they tell us that we are more than likely heading for another war. Whatever, war or no war, that young man intends to join our army with good recommendations from his cadet sergeant. If he is willing to fight for your country while you stand there safely behind your racist bar then I am more than sure he can have a drink here. So do as I ask and pour the beer!"

The surprised radicalised barman hesitated.

"Did you not hear me? I mean now!" Stella meant business. Stuart knew not to cross his wife.

The barman looked around for support but received none, although a few customers, deep down on his side, said nothing. A wrinkle faced old woman sitting by the window with her husband broke the ice. She stood up and shouted across to the beleaguered barman. "Pour him the beer and I will pay. Years ago when I was very young I went with a black man and it was the best sex I ever had. The young boy deserves to be in here if he's going to fight for Britain. Pour him the beer!" The old lady was adamant.

She sat back down next to her husband who was trying hard not to laugh. There were now mutterings and giggling. The reluctant barman began to pull the pint and a great cheer went up. He handed the beer over but for no known reason refused to take any money. Soon the bar was back to normal although the atmosphere was tainted. Stella went to the old lady and thanked her and then asked if the story was true. Unabashed the old lady confirmed the story.

Her husband's expression said everything, he didn't disbelieve his wife. "No-one's been able to satisfy her since," he said laughing.

Before leaving, all the party-goers went over to the old couple and thanked them sincerely, especially Mark. After a long pub crawl around the district they staggered back to the 'Gin Palace', if only to annoy the barman. Before they left to catch the last train back to Bath, Mark's father collected him outside because parts of Bristol were not safe for any man or woman of his creed to walk home alone late on a Friday night in Bristol.

The rest of the party were lucky, they were all allowed to board the train because some were in a bad state of health. Drunk and disorderly on the rail system was a punishable offence. Stella's forthrightness and willingness to oversee any mishaps persuaded the guard to allow their passage. She bribed him with some of the residue from the young men's pot. The rest of the money was to pay for the taxis to distribute them around the city when they arrived back in Bath.

Having seen them all off safely, Stella, with her husband now in a Scottish stupor, and their overnight guest Daniel, decided to traipse back up to the Bear Flat where the couple lived in a house on Shakespeare Avenue. There was a long arduous uphill walk.

Stella helped her husband up the stairs whilst Daniel stood behind should they fall. Stuart fell fully clothed on the bed and in seconds was asleep and Stella left him, returning to the sitting room where Daniel was studying the photographs on the mantelpiece. He swung around as she entered the room. She appeared pleasing to the eye and he smiled at her shyly. Something stirred inside him whenever he looked at her or when they spoke together. Most of the evening he had shot secretive glances towards her which Stella had returned attentively.

"Would you like a glass of wine or have you drank enough?" she asked him temptingly.

He thought about his current condition and weighed up the situation with the company he was keeping. "Yes please. I don't mind having a nightcap with you, thank you," he told her politely.

Stella went to the parlour and he heard the cork pop. She came back with two cut glasses and a bottle of German red wine and pointed to the settee inviting him to sit down. Having showed him the bottle, given him a glass, Stella asked him to try a small amount. He read the label but in ignorance didn't know what was good or bad wine and merely told her red was fine.

Settling herself comfortably into the armchair she asked him the question which everybody wanted to know the answer. So which regiment have you decided to join?"

Daniel knew that now the party was over he'd have to make his mind up but he still hadn't fully decided. Stella had put him on the spot. He sipped some wine cautiously as he knew that red wine could stain his soft lips. "I am seriously considering staying local and joining the Wiltshire's. Rob Goode made the suggestion to me but I can always move over to a more specialist corps if I do well. At least my mother will know where I am, providing there isn't a war on." He chuckled.

"Stuart is more than certain something will happen. The war I mean. He's considering rejoining the Seaforther's. He doesn't really enjoy civilian life. The army is in his blood, on his mother's side." Stella was pensive. No-one relished losing their loved ones. "He'd sooner rejoin than be conscripted and end up on the bottom of the pile starting all over again. If he re-enlists as soon as possible he might then attain his original rank."

"Does that worry you?" Daniel asked her naively.

"I met him when he was in the army. Before our relationship even began to grow he warned me what being married to a soldier entailed." Stella smiled to herself and stared down into her glass swilling the remaining contents around and around. She looked up at the ceiling and then across to Daniel. "I'm worried, definitely worried Daniel. Do you believe there is going to be a war?"

He could see she was becoming slightly melancholy. 'A woman's prerogative with alcohol' he thought, knowing his mother's mood swings. "Personally I am convinced something will happen. Without a doubt there will be a war, but when the first serious move begins and the gauntlets are thrown down is anyone's guess. Hitler has high ambitions for Europe. He desires complete control of his own people and eventually producing a master race which will systematically eradicate any others that might stand in their path." Daniel went quiet. He was relaxed. He then looked Stella in the eye. "There will be a long war and not only contained in Europe. Everywhere the British have emplacements within their empire they too will be involved. The Germans are in Africa and will want to prise our possessions from us. The conflict will spread far and wide. The Italians are in cahoots with Hitler. Mussolini has already occupied Abyssinia which places a large part of our African empire under threat." Daniel suddenly stopped. He was thinking and stared down at the patterned rug on the floor.

Stella rose from her chair and partially replenished his glass. The sound of bottle neck on glass brought him back into reality. "Japan invaded China last year." Again he appeared to drift into his own world. "Where will this all stop? No-one knows do they? Actually, to be perfectly frank, in Europe war hasn't really started yet. There has been no bloodshed so far." He smiled as he stared through his glass of wine.

The unlikely pair drank wine into the night, talking of many subjects. On their own together Stella found Daniel interesting, definitely anti-Hitler, but one thing which disturbed her was his willingness to go to war. What gave him the desire to fight in earnest she couldn't understand. One thing was sure and that was he didn't need to go to war because his family was in the agricultural business. He was a good healthy looking young man for whom she had a lot of admiration, and certainly her husband did as well.

Now spread across the sofa Daniel began to lose concentration and slowly he drifted off to sleep. The evening had been long, now stretching onward into the middle of the night. Stella watched him with a feeling of pleasure. Her mind stirred up the past, Daniel was so pleasant and intelligent. She wiped a tear from her eye.

Stella went quietly upstairs and from a cupboard drew some blankets. She tiptoed back to the sitting room and placed them over her young guest. Before leaving she bent over his sleeping body, gently rubbed his abdomen, felt his genitals and kissed him fully on the lips for a few seconds.

Her provocative actions briefly woke Daniel and the last he vaguely remembered was seeing Stella leaving the room and turning the light out before he fell back to sleep. He had been stirred.

Chapter 09
The Course to War

Stuart Sinclair woke at the sound of knocking on the door. He was confused. Stella slept soundly beside him with her head almost buried beneath the blankets, but breathing slow and steadily. The sun was high indicating the time was at least mid-morning. He rubbed his bloodshot eyes. In his ear there came another more emphatic knock on the door. Still dressed from the evening before he eased off the bed and crept down stairs into the hallway. He could see a figure behind the two frosted glass panels of the front door which he opened trying his utmost not to make too much noise.

"James! You're early," he exclaimed holding his hand over his mouth.

James eyed him up and down and smiled. "I'm actually late Stuart. I think the time is about ten thirty. You look like you had a good evening out in Bristol."

Stuart realised his clothes were creased having slept in them all night and apologised. He invited Daniel's father into his home.

Daniel was still asleep on the sofa snoring gently and they moved on into the kitchen. On the draining board were two wine glasses and one and a half empty bottles of best red wine.

"You live in style." James remarked whilst reading the label on one of the bottles.

Stuart tried to defend himself. "Believe me that was not me, that must have been Stella and your son. No wonder they're both still asleep," he paused for thought, "I can't even remember coming home. What would you like, finish off the wine or a cup of tea?"

'Much too early for wine', thought James. He opted for tea although he did sip and sample the wine.

Stuart lit the gas stove and put the decrepit kettle on. "Excuse me a minute." He went out of the already opened back door and relieved himself in the karsey.

When he returned James had prepared the teapot and four cups he had found in the cupboard. "I'll wake him up," he said, referring to his son. He left the dishevelled Scotsman to finish brewing the tea and find the milk and sugar.

Daniel struggled to wake up. When he finally came around he appeared to be a mess, his mouth was dry and lips were stained red. His eyes were much the same. He quickly went straight outside and urinated up against the privet hedge, watched by an indignant neighbour from a bedroom window, ironically with a West Highland terrier cradled in her arms. Stewart brought in the tea and the three sat around the table saying very little, just sipping their insipid liquids if only to regenerate the fluid in their bodies. Noises were heard from upstairs and shortly afterwards Stella appeared in her dressing gown. To Stuart and Daniel she looked decidedly worse for wear, unkempt and disorientated, so much different from the night before. The appearance on her face was one of aghast when she tried to drink the tepid contents from the porcelain pot and she went back to the kitchen to try and rejuvenate the pale infusion.

Eventually Stella returned and topped up each cup with some more satisfactory brew. Daniel avoided eye contact with her. In his mind, her kissing him late in the night embarrassed him somewhat, young as he was. He vaguely remembered what had happened.

It was Stella who spoke first with any conviction. "The Wiltshire regiment. I think Daniel wants to join the Wiltshire regiment." She smiled at him.

He was shocked that she would say anything in front of his father. They all stared at him expecting an explanation. "Maybe, I'm not sure yet," he hesitantly told them.

"Why the Wiltshire's Daniel? There are plenty of other options. Don't be too hasty." Stuart willed him to think before he jumped, and so eventually make the right decision.

Daniel watched the three of them cautiously and then answered. "I'm from Wiltshire. I was born in Wiltshire. So joining the 'Wiltshires' is the rightful thing to do." Daniel looked at them almost accusingly as if they had no right to question his decision.

Stuart knew from past conversations with James where Daniel had been born and his reason for being, but now he tested them both. "You could join one of the more formidable regiments such as the Scottish Highlanders, the Irish or Welsh Guards. Regiments with great reputations. Why not?"

James realised where Stuart was angling towards. He was interested to know if Daniel knew he had been born in Wales, or indeed why.

Stella raised her eyebrows. She knew the story from her husband, and promptly told Stuart to go and wash and change if only to have him out of the room, scolding him, telling him they were going out quite soon. He obediently left the table without saying a word.

Soon after they bid farewells and after all things said Daniel was being driven out of Bath with his father.

As they walked down to the city centre Stella eyed her husband up and down. "You look terrible. Why do you have to get so drunk?"

"I can't say the same about you, can I?" he replied sarcastically, trying to smile but finding mirth difficult. "A Scotsman is entitled to have a drink every now and again. Where are we going anyway?" he asked.

"I have six weeks off before the schools go back so we're going up to see your parents. I've never met them, but now I have the time. We'll go by train, so by booking early we can apparently buy the tickets cheaper." Stella watched Stuart's anguished face.

Unknown to Stella he hadn't seen or spoke to his mother or father for some considerable time and he had no intention of doing so in the near future. He had met Stella in Warminster nearly three years previously and after a whirlwind courtship married the girl. Very shortly afterwards he demobilised himself, and much to his regret of leaving the army, they moved to Bath. Solemnly he walked towards the footbridge which would take them over the river Avon and then under the rail track to the station.

In the foyer of the railway station Stella joined a short queue. Stuart made his move and tugged at her elbow indicating to her that he wanted a word outside. At first she was reluctant to move having been the next in line to be served, but he pulled even harder.

"Please Stella not in here. Let's go outside, or even better into the Station Hotel. We'll talk about going to Scotland there. We have plenty of time." He pleaded with her not to make an issue in front of everyone.

Stella glanced around and she reluctantly left the station and went across the street through the taxi throng and entered the hotel lounge. There was a look of anger on her face as he returned from the bar. "What's this all about Stuart? I want to know!"

He placed a glass of wine in front of her and sat down opposite. After gulping down some large mouthfuls of beer which he nearly deposited on the floor, Stuart began telling her what was troubling him. "I'm twenty eight now and have done six years with the Highlanders. I've told you this before. What I haven't told you is the reason why I joined the army. Petty criminality basically. The Scottish judiciary gave me the choice of either going to prison or sorting myself out and joining the services. My mother and father haven't seen me since before I was given those options. Nor my brother and sisters. To be perfectly honest Stella I am too ashamed to go back home."

Stella gazed out of the window whilst tapping imaginary tunes on her wine glass and suddenly turned to him, "so what did you do?" She wasn't quite so livid but annoyed he had never told her about his criminal past before.

Stuart took a deep breath. "When I lived at home, burglary and house breaking. I was a thief. The police were on to me and that was when I left and moved to Edinburgh. Soon enough I was involved with a gang. We did well out of our booty but that wasn't to last. Someone grassed us up and we were caught in a warehouse near Musselburgh. I was the youngest and for some reason the judge took a lenient view, then he gave me my options. Join up in the army or go to prison," Stuart went quiet for a short while and then looked up at her, "Stella I am not yet ready to visit my family by any means so please don't force me back home right now."

"Why didn't you tell me in the first place. I could have accepted what you had done," she said sorrowfully.

You've said everything Stella. 'You *could* have accepted my misdeeds'. But would have you? I didn't want to lose you. A beautiful young woman. I never lied to you, I just didn't tell you the whole story. Besides I've made up for my crimes haven't I? Been out of trouble for years and then reached the rank of sergeant. I look after those lads in the cadets. I know they respect me. I just don't want them to go the way I did when I was their age." He leant back circling his fore fingers hoping she would support him all the way.

Stella's eyes were sad. "Your mother might be proud of you now, why don't you just go and see her?"

Stuart stood up and stared up at the chandelier. He took some deep breaths. People at the bar wondered what was happening between the pair. "My mother and father are staunch Presbyterians. Deeply religious and regular attendants of the church." Briefly he stopped talking. His mind thought back in time and he wasn't proud. "The first time I ever stole something was when I was about thirteen." He stopped again.

Stella waited for him to explain what he had done. "Well?" she asked.

"I went into the church and stole the money from the collection box." Stuart stood up, turned, and went to the bar and finished his drink. He ordered another for himself giving time for his wife to dwell upon what he had just told her.

When he returned she asked. "Why did you start thieving Stuart. Why?" She looked deep into her husband's eyes.

"Life isn't easy up there in northern Scotland. People have families of eight children and often more. As much as my parents tried their hardest they had desperate times. Every penny counted. I didn't begin to steal for myself. I stole for my mother, father and siblings. I remember her one day staring into her purse in bewilderment and finding more money than she thought she had. Her face was one of incomprehension but she never admitted to anyone that the extra income existed, she couldn't afford to say anything. I have three brothers and three sisters and in those days, we all needed feeding. When eventually mother realised from where the money had appeared, from my nefarious activities, she was flummoxed. Mother had spent the money to help feed and clothe my brothers and sisters. In desperation to sustain the family she said nothing but continued to go to church. Poverty Stella! My activities were all derived from abject poverty. Over the years rumours were rife and the people in the village knew what was happening and then I realised the time was for me to move south. Any money which I had accrued from thieving, went into my mother's household. Even when I went to live in Edinburgh I sent the proceeds back. Now most of my brothers and sisters have left home but my father can now live off his paltry earnings from the estate." Stuart sat back waiting for Stella to absorb his criminal revelations.

She was completely bemused and gazed around the bar wondering what to ask or say next. She suddenly looked him in the eye. "Is there anything else you might want to tell me?"

As if his day couldn't develop into anything worse he had to tell her even more ignoble news. "I've contacted the regiment and offered to re-enlist. Subject to a medical, I shouldn't have any problems."

Stella peered out of the window and up along the busy street. She was deep in thought. At least she'd saved herself money on two unnecessary rail tickets.

James and Daniel never spoke at all as they headed back to Colerne. As they entered Batheaston James suddenly veered off left from the main road and took the lane towards Northend. Daniel glanced at his father. "Why are we going this way?"

He never answered and continued along an ever narrowing lane ignoring the right turn back to Colerne and headed up the St Catherine's valley towards the tiny hamlet of Fuddlebrook. However Fuddlebrook wasn't his intended destination and soon he attempted an extremely tight left hand turn off road up a well worn track. The wheels of the Austin screamed as the car tried to grip the dusty surface but eventually there was cohesion and they parked up in front of the unique Sandybanks Inn.

The weather was beautiful with hardly a cloud in the sky and barely a puff of wind. Daniel was reluctant to have a drink but his father insisted and soon they were each sat outside with a fine pint from the famous Bristol brewery, George's. "The name is nothing to do with your grandfather," James remarked, jokingly.

"So why have we come here? I need to go home and have a wash and brush up." Daniel was agitated.

"When I return home I want to be able to tell your mother what you are doing next and where you are going with your short life. You don't understand what she's been like over the last months, especially as time ambles on and another bloody war looms on the horizon. I have the impression everyone else knows what you are up to except us." James raised his eyebrows demanding some truths.

Daniel sipped at his drink and then looked up at his father. "I've made inroads into joining the Wiltshire regiment. Subject to what I achieve at school, a medical and an interview, the military authorities will take my qualifications from there. Sergeant Sinclair says judging by my background I should have few problems in joining any regiment's officer cadets." He took some more tentative sips at his beer.

"You would be more helpful to us at the farm." James told him, almost pleadingly.

"From what I can gather if we don't stand up to the Nazi menace soon we won't have a bloody farm to protect." Now Daniel had his turn to raise his eyebrows and await an answer in anticipation.

James stared across the valley. He swirled his drink around in his glass trying to contemplate the future, not only that of the farm and his family, but the whole of Europe as well. Deep down he knew what his son was insinuating but now had to come to terms with the fact that what he had done those many years before, his own son was about to re-enact, although probably, in a more responsible manner.

"So I can tell your mother that is your final decision?" James asked him hopefully.

"Tell her what you want. Whichever regiment I join nothing will make any difference. First of all I will join the Wiltshire's as an ordinary soldier, spend a couple of years there, earn some stripes and then specialise in a particular corps or division. I should be signing up in September." Daniel was adamant.

"Alright. That's fair enough. Now I'm going to ask you some questions which you might not know the answers. When you sign up are you going to say where you were born?" James almost smiled.

"Wiltshire, where else?" Daniel was bemused.

"And who is listed on your birth certificate as your mother and father?" James hardened his attitude. Daniel couldn't answer and now the boot was on the other foot. "And what is your name on your birth certificate?" his father asked him.

"What are you insinuating Dad?" Daniel went to stand up and move away.

"Sit down! Now begin to have some respect and I will tell you what happened eighteen years or nineteen years ago. Are you now going to listen?" Daniel nodded his head slowly not knowing what he was about to hear.

James started at the very beginning. He explained why he himself had left home to join the army, taking his brother's conscription papers because he felt his older brother, Jimmy, was less suited and too small for military life. The decision eventually led to the incident of James' knee injury having being shot by *young* Daniel's uncle during the war, with the intent to prevent the itinerant underage soldier from 'going over the top'. James described in detail his travels which brought him to Colerne and himself falling in love with his mother, Joy. Then there was the initial persecution from George, Daniel's grandfather, and the military police's over exuberance to take him to trial. He paused every now and again and thought back in time. James mentioned the court martial and his own father, whom he had never ever seen, being there as a witness, then the feeling of being found not guilty and the euphoria on the steps outside the courthouse. Everyone appeared to be on his side. He mentioned a car that had pulled up in which he had no idea who was inside.

"I hadn't by this time seen your mother for some time. Nor your grandfather or grandmother, although George did go to the trial but I actually believed he was there just to see me put down. Your grandmother, Helen, had been ill for a long time, stressed perhaps from your uncle Daniel's death. Your grandmother was the woman who first stepped out of the car with a tiny baby, she walked over to me and placed the child in my arms. Everything went so fast, and I didn't know what was happening. Suddenly there I was with a baby in my arms and I looked around for some encouragement and then your mother stepped out of the car. She came over and told me that you were ours." James paused before he carried on, tears rolled down his cheeks. "Not that your birth place makes any difference, but you were actually born in Pembrokeshire, not Wiltshire. On your birth certificate, which you haven't seen, you are registered as Daniel O'Dell because me and your mother were not married at the time, so be careful when you sign up, make sure you use the correct name." James wiped his eyes and smiled at his son. "So now you know. You were born a bastard! Believe me Daniel I don't care what people think about the circumstances of your conception or birth, you are mine and your mother's son and we both love you dearly. I was lucky and came back from that awful war. Many didn't. I would sooner be an alive 'bastard' than an inscription on a memorial stone, whichever side I was fighting for."

There was a sound of hooting coming up the lane. James looked across at his son who was struggling with his beer. "That could well be Rob and Herbie. I'm supposed to be meeting them here." He tossed his son the key to the car. "Do you think you'll be able to manage to drive the Austin home on your own after last night?" he asked. "I need you to do two things for me? Speak to your mother because she is your best friend. Secondly milk the cows this afternoon please." James turned away and then turned back. "Oh! and wash the lipstick off your face."

Daniel frowned, he said no more and went home. The last thing he wanted that day was to confront his mother and then end up milking the cows. They were all cantankerous in the summer sun.

Chapter 10
Hitler's Intentions

Daniel sat in the window of the Station Hotel reading a copy of the German journal the 'Voelkische Beobachter'. He had obtained the paper from his old German teacher who had a friend working in Germany and occasionally posted him a copy through devious hands. The journal was about a week old but the headline spoke of Hitler's crossing of the Czech border and annexing the Sudentenland on October 1st. He smiled to himself. The school debating club had been correct, but how long now before the German dictator took over the rest of the country, if not the whole of Europe. 'Where would he turn his attention to next' Daniel thought to himself.

Daniel glanced at the clock behind the bar. The time was just after twelve, lunchtime. He was awaiting the arrival of his friend Mark who was coming from Bristol into Bath on the train. Their intention was to have a few beers in town and then go up to Colerne for his leaving party. On Monday he would finally achieve his goal and enlist in the army with the Wiltshire regiment. He had done what his father asked and worked on the farm throughout the summer and early autumn until the harvest was complete. In two days he would begin his military travels. He became engrossed in the paper and failed to notice the passengers vacating the station. The next thing he knew Mark was sat beside him with two beers on the table.

"Ei gude wie Herr Hitler?" Mark asked him with a large grin on his face exposing his brilliant white teeth.

"I'm fine thank you. Did you learn that just for today?" Daniel replied.

"I did actually. I happened to meet someone from Germany who told me what to say and how to pronounce the words. Poor bloke was worried to death about what might happen to him if war does break out. He was perturbed as to whether they would let him go home to Germany or incarcerate him here in an internment camp." Mark had actually been uneasy for him. "He wasn't sure at all as to where might he be safer?"

"Did he tell you where he actually came from because the dialect sounds like he is from the Frankfurt Mannheim area judging by your pronunciation," Daniel explained.

"He does. How do you know that?" Mark was astonished.

"The dialect is known as Sudhessisch from around that district." Daniel informed him, trying not to sound conceited. "Comparable to listening to a Geordie or a west countryman."

Mark shook his head slowly and said nothing more on the matter. The pair sat chatting about the latest news, most of which was about a possible war. The economy and local gossip paled into insignificance. They both agreed Hitler would annexe the whole of Czechoslovakia eventually and then he would invade Poland, using the excuse that he wanted to reunite Prussia with her so-called 'mother country', Germany.

People socialising at the bar were quite amused listening to the two young men in the window debating the state of Europe, especially as one was black and the other white. They wondered where their allegiance had developed. Out of earshot the barman quietly explained who Daniel was, a farmer's son from upon the hill at Colerne, but couldn't place his friend with the slight American accent.

"I've had some bad news in the last couple of days." Mark nervously tapped his fingers on the table and kept glancing out of the window.

Daniel looked at him sullenly. He almost knew what was coming but never the less asked him what he had heard, more than probably through a ministerial brown envelope. 'Ironic, a brown envelope' thought Daniel'. He smiled to himself.

"They won't let me join the army." His expression revealed his disappointment.

"Why, what did *they* say? What excuse did *they* have? You were as good as the rest of us in the cadets! In fact better than most." Daniel took the news personally every time Mark was thwarted from doing something because of the colour of his skin.

"Their excuse is I don't have a British passport. I am British by birth, actually born in Bristol. I was adopted immediately. They kept quoting my parents nationality, American. I cannot convince them I was born in England. Then they kept telling me about how things would be tough in a British regiment especially because of my colour. If they only knew what it's like in the American army. Blacks and whites are segregated. The blacks have to do all the menial tasks like cleaning the mess halls and toilets. None of the likes of us ever become mechanics or artillery men, jobs with trades. We're not even allowed to drink out of the same fountains as the whites. Racism is rife and starts at the very top." He leant back in his chair with his hands behind his head and gazed out of the window. His powerful biceps twitched uncontrollably, exposing his exasperation.

Daniel felt so sorry for him. He thought about Marks' dilemma for a while, trying to think of who might be able to help and soon came to a conclusion. "Come on! Drink up! Let's go and find a bloke we both know who can be more than useful in the circumstances. He has many connections." They drank up and politely acknowledged the staff as they left the premises. The unlikely pair walked along Manver street and crossed the road heading towards the Edinburgh Castle. Most people walked past them with their heads down avoiding eye contact. Daniel smiled ironically. Here was his friend, desperate to join the British army and fight against the Nazi scourge, and they didn't even want him in the country.

In the 'Edinburgh Castle' they bought a drink and then asked where Herbie might be. A wizened old lady turned and studied the clock for a few seconds.

"Could be in the Saracens or maybe the Bell in Walcot street. Around that area anyway," she told them in a strong west country accent.

"Try the Old Green Tree." A middle aged man, Henry, with a hand missing was rolling a cigarette. As he ran his lips over the fragile paper he eyed the two young men. He was adept with his disability and soon he was puffing on his frail roll up. "Herbie is out with Rob, that's what he told me. Not for long though, there's a party somewhere tonight."

Daniel and Mark turned towards each other and raised their eyebrows simultaneously. Without saying a word they began to drink up as quickly as possible.

The one handed man spoke again. "Take your time boys. Take your time. Life is short. We've another war on the way so enjoy yourselves while you have your freedom. Savour every moment." He raised his stump. "I had a highly skilled job before the last war, afterwards there was no possibility I could work with one hand. I can't even clean the streets. Ever since I've been in poverty. My wife left me and I've lived alone for nearly twenty years. The only thing that kept me alive was the hostel next door but even that now is finished. There's no money from the government or local sponsorship." He dragged on his cigarette, took a mouthful of beer and looked at what was left in his glass. "You try living on handouts."

The despondent old fellow looked away. Mark bought a beer for him and he and Daniel left.

The barman looked across the near empty room at the man with one hand. "Henry why didn't you tell them you lost your arm in a work accident at Stothert's and not in the war?"

"I didn't tell them I lost my hand in the war. Anyhow, war or Stothert's, nobody cares where my hand was lost, life is still short and I am still living on handouts." He stood up and asked for the beer that had been so graciously put in for him behind the bar.

Herbie and Rob were discussing the success of Arsenal football club when Mark and Daniel entered the smallest pub in Bath, the Old Green Tree. General banter went on between the four and they settled down having a general discussion about the economy. Soon the subject of German expansionism came up. Daniel had been studying the maps and reading the history books. He had become fully aware of the divisiveness of all the nations in Europe. Stretching over hundreds of years they could be on each other's side one minute and the next minute would suddenly be in conflict.

"Hitler intends to turn Germany into the most powerful nation in Europe with his people completely in control. He has a vision that the Teutons will rule over the whole of Europe and possibly one day, the world," he paused for a moment, "in the new year the whole of Czechoslovakia will fall and then he'll set his sights on regaining eastern Prussia bringing the area back into the German fold."

Rob interrupted him. "That would mean invading Poland and would certainly mean dragging us into the war, including the French but what about the Russians. Would the Bolsheviks want an aggressive German army on their western doorstep?"

"I don't know. I doubt whether they do, but is Hitler ready to take on such a sphere of action? He might come to an agreement with the Russians." Daniel would find out in the future. His appetite for the subject was never ending.

Both Mark and Herbie said very little during the conversation. Their job was to keep replenishing the table with beer.

One other subject Daniel brought up was the state of the British Navy and the menace of the U-boats. "The number of U-boats the Germans have is not known but an estimation of possibly as many as fifty has been broached. Now this is significant because obviously some will be deployed in the North Sea, but more importantly, most out in the Atlantic."

"Why?" asked Mark.

"Britain is far from self sufficient and we will need all the supplies we can get from abroad especially from America. We have our colonies across the world which will undoubtedly help but if they become embroiled in regional wars then they could easily be cut off from the 'mother' nation. If the U-boats gain control of the seas then no doubt we will be starved into submission. With all these threats of war we should now be, in haste, rebuilding and re-arming our military fleet to protect our merchant shipping. We have thousands of merchantmen out on the seas but also we have many coastal traders which will need safeguarding, especially on our east coast."

Again Rob interrupted him. "The government will have to re-instate Churchill as First Lord of the Admiralty. They ought to now *and* create a war cabinet."

"I couldn't agree with you more Rob. The government has dithered for too long now and the newspapers keep telling us they hope to appease Hitler with a series of treaties or agreements. He signs the documents and then completely ignores them. They are not worth the paper they are written on. If Hitler does attack Poland are we going to act only then, or do we start preparing for war now?"

All the listening parties agreed that something should be done straight away although few knew where to start.

Daniel began again. "One other thing we should bear in mind. Going back to what was said earlier about the U-boat fleet, which leads me to think that after Hitler's assumed Polish campaign and the Poles capitulate, his next target will almost certainly be heading northward through Denmark and then across the Skaggerak to Norway."

His three friends appeared a little bemused but then Rob understood the thread of his rationale. "Do I understand that you believe the Norwegian fiords will be used to harbour and re-supply the German U-boat fleet?"

"I am almost sure that will happen plus they will have easy access into the Atlantic, and of course, the North Sea. We will have to wait and see. Another good reason is the supply of iron ore. Norway is an important source for the Germans and they will have to keep the ports open, especially Narvik." Daniel rose to stretch his legs. He went to the bar but not before telling Mark to explain his own personal plight to Rob.

After a traipse around other establishments in Bath they split up and made their way home. They would all meet up in Colerne that evening for Daniel's leaving party whilst Mark would be his guest of honour.

Daniel doggedly steered his father's car out of Bath and began the familiar route up Bannerdown hill. He found difficulty in concentrating as the drinks had taken their toll. Mark remained quiet as he mulled over in his head what he'd heard that afternoon. They approached the turn off to Colerne and Daniel managed to slow down enough to take the notorious right hand fork at Giddeahall, rather than carry on along the Fosse road. Not four hundred yards further on he veered off left onto a bridle path. The ground was rough but navigable. He kept his speed very low as he coaxed the Austin along the rutted old track used only by tractors or horse riders at leisure. His father would go mad if he found out where he'd driven his car. Some way along at a gateway he parked and they took the much needed opportunity to relieve themselves of their lunchtime intake of alcohol.

As they leant on the twisted wooden gate which hung off only one hinge Daniel spoke for the first time since leaving Bath. "I found out the other day that all these fields in front of us as far as you can see and the few behind were surveyed a couple of years ago in nineteen thirty-six. The surveyors have been back here recently," he hesitated, "guess what for Mark?" Daniel smiled, because he knew he'd have to tell him and didn't give him a chance to answer. "Military purposes. An airfield for the defence of Bristol and Bath," came the cocksure reply, "and this one won't be the only one around here". Daniel kept gazing across the fields when he suddenly asked. "What did Rob say when you told him about not being able to join the army?" Daniel wanted to know.

"First of all he asked me why I didn't go to America, and under my father's surname join there but I told him what I have told you. He seemed to understand the problems we blacks have and thought about our problems for a while, but then he asked me a strange question."

Daniel raised his eyebrows waiting to hear.

"He asked me if I only wanted to go to war or fight merely for an ideology. He mentioned the Spanish civil war whereby people came from all over Europe to fight against a right wing government, a dictatorship, and that the rebels were mostly communists. He mentioned a group, the International Brigade. I didn't understand who he was talking about and told him I had no particular ideology but would always fight on the side of righteousness. I felt as if I was being interrogated by the same people who refused to let me join up here."

Daniel smiled. He knew Rob would want to know where Mark's heart really lay. With the 'Empire'.

"Daniel! I just want to be a soldier. Especially along side you but I know now that will never be the case." Mark was desperately unhappy, thwarted by a biased system.

"How did he leave the subject with you? Was that the end of the conversation?" Daniel was surprised Rob hadn't reassured him or at least given him some sign of hope.

"He did say he still had strong contacts within the British army but wouldn't elaborate. He told me to be patient and not to expect an answer when he appears at your party this evening." Mark turned and stared back across the fields trying to imagine how the fields would look like as an aerodrome or army barracks.

Just as they were about to squeeze back into the Austin Seven Daniel stood on the footboard and spoke across the roof. "Believe me Mark if Rob thinks you genuinely want to enlist in our army he will make some arrangement. Just remember this conflict isn't going to be confined solely in Europe."

The party went well. People spilled into the car park, but no-one cared about the cold. The only thing that spoiled the evening for Daniel was his grandfather's degeneration. Lately his health had been deteriorating rapidly. His mother didn't stay long as she was concerned for her father. She left early with doctor West. Both Daniel and James watched their quiet departure and acknowledged the problem. Anything might happen, but under guardianship George's health was hopefully manageable.

A little later Mark tapped Daniel on the shoulder. "There's someone here to see you," he told him warily.

Daniel scanned the room and caught sight of Stella standing just inside the door. She had a friend with her and he made his way over to them both and courteously pecked Stella on the cheek. "I didn't expect to see you here. What a surprise." He quickly eyed her up and down. Her attractiveness stirred him briefly as she did the others in the crowded bar.

Stella introduced her friend to him. "Daniel this is Karen."

"I've heard so much about you Daniel. I'm pleased to have met you." Karen glanced at Stella and smiled, quickly shrugging her shoulders as if to agree with Stella about his persona.

Daniel felt awkward but quickly changed the course of the conversation and persuaded them to have a drink. They struggled to the bar and after being served the two women preoccupied him for most of the evening.

Daniel learnt that Stuart would rejoin his regiment the Seaforth Highlanders and had sent his best wishes on his own enlistment with the Wiltshire's. Stuart had already returned to Scotland. First he would visit Edinburgh and spend a couple of weeks there with old friends and then travel to Fort George, Ardersier, home of his regiment.

"So what are you going to do Stella? Follow him?" Daniel asked.

"There's no point. I can keep my job in Bath. If what the omens suggest are true then he'll be away for some time. No! I'll be staying in Bath, our home now. He's going to have to leave the army for good one day and we'll have to settle down somewhere, so why not Bath." Stella was happy with the arrangement.

Daniel excused himself and made his way across the car park to the toilets. Robbie Goode watched him go and then followed him. As they stood peeing up against the wall Rob asked satirically whilst smiling, "she's getting her claws into you isn't she?"

"Who?" Daniel asked, surprised.

"The woman you're talking to. The one that drinks the red wine," he answered sultrily.

"Who do you mean? Which one?" Daniel didn't understand.

"The one with the dark hair. You know who I mean. Most of the pub knows she's after your cock, except you."

"She's not my girlfriend she is Stuart Sinclair's wife. You've met her anyway, the night we went to Bristol," he answered, rather annoyed.

Rob thought back but couldn't remember. He went to leave but nodding his head made a final remark, "I think she fancies you."

Back in the bar Daniel was relieved to find that some others were talking to the two women and he grabbed his glass and left them to their conversation. Not long afterwards Stella re-attached herself to him and he began to realise what Rob had said appeared to be true. He introduced her to Rob and crept away hoping he would keep her talking for some time, but again there was no time before she was at his side again. Daniel couldn't be discourteous and so he went along with the situation although he couldn't keep Stuart out of his mind. What would he think? Then he remembered the night he'd stayed at their house and had thought she kissed him goodnight. The scenario was beginning to add up. Something was on her mind, but were there sexual connotations?

Much to Daniel's relief Karen broke the union. "Come on Stella I have to be home by midnight."

Soon after, Daniel was seeing them off in Karen's badly maintained car, but not before Stella had drawn him towards her and kissed him passionately. "Good luck! Ring me when you get your first leave. I'm going to miss you."

The ladies battered old car chugged out of the car park, back fired a couple of times and disappeared around the corner into the night. Daniel went back inside and the whole pub cheered him, much to his embarrassment. The celebrations continued. As the local policeman was at the party, the drinking went on into the early hours of the morning.

Chapter 11
The Morning after the Night Before

Mark woke with a start, not knowing where in hell he was. When he moved, his body created a rustling sound. His neck and face itched and he realised he still had his clothes on from the night before. After a while his eyes adjusted to the gloom and he could see a very dim light enter underneath the barn door. The longer he kept his eyes open a general picture began to evolve. Near his feet, parked in the middle of the old stone building, was a worn out old tractor. Sacks of grain and bales of hay and straw were everywhere. Farm utensils of every kind lined the end wall. Unknown to him he was being watched by a ghostlike white bird perched motionless on a dusty oak cross beam. The owl's faeces below was long dried out suggesting the longevity of the bird's co-existence with the owners. A large brown rat scurried across the floor but the owl paid no attention to the rodent as he was pre-occupied with his guest's intrusion.

Daniel sneezed and broke cover from his bed of loose hay. He too sat up and surveyed his predicament after rubbing the sleep from his eyes.

"What's the time?" he asked, but Mark didn't know.

"My ol' man will kill me. I was supposed to help with the milking." He struggled out of his dried grass camp bed and went to the small opening in the barn door and let himself out into the yard. The cows were trundling back down to the fields, oblivious of Daniel's idiotic appearance, being covered in hay, straw, chaff and seeds. Two of the animals peered at the ridiculous pair when Mark followed him, stumbling out into the cold open air.

The forever reliable Albert appeared from the bottom shed. He didn't know what to say, and struggled to hold himself back because not laughing was difficult when he saw them both in such a state. Black people never came into his sphere of operations but to see Mark and Daniel as they were he felt he couldn't have written a better comedy script.

"I've finished the milking. All you need now is to clean everything up. Your father said you were going to help." Albert looked at him sternly. "Never make promises you can't keep especially when you're drunk." He turned away smiling to himself wondering what Daniel would do or say next.

"Alb! Alb! Wait! Wait a minute please." Albert turned around and stared at Daniel expecting him to beg forgiveness.

"Albert I have to take Mark up to the market square. His father's picking him up soon. I'll have to take the tractor. Please finish off the cleaning and I'll be back to help you out."

"What! In those clothes on the tractor. I'm not letting you take the Ferguson. No! I'll tell you what. You clean everything up and I'll drop your friend off up in the village. Do you want his father to see you in your state, let alone his own son?" Albert had him eating out of his hand.

Mark couldn't understand the hierarchy in Daniel's family and stayed well away from the diplomacy. All he wanted was to be in the market square when his father arrived. Mark looked pleadingly at Daniel and nodded his head in agreement. Daniel reluctantly went along with the arrangement.

The two friends bid farewell emotionally and vowed to keep in touch. Albert manoeuvred the little old tractor out of the barn and Mark climbed on board. Daniel opened the gates in front and allowed them out onto the lane. He turned back. In the parlour he donned an apron, changed into some Wellington's and began washing down the sheds. 'Tomorrow', he kept telling himself, 'he would begin his new life in the British Army'.

Albert arrived back a half an hour later.

"Was he alright." Daniel asked.

"Yes he was fine," but then he went quiet.

"What's the matter? What happened?" Daniel felt there was something wrong.

"I don't think that was his father who picked him up," he looked at Daniel suspiciously.

"Why, how do you know?" Daniel was worried.

Albert was matter of fact. "He had no qualms about getting into the car. They spoke as if they were lifelong friends and then drove off."

"Why don't you think his father picked him up?" Daniel wanted to know his friend was safe.

Albert paused for thought. He was as equally intrigued as well, "because whoever picked him up was a white man."

Chapter 12

The Message

The telephone rang startling George from his whisky induced sleep. He muttered something incoherently and when Joy picked up the receiver he slowly fell back into the slumber which separated him from the real world.

"Hello! Joy speaking," she answered with the perceived voice of an eloquent office receptionist.

"Joy! It's Rob. Lovely to speak to you. Have you heard from Daniel?" he went straight to the point.

"Only once when he arrived at his new barracks. Why? Do you need him?" she asked inquiringly.

"Well no, not really. I'm after Mark actually but I've been unable to make any contact and have an important message for him. I just wondered whether you would know how I can get hold of him. Did Daniel ever have his phone number?"

"Strange you should say that because Mark rang here last week. He sounded a little bit emotional. His parents had to move home for some reason, although he didn't explain why. Hang on, I'll see if I can find his new number." Joy rummaged around amongst the pile of paperwork on the small table where the phone was kept. "Here, have you some paper and a pen?" Joy gave him the number. After a few words in exchange they replaced their receivers, both curious.

"Mr. Campbell. Hello is that Mr Campbell. Rob Goode here." Rob was frustrated. For three days he had been trying to help someone but kept coming up against a brick wall, or so he felt.

"Yes. Why? Who is that?" Mr. Campbell sounded extremely wary which made Rob equally suspicious.

"Is there any chance I can speak to your son Mark?" Rob was on the point of giving up.

"Just at this moment he is not available. Please give me your number and I will ask him to ring you as soon as possible."

"Mr. Campbell! If Mark is with you now, please tell him I am Rob Goode, he knows me, I have some important news for him. He asked me to do him a favour and now I think I may be in a position to help." Rob began to feel there was something underlying in Mark's background, but what, he couldn't fathom out, 'possibly his colour', he thought.

There was a pause and he could hear someone talking over the shoulder of Mr. Campbell. Someone had been talking in the background, then a woman spoke, "yes that is alright, hold on and we'll just go and fetch him." She was Mr Campbell's wife.

"Rob I am sorry. There has been a misunderstanding. My parents don't know you and they are reluctant to give any information to people on the telephone. We've been under some pressure of late, just one of those things at the moment. We've moved house and hence the new number." Mark was very apologetic.

Rob's sharp mind immediately thought there were definitely racial undertones involved. Bristol had historically played a large part in the slavery of black people and old attitudes within the communities die hard. "I'm sorry to hear that but just listen to me please. I have a friend who has extensive connections in east Africa. He also has an insight into the British army there as well. In fact he owns a considerable amount of land in Kenya. He is over here in England at the moment and I have told him about your plight. We are meeting in a small public house in north Wiltshire called the Old Spotted Cow at Marston Meysey. I am prepared to take you along so you can talk to him yourself. He is very amiable and I am more than sure he will be able to help you enlist if that is what you really wish." Mark went to interrupt him but Rob was having no more. "Wait! First of all he will have to employ you or find you employment. That will not be for long but then you will have the entitlement to be British, up to a point. Then you can enlist but you will probably be in the King's African Rifles. They are a renowned regiment. Their headquarters are in Kenya at the capital city, Nairobi.

Mark if you are happy to accept then we'll pick you up next week. One other thing, if you decide to come with me, read up on the regiment, the more you know about them, the better. They have a flamboyant history. You'll only get one chance which you'll have to take, if that is really what you want."

Mark didn't throw his opportunity away and organised to meet Rob for their visit to the obscure village called Marston Meysey.

Chapter 13

The Christmas Present

After six weeks of basic training Daniel arrived back in Bath on Christmas Eve. He had a mere four days off, and then would have to return to Catterick barracks and prepare to go to Palestine, joining the 2nd. Battalion some time in the early new year. The journey south had been arduous. Celebrating or moody servicemen were everywhere, many already intoxicated. The train had been completely sold out and he had to stand all the way after, as a well mannered young man, offering a tentative young woman and her child his seat. The short passage from Bristol to Bath had offered some respite but now he was sitting in the familiar bar of the Station hotel waiting for his father to pick him up. Snow was falling and he began to think that if his father didn't come soon they would never make the journey back up to Colerne, the 'village on the hill'.

The noise of a car horn drew his attention away from the bar and onto the street outside. His father had arrived and he quickly drank his beer and left.

There were many people about which slowed their exit from the city. Snow was falling but not settling. At the bottom of Bannerdown hill their problems were about to begin.

"Down here the weather is not so bad," James told him, "but the higher we climb the snow thickens and is settling." He brought the car to halt and asked Daniel to sit in the back so as to increase the traction over the back wheels. "If we begin to slow and slide, bounce up and down on the back seat that will probably help."

They set off and after gathering up enough speed veered off left up the notorious hill. The wheel tracks in the snow showed that someone had gone before them but whether they had driven to the very top remained to be seen. Whatever, James had little choice but to follow the mystery vehicle.

The first bend was crucial, a relatively steep and long incline. A danger was other cars coming in the opposite direction, losing control and colliding. Daniel bounced up and down like a child having a tantrum but his antics worked and they reached to where the gradient was less steep, moreso a slope. Here they managed to gather pace for the assault on the final climb which would eventually offer a treacherous bend and a long haul to the summit. The snowstorm was worsening as the altitude increased and their visibility was poor. The wipers struggled to remove the excess snow and James drove with his nose almost touching the windscreen. The car slewed from side to side and the engine raced from the little traction gained from the cold, buried road surface. No-one else had appeared to have attempted the final hill climb and James began to wish he'd brought the tractor into Bath instead. Perhaps though, the cold would have been almost unbearable, but they would have conquered Bannerdown Hill with relative ease.

Daniel bounced up and down frantically and slowly but surely they approached the top of the hill. They both cheered when the little Austin made the summit, levelling out, and they began the last three miles into Colerne village. The old Fosse road was as straight as a die and visibility down to about ten yards but James pressed on, keeping to the middle of the road assuming no other fools would dare venture out on such a night. Soon they were negotiating the small lanes into the village and finalised the hazardous journey to the Fox and Hounds where they parked the car for the evening not wishing to miss out on a drink and chat. After a few beers and long discussions, on foot they began the trudge home in the ever deepening snow to a worried wife and mother.

Some time after ten o'clock there was no sign of James and Daniel. Joy only imagined the worst. She hoped they hadn't taken the risk of returning from Bath and had decided to stay in the city for the night. She rang Rob and then Herbie but neither had heard from them, let alone seen them.

Outside the snow blew in from the north east and swirled around in front of the cottage. The meagre outside lights painted a pretty winter picture amongst the Cotswold farm buildings, but underlying was the overwhelming danger of a freezing encapsulation. The children had stayed up waiting for their brother, not to mention their father. No longer did they become over excited at the thought of Christmas day as they approached their older years. Joy had managed to persuade her father to have a bath, and under much duress and effort he took up the challenge, but obstinately refused to admit how much better he always felt afterwards.

The Christmas tree in the sitting room had been dressed by Robert and Helen and various presents of all shapes and sizes were laid underneath, gifted from each of the family members. Hand made decorations hung in chains from the ceiling. The new oak drinks cabinet was full. A large cockerel sat on the side in the kitchen already prepared and stuffed with breadcrumbs, thyme and parsley. Vegetables were soaking in pans of salted water. Everything was ready for Daniel's short homecoming and a family Christmas dinner.

George stared at the clock on the wall. In the meantime he had refrained from his whisky tipples awaiting his son-in-law and grandson, although he had an inclination as to where they probably were. They would make the excuse that the weather had deteriorated so badly that there was difficulty reaching home, citing snow as the reason why they were late. He smiled to himself but desperately wanted to see Daniel before drinking himself to sleep.

The dog, with no name, at George's feet looked up and growled. He'd heard a noise out of the ordinary. Joy opened the door and thought she could hear the voices of James and Daniel. Sure enough the pair appeared from around the bottom end of the cottage as if they were two stumbling ghosts. Helen ran out and jumped all over her brother. Robert, almost as excited, slipped over in the snow laughing. Daniel helped him to his feet. At the door the two living apparitions removed their borrowed coats and shook them off. Joy hung them up as they took off their sodden footwear. Daniel's baggage was thrown into the sitting room. The pair were laughing and joking and then Joy realised where they had actually been. Up the pub. She didn't say anything. Christmas was almost upon them and having a drink was their prerogative. The season was one of goodwill but more importantly they were both home safe and well, although slightly inebriated.

Daniel hugged and kissed his mother. She was delighted he was back in one piece and he looked fit and well appearing even taller and bulkier than before. He sat down on a stool next to George and explained to the old fellow everything he'd been doing and where he had been. George was pleased to see him and even happier when James handed him a large glass of whisky. Shortly afterwards he began to close his eyes and then, as usual, in no time he was off to sleep.

The five sat around the table and Daniel, far from the first time that evening, explained his story again over a glass of wine. Joy found her son sitting with her dressed in his Wiltshire Regiment uniform, quite strange. She asked why he wasn't based at Tidworth or Warminster instead at Catterick in Yorkshire. He shook his head, he had no idea how the army worked.

Before retiring to bed Joy persuaded her father to use the toilet. He objected at first but when reminded of his recent accidents took her advice. James and Daniel helped him achieve his goal. After they settled him back down into his armchair, giving him one small drink, and wishing him a restful night, he responded, 'Good night Helen I'll see you in the morning'. He was smiling. Joy stared at her father whilst both James and Daniel watched the bemused expression on her face. She hoped he was talking about his granddaughter and not her mother, his dear wife. Age was now creeping up on George. His mental state was worrying.

Christmas morning came and the snow had ceased falling, although the white flakes were nearly a foot deep in places, especially where the wind had caused drifts up against the walls and hedgerows. James had wisely accepted the decision from George to keep the cows penned up. When he entered the sheds to wash the animals down, the small stone buildings were comfortably warm from their body heat. Daniel was soon along side his father and then Joy followed after caring for George. Between them they acted as a team whilst barely speaking to each other. These were tough days for small hill farmers and whole families came together as one. As the day brightened, although under a thick blanket of white cloud, both young Helen and Robert took up their chores of managing the pigs and chickens.

James went to view the scene in the valley below. He felt there was no chance he could allow the herd out, and decided to release the cows into the yard while they thoroughly cleaned the stalls. The children enjoyed tossing the turnips into the manglewurzle whilst Daniel used all his strength to turn the handle and slice the root vegetables up into edible pieces. The difficulty was keeping the hungry animals at bay.

Penned back up, the cows enjoyed their unexpected surprise and settled in for another day in the sheds with straw at their feet plus hay and turnips in abundance. How long they could be sustained in the current climate, only George knew. One other serious problem they had was whether the milk could be collected and eventually distributed. The income was dangerously disrupted.

Christmas lunch went well. A family affair and then the children set about passing around the gifts. Each were excited. Daniel passively sat smiling to himself, wondering if his siblings realised what might be in store over the next years. The less they knew the better, the pair didn't know what boiled in his mind. He hoped any conflict would be ended by the time they reached their later school years.

Joy slid two envelopes towards Daniel as the others were pre-occupied with the gift sharing. His mother told him they had coincidentally arrived three days before. Without opening them he studied the handwriting. One he recognised as Mark's but the postmark was obscure. He glanced up at his mother. She looked on inquisitively. The other he didn't recognise but had arrived from Bath. He bent them back and forth gently, assuming neither were Christmas cards. James sat back down at the table with raised eyebrows as he didn't understand what was going on between mother and son.

"Well! are you going to open them?" his mother asked.

James, then realising Daniel wanted to keep any personal letters to himself, took Joy by the hand and led her into the sitting room with the children.

Daniel slid a clean knife through the first and read with interest. Mark was still in England. He was bound for east Africa in the new year and he mentioned enlisting in the KAR.. Daniel racked his brains as to what it meant. Mark told him to keep in touch through his mother and father in Bristol and left their new address. He called through into the sitting room. "Dad! Who are the KAR?"

James wallowed back into the kitchen. "Well! I'm surprised that you don't know of all people. They are the King's African Rifles. They are a black east African regiment who are commanded by white British officers. Why?"

"I think they are with whom Mark has enlisted." Daniel pushed him the envelope and letter across the table and gestured for his father to read the short message.

James perused the letter then passed it back. "Good luck to him. That will be a great adventure!" He smiled at his son but noticed the other letter had disappeared out of sight.

Later that day the heavy clouds cleared in the afternoon sky, but the temperature dipped considerably as the sun began to disappear over the horizon. They had all wrapped up warm and went about their business in the hope that there would be no more snow and perhaps a thaw. James could only estimate how long they could keep the cows in as the emergency supplies couldn't last in a long winter. He did, however, have a field of kale up on the top ground but was reluctant to begin using the crop prematurely, ahead of time. James would still take George's advice, if and when the old man was coherent.

That evening the family sat around the table drinking wine and playing games which the children had been given for Christmas. They retired early as Boxing day would be another long and toilsome day. Animal husbandry offered no respite in any conditions, and there were no days off.

Halfway through milking that morning Daniel excused himself and went down to the cottage. From his pocket he took out the letter which he had kept away from everyone. He picked up the telephone receiver and dialled the number at the bottom of the page.

The morning was still very early and he didn't expect a reply but he could ring without his mother and father knowing. George was gently snoring but Daniel was more than sure he wouldn't say anything if he overheard his conversation.

The dialling tone went on for what seemed an age and then there was a connection.

"Hello. Stella Sinclair speaking," she sounded weak and tired as if just being woken up.

"Stella. Daniel speaking. Sorry I'm so early but mum and dad are out of the house so I took the chance to ring you. I received your letter, how can I help you?" he asked warily and businesslike.

"I'm travelling up to Scotland for the new year the day after tomorrow. Stuart is in Edinburgh to meet some old friends. I just wondered if you would like to come to lunch with me before I go," she went quiet, hoping he wouldn't refuse.

"When exactly?" Daniel asked her, unsure of what to do.

"I've only tomorrow lunchtime spare. Will that be alright?" she asked, hopefully.

"Providing the roads are open that will be fine because I have to return to Catterick the day after. I'll ring you if I can't get into Bath."

They arranged to meet first of all at the 'Coeur de Lion' in Northumberland Passage and then go on from there. Daniel replaced the receiver and immediately had misgivings about the arrangement. He couldn't get Stuart out of his mind, not wanting to let his mentor down especially after all the things he had done for him. Being seen with his wife, or any another man's wife for that matter, was not morally correct.

The next morning the weather had changed and a gentle wind blew in from the west. There were few clouds and out of the shade the sun began to soften and thaw the snow. The bus was running into Bath and rather than ask his father if he could have a lift, Daniel thought that taking the local transport would be better and more convenient. They both walked up to the village together and James retrieved his car. The bus was a little late due to the road conditions but being the first public vehicle out of the village since before Christmas, a few people were glad to board and travel into the beautiful Georgian city.

The Coeur de Lion was a small but cosy public house which nestled among a row of all different kinds of shops in the 'Northumberland Passage', in which it was built. The ancient walkway was always a popular place. Once Stella and Daniel had met they settled in the corner and discussed the whereabouts of Stuart.

"The army has created a Highland division should war break out which includes the Seaforth's and four other Highland regiments. They have been training hard already. When Stuart sends me letters he writes in precise detail unless he's not allowed to mention some of their plans. Other than that he's healthy but can't wait to see me, or so he tells me."

Daniel explained what he'd been up to, and where he was going in the new year.

They talked for an hour and then decided to have lunch at the Empire Hotel. The establishment was sumptuous and they both felt out of place with their dress sense but Stella reminded Daniel that the clientele would still expect him to go off and fight in the war on their behalf. The food was of the highest quality and, along with the German red wine, was justifiably expensive.

Daniel explained to her about the farm, the bad weather conditions, and difficulties of keeping the stock fed. Together they were happy, appearing to other customers as a courting couple.

While they ate two gentlemen and a woman sat on the table next to them. Stella kept staring coldly across at them and told Daniel she couldn't understand their language. The trio chatted idly, convinced that no-one would understand what they were saying. Daniel leant forward and spoke quietly to Stella. "They are German. Listen carefully and every now and again they mention Hitler or Ribbenthrop. They are discussing Hitler's plans for Germany."

One of the three spoke good English and they ordered food, but when they asked for German wine they were told there wasn't any available and difficult to come by because of the sanctions. They joked and ordered French wine, quoting that one day the French wine would be theirs anyway.

Daniel enjoyed his time with Stella as well as having the opportunity to overhear the opinions of his potential enemies. The wine was taking hold and Stella picked up her handbag and went to the bathroom seemingly glad to move away from the people at the adjacent table. On her return, at the bar, she paid the entire tab which annoyed Daniel who offered his share of the bill. Stella insisted the cost was affordable to her purse. The bar had closed and the pair left. Outside the temperature was dropping. The hills around the city blocked out any chance of late afternoon winter sunshine. They crossed the road and she hailed a taxi.

"Where are we going?" Daniel asked innocently as they clambered in the back.

"Well there are no pubs open until six o'clock so we might as well go back to my place. I have plenty of wine in the larder." She smiled at him and took his hand. Soon she was resting her head on his shoulder. As they drove through the dimly lit city Daniel felt extremely uncomfortable.

Careful not to fall on the icy path Stella searched for her keys. She was giggly and excited, far from how Daniel felt. The feeling of guilt ran through his head knowing he shouldn't have cornered himself into a very awkward position. Now he had to extricate himself from the situation without upsetting her, but he didn't know how she would respond, especially as she had drunk too much. He fully understood his mother's moods but would Stella be the same?

Inside she stoked the fires up and politely asked him to sit down. He stayed on his feet imagining that he would be safer. She brought two glasses and a bottle of her favourite German red wine from the kitchen, even though she appeared to have drank enough already. She poured the wine and handed one to Daniel and said 'cheers' whilst clumsily chinking the glasses. Stella suddenly went quiet and turned away and stared briefly out of the window. Her mind was melancholy.

"I'm lonely here on my own but you make me feel happy Daniel. I'm glad you could come today. Aren't you?" she asked him.

"Of course but I can't stay for long because I need to travel back to Colerne. The bus service is poor." He was telling the truth.

Stella placed her glass on the mantelpiece and put her arms around him. "Come on. Don't be afraid. Let's go upstairs. I know you want to, that's why you came to see me?" She spoke softly and alluringly and looked up at the handsome young man before her and squeezed him gently. They stared into each other's eyes and soon their lips met and they kissed passionately.

Daniel thought long and hard and then placed his glass next to hers. He was reluctantly led upstairs to the marital bed.

Stella had prepared the room with candles and lit them using an elongated matchstick. The odour of the spent match permeated the air. A small coal cast iron fire flickered in the corner and along with the waxen light created a warm sultry atmosphere in which Daniel was about to succumb.

The woman he had personally vowed to stay away from became irresistible. Her sexuality was magnified under the dull but sensuous light. Stella approached her young man and ran her hand across his flawless face. She pulled him down towards her and their lips and tongues once again became entwined. The feeling was one that Daniel could not resist. Her sexual femininity oozed in the warmth of the bedroom. Twice before he remembered she had stirred his inner self like no other woman but this time was different, Stella showed unbridled promiscuity. Her hand felt its way beneath his shirt and he stood back and eyed her up and down. He re-approached and slowly began unbuttoning her blouse revealing her shapely upper body. His tongue explored the softness of her neck and gently sucked on the pale skin. Stella was impatient and tried to tear Daniel's shirt from his back but he stood back and undressed himself slowly in front of her. She stared as he stripped to the waist and revealed his powerful torso. He pulled her towards himself and spun her around in front of the long vertical mirror hanging on the wall. Untying her pale cream bodice excited her and Stella's breathing deepened. Daniel dropped the clothing to the floor. His hands ran over her shapely breasts and she tried to turn towards him but his muscular arms held her firmly in front of the ageing mirror. As he kissed her down her back he undid three buttons which allowed the dark brown skirt to drop to her ankles and then he released her stockings and suspender which she couldn't wait to step out of. His right hand slid down inside her white panties which clung to her so tightly and he gently caressed her pubic hair. Stella tried to watch in the faded mirror but her head bent backward into Daniel's chest seemingly having never felt anything similar before. She could feel Daniel's sexual prowess pushing into her from behind. He pulled her panties down and she stepped her legs slightly apart allowing him to explore her dampened genitalia where he soon found her sensitive spot. He stroked her continuously with his middle finger all the time watching her in the mirror whilst his left hand caressed her breasts gently, causing her nipples to harden. Daniel was in control. She couldn't resist him and suddenly with her eyes closed she threw her head back and took massive breaths one after the other as she came to her own ultimate orgasm whilst holding his erect penis behind her. She implored him to stop and he ceased his powerful grip and they both fell onto the bed. In no time he was also completely undressed. She lay with her legs wide open willing Daniel to penetrate. His tongue explored her all over, eventually again finding her clitoris, and bringing the woman he was falling in love with to a second climax. Stella lured her lover on top of her and irresistably he physically invaded her wanton vagina. They made love with fervent passion.

Neither wanted to give up but Daniel's resolve wasn't as strong as Stella's and soon they lay staring at the ceiling. Nothing else was said and they fell asleep.

Daniel woke with a start. He turned and Stella was standing watching him dressed in a loosened negligee. She gently caressed his face and hair.

"It's not late. I have rang for a taxi." She climbed back into the bed, ran her hands all over him. They made love again and young Daniel lovingly lingered a little longer.

The taxi driver sounded his horn outside the house in Shakespeare Avenue, and Daniel left to return to Colerne.

Chapter 14
Poland

Many political changes began to occur in the early months of nineteen thirty nine. There was the 'Dutch War Scare' whereby people broached that the Germans would invade Holland with the intent to use their airfields to attack Britain. The rumour wasn't true but the British government changed its view about the developments on mainland Europe. Churchill continued to press the cabinet to consider any implications by which the Germans might spread their power east or west. *'We must be ready'* he emphasised to the disbelievers.

The Spanish civil war was more or less concluded except for sporadic fighting in outlying areas and General Franco had created a new government so all eyes in Europe were then focused on Hitler and his Nazi party.

Intelligence suggested that Hitler was planning an invasion of Poland, thus bringing eastern Prussia back into the German fold.

Summer came and Hitler's patience was at an end, confident Britain and France would not react to his next dastardly military deed. He had signed a pact with Stalin and between themselves had agreed to divide Poland into two, one controlling the east and the other the west.

The time of year was now late in August and Neville Chamberlain recalled the British Parliament for urgent talks. The signs in Europe were menacing. Britain was placed on a war footing.

The omens were not good. Poland had mobilised her army but they were considerably weak compared to her now aggressive westward neighbour as well as the ominously lurking Soviets on her eastern border.

Cut off from other dithering western European governments she was effectively on her own. France nor Britain were in a position to physically assist their ally and continued to pursue a doctrine of peaceable negotiations most of which Hitler agreed with on paper, but totally ignored in principle. In his own mind his intentions were clear, Europe would be ruled entirely by the Germanic speaking people.

In the early hours of September 1st. 1939 Germany attacked Poland. An ultimatum to retreat was given to the aggressors by the British that morning and again two days following. None were heeded, and Hitler continued his onslaught. The Prime Minister, Neville Chamberlain, announced on the 3rd. September that we were *'at war once again with Germany'*.

Life in Britain had changed dramatically for the worst. Fear spread amongst an incredulous population.

The Prime Minister summoned Winston Churchill to his office after the parliamentary session of the day and offered him a place on the war cabinet and also control of the Admiralty. Stoically he didn't refuse. On hearing the news, a message was relayed to the fleet, *'Winston is Back'*. For the second time in his life he became First Lord of the Admiralty and he immediately set about organising the defence of Britain and her surrounding waters.

Under the Command of General Lord Gort a British expeditionary force was mobilised in readiness to be sent to France in support of her allies in case of a German attack. The expeditionary force consisted of three corps, comprising nine divisions. The Royal Air Force would also be in attendance with several hundred aircraft. The First Army Tank Brigade were fully equipped and ready to board ship at a moment's notice.

The British war machine was on guard waiting to travel to France for the second time in a quarter of a century. Britain would face the same foe who had been previously subjugated to a humiliating defeat during the 'Great War'.

The general consensus of the British people was how did the fools in government allow another war to develop a mere twenty years after the last disastrous conflict against the same aggressor. The wives and mothers of Britain dreaded the thought of their husbands and sons being conscripted and sent to their deaths, or more leniently, mutilations.

The country was in for a long fight.

Chapter 15
The Birth

Stuart Sinclair, now re-enlisted with the Seaforth Highlanders, was back in Bath on compassionate leave. He impatiently paced up and down in the front room of his home. Having few friends in the city didn't help as he needed someone to talk to, a shoulder perhaps to lean on. From upstairs he could hear the midwife and her assistant coaxing his screaming wife Stella through a particularly long delivery. The phone rang and he hastily picked up the receiver.

"Stuart is that you?" a worried voice asked.

"Yes! Who is that?" he answered, only too pleased someone had rang.

"James. Joy said you had called asking after Daniel. What is it?" James hadn't heard anything from Stuart or Stella for many months.

In his clear Scottish lilt he explained. "Stella is about to give birth and I wondered if he might be back in the country. Just someone to talk with, that was all."

"No he's not. He's still in Palestine on a peace keeping role. We had a letter from him a while back saying he is fine but rather bored. The conflict has died down. We haven't heard from him since, besides, he isn't allowed to say too much when he writes."

The noise upstairs became frenetic, and even James could hear from his end of the phone. "Stuart!" he shouted down the phone more than sure the Scotsman wasn't listening, "concentrate on Stella and the child. I'll come down and see you!" James thought giving him some moral support was the least he could do in the circumstances.

James replaced the receiver, grabbed one of George's bottles of Scotch and set off into Bath. Joy stood by perplexed as she watched her husband leave the cottage.

All the lights appeared to be on in the house when James arrived outside, even though the time was nearing midday. He assumed the labour had begun during the night and nobody had noticed the illuminations. He approached the door with apprehension and knocked quietly not knowing whether the 'labour of birth' was over. He knocked again this time a little louder and was answered by a meek old lady who kindly ushered him inside.

James placed the bottle on the mantelpiece whilst she went upstairs to inform Stuart of his presence. The atmosphere was mellow and James thankfully assumed the child's delivery was successful. Stuart came down the stairs and confirmed his convictions.

"It's a girl. They are both doing well. Stella is rather tired but after eight hours in labour what do you expect." The Scotsman was more than pleased, he had become a father.

James shook his hand and embraced the delighted Highlander. "I've brought some whisky. Do you fancy a dram?" he asked jokingly.

"Why not, but I have to be responsible tonight. The midwife is about to leave, after making sure they are both comfortable, although her assistant said she'd stay until the morning, if need be."

They held a toast to the child's health and future, a future which brought about the subject of the war. James asked him how the situation would be with him being in the army, and Stella here alone in the city with the baby.

"She's staying in Bath. Her job at the school is well paid and so we are employing a live in nanny to help. Luckily they've allowed Stella some time off to let her get back on her feet. My regiment could be deployed anywhere so there is absolutely no point in her following me around. Anyway, from what I heard just before I travelled back down from Scotland is that in the new year we are going to France. That is almost definite. We are training full time and that is a positive sign, or negative if you are not a warmonger. That depends on which way you view the scenario I suppose." Stuart took a swig of whisky and shrugged his shoulders.

"I think that may be the case for Daniel as well, although I cannot be definite. As I said on the phone we had a letter from him. He's in Palestine on permanent guard patrol. He says the job is tedious but has heard they are returning to England for which he can't wait. He wants to see some real action, adding much to his mother's consternation." James raised his eyebrows. He was more worried about Joy's moods than Daniel going to France.

"By the way do you know how is he coping in the Wiltshire's? We haven't heard from him," Stuart asked out of interest.

"As it happens he's doing well. He's already been made up to Corporal, quite unusual in such a short time." James was rather proud of his son.

Stuart approvingly nodded his head. "He was a damn good cadet. Why he didn't apply for a commission I don't know, but I'm sure one day he'll be offered one. If they find out how well he speaks the German language everything will change for him anyway. There is no way they'll waste that kind of talent, especially in the current military climate."

The pair stopped talking as the midwife entered the room. "Your wife is comfortable and the baby is fine. She has one blemish. A large mole on the top of her leg but few will ever know. At least it's not on her face. She's a beautiful child. Everything is clean and nurse Chandler will stay the night. She is very experienced, so do not worry."

Stuart thanked her very much and placed a half crown into her hand which she tried to refuse but he insisted and squeezed her fingers closed. 'His wife and child were safe' he thought 'and a little remuneration was the least he could offer'. He showed her to the door, thanking the lady profusely.

After two or three more drams James made an excuse to leave and wished them all well as he left. He took his time as he drove home but was deep in thought about Daniel. The baby had been born one week before October and he kept counting up chronological numbers in his head and became fairly convinced there was something amiss. He recollected how his father was brought in as a witness and had recognised him at the court martial all those years ago by quoting the mole which he had on the inside of his leg. His father had last seen him when he was merely three months old, about eighteen years before. Stella's newborn child has a similar mole in relatively the same position.

Was the midwife's remark co-incidence, or was the child Daniel's? Daniel had been seen in Bath with Stella during the Christmas period, nine months previously, while Stuart was in Scotland. He decided the less said would be for the better and he would keep his thoughts to himself.

Chapter 16

Return from Palestine

James and Daniel sat in the 'Edinburgh Castle' talking about his exploits in the Middle East, boring as they had been, whilst waiting for Rob. Herbie pottered around behind the bar.

"The problems out there have been going on a long time now. The Palestinian Arabs are fed up with the thousands of Jewish people emigrating into what they see as their own territory and being able to buy up the land at low prices. They've been attacking the Jewish communities, burning their homes and have refused to pay taxes as long as they remain on Palestinian soil. There is an oil line coming from Iraq which they have repeatedly blown up, disrupting supplies into the port of Haifa. Palestine is obviously one main source of oil to the British mainland and in the current political climate we're going to need plenty of the 'black stuff' now." Daniel stared out of the window only to see the dim unprotected lights from the bar reflecting back at himself. He turned back towards his father. "How is George?" he asked with an uneasy look on his young but tanned face.

James couldn't help thinking how out of sorts his son would appear back in Colerne. "He's not good but don't disregard his age as he's quite old now. His mobility is extremely poor. Your mother helps him to bath and use the toilet but unfortunately he doesn't always last through the night after we've retired to bed. He's not well Daniel I'm afraid."

Daniel peered solemnly into his father's face. "Have you heard from Stella and Stuart?"

James immediately wondered what was on his mind and didn't quite know what to say to him. "Only briefly. Why do you ask?"

"Oh! nothing. When you are away you lose all touch with your friends. I haven't heard from Mark since last Christmas. Twelve months ago probably?" He raised his eyebrows hoping his father might be able to shed some light on his past friendships.

"There are a few letters at home for you which we felt better not to send on in the circumstances." James was sceptical about his enquiry. "There are a couple from East Africa, one or two from America and the rest local. Bristol and Bath. You're obviously well known around the world and have a lot of reading to catch up on." Although worried about him, James smiled as he was still proud of his son.

Rob arrived through the door and joined them. Daniel noticed how he had deteriorated. He wasn't as jovial as normal and had definitely declined physically. His father's facial expression had the same opinion and James appeared perturbed about the man who had instigated his own freedom nearly twenty years previously.

"What's happening next door at the hostel Rob?" was the first thing Daniel asked.

"That is a good question. The authorities closed the place permanently last March but in view of what's happening abroad, revamping and reopening the building would be a good idea. The trouble is now there are no sponsors and whether the government would help financially is doubtful. Another hostel would have to be operated on a voluntary basis aided by charities." Rob was glad that the hostel had closed. The building had served its purpose after the 'Great War' and now, ageing himself, he didn't have to visit there anymore. The place was for younger people to become involved. The original project was the end of another chapter in his life. "So how long are you home for Dan? Until after Christmas?"

"Yes I have three weeks leave and straight away after Christmas before the new year we are sailing to France as a part of the expeditionary force," he leaned back, "we might now be able to put all our practise and training into use at last."

James conceded, he had heard from Stuart and had indeed met him. "Did you know Stuart is going over as well?" James watched his son carefully, "he did ring me about October time to tell me. The Seaforth's are a part of the 51st. Highland Infantry Division and they are sailing from Southampton in mid January. He believes they are going to Le Havre, but where then only the army hierarchy are privy to that information."

"I haven't seen or spoken to him for well over a year now. A year last summer probably." Daniel didn't want to see him. He didn't think he could face him after fornicating with Stella. The shame was embedded deep in his mind.

Rob didn't help when he asked him, "have you heard from Stella?"

Daniel could not refuse to answer because unbeknown to James his mother had sent on some letters delivered at the farm and his father would have known they had been posted in Bath. "Twice, but not for a long time now. She didn't say much, just asked me to keep in touch."

James latched onto his answer. "So you knew she was pregnant then?"

The question hit Daniel hard. He was shocked but tried not to show any emotions. "No I didn't," he meant what he said, "good for her and Stuart, I bet he's pleased."

"Was pleased." James told him.

"What do you mean, was pleased?" A frown appeared on Daniel's forehead.

"*Their* baby girl was born in late September." James emphasised the child was their baby. Daniel wasn't sure how much his father and Rob knew of his relationship with Stella.

"Seems like you have some visiting to do," Rob insinuated, as if the baby was Daniel's.

Both Rob and James had spoken of the possibilities in the past but only in a satirical manner. Neither could actually confirm that he had been around her house, but Daniel didn't know whether they knew he had been around her house either, let alone what had gone on. 'How would they know'? he thought. Someone would had to have seen him.

He tried to change the subject but James butted in. "I assume your mother sent some letters on. As I told you earlier, back home there are quite a few letters waiting for you. There are some from Bath but also there are two or three post marks from which look like Nairobi."

Rob smiled. "They will be interesting. They're almost bound to be from your old friend Mark. I keep wondering to myself how he's getting on."

Daniel was deep in thought and Rob and James didn't have to wonder why. They talked about all manner of things but Daniel couldn't concentrate and just wanted to go home, if only to read the contents of his letters. Besides that, he wanted to change and put his uniform aside for the next three weeks.

They finally left the pub, but before separating they arranged a night out in the city. They bid their farewells.

"Rob doesn't look well does he Dad?" Daniel had been quite taken aback when he saw him walk into the 'Edinburgh'..

"He is a lot better now. Four months ago he had pneumonia. He was very ill, 'touch and go' was how the doctors described him at one time but he pulled through thankfully." James was glad he hadn't lost such a loyal friend. "On the subject of illness, while you are home, and before you leave, we have to try and move George upstairs. We need to get him into a bed. I should have told you earlier but he isn't expected to live much longer. Maybe a couple of months. Having a bathroom upstairs now will be much more convenient for your mother, and the nurse, that he is up there."

They continued their journey back to Colerne in silence. Daniel had too much on his mind and he already wanted to return to his regiment, out of the way.

Chapter 17
The Letters

After all the jubilance of homecoming Daniel made it into the bedroom which George would eventually tenure for probably the rest of his life. His mother had decorated and prepared the room for both, although Daniel would stay there temporarily. He was glad to take off his wearisome uniform and boots. In the new sparkling white bathroom he performed his regimental ablutions with military precision whilst wondering how anyone had had the strength to manoeuvre the cast iron bath up the awkward staircase. Trying not to wake anyone he trod carefully back along the creaking landing and settled into the bed in which he knew his grandfather would eventually pass away.

He studied the envelopes his mother had given him, slowly passing one behind the other and trying to decipher the postmarks or recognise the handwriting. His father was right about whence they had come, but which should he open first played on his mind. Daniel was tired. Falling to sleep was easier than trying to read several letters but the insinuations towards him that evening played on his conscience.

He shuffled them like a pack of cards but kept coming up with the wrong suit. Stella was on his mind and he passed them back and forth until he found one written in her hand, elegant and professional. He slid his thumb through the flimsy envelope and drew out one single piece of paper. The date was March, nine months before.

My dear Daniel   *3rd. March 1939*

Just a short line. I am so pleased because we have found out I am pregnant. Stuart is over the moon. We now have to seriously plan our lives ahead. He is away at the moment in Scotland but will take his leave and come to Bath whenever he can. I do look forward to seeing him.

I can only send you any letters to your parents home and hope they pass them on but will try to keep you informed as to what is happening. We think the baby is due near the end of September. I'm sorry it's such a short note.

Love you!

Stella.

Daniel rested his hand on the bedspread with the letter between his thumb and forefinger. About Stella being pregnant was the last thing he wanted to read. So vividly he remembered that afternoon with his friend's wife and now the indiscreet incident was coming back to haunt him. 'Why hadn't he had more self control' he asked himself. He was convinced that she was the temptress and the sexual altercation was not his fault but when he thought back, his desire for her made him feel no less innocent. She was attractive and he assumed she had not changed. He dropped the letter on the floor and reached out to turn the off bedside lamp. His thoughts of his permissive clash with Stella Sinclair, her exuberant sexuality and a combination of alcohol eventually sent him to sleep.

Daniel's father tried creeping down the stairs in the early hours, but the ancient woodwork creaked under James' weight and woke Daniel. He heard the door close and waited a couple of minutes, eased himself out of the bed and then turned on the solitary light bulb. First of all he went to use the bathroom, and returned, climbed back into bed and picked up the letters again. He began reading them in chronological order starting from the earliest date.

Hello Danny,   *11th. April 1939*

I can't imagine where you might be, but I hope it's a good posting. Are you well?

I am currently in America staying at some friends but not for long. Soon I will be leaving for Africa and working for some archaeologists in Kenya. Imagine that, me fossil hunting. The people who I will be working for have strong connections with the King's African Rifles and they are more than sure I will be able to enlist with them.

I will send any letters back to the farm.

Hope to see you again one day soon. Good luck.

Mark.

Daniel felt a twinge of sadness that he couldn't be with his old friend but he was confident that they would one day meet again. Mark had written his American address on the back of the letter but trying to contact him would be futile as he would now, in all probability, be in Africa, as his letter suggested.

He read another one from Stella. She mostly described her pregnancy and the whereabouts of Stuart. Apparently they rarely saw each other. She insisted that when Daniel was next home he should pay her a visit. The letter was written in August.

Mark's letters sent from Nairobi told him how he'd been fossil hunting in some massive gorge in Tanganyika. The weather was extremely hot but was manageable and he was being properly looked after. In his last letter dated the 1st. September he told him of his success at joining the KAR. He had been with them for six weeks and they believed he was showing promise. Mark could only thank Stuart for his expertise, Daniel for standing by him over the months, and Rob for making his dream possible.

Daniel smiled. Mark sounded extremely happy. He wondered where he was now or what he was currently doing.

A letter from Bristol was from Mark's parents, basically telling him what he had just read but left their address should he want to contact them.

The final letter from Stella had another affect on him.

My dear Daniel   *30th. November 1939*

I do so miss you. I haven't heard from you for such a long time. Please get in touch as soon as you can.

Stuart comes home Christmas Eve for three weeks and then he is off to France. He would be disappointed if he didn't see you and you were only eight miles away in Colerne. I am sure we could make some arrangement.

You must know now we had a little girl and we have called her Caronwyn. She has blond hair. She is pretty and already putting on weight. Stuart rings me often and can't wait to come home. He won't recognise her when he eventually arrives here.

I hope you and your family are all keeping well. Please don't hesitate to come and see me when you get back as I have only the nanny to speak to and I so much want to hear your voice.

All my love xxxx

Stella

What she wrote unnerved him. She implied she wanted to see him before Stuart returned from Scotland. Daniel didn't know what to do. He didn't want to face Stuart for one thing but going to see Stella shortly before his arrival home was another. He could only wait and see.

Other letters were from some old school friends and the lads he had met in the cadets. After he finally read them all he slid out of bed, put on some work clothes and went to the milking sheds to help his father. Daniel's mind was in turmoil. Although the dates on his letters were months old, to him they were rather confusing. Stella never implied that Caronwyn was his child but never the less, the conception was a possibility he could not erase from his mind. The letters from Mark were poignant, and he wished he could be alongside his old fellow cadet who he had taken to straight away when they had first met. Such was friendship but it was not to be.

Chapter 18
Karina Koster

Karina Koster walked down the Westerstraat with her two school friends, all three were heading home on a bitterly cold day. The north wind had drawn in the arctic temperatures and although the sky was clear and the sun was still just above the horizon there was no offer of respite against the exceptional chill.

She left her friends at the junction with Harkesteiger and continued home to Clarissenplaats where her father had his medical practice in a modest home in the town of Enkhuizen, Noord Holland.

Karina walked through the door into the tiny foyer, where three patients sat in silence, fidgeting, waiting for her father's attention. Two smartly dressed middle aged ladies with their handbags on their laps and an old man also clean and tidy stared straight at the wall in front paying no attention to the posters displaying the perils of tuberculosis and influenza. None spoke or appeared to be unwell. Karina could never understand why people always put their best clothes on when they visited the doctor. They gave her the impression that to be ill was a crime.

When the evening practice finished Karina and her father would sit down and have dinner together. The young woman would begin preparing the food after changing out of her bottle green uniform into something more comfortable and less formal.

Dr. Koster saw his last patient out of the door just before seven. He sat back down at his desk finishing off the day's paperwork. The light was dim and he struggled to read clearly through his worn glasses. He hoped there wouldn't be any phone calls whereby he could be called out into the freezing weather. Unfortunately most of his patients were suffering from chest and respiratory problems due to the extreme cold and his chances of a restful evening, he thought, were probably slim.

Karina peered around the door of his office. She knew he was tired. "Come on Pappie. You need to rest. Five minutes and the dinner will be on the table."

He looked up over the top of his reading glasses. "Thank you my sweet child, I will not be long."

Father and daughter sat at the table eating smoked herring and mashed vegetables. Dr. Koster was never keen on the local delicacy but conceded that his daughter had an acquired taste for the recipe and she cooked well for her age, he didn't complain.

"Has anyone said anything to you at school?" he quietly asked his daughter and wiped his mouth with a napkin.

Karina picked up her small glass of Reisling, took a small sip, and asked what about, then continued eating.

"No-one has mentioned your place of birth?" he asked warily not intending to put odd thoughts into her mind. She was fourteen. Still young and naïve, or so he believed.

"Not really. Everyone at school know I come from Germany but that was along time ago. I was eight when we came here. All my friends are from Enkhuizen. What is the matter Pappie?" Karina was becoming dubious of her father's questioning.

"Nothing. Nothing." He waved his hand. " Finish your meal. I am sorry I asked." He didn't want to upset her. He was amused that she thought six years was a long time ago. Many things had happened since then.

Karina cleared the table and washed the plates. Her father was proud of the way she had adapted to her new life in Holland. He would one day have to explain why he and her mother had actually moved.

Karina sat back down at the table and picked up her remaining wine. "Some people did speak to me in the street the other day."

A suspicious thought suddenly struck her father as would a slap in the face. His eyes became intense, and eyebrows dropped. "Who?"

She described them to him. "Two men. Only one spoke, the other turned away watching along the street, lighting a cigarette."

"What did he say?" The doctor tried to stay calm.

"He just asked me if you were my father. That was all." Karina shrugged her shoulders.

"And then what?" his concern was obvious.

"Nothing. I just turned away and carried on to school."

"Were they Dutch? Did they speak Dutch?" He now wanted to know everything.

Karina hesitated. Her ability to speak German, Dutch and Flemish made everything sound simple to her. "Whoever the man was that asked the question, I just answered back and told him that you were my father. He spoke Dutch but with a slight accent. All I can say is he was not Flemish. Perhaps he was from the north or something. I don't know." She looked at her father. He stared out of the window. Something troubled him but she didn't know what. "Tell me Pappie? What is it? What is on your mind?"

He turned back towards his daughter. "I do not want to worry you Karina. You are too young. I want you to be happy and free."

"Pappie. When I walk away from this table and you still have not told me what is happening I will worry even more. Perhaps I should know what I am facing, rather than be looking over my shoulder all the time wondering who might be watching me."

Dr Koster understood what she meant. If he didn't tell her there may be a psychological adverse effect on her. He knew only too well what was developing politically in his homeland and the consequences bestowed upon large parts of the population. He decided to tell her the whole story.

"Karina my darling, I qualified as a young doctor in nineteen seven and worked at a clinic in Berlin owned by Dr. Julius Wolff. There I began work as a junior orthopaedic surgeon. I gained much experience working alongside great men such as Dr. Jaques Joseph. With them my skills improved enough to take on other more senior posts until the war broke out in nineteen fourteen. The military were looking for skilled surgeons and just out of sheer devilment I joined. The experience was second to none. Never before could I have imagined the horrors brought about by, what was then, a modern war. I began to realise the futility of the conflict from both sides when often I would be treating enemy soldiers from all over the world, if not my own people. I worked tirelessly alongside surgeons from France, Britain and America, plus Canadians, Australians and many more places on this Earth. One man comes to mind, from England, a fantastic surgeon, not old but extraordinary and brilliant. I cannot remember his full name, just Andrew. My attitude began to change towards everything. All the soldiers, whether ours or our opponents, were of the same opinion, each of us just wanted to end the war there and then, but the politicians were not listening or more to the point, were too far away from the battlefields to take heed and understand."

Dr. Koster rose from his seat and nervously walked around the back of his daughter who was listening intently. He touched her affectionately on the shoulder, continued his circumnavigation and then sat back down.

"None of us could understand why always the poor people suffered in these hostilities, but then one day we heard there had been a great revolution in Russia. The peasants and workers had overrun the monarchy, their rulers, and murdered them all. A group of people claiming to be 'Marxist' had secretly organised the rout and the ordinary people would be in control of their own destinies and not dominated by a royal family minority. Suddenly the demand in Germany for any of Karl Marx's writings went sky high especially 'The Communist Manifesto', but most of his publications were banned even though he himself was a German." Dr. Koster went quiet and took a sip of wine. He was reminiscing, unexplained thus far was Karina's mother's disappearance.

"After the war I returned home to Germany from France and found a post quite easily at the Berlin Memorial Hospital, there I met your mother. She was working as a nurse. After some while we slowly began to get to know each other but eventually our relationship blossomed." He smiled, thinking back to those happier days when as a young couple they courted flirtatiously in their own capital city.

"Aside of our jobs we also had something in common. We both had a leaning towards left wing politics and often we would debate the subject long into the night. We were never at this time activists but were definitely supporters of communism. Our attitudes hardened when in nineteen nineteen the Communist Party of Germany was formed under the leadership of a woman called Rosa Luxemburg and a man, Karl Liebknecht. They attempted a coup but failed. A second revolution was proclaimed but the Social Democrat leader Friedrich Ebert ordered the Friekorps to put an end to the uprising. Along with the two leaders, Rosa and Karl, hundreds of Communists were assassinated. Fortunately for us neither me nor your mother were members on paper. Had we been, we would probably have lost our lives along with the rest." Dr. Koster clasped his hands behind his head.

"Pappie this is so long ago, why has the past anything to do with you now? Karina was a little bewildered.

He placed his elbows on the table and continued, "at the same time there was also another new political party forming called the National Socialist German Workers Party. They believed that anyone not born pure German is not worth a life, for example Roma's, Slav's, Jew's etcetera, and also communists. In Europe their members collectively, as you probably well know, are known as the Nazi party. Hitler became involved with them immediately after the war and rose to prominence in nineteen twenty one as their overall leader. He was then a charismatic individual with excellent oratory skills but ruthless by nature. People seemed to appreciate his opinions. The party dropped the word socialist from their title as the implications were that they were left wing and communist. Hitler controlled everything within the party. In nineteen twenty three he attempted to overthrow the government but wasn't supported by the local militia and was subsequently jailed, but not for long."

Dr Koster went to the cupboard for another bottle of wine. Karina said little as she still wasn't sure where her father's story was leading. After replenishing her glass he continued.

"There is a long story between the year of your birth until nineteen thirty three but basically had there never been a 'great economic depression' the Nazi's would never have come to power. Unemployment was so high and the underlying poverty turned the people towards Hitler and his Nazi party as a last hope. At an election he was voted in as Chancellor, overall leader of the German state. Myself and your mother knew we would be persecuted because of our beliefs, which were widely known by then, and we decided to leave

Germany, our home, and we came to live here in Enkhuizen." He sighed and tried to gather his thoughts.

"Under the command of Heinrich Himmler, Hitler formed the 'Gestapo'. The Nazi Party's secret police. Anyone Jewish, communist or anyone who they detested and threatened their power base were placed under surveillance. Everyone was being watched. Activists went missing never to be found. Workers against Hitler's party were taken away and questioned, possibly tortured, but never returned." Karina said nothing as her father took a large gulp of wine.

"One day we had a message that your grandmother was ill and your mother decided to risk returning to Berlin to see her," his eyes welled up, "I remember seeing her off on the train from Amsterdam to travel to Berlin." Charged with emotion Dr. Koster struggled to speak.

Karina butted in. "But we never saw her again Pappie, she died in an accident."

"You were very young then and that is what I told you my dear child but the story is not true. Your mother is one of those missing thousands." He held his hands over his face while Karina tried to understand her father's story.

He gathered himself and began again. "I should have known better. Your grandmother was apparently perfectly well, nothing wrong with her, or so I found out later. We had been duped." He stared at his daughter hoping she had understood.

"Pappie we are safe here in Holland. There is not a problem. They cannot come here can they? This is not their country." She was beginning to look distressed. Her eyes were opened wide.

"My dear Karina. They have already invaded Poland. Who do you think were the men who spoke to you the other day asking after me? I am afraid I believe they are already amongst us. The Gestapo has already spread their evil tentacles throughout central Europe. They have spies everywhere. Many Dutch people wish to become a part of Germany. Your mother and I were on their list of subversives and I am more than sure my name will not have been removed. Hitler will spread and create a Germanic empire which will rule at least the whole of Europe. He is merely doing his groundwork before he sends in his army but where he makes his next move I don't know."

Dr. Koster wasn't sure he should have told Karina. He went to her and held her tightly as she sat. She was quiet and seemingly unperturbed.

"We must do something Pappie. Why not leave and go somewhere else?" she asked.

"Where can we go? Not to Germany. I cannot work elsewhere because of the language barriers. We will have to wait and see. Hitler gives great promise to the Dutch government that they are friends and has no intention to attack and overrun us here. We do not believe him but we will just have to wait and see the outcome over the next few months."

Neither spoke for some while but the doctor broke the silence. "From now on Karina be careful who you speak to. Try not to be afraid. Anyone could ask a question which you might think is innocent but they could also be gathering information. Even your friends. As I have said there are many Dutch people who are on the side of the Nazis who could well be your friend's parents. I am not saying that is true, but anything is possible."

Karina nodded her head in appreciation, fully understanding what her father had told her, but with youthful trepidation.

Chapter 19
Rob and Daniel

Daniel waited impatiently for his father's best friend. He himself was eager to get away. The Green Park Tavern now teemed with engineering workers stopping off on their way home. Although retired Rob Goode would soon be following them. When he did walk through the door most people spoke to him, such was his popularity. Many admired how he coped with his plight. He bought his beer and was soon sitting next to the irritated young soldier.

"So what's the matter?" he asked Daniel, knowing something must be wrong.

Daniel pulled out a letter from his breast pocket. The address was written out to Mark. "He has sent me letters but now I don't know where to send any replies. I just hoped you might be able to make sure this reaches him." Daniel looked hopeful as Rob read the scant address on the envelope.

"Is that all you want?" he asked him, "you've come all the way into Bath to ask me that?"

Daniel tried to explain but Rob was not impressed. He had already noticed him clock watching. "Can't you wait to go? You've dragged me down here just to post a letter for you. Is that all?" He wasn't annoyed with him but certainly wanted to know what was affecting him since he'd been back home. Even his mother had rang and asked for him to try and find out what was on her son's mind.

"Where are you going after you leave here? Home?" Rob studied the expression on his face knowing he was guilty of something.

"I'm going to meet some friends and have a few drinks. I'll probably stay with one of them for the night." Daniel knew he could not convince Rob.

Rob was no fool. "How loud do you want me to speak?" he asked Daniel.

"What do you mean?" Daniel was taken aback. He glanced around the bar. They had no audience.

"You tell me what you've been up to or I'll start shouting out loud what I think you've done." Rob was almost holding a psychological gun to his head.

Daniel raised his hands trying to quell Rob. "No don't please!" he pleaded.

Rob had him cornered." Well tell me then!" He tried to smile but couldn't, his face hurt.

Daniel rubbed his hands together in anxiety but never answered.

"You've been shagging Stella haven't you?" His one eye peered menacingly at his naive adversary.

The question seemed to calm Daniel's nerves. He stood up and looked at the clock again and in the same motion offered another drink, which Rob didn't refuse.

Daniel was a little bit indignant when he sat back down. "No I haven't been shagging her for your information. I've been in Palestine for most of the year."

There was no way out from Rob's scrutiny. "No! But you have shagged her haven't you?" His one eyebrow was raised and he anticipated Daniel might tell the truth but was met with complete silence. "I'll tell you what we think!"

Immediately Daniel asked him who else knew.

"Your father for one. Your mother doesn't know but soon she will. There is a child involved, now don't forget." Rob slowly weeded the truth from the worried young soldier. "Daniel you have had an intimate time with Stella, haven't you? and now you want to talk to someone about your misdemeanour, and you have come to me to try and ease your conscience." Rob waved his letter to Mark in front of him. "Your misdemeanour has little to do with this letter, but I will pass your communication on. You don't need to make excuses to come and see me for a private talk. Now tell me what is troubling you."

Daniel wasn't sure where to start. "I don't want Dad to know."

"I think you'd be surprised how understanding he would be, in fact you should be confiding with him first not me. You tell me your story and I'll tell you his." Rob assured him.

Daniel told Rob of all the things that had happened, culminating in the afternoon when he stayed with Stella at her house. He mentioned the letters she keeps sending and the invitations for them to meet clandestinely.

"So Shakespeare Avenue is where everything happened, I assume." Rob asked him.

"Yes." Which was all Daniel said as he wasn't going to elaborate any further.

"So what is the problem as long as Stuart doesn't find out? She's not going to tell him, and I assume I am the only other person who now knows, officially I might add." Rob didn't see any difficulty as long as nothing more was disclosed.

"Our encounter happened the day after Boxing Day, last year." Again he went quiet.

"Well? What has that to do with anything?"

"Stella had the child near the end of September as you know. The child could be mine."

"Where was Stuart when you went around her house last Christmas?" He was becoming a little anxious for his young friend.

"He was in Scotland with his regiment and rather than travelling down to Bath for a couple of days and then returning, he stayed up there and Stella went up for the New Year. She journeyed up the day after we met." Daniel shrugged his shoulders. He couldn't tell Rob much more.

"Have you seen her since? I mean, since she went to Scotland." Rob was inquisitive.

Daniel glanced at the clock. Rob realised straight away that after their own personal encounter he was on his way to see Stella. "No I haven't seen her at all. I told you I've been in Palestine but I've had a few letters sent to the farm. Stuart's back this Christmas Eve." He showed Rob the last letter she had sent and waited for his opinion.

He looked up. "There is then a possibility that the child is his. She must have been with Stuart at the most two days after you were with her. The fact that the child is a girl helps because she will more likely inherit her mother's traits. At least if she does take after her father the child's features won't be noticeable for some years. She definitely wants the best of two worlds though, a husband she wants to keep and a young lover."

"I feel so guilty though. Everyday I think of what I've done. He was a reliable friend and damned good instructor but I've let him down. I've let myself down as well, what I did was morally wrong. If mother ever found out she would go crazy." Daniel hated himself.

"I'm more than sure you don't understand your parents Daniel, and there is definitely something you need to know. I'll speak to your father and tell him what you've told me and we'll let him decide whether he tells your mother. Trust your father. He is a good man. You can't keep bottling this up." Rob smiled to himself. He thought if Daniel didn't have a Christian conscience he knew who passed his atheism down to him.

Daniel now accepted that his father would now find out. He and Rob soon shook hands and parted company.

Daniel began the long climb up to Shakespeare Avenue hoping the nanny would be in attendance so nothing could possibly happen.

Rob sat with another pint pondering over what he had just heard. His mind thought back over twenty years before and he visualised all those dead or horrifically injured young men, most had never had the experiences of any sexual encounter, except perhaps, with themselves. Daniel didn't know how lucky he was.

Chapter 20
The British Expeditionary Force

The British army had hastily began to deploy her advanced parties of troops to France four days after Hitler's invasion of Poland on September 1st. 1939 and through specifically chosen ports. Aware of the long range ability of the Luftwaffe, troop movements were to be made through Cherbourg. The German preoccupation invading their eastern neighbour, Poland, made the British task a relatively easy operation.

The ports of Brest and Nantes in Bretagne situated in the far west of France were used to bring both mechanical and stores supplies into the country. A general headquarters was set up at Le Mans, and along with the nearby town of Laval, there were assembly points for the incoming British army. British military personnel were made most welcome by the French, although discipline was of paramount importance.

By the middle of September until the very beginning of October both 1st. and 2nd. Corps had landed and were making their way eastward to the frontline where there was confirmation that they would strengthen the line south of the town of Lille in Nord Pas de Calais.

Daniel was to leave immediately after Christmas, rejoin his battalion and travel to France where he would become a part of the 5th. Division, a combination of the Wiltshire's, Royal Inniskilling's and Cameronian's known as the 13th. Infantry Brigade.

Stuart on the other hand would have to wait a while longer as his scheduled deployment with the 51st. Highlanders had been delayed until the end of January or even the beginning of February.

Neither could wait to set off. Both were physically at their prowess, alert and desperately wanting to see action.

The Naval task had already begun and the sinking of British merchant shipping increased. U-Boats became a menace and the admiralty under the direction of First Admiral, Lord Winston Churchill, worked frantically to offer a solution. Protected convoy systems were put into place along with complicated strategies to prevent German warships and U-Boats from operating in the North Sea and Atlantic Ocean. Scapa Flow where the British fleet held their operational base was heavily protected.

The Royal Air Force was on perpetual guard with reconnaissance flights and attacks on enemy aircraft and shipping.

The whole of the British and French military was preparing for a showdown with Europe's most organised and aggressive army.

Chapter 21

Compatriots?

James could see the apprehension in his son's face as they waited for Stuart Sinclair in the Devonshire Arms on the Wellsway in Bath. The public house was a mere ten minutes walk from Stuart's home in Shakespeare Avenue where Daniel would be having dinner with his ex-cadet sergeant and wife Stella. Here was a last chance for them to meet before Daniel set off to France with the expedition force. This was a Boxing Day which Daniel did not relish, especially the next five or six hours but had been persuaded to attend, if only to put his mind partly to rest.

Stuart came through the door and looked around before setting eyes on the father and son. They shook hands and embraced. Stuart held Daniel at arms length. "My god! you have changed since I saw you last. A lovely sun tan as well." He was beaming all over.

"Let me get a round in." James smiled at Daniel. 'At least for now the ice had been broken', he thought.

James stayed for another hour during which, between them, they chatted about life in general. He then left, telling Daniel he would pick him up at Stuart's and Stella's house at five o'clock.

The two friends remained at the bar and drank steadily. Daniel was fearful he would have too much alcohol and say the wrong thing in front of his host and Stella. They decided to walk back down onto the 'Bear Flat' and have a drink. After a couple more pints and a 'whisky chaser' they left as Stuart was under orders to be home by two-thirty. They walked back up the hill, a little worse for wear. The Scotsman put his arm around Daniel's shoulder and kept repeating how glad he was to see him. Keeping himself upright was probably more to do with his over friendliness Daniel thought.

The nanny answered the door and let them in. She wasn't overwhelmed to see Daniel but said absolutely nothing. Stella embraced and kissed Daniel in her usual provocative way. She was always pleased to see her lover.

Stuart poured three glasses of wine and they toasted Caronwyn's health. He explained the choice of name. He was Scottish and Stella was English so they had chosen a Welsh name.

The nanny was also the cook that day but all the way through the meal she never uttered a word as she pottered in and out of the kitchen. All in all the afternoon passed quite positively. Stuart appeared not to know anything of what had occurred in the past, and as Rob had mentioned, wouldn't be able tell who the baby resembled.

James turned up exactly on time as he knew Daniel would want to escape from his enclosed environment at the first opportunity. He refused to enter the house for a drink, citing other work to be done on the farm. After emotional scenes on the threshold, Daniel departed.

In the car James immediately asked Daniel how was the afternoon. "I suppose everything went well except one thing. Stella made us both stand together with the baby and she took a photograph, the only one taken."

Chapter 22
Farewell

The day before Daniel left to go to France George took ill with suspected pneumonia. He was taken to hospital in Bath. Before leaving Daniel tried to speak to his grandfather but he was weak and delirious. As Joy and James followed the ambulance into Bath the farm was left in Daniel and his two siblings control. Helen was to prepare the evening dinner while Daniel and Robert were to milk the herd. Their parents returned at six that evening fearing the worst for George. Daniel reminded them what a tough 'old devil' his grandfather was, but deep down he too believed the end of George's life was nigh.

Dinner went well and James made a point of congratulating Helen on her first culinary test. He tried to persist with a diverse conversation but both Joy and Daniel were sullen. He opened one of the wines and poured the contents into five glasses allowing the children a large mouthful each. Their minds were soon oiled and they began chatting incessantly about George and then Daniel's journey to Southampton the following day.

"Will you have much time off," his mother asked.

"Yes, but probably not enough time to travel home. They will move us back behind the lines and we can rest up safely in the nearest town. Everything depends on how the war progresses though. We still don't have a fully equipped army, up to full strength. Besides that we don't even know if Hitler intends to invade France. Hopefully he'll go eastward."

Daniel seemed laid back about the situation but James knew that underneath his nonchalant exterior the outcome worried his son.

No-one had envisaged a full scale war but that was the way Europe was heading.

Joy quickly drank her wine. Both Daniel and his father thought she was acting oddly. She slid her glass towards what was left in the bottle and James reluctantly filled the vessel and then watched her response. Robert and Helen were not paying any attention and he politely asked them to wash the dishes while they talked. Neither wanted to, but they did as they were told.

Joy tapped out an imaginary tune on her glass as she stared down at the table. "Has your father told you about the circumstances of your birth?" she asked Daniel.

"More or less I suppose." He could only assume his father had told the truth.

"Doesn't the circumstances of your birth concern you?" His mother stared into his eyes.

"Why should I be plagued by a conception over which I had no control? You both loved each other didn't you? That was what was important. I have lovely parents who care about each other, unlike some parents of friends I had at school. Of course I'm not bothered. I also had grandparents that cared, and one still alive, who still cares." He was a little annoyed at the futile questioning. What had happened in the past was not his fault. Daniel merely felt he was the end product of what George had perceived, in those days, as an illicit love affair, although even his grandfather had forgiven both his parents in the end.

James popped the cork on the other bottle of wine. He helped himself first, fearful that Joy would inevitably drink too much. Robert and Helen began messing noisily around by the sink and he told them to go upstairs to bed and read.

"I'm so scared Daniel that you won't come back. When your uncle left here against dad's wishes we didn't know where he had gone. His disappearance was a nightmare." She stood up abruptly. The chair scraped across the flagstone floor. Joy held her hand across her face trying to hide her tears. Daniel went to console her as she went into the living room but his father pulled him back into his seat shaking his head.

"Leave her," he whispered, "she'll be alright in a minute. Let her come to terms with your departure on her own. She hasn't had a good day at all."

Joy calmed down enough to sit back at the table and sip some more wine.

"Have you packed all your things ready to leave in the morning?" she asked him, as a mother would, sending a child off to school.

"Off course I have mum and I've done my ironing. Like all good soldiers, ready for action." She hadn't wanted to hear his last remark.

The cottage went quiet. The children had gone to sleep upstairs. Only the sound of the clock could be heard. A house spider silently watched the proceedings from a corner above the wall cupboard. Both James and Daniel wondered what she would say or ask next. Nothing they hoped.

Joy went upstairs to check on the children. Fresh air and hard work had sent them to sleep early. She crept into her own bedroom and rummaged around under the dim light and produced a letter. She hid it inside her clothes and returned downstairs.

"When your father returned from the war, he went on the run. When he was eventually caught he gave himself up in this very room at this same table. Did he tell you that?" she asked Daniel.

He looked at his father for confirmation. "No, I didn't know," Daniel told her, shaking his head.

"Did he tell you that he brought three letters back? All written by your uncle Daniel," she sullenly asked. "Did he explain what happened during those last minutes of his participation in the war?"

Daniel wasn't sure where his mother was leading. He looked at his father hoping he might elaborate but James was as baffled as Daniel was, although just as interested.

"Carry on," James told his obviously distraught wife.

"Your father brought back three letters. One was for Julianna, your uncle's girlfriend. Another to your grandmother and grandfather, George, and one for me." Joy was becoming distressed again. Both father and son waited patiently.

Joy pulled out the letter she had in her possession. "This letter is the one he sent to me. It is the last time I ever had contact with my brother. They are his last words to me," she began to sob, "and now tomorrow I am sending my son to an equally horrible war where I fear, as well, you will never come back." Joy broke down again.

James went around the table and held her tightly trying to persuade her the current conflict would never be such a bad war as the last.

Daniel sat passively believing that if people with a similar attitude to himself didn't enlist then no-one would survive. He broke the silence. "I've read the letter that he sent to George and my grandmother."

His parents briefly stared at him in silence. "When?" James asked, almost shocked.

"George gave the letter from uncle Daniel to me quite some time ago and then told me I was to look after the note as a keepsake. Years ago when I was a young boy he told me what had happened. I didn't fully understand what he was saying at first but as I became older everything began to fit together but there were always parts missing from the jigsaw." Daniel shrugged his shoulders.

Although James had brought the letters back from the front line he had never been privy to what was in them. He looked from one to the other, his son, and then his wife. The sequence of events was similar to watching a tennis match, which one would concede first.

"What are you going to do with the letter your uncle Daniel sent to my mother and father," Joy asked meekly, still distressed.

"I am going to do what George asked. Take the letter back to the front line. He told me, and believes so, that if the letter survives at the battle front again, then the letter would remain in the family archives forever, myself along side. A lucky charm was how he described the incredible final note." Daniel waited to see what his parents would say.

James and Joy stared at each other incredulously. George and his grandson were in cahoots together, or so they seemed.

"What about the letter you have then mother. Are you going to show Dad what uncle Daniel said?" Young Daniel was incredibly calm considering the next day he was to travel off to war. A little wine and a few things off his chest relaxed him. His mother pushed the letter to

James which he believed had been destroyed years before, or perhaps even lost. James read out aloud the contents;

My dear sweet sister,

I haven't much time to write, but just to let you know that I am fine. We are on the front foot and hope to be home in the new year.

I look forward to hearing your lovely voice and sitting on the wall together overlooking the valley across to Euridge. There are no birds left here bar the scavengers and rats. All the trees have been blown away. It is a desolate landscape.

There is a young soldier under my command who I am sure you would like and after the conflict I have told him to visit Colerne. He would appreciate the scenery and probably your company. I have one worry and that is he might be an under age soldier. Before we engage the enemy again I will hopefully have some more information and be able to take him out of the front line.

A very pleasant Scotsman has also joined us and between us all we have an interesting group of hard fighting men. Soon, I am sure, the war will be over.

I am afraid my letter has to be short. I will see you in the New Year.

Love you all my life Joy, little sister.

Daniel.

James put the letter back down on the table stood up and stepped into the sitting room. Everything flashed back at him. The last incidents of his war. Captain O'Dell telling him not to leave the trench. He had disobeyed, probably resulting in the man's death of which he still felt guilty. He visualised the sightless eyes of the dead and dying. Second Lieutenant McLaren staring at him motionless. Eddie Gardiner, Freddie Pond and then Captain Daniel O'Dell dying in his arms. The carnage was so vivid as if he was there again. A nightmare he had lived with for twenty plus years. The screaming of the wounded and dying from both sides, whether they were British, German, Americans, Aussies, Canadians, whoever. Many were never going home. The rat-a-tat of the guns and explosions from the artillery. Just six weeks later there was a truce which rendered the last battles of the war as futile. Second Lieutenant McLaren's young son had lost his father. James recalled how the Scotsman used to say how proud of his son he was and the day before telling himself the war would soon be over. Now he was dead. Uncontrollable tears ran down James' face. He only came around when he felt Joy pulling him around the waist. He still hadn't fully taken in that Captain O'Dell was his wife's brother. Nothing seemed possible. Joy comforted him until he calmed down and then led him back into the kitchen.

In all of the last few minutes young Daniel had remained composed. He had poured himself and his father a large whisky in the belief that George wouldn't be needing the 'tartan spirit' again. "Rob told me quite a bit, so did Herbie but they only confirmed what Grandad had told me. I basically know your story dad and that of uncle Daniel. I can only say I am proud to be a member of the family.

The three sat talking late into the night in the cottage kitchen watched impassively by the spider. The arachnid was imperceptive to the heartaches which the 'Great War' had caused.

The next morning, as Daniel had requested with no fuss, James dropped his off son at the Market Place to catch the bus to Bath, where he would board the train to Southampton. As he struggled out of the car with his kit Daniel briefly turned back to his father, and a mere handshake sufficed.

Chapter 23

Southampton Docks

Daniel had taken great care to wash and iron his uniform and spare clothes before leaving Colerne. He was clean, tidy, and his boots were shiny black. His kit bag by his side was full. At the top were sandwiches wrapped in brown paper made by his mother for the long journey ahead. Her final hope, having kissed her son affectionately, when he had left home was that they were not the last meal she would ever make her dear son. Joy had been distraught.

He was far from alone on the platform. There were several other soldiers of all junior ranks and some very young looking officers, all waiting for the same train. All were sombre having spent their last evening of freedom on home soil, but also sinking in was the realisation that heading to war was approaching fast. From relatives and friends experiences, first hand or merely read about in journals, they had all been reminded of the last war. Death and destruction! They were fit and healthy and had been 'raring to go', but now, approaching fast, was the 'day of reckoning'.

The station clock ticked on slowly. Pigeons chased each other, or coherently swooped across the tracks alighting on the faeces strewn girders which supported the Victorian roof. Sparrows scavenged around the waste bins and the feet of hungry soldiers. There would be a long journey down to Southampton, stopping at every small town or village.

The train approached the station and slowly slid to a halt. There was the familiar sound of doors clicking open and clunking shut. A few men squabbled, some were polite but most merely boarded as if Europe was their final destination. Few had anyone to see them off. Few soldiers wanted a sentimental send off, no emotional outpourings, just simply board the train and leave.

Daniel found a seat in a compartment with two other men who sat opposite each other, proudly wearing the same regimental badge. They respectfully acknowledged one another.

Daniel stared out of the window and caught sight of Stella dressed in red with a beautiful maroon coat and black stilettos. She looked out of place as she paced up and down the platform trying to see into every carriage. Daniel remained seated and disinterested. In his mind, one of his travelling companions wished she was seeing himself off. The guard blew his whistle and all who were left outside stood back. Just as the train began to pull away Stella caught sight of Daniel, and ran up to the window waving frantically and blowing kisses. He waved back, half heartedly, but soon, much to his relief, she was out of sight. The two soldiers glanced at each other, raised their eyebrows, but said nothing.

Daniel's mind rocked to and fro. One minute he was thinking about Stella and Stuart, and then had mental visions of what France would resemble. He thought of his mother's distress and his father's seemingly indifference. Palestine cropped up in his head and then the farm back home. Always his thoughts reverted back to Stella. Why was she haunting him, he asked himself time and time again. He should have never gone back to her place a year ago. Had he not, his conscience would be clear. As for Caronwyn, he didn't know if he was her father.

The train sauntered on. At every station on the way to Salisbury the train stopped. The wooded Avon valley outside of Bath was a picturesque winter landscape. Soldiers and the odd sailor held their heads out of the windowed doors admiring the view knowing the landscape could be their last sight of England for quite some time. The corridors were freezing. The grey clouds summed up the mood of the train's occupants.

After the ancient wool town of Bradford the river meandered north eastward and parted company with the railway. The train headed towards Westbury under Plain via the important county town of Trowbridge. At Westbury two great train lines crossed and Daniel sat for twenty minutes before they were on the move again. Many of the previous incumbents had left the train, no doubt heading by bus for their barracks on Salisbury Plain. The remaining soldiers, sailors and new passengers were undoubtedly off to France.

Through the Wylye valley the train chugged out smoking black carbon onto the surrounding fields. Here there was little more than rolling hills dotted with all weather sheep. Few trees could be seen except for the everlasting willows along the valley, dipping their leafless branches into the chilled shallow waters.

The great cathedral came into sight and they were on the outskirts of the only city on their journey prior to Southampton, the architecturally beautiful Salisbury.

A few more military personnel crammed on board, and shortly, with precision timing, the old steam engine pulled out of the station. At Southampton the military personnel were asked to stay on the train unless they had any other business, otherwise they were to be shunted straight on towards the docks. There was a buzz of nervous excitement.

Carriage doors opened before the train had halted. Here there was no platform and to jump with full kit risked a broken leg. The shouting and chatter reached a crescendo and finally they were able to clamber down onto the dockside and stretch their tiresome limbs. They were greeted by the forever hungry seagulls and watched by the forever artful military police.

Daniel remained in his seat until almost the last man had evacuated the train. He was about to leave when the guard came along with one of the policemen. They were looking for shirkers. The guard stood aside as Daniel was none of his business, he was a mere employee of the train service.

"What's the matter with you lad? Do you want to go home already?" The military policeman insinuated cowardice.

Daniel stared hard into his ageing face but said nothing.

"Well! Why aren't you off the train? Answer me?" He was irate with Daniel's supposed insolence.

"There's not a struggle now everyone has gone is there?" He was challenging. "I walk along the corridor, step down in an orderly fashion, no hassle. I wander around and find my regiment. We sail this evening. The time is now only two-thirty in the afternoon. Why are you so concerned? Am I holding up the train?" Daniel almost smiled, testing the military policeman's nerve.

"Who do you belong to? Which regiment?" he asked him.

"I assume you can't read the badge but I belong to the Wiltshire regiment, Duke of Edinburgh's, sir!" Daniel answered him sarcastically, as he understood, he had done nothing wrong.

"Come on! Get off the train. We'll deal with this outside."

They stood alongside the carriage and Corporal Daniel Godwin had to give him his name and number. He would be reported to his senior officer for insubordination, in the impending circumstances, a minor charge, he was going to war.

As the police sergeant jotted his details down on a scrap of paper, shouts were heard. "Glen! Glen!" They came closer and a breathless young military policeman came into sight. "Sergeant Paignton, sir. You are needed sir. There's a fight broken out between some squaddies from two different regiments over by the far troopship."

The policeman stared at Daniel. "You're lucky son that this might not go any further."

Daniel watched the old policeman walk away, too old to run even in the circumstances. He kept his eye on him until he was almost out of sight amongst the military throng but suddenly the sergeant turned back and looked towards Daniel. The sergeant glanced at the name on the piece of paper. Something had jolted him. Had he missed something?

Daniel watched him disappear out of sight.

Chapter 24

The Enigma

Every year since nineteen twenty the people who were involved in James' court martial had met for dinner in a Bath restaurant depending which establishment at the time was in fashion. The reunion was normally arranged around the third week in May but this particular year they decided to bring the date forward. The main reason was the general belief that Germany would any day now attack France and travelling in England might be rendered more difficult with tightening security. Fittingly they decided to hold the dinner on the 11th. April, James' thirty eighth birthday. The year was also the twentieth anniversary since his temporary incarceration.

The men were required to wear dinner suits and the ladies, evening gowns. Rob and James had pre-booked at the Empire bars on hearsay that the food and service were currently the best in Bath. Even Daniel had recommended the rendezvous. Dinner was at eight-thirty but to begin with they would all meet at the 'Edinburgh'.

In the Edinburgh Castle Rob and Herbie chatted at the bar along with their guest Ed Moses, Ed being one of the military policemen who along with his colleague Glen Paignton had arrested James those many years before. Although they were in the pub before opening time, Herbie was expecting the Thursday night rush at six o'clock as the weekly pay day had arrived. All three, dressed as they were, looked out of place in the bar and would appear even more bizarre when workmen and builders from all different areas of Bath converged on Herbie's pub, all flushed with cash.

There was a tap on the window and Herbie shifted off his seat to investigate. They were Andrew O'Dell and his wife, along with his sister Elizabeth and her partner. They had been visiting the farm at Eastrip but then had driven back to their hotel in the city to change. Shortly afterwards James and Joy followed. Herbie opened one half of the front door, looked up and down the street, and then quickly ushered them inside. Not long afterwards James' brother and sister , Jimmy and Jennifer with their spouses were tapping on the door. Rob persuaded Herbie to leave the door open, as opening time approached. All sorts of people then poured in and the bar filled rapidly, but fortunately Herbie had foreseen the situation, having extra staff at the ready.

Sarah came down from upstairs. Considering her age, she looked stunning. All eyes turned to her and everyone stood back as she made her way through. She wore a shimmering turquoise tight fitting dress which emphasised her well kept figure. With high heels and her light coloured hair formed in a classic bun, she resembled royalty. Rightly so, Herbie was proud of his wife.

Over the years, many invitees of the private party couldn't be there because of illness, old age or had other preoccupations. There was always a hope that the annual social gathering would be a full house, although Rob's father and mother had declined the offer this particular year due to 'general old age', as Rob had described the dear pair. Some of whom hadn't been seen for some years were *half* expected to turn up.

Sarah spoke into Herbie's ear. Her husband nodded discreetly. She pecked him on the cheek, wrapped a shawl around herself and went out onto the street alone. Sarah headed for the Station Hotel.

The Edinburgh entourage finally decided to leave and make their way to the Empire Bar. The working lads wished them all a good evening. By request, taxi's lined up outside and the party set off to an evening beginning with dinner and followed by light entertainment.

Inside the Empire bar they were reserved the grandiose table with two beautiful chandeliers above. Most of the entourage, at first, latched onto the bar, but gradually took their places at the table Rob nor James knew exactly how many would attend. Sarah still hadn't arrived from the Station Hotel. Wine was brought to the table and a few irrelevant toasts were made, one in particular was Daniel's absence. A prawn salad first course was delivered in silver plated dishes and everyone began eating. Most talked of the surprising availability of the seafood dish.

A solitary young woman, pretty but very slight, sat close by. Simultaneously she took food from her plate and browsed through a copy of the 'Times', deep in thought. Her dark brown eyes studied the paper, her mind contemplating the situation in Europe. James couldn't keep his eyes away from the attractive lady. Absent of company she had no conversation and James could not ascertain from where she might hail.

His thoughts were suddenly distracted.

Sarah appeared through the glass doors which were now draped inwardly with black out curtains and she caught sight of Herbie and Rob. Sarah beckoned them to the bar area, obviously intent on supplying information.

"What's the matter darling, you look flustered?" Herbie was troubled about his wife.

"I went to meet Alfie and Glen as planned," she glanced around the room hoping no-one could hear, "they were enjoying themselves when I arrived, but guess in whose company?" Sarah half expected them to know. Both shook their heads and shrugged their shoulders.

"That Stella woman! Glen has asked her to come along. They're on their way here now."

Rob moved into James' view and signalled him over. Glen, and especially Alfie turning up at the informal event after years of absence were supposed to be the surprise guests of the evening, but Rob had to warn James about Stella.

Fortunately James saw the funny side. "Except for us, and I assume Judith is aware, we're the only one's who know about Stella and Daniel. Even Joy is oblivious to Daniel's apparent misbehaviour, but she would be completely hypocritical, if she said anything! Tonight, as long as we say nothing, we'll just have to play along with the melodrama. Stella must be unaware that we both know that Daniel has been shagging her. Possibly the way she wants the situation to be! Silence hopefully."

Shortly after he spoke Stella walked through the door with Alfie one side and Glen on the other. James was over the moon for seeing Glen and Alfie after so many years. He eyed Stella up and down, "and who is your friend?" he asked knowingly, with an admiring smile on his face.

Both men tried to explain but made little leeway as others rose from their seats and greeted them. After some time rearranging the furniture and tableware they were asked to take their places and Stella sat between her two new found companions, knowing exactly where her place at the table was.

Dinner went exceptionally well. Coffee was finally offered but the men kept to their normal drinking habits. Decanters of expensive port were brought to the table and Rob rose to his feet and demanded attention. Each by now had a glass of fortified wine either in hand or on the table in front of them. He intended to make a short speech.

A waiter came across and whispered something into his ear. Rob looked up and waited for the door to open and with the aid of two walking sticks, in hobbled Arnie from the Fox and Hounds, helped by his wife Maggie. A cheer went up and the big fellow apologetically struggled over and he and his wife took the seats on offer.

Rob continued. "As usual I will make a short toast which will encompass most of us in our fold."

Someone called out. "Hear! Hear!"

He went solemn. "To our friends who died in the 'Great War', and the injured, to the young men and women who now also face a formidable future but above all let us toast the righteous and hope that human justice will prevail." Rob raised his glass and they made the toast. "We've eaten, we're drinking so now let us be merry."

A brass quartet struck up in the corner. Slowly, some raised enough courage to dance. The celebration became infectious. People from the bar were invited to join the jollification. Stella remained seated, herself waiting to be asked to dance. Andrew approached her after his wife took up with another partner. He was graceful on the floor and she was an equal match. Neither spoke, they merely trod a measured whirl.

Rob, James and Herbie continued to contemplate why Stella had latched on to the absurd celebration. Joy watched them all from a distance and coyly tried to understand their connection with the sexually attractive woman.

Stella was a party gatecrasher but had soon made herself known, especially to the men. She wasn't the most beautiful woman but she had a lure about her which none of the men seemed to be able to resist, besides she had been picked up, cavorting in the Station Hotel on her own.

Joy took James by the arm and dragged him onto the floor. "Who is that woman? You men all appear very interested in her. Who is she, and what is she doing here?"

James sighed knowing there wasn't going to be an easy explanation, especially to his wife. He glanced up at the ceiling not knowing what to say. "I can't tell you here on the dance floor, there are better places to answer your question, especially because of this evening, but give me time, and tomorrow I'll tell you the truth. Tonight is not a good time to ask."

Joy pushed him away and loudly demanded an immediate answer. All eyes converged on both of them. The experienced quartet changed to a livelier piece of music while James pulled his wife towards him. "You have obviously never met her, but she is Stuart Sinclair's wife, Daniel's ex-cadet sergeant. You must know *his* name surely. Apparently she was in the Station Hotel and met Alfie and Glen. *They* invited her up here, not me! Whether she knew what was our reason for being here this evening we don't know, but please don't make an issue of the situation because she is a mystery woman. We are trying to find out why she is here. Please relax and just enjoy yourself." They awkwardly finished off their dance and returned to their seats. Joy couldn't keep her eyes off Stella, although she didn't know her, she watched her every move.

Few were left embracing during the final slow dances on the tiny dance floor. Most were now sitting, reminiscing or wondering what future was ahead of them. As the waitresses cleared up and the doorman refused entry to anyone else, the conversations were solemn. Each had had enough beer, wine or spirits.

The end of the evening came and Stella was sitting talking to Glen and Alfie when the hotel manager came over to her and whispered in her ear. A concerned expression came across her face and she looked straight across to James, grabbed her handbag, and left abruptly without saying a word to anyone.

Joy was watching her husband as she departed and he subsequently glanced across to Rob. Deep down Joy was seething and wanted to know what they knew about the woman. All the men folk who had been around her were hiding something, or so Joy believed. A jealous woman was difficult to appease.

At the exit for the umpteenth time that evening Joy explained, when asked, how her father had recovered from his dice with life and death against pneumonia. Daniel, as far as she knew, was fine and her twins were growing up fast. They finally saw everyone off and had the privilege of a last drink with the manager whilst they paid the bill. A courtesy car was arranged to take them both home in respect of the business they had brought to the establishment that night.

Back home in the cottage the lights were still on downstairs. Joy immediately crept upstairs checking that George and the twins were sleeping soundly. Downstairs James struggled to open a bottle of wine. When Joy returned the pine table was stained from his feeble efforts. They sat opposite ends of the table and the interrogation of her husband began.

"Come on then, tell me who is this woman you men were all infatuated with tonight? I want to know. Stuart Sinclair was in charge of the army cadets. So what has she to do with all this?" Joy was angry. "Why was she there this evening?

James drunkenly twisted his glass around and around between his forefinger and thumb, small pieces of cork floated on the top of his wine, although he was past caring. "We don't really know. Perhaps the encounter in the Station Hotel was a mere coincidence when Alfie and Glen bumped into her. Please Joy! she did no harm. In fact she was good company for everyone."

Before he could say any more Joy retorted. "Who else knows what is going on? Rob! by the look of his face, probably Herbie. Come on who else? You know something about her don't you?"

James decided to wind his wife up. "I'm not sure now is a good time to tell you. You've been drinking and you know how your attitude changes!" he told her sarcastically. He slurred.

"Have you been shagging her! Have you!?" Joy was livid but tried hard to keep her voice down. "You have! haven't you?" She stood up at the end of the table with her palms flat down on the top, leaning forward and staring at him demanding an answer.

"No!" He shook his head half smiling. *No! I haven't.* That is far from the truth. Now don't start getting jealous over something that has never happened."

"Well then tell me what has happened?" Joy was frantic to know the truth.

James wound her up even more. "I will tell you if you promise me one thing."

Joy was not up for promises but couldn't resist to hear what he had to say. "Go on then! What?" she asked vehemently.

He again slurred slightly. "I'll tell you the truth, but you get up and do the milking in the morning and let me lie in bed."

"You're going back into town tomorrow lunchtime to see everyone off and you want me to stay here all day and sort the farm out on my own. Who do you take me for. What kind of deal is that?" She held her hands out as if she was the loser.

James decided enough was enough. Joy didn't want to listen and so he was retiring to bed. She went to say something but he rebuked her. As he opened the door to go upstairs she stopped him in his tracks.

"Alright I will! I *will* do the milking." She glanced at the clock which said two-thirty, meaning only two hours sleep. "Now tell me what is going on!" Her eyes pleaded to know.

James relented, shuffled back to his place and settled his behind down on the edge of the pine chair and poured some more wine. Forgetting his manners, he stood again, he went to his wife's end of the table and poured out the residue of the bottle, returned to his seat and sat back down again. He felt rather pleased with himself. Joy looked at him with her head half cocked not knowing what she might hear or whether there was going to be any truth in the statement or not. She only imagined her husband was screwing someone else's wife.

James suddenly sat bolt upright. He tried to shrug of his slovenly appearance and act sensibly because he knew, at first, she wouldn't believe him. He didn't know whether to explain like a fellow soldier or tell her the story as an officer and gentleman would describe. He chose the latter.

"Daniel has had an affair with the woman of whom you are jealous. Not me. Daniel, your own son." James was matter of fact, but relaxed.

Joys face slowly twisted up trying to construe with what her husband had just explained. She disbelievingly shook her head, spelling the story out in layman's terms, Joy spoke slowly, *"Daniel has been screwing Stuart Sinclair's wife."* Her eyebrows were extended upwards, her mouth agape

James didn't know if her words were an utterance or a question. There was a long silence which James broke. "Yes and he told us that the baby she had, Caronwyn, might be his, or so he thinks, unproven though, either way."

Joy was stunned. She knew that Stuart Sinclair had become a father, but not that her own son possibly had some connection to the child's conception as well. "How could he do that to his friend's wife? Is he old enough to understand the consequences? Caring for a child for the rest of his life."

James smiled. His wife had a short memory, especially with regard to the circumstances of Daniel's conception. "He won't have the problem. Stuart Sinclair believes the child is his own, which is quite probable. Obviously Stuart knows nothing about Daniel's involvement with Stella. While Stuart is away they are hiring a nanny to help around the house." James could say no more and after more obsolete and unanswerable questions, finally persuaded Joy that they should go to bed.

As they lay there initially prior to falling asleep he placed his arm around her and reminded Joy of the agreement at the table. She told him in no uncertain terms to leave her alone which he did chivalrously and turned away, thankfully intoxicated, he quickly fell asleep.

Seconds before he did pass out, he thought of Albert who he had asked days before to help out at milking that morning. Unknown to James, Joy had also asked Albert the same favour.

Chapter 25
The Fall of France

The news from the continent was dire. The German army had swept into Holland and Belgium on 10th. May. Information was already coming in thick and fast. With the use of the Luftwaffe and airborne landings they were able to capture vital Dutch airfields and bridges which would enable a speedy advance towards the west.

On the same day in Belgium an extraordinary assault was made upon the strategic Fort Eban Emael in the east. Gliders were used initially to land troops, who carried flamethrowers and specialised explosives which dislodged any resistance from within, and after twenty four hours the fort's protection was overrun by the superior German forces.

Meanwhile the French and British line of defence moved forward with the intention of protecting the Belgian capital, Brussels.

The 51st Highland Division however were deployed near the French-German border south of Luxembourg with the objective of holding back any German attack directed across the Maginot line. The superior weight and mechanisation of the German army was unstoppable and forced the French armies south and west. This included the Highlanders who were ordered back to a new defensive line at Etain. After a week of heavy fighting there was a short respite before the Germans struck again.

Luxembourg and Belgium were now entirely under occupation. The unexpected advance, over the supposedly impassable Ardennes, had taken all by surprise. Hitler's troops were forming a pincer movement to cut off any retreat by the British and French armies. After ten days they had taken the strategic town of Noyelles situated on La Manche. At this point of time Major General Fortune realised his Highland division were cut off from the rest of the expeditionary force.

General Gort attempted a rescue mission with a depleted armoured brigade to link up with his French counterpart General Weygand, but only succeeded in isolating more of his own troops. The allies were overwhelmed.

General Fortune attached the Highlanders to the French 10th. army with the resolve to defend the northern ports of Le Havre and Cherbourg but the pressure was immense. The German advance was rapid. A total surrender was imminent but Fortune knew his division would refuse to capitulate come what may. General Gort's problems were entirely different. He had more than a quarter of a million men to deal with and the unfamiliar word from both sides of the channel was *'evacuate'*.

The fighting intensified as the British army fought on the back foot. Brave men held off the German advance as others escaped the onslaught. The scenes at Dunkerque were chaotic as more and more troops poured into the town and onto the beach desperate to avoid the unstoppable onslaught.

On the 25th. May, the Royal Navy, under emergency orders from the newly installed Prime Minister Winston Churchill and his war cabinet, began the process of withdrawing the troops from the beaches of Dunkerque. The job at hand had been designated to Admiral Bertram Ramsey. For some days previously, every English dock and coastal town were scoured for all types of small and medium sized boats, which could be used to ferry the troops off the beach at Dunkerque to the larger ships waiting further out in deeper waters. Pleasure cruisers, fishing boats and commercial boats came into use from as far away as Manchester and Glasgow. Under the protection of the Navy, the tiny flotillas began their precarious voyages across the English channel. There was no time to be lost as the fighting intensified and both the French and British armies were coming under severe pressure.

"Sarge!" Corporal Godwin shouted across to his platoon Sergeant. "Sarge! how much longer do we have to hold off these Krauts before we're overwhelmed?"

"The lieutenant said that Gort has sent General Adam to create a defensive perimeter around Dunkerque. We're here to defend this ridge until the end if necessary. They're sending up a couple of brigades from the 4th. Division to help us out. Once the evacuation begins in earnest we start retreating, fighting on the back foot, I assume." Sergeant Willie Myer realised how acute their position had become, but needed to keep up his troops self-confidence. "We'll be home in Blighty next week!" he shouted back across to Daniel.

The 10th. Brigade, mostly the 2nd. Bedfordshires, arrived to relieve the 5th. Division and the Germans were found to be closing in on the British artillery. Together with the 11th. Brigade they cleared the Messines ridge and dug in to hold off any further German advance whilst their comrades in arms made their escape towards Dunkerque.

The road to Poperinge was calamitous. Any transport available was in use. The wounded were first priority, but as their trucks approached the town a massive traffic jam built up as both the military and refugees headed in the same direction.

"Danny! get our men off the trucks. We're going nowhere. Start marching. We'll try and organise some sort of thoroughfare through the town." Willie was determined not to be held up and deeply concerned about the consequences if the traffic became over-congested.

German planes regularly flew over, heading towards Dunkerque eventually strafing and bombing the helpless troops. "Willie and Daniel kept their men moving, running, jogging then walking, running, jogging then walking. Every time the Luftwaffe were heard they stopped and fired if only to cause minor damage had they succeeded in a hit. Within the hour they were in the town directing the traffic across the Yser canal. Traffic began moving a little more quickly but time was running out fast.

The Luftwaffe realised the bottleneck was an impediment to the retreating soldiers and began bombing the town. All roads led to Poperinge at this point. Everything came to a standstill as most of the transport was laid to ruin. Any vehicles blocking the route were shunted out of the way. For two hours the bombardment continued. The small remaining section of the Wiltshire's continued to usher through the despondent retreating troops urging them to keep going. There were men on makeshift crutches, helped by others. Some with gaping head wounds and the partially blind.

'Come on lads, Dunkerque's your only hope. Get out of Poperinge and there's an open road.' Daniel and Willie urged them on.

Just when they thought the daylight bombing had finished in came the Luftwaffe again during the night, dropping flares and following up with more attacks on the town, with its desperate locals and unwanted visitors. The burning trucks could be seen for miles in the night sky but as the Germans relented the Wiltshire's began to clear another route through the beleaguered town. They commandeered all other fit, healthy and willing troops to help in the task, from whichever regiment. They were all stragglers.

A captain approached Willie and spoke with a university educated accent. "Damn it man who's in charge here?"

Willie turned and looked at Daniel. Both shrugged their shoulders. "We are I suppose sir." Willie answered sarcastically, having little to lose.

"But you have no rank. Where's your immediate superior?" he asked haughtily, oblivious as to what was happening in Poperinge.

"We have none sir, I request you keep your troops moving before you create another backlog." Willie looked up at the skies expecting another strafing at any minute from the formidable Stukas.

"I insist you have an officer in command. Now stand aside," he went to brush Willie out of the way.

Daniel pushed in front of him and spoke in German. He held the point of his gun to the Captain's throat. He spoke again in German and then reverted to his own language. "You don't understand me do you. We are special operations executives looking out for German spies trying to infiltrate our troops and you are holding us up." Daniel was emphatic.

The captain, unsure whether to believe him, conceded. He turned weakly and addressed his tired men asking them to move on.

'Thanks lads'. 'Well done boys'. 'The man's a prick'. 'Good on y'er'. As the captain's long suffering troops passed them by, they only had praise for Willie and Daniel's makeshift troop staying behind to sort out the chaos.

Willie and Daniel stood watching them leave. "What did you say to him?" asked Willie.

"Nothing really. I asked him if he'd heard the latest football results. I knew he wouldn't understand. He's tired and harassed. As soon as he realised I spoke German, he assumed I was telling the truth."

Willie went to walk away. Daniel stopped him. "How long are we going to stay here Willie?" Daniel spoke on personal terms.

Willie swung around and walked back towards his young corporal. He too was tired and the stress showed in his face. "We've hardly any contact now but from what I can gather is the 44th. Division have just passed through but now there is a lull. Your non German speaking friend must have been a part of them. We'll try and hang on for the 3rd and 50th Divisions. Then we have to think about saving our own skins." Willie turned to go but again suddenly turned back, "I thought the football season finished six weeks ago?"

Daniel shrugged his shoulders and smiled. "Willie I'll stay here and wait for the Bedford's. They came and relieved us upon the ridge. We can't do any less than that. You take our boys back to Dunkerque." Daniel watched him passively as he thought about what he had said.

Willie took his helmet off and ran his hand through his unkempt hair. "Danny when we leave, we leave together. If we can muster up enough willing men to stay long enough we will. I don't care which regiment they belong with, but if we can offer the others safe passage through, then fair enough. I'll find out what weaponry we have available and set up a defence. Please! just keep the traffic going." Willie Myer left with a serious mission running through his mind, practical or not.

After hard work and limited sleep the two hundred or so soldiers left behind formed a defence around Poperinge to enable the remnants of the British expeditionary force to pass through. Surprisingly the German assault had relented and they had diverted their attention towards other strategic gains. Some of the Bedfords who limped through were hurried on towards apparent safety. Then Willie, Daniel and their ragamuffin troop began their withdrawal. They had since learnt that the Belgium government had capitulated under the continual assault. Their need to reach Dunkerque was paramount for their survival. German Panzers could be heard everywhere and sporadic fighting began to increase. The loss of men through injury hampered the retreat but little could be done but to stave off the powerful German advance.

With few options open the injured were left at the mercy of the enemy in the belief that they would be spared. Caught on almost all sides, the British and French fought on the back foot. France's finest troops held off the German attack to allow the British to evacuate as many men as possible.

At Dunkerque Stuka's bombed and strafed the soldiers who waited on the beaches. Ships were sunk at sea. The Royal Air Force fought back with pugnacious tenacity to repel the superior enemy. Soldiers waded chest deep into the sea to embark on waiting transport ships and boats while the Navy attempted to bombard the German inland positions. There were thousands of injured troops and their numbers were increasing by the hour. Soldiers fired their guns at all enemy aircraft and occasionally a great cheer would go up if smoke suddenly poured from a Stuka engine. Collectively they would claim a hit.

Too hungry to sleep Sergeant Willie Myer led his band of soldiers into Dunkerque. Here was to be their last battle. There were few behind them and the road to safety was now nigh on empty. They had just passed through the French manned defensive perimeter with the Germans barely two miles behind them. Many were walking wounded and some were carried on makeshift stretchers. Each brave soldier had a job to do.

"Danny take the men straight to the beach." As he spoke three bombers screamed overhead and let loose their deadly cargo. Spitfires challenged them in the sky and one Stuka was shot down. Guns rattled continuously. German artillery was now within striking distance from the town. "Get them to the beach and into the boats! I'm going to try and find the rest of the battalion." For days now Willie and his platoon had been separated from their unit and a week had passed since the evacuation had begun in earnest.

The bombers came in again randomly hitting the town and beach. Taking cover was a lottery. The local population were as much at risk in their own homes as they were on the streets. Hundreds had already died and many more would probably do so before the end of the evacuation. The whole town enclosure was terrifying for everyone.

The scene at the beach was one of attempted organised evacuation and destruction. Bodies were neatly laid out on top of the sea wall. The padres and pioneers were carefully taking notes and removing any articles which might be sent back to their next of kin. Queues of soldiers in regimental order waited patiently for the next small boat to take them to the relative safety of the larger ships moored further out. Many defenceless small boats had been sunk by the tenacity of the German fighter pilots, although they didn't have the battle all their own way as their losses were also excessive. The Royal Air Force had fought a great aerial battle, and still continued to do so, but not without loss themselves.

Daniel first found the queue which took only the wounded. There were military and civilian doctors and nurses, most of whom were French or Belgian. He wished his wounded comrades luck telling them he would see them on the other side. None knew if he meant heaven, hell or home.

"Sir! Are you Captain Tennant sir?" Daniel asked the man before him who was staring out to sea watching how the evacuation was going.

The officer in charge of the operation swung round. "Indeed I am Corporal, how can I help you?" To Daniel he seemed very congenial.

"We've just arrived back in Dunkerque sir. We are a part of the 2nd. Battalion of the Wiltshire's. There are about twenty of us fit sir and our wounded are waiting to embark on the hospital ship." Daniel really wanted to know where he should take his men from there.

"I can tell you now the bulk of the Wiltshire's left here yesterday. Where have you actually arrived from?" the captain asked.

"Over the last week we were trying to hold the Messines ridge, but since then we've been fighting our way back here. We were with the Royal Irish Fusiliers and the Cameronians in the 5th. Infantry Division but we've lost them as well." Daniel sounded tired. All his men needed food and rest.

Unfortunately the captain could only offer rest for the time being. He also knew that Daniel's division had had a tough time of late and desperately needed some respite.

"Take your men and shelter under the sea wall." He pointed to an area where he would be able to find them. "Keep your heads down as the Stuka's appear at anytime. "Just rest. I know that will be difficult in the circumstances but try and get some sleep. I'll be back as soon as I can." Captain Tennant left him to his own devices and went to find his radio operator.

Daniel observed the bizarre scene down below in the water. Hundreds of soldiers were wading up to their waists and some even up to their shoulders in the green brown sea, many in areas stained with the blood of the unluckiest, not one mile from the safety of the large ships. Many had been in the water for hours. Bodies floated gently in the calm sea awaiting recovery by the Pioneers. Small boats came, picked up their despairing passengers and then set about delivering them to the ferries, cargo ships and coasters. There were even Dutch barges on hand and many other small boats which would suffice to take them back to England. Artillery shells began dropping into the water indicating the nearness of the German troops. The air was acrid from the smell of the burning oil tanks in the docks and the exploding shells. Behind Daniel the German salvoes increased and were hitting the town continuously. They had found their length and line.

Daniel watched the Spitfires pursuing the Stukas around the ships further out at sea. He likened it to the swallows chasing the flies around the barn in front of the cottage at home, only on an entirely larger scale. The swallows took no prisoners. He began to slumber and his mind became remote and he no longer heard the bombing and strafing. Obscurely, he dreamt of home and all it's creature comforts. Occasionally his body jerked and he half woke only to slip back into his delirium. Exhaustion had overcome his psyche.

A hand gently touched his face, and he sprung as a serpent does to his prey, and gripped the wrist of his assailant. Willie Myer had already placed his foot on Daniel's gun in case he blasted off spontaneously. Daniel's eyes compared to those of a drunk just passing into oblivion.

"Danny it's me! Willie! Wake up! Come on! son wake up!" Daniel came to realise where he was and with the help of his sergeant rose to his feet. He tried to apologise, but Willie wasn't listening.

Captain Tennant stood next to Willie Myer. He stared at him hard in the face. "Tell him please."

Willie wished he had never said a word. Daniel was bemused. 'What were they talking about'?

A Stuka flew over low and they all ducked. In the din Willie shouted out his instructions. "I'm sorry Danny but I mentioned that you can speak German. He wants you to stay here with him until the end so you can co-operate with the Krauts if the remnants of the army are captured." Willie was shouting at him as the din from more Stukas flew over, followed by exploding artillery shells. "I shouldn't have said anything." His face portrayed a guilty man. He'd let his corporal down. "At six-thirty this evening Captain Tennant has organised that the rest of us will be leaving. I wanted to stay as well, but he won't let me. I'm sorry Danny, I shouldn't have said anything."

Danny peered over Willie's shoulder at Captain Tennant. He then looked back at his sergeant. "I trust you both Willie. The army is my job. I'll see you off this evening and perhaps meet up with you in two or three day's time." They shook hands, both were sorry that their working relationship was coming to a temporary end.

The Captain took his new corporal aside. "I am not normally allowed to confide with the lower ranks but we are receiving more and more German speaking refugees and we need to be able to find out who are genuine and who are disingenuous. There is little time. Tonight hopefully the last of the British troops will have left and tomorrow morning I can telegraph back to England that the evacuation has been a success. Success is probably not the right word, 'completed' would be more appropriate," he stared around at the carnage. "I can tell you now our government wants to treat these expatriates well so as to use them as a part of their propaganda machine." He held his hands up, resigned to how the 'powers that be' worked.

Daniel spent most of the afternoon talking with the refugees. He didn't begrudge them at all from trying to escape from an inevitable death sentence. They were mostly families with children caught between a yearning to improve their lives wherever they lived and an ideology bent on social destruction. The majority were Jewish. The conversations he had that day changed his attitude forever.

The water was calm. Sergeant Willie Myer waited under the sea wall with his diminutive troop. They would be the last of the Wiltshire's to leave the beleaguered Dunkerque beach. A signal arrived as a small boat appeared some way out and his men stood and prepared for their evacuation. Daniel spoke to them all and then finally Willie. "I'll be watching until you are all safe. Believe me." The two men embraced. Hard soldiers as they were there were tears in their eyes. Neither knew if they would see each other again. As in war, they lived in hope.

Willie ordered his men forward. Each were aware that they had to wade into the water and reach their designated rescue boat before she floundered in shallow water. As he met the ebbing tide Willie turned and urged them forward as quickly as possible. "Keep your guns dry above your heads!" he shouted.

The deeper they went the more arduous wading became. Willie followed, trying to persuade them to move as fast as possible. The rendezvous boat approached at one pace, sailed by a brave civilian. A Messerschmitt 109 appeared from over the town and strafed the platoon in the water. Daniel watched, completely helpless. He picked up his gun and attempted to fire at the enemy aircraft. He ran down to the water's edge as the plane flew in on another run. The German plane fired onto his helpless men in the sea and this time killed two instantaneously and shattered Willie Myer's right shoulder. The impact rendered him unconscious and he lay face down in the bloodied water.

Daniel waded in to his rescue. Two colleagues turned him over to allow him to breathe not knowing where he was injured. Frantically Daniel eventually reached him and barked his orders at the others to take the boat. Blood poured from a massive wound in Willie's shoulder.

One of the lads shouted at him. "Danny! Danny! For fuck's sake bring him here. Get him in the fucking boat! And you! Get in as well!"

Daniel took heed. Willie's weight was nothing in the water and he dragged his unconscious body the last few yards. The boys hauled Willie Myer's limp body into the little pleasure boat. The Stuka attacked again and Daniel felt as if he'd been hit with a hammer in the left side of his back. The cannon splintered the little boat but not below the waterline although two more died. The Royal Air Force saw off any other offensive attack.

'Come on Danny get in. Get in for fuck's sake!' They held their hands out but he was not listening.

Daniel stared up at them from the crimson sea. "I can't. I have another job to do." He turned and headed back to the shore as blood poured profusely from his wound.

Staff Sergeant Stuart Sinclair headed back to his men. He'd just been briefed by his commanding officer. They were dug in, overlooking the town of Abbeville. He gathered them around. "I have good news and bad news to tell you. First of all most of the expeditionary force have escaped back home through the port of Dunkerque. By today or tomorrow they will have all been evacuated including about thirty thousand French soldiers. That's the good news.

Secondly we are the only British infantry division left in France and we are now attached to the French 10th. Army. Now that there is little left of an opposition force, the Germans are almost certain to divert their attention to us. There has so far been no word from London as to what we are expected to do, whether we withdraw as the rest of the army has, or stay and fight on."

A private interrupted him. "Why should we stay here and fight if the French have given up? It's not our war!"

"I don't want to get embroiled in politics but France is our ally. Just remember that if Hitler succeeds in taking the whole of France then he is almost sure to try and attack the British mainland. Ultimately, he wants control of the whole of Europe. Here is one of our first lines of defence. Believe me, I don't like our situation any more than you do, but we are soldiers of the realm and we do as we're asked. In the next day or so we will almost certainly find out what our fate is." He dismissed his men. Never once had he kept his men in the dark about what was happening, that wasn't the way he operated. At least they knew who they were fighting for, or against.

The Highlanders were actually dug in just south west of Abbeville near the mouth of the Somme. Their line was thin as it stretched for over twenty miles. The town itself was an important bridgehead on the northern coastal route.

A battle entailed but was futile and soon the French conceded the town and together with the Highlanders and a few stragglers from other regiments, they began a long retreat to the coast. Eventually the last pockets of resistance were holed up in and around the fishing village of St Valery en Caux.

During the retreat Major-General Fortune had asked for Royal Navy assistance to evacuate his troops from St Valery.

Unknown to the general the Navy had approached the harbour the day before and finding no-one there, pulled back out to sea. After coming under heavy aerial attack they moved even further seaward. Fog shrouded the coast and a decision was made from London not to risk a rescue.

The very next day General Fortune issued his orders to the commanding officers explaining how the evacuation would take place. Little did he realise the Navy were steaming north back to England.

That afternoon the Black Watch took a heavy bombardment at a small village east of St. Valery losing more than fifty men. They were aided by a brave French cavalry unit but to no avail, and were overrun in the early evening.

At midnight artillery fire bombarded the town. The German's had restocked their ammunition and were convinced that the Highlanders and their stragglers would capitulate. There were a few Norfolk's and Kensington's in the village all doing their best to keep the German's out but the position was becoming untenable. After another four hours of continual bombardment a rumour spread that the French were to surrender at eight o'clock, which they duly did.

Detached from the main group, the Seaforths heard none of this and were determined to fight on. Two kilometres away the bombardments had almost ceased. At the tiny hamlet of Le Tot, however, the defended ground became smaller and smaller. They took refuge in any building possible knowing one direct hit could wipe out many men.

Stuart Sinclair lay low in in a pig sty with three others. He constantly asked his men to concentrate their fire on strategic targets and shouted words of encouragement. "Don't waste your ammunition! Fire only at guaranteed targets!" he shouted constantly, "and keep your fucking heads down!" as artillery fire came soaring over.

The German infantry were now easily in sight and mortar bombs started to find their range. His lieutenant considered a counter attack but they lacked the fire power. Stuart persuaded him to sit out the current onslaught and hope for a rescue.

Mid morning came and the losses were horrendous but not one Seaforther wanted to surrender. Bullets whined everywhere but the Seaforths' now had little to offer in return. A renewed attack by the German artillery ended Stuart Sinclair's war. A shell hit the pig sty directly and the last he remembered was being thrown through the air like a rag doll at an unruly children's party.

There was quiet for once. The sound of sea birds was once again apparent. The remaining Royal Scots Fusiliers rummaged around searching for the living under the guard of the German infantry. The dead they solemnly buried. Each grave they marked and listed.

That morning of the last battle the British army conducted on French soil, Major-General Victor Fortune surrendered his troops to General-Major Rommel. His choices were stark. He knew they couldn't escape and one option was to fight to the death but that would have been a needless waste of the lives of so many tenacious soldiers, respected even by the enemy. The 51st. Highland Division surrendered to German command on the 12th. June 1940.

Chapter 26
Convalescence

Whenever a hospital ship was due in at the Queen Victoria, the hospital itself became a hive of activity. Preparations were made in advance for the 'mercy ship' to arrive. Those not so ill or badly injured were moved quickly to other medical centres or sent home to convalesce making bed space for the new incoming wounded. The operating theatres were cleaned meticulously by hard working nurses in readiness for the surgeons to perform their procedures. No two wounds were the same and the skills of the surgeons were second to none, many of whom were veterans of the 'Great War'.

When the ship arrived the information gathered on each patient was brought ashore immediately and those who needed immediate and preferential treatment were attended to first. Specialists were brought in from afar to deal with the most complicated anatomical operations. Everyone had a job to do and their organisation was paramount to the hospital's success.

Daniel woke in a ward. As he wasn't thought to be in any great danger he had to wait some time but the morphine helped, and he kept drifting in and out of sleep. When he was fully awake he couldn't help but notice that everyone who left his ward, none of them had come back. 'Worrying' he thought. A pretty young nurse who he had met on the hospital ship came to visit him, perhaps to reassure him.

"How are you feeling?" she asked him calmly as if talking to a little boy in a children's ward.

"I'll be alright," he answered quietly, although he did feel extremely uncomfortable.

"You'll be taken down to have an x-ray soon. We normally bring the apparatus to you, but providing you are not too unwell we'll take you there. You are lucky, these machines are brand new and produce some good and accurate results." She puckered her lips into a slight smile and gave him a sympathetic look.

"Tell me what your name is please?" he asked her and then grimaced as his broken ribs grated against each other.

"Nurse Mahoney and that's all I am allowed to tell you," she stared at him for a few seconds, but added, "for now." She walked away smiling but didn't look back.

Half an hour later the men in white coats took the brake off his bed and wheeled him along the corridor. Such was his intake of morphine he fixated on the upside down images walking towards him, reflected off the polished linoleum floor. He began to fall asleep but was awakened by the need of the radiographer to position him to take the best picture of his injured ribs. They didn't give him anymore morphine and wheeled him into the bay outside the operating theatres. He was lying flat on his back and the last he remembered was vaguely seeing two men either side staring down, masked up to their eyes. They spoke to him reassuringly telling him that when he woke up his problems would be over. After an injection they were the last words he heard that day. The effect of the anaesthetic was immediate.

A well suited man walked into the recovery ward, and his white coat billowed out behind him like the sails of a Solent racing yacht as he pushed his way through the heavy double doors. The bed traffic caused by the last of the Dunkerque evacuees was slowing up and he had some time off to go visiting. He was tall, grey haired and in his mid fifties. About him was an air of authority, although he wasn't a military man.

At the desk he asked. "I am looking for a Corporal Daniel Godwin. He's had an internal injury relating to his kidney. Can you possibly help me find him?" He was pleasant in manner and stared down, concernedly, at the young woman who slid through the paper work before her.

"Can you wait one moment please sir?" He duly agreed and she went off to find the ward sister.

"How can I help?" A matronly figure asked, attracting his attention when he was reading the paraphernalia pinned on the wall about ward cleanliness.

He turned quickly. "Oh! I do beg your pardon. I am looking for a patient. Daniel Godwin. Corporal Daniel Godwin. I was told I might find him here."

The young nurse agreed he was there but the sister wasn't sure what the connection was. "I am afraid he hasn't come around from the anaesthetic yet. Can I help?"

"No! Not yet. I'm obviously too early, but can you inform me when he is fit enough to talk, and then I will come back. Please don't rush. I appreciate you have more than enough on your hands." He gave her a card with his name and number. The sister read the card with an expression of awe on her face as he returned back through the double doors.

Daniel slowly came back to life. He shivered uncontrollably. At first he had no bearings. He was being watched over by a portly woman who gently held his wrist to prevent him from thrashing around. The pain in his side had decreased but she whispered to him, persuading him to lay still until he became fully awake. Behind her stood Andrew and he politely asked her to step aside.

"Daniel," he questioned him quietly. "Daniel. I'm Andrew. Andrew O'Dell, your uncle. Try and wake up."

The nurse standing by the bed recommended he should come back in about half an hour.

Daniel could hear their voices but then drifted off, back into a comfortable slumber. Slowly he came around. When he did there was nobody near except his other unfortunate inpatients. His mouth was dry and he desperately needed water. At first they were reluctant to give him anything as he might vomit, but they relented and allowed him a tiny amount to wet his parched tongue.

An Austin Seven pulled up outside the grounds of the Queen Victoria Hospital and then turned and parked some distance away. The occupants, smartly dressed, walked the half mile to the spectacular red brick building. The structure was immense. Ninety years old and still fully operational. Which part of the hospital they needed was scribbled down on a small piece of paper taken from a telephone message the day before. Joy walked on hurriedly. James tried to hold her back, asking her to calm down but she shrugged him off. Seeing her son was of paramount importance.

Inside they asked at the reception desk and were directed up the twin staircase onto the second floor. There was a long corridor to their left where the end was practically too far away to focus. The passage way was busy. Nurses pushed wheelchairs back and forth with wounded soldiers who paid little attention to their surroundings. One had lost both his legs and sat, sullen faced, oblivious to what was happening around him. For James his injuries brought back terrible memories but reminded him of all the hard work done at the hostel in Bath. Soldiers in regimental uniform searched the corridor for wards where they might find their wounded comrades. Their shining boots squeaked on the mansion polished floor.

Halfway along they turned right again and there they came upon the Edward Jenner ward. Here they were confronted by a powerful and grim looking matron.

"How can I help?" she questioned them both whilst looking at the large clock above the door which told her the time was twenty five to two.

"We've come to visit Corporal Daniel Godwin," Joy asked timidly.

The matron looked her up and down. "Are you his elder sister?" scarcely believing that she could be the mother of a twenty year old.

"No! he's my son," Joy answered surprised.

The ward disciplinarian then turned her attention to James. "I suppose you're the father," she retorted, disbelievingly.

"Yes I am. We are his *proud* parents. Now where is he? if you don't mind. We have come a long way."

She looked back up to the clock. "I am expecting him here at any time now. Visiting time is not until two and we adhere strictly to that rule. If you would like to go and have a look around the hospital or have some fresh air by the time you get back we will probably have him made up and comfortable."

James turned to Joy, and without saying a word merely shrugged his shoulders, suggesting they had no options. He took her by the arm and led her away before she could say anything out of order. 'The Queen Victoria' was a military hospital, with military discipline.

Wandering around for twenty minutes seemed an age to Joy and to make matters worse Daniel had only just been received onto the ward when they returned. The matron would only allow them in when he was made fully comfortable, and all the necessary checks had been completed. Fortunately Andrew appeared and he briefed them on his condition.

"He was strafed and the bullet passed through his side shattering a couple of ribs which subsequently bruised his kidney badly. Don't worry Joy he will make a full recovery and will be raring to return home in no time." He tried to reassure his sister but motherhood was more powerful than her brother's assumptions, however exceptional his qualifications.

A nurse peered around the door, a completely opposite character to her dominant supervisor. "Mr. and Mrs. Godwin you may come in now," she told them sweetly.

As only two were allowed to visit at any one time Andrew excused himself having had other work to complete at the hospital and needed to return to London that night. He saw them through the door and went to depart.

"Doctor O'Dell," the matron had called out, she knew him from his ward visits.

Andrew swung around.

"You obviously know them. Are they the young soldier's parents?" she asked inquisitively.

"Most definitely. She is my younger sister and Daniel is my nephew," he smiled at her and as he walked away he emphasised, "oh! and by the way, they *are* married!"

Joy and James had to be out by three o'clock but oddly enough the Matron gave them a ten minute concession. Daniel told them as much as he knew and how he felt. He struggled to stay awake and the Matron kindly asked them to leave as he needed rest. Joy kissed her son as he slept and James tapped him very gently on the shoulder reassuringly and then they left, much more encouraged having seen his condition.

As they walked back along the corridor, in no hurry, James asked Joy, "did you notice how the matron's attitude was completely different when we left?"

Joy wasn't listening, her mind was concentrated on her eldest son's welfare.

Two days after his operation Daniel felt much better and had weaned himself off any pain killers. From medical advice he drank water profusely in order to flush his injured kidney through, and his determination to free himself from hospital almost overwhelmed his reasons for being there in the first place.

Nurse Mahoney paid him a visit. She spoke quietly to the sister asking if she could take Daniel for a short trip outside in a wheelchair. The sister then laid the law down about his absence from the ward. "I know it is hot outside but do not let him sit in a draught. Make sure he has enough water to drink and take a bottle for him to urinate in. You have forty five minutes. Don't be late."

Daniel had no objections to his excursion or the company he would be keeping. She took him out to the front of the building and wheeled him first of all to the north side and then the south side of the hospital. The building amazed him, the overall length, design and position by the side of Southampton Water. Built purely for the homecoming wounded from past conflicts. They stopped at a bench dedicated to the nurses of the Crimean war and she applied his brake and sat down.

After gazing out for a minute or so across the dirty estuary waters he turned to her and asked, "would you do this to me 'for better or for worse'?"

She thought for a second or two without taking her eyes off the passing freight ships. "How many times do you think I've been asked a similar question since I have worked here?" she glanced at him, smiling ironically. "I've just spent nearly three weeks involved with the evacuation at Dunkerque. Men, any age, very badly wounded but mostly single, always ask us young nurses to marry them. Perhaps they think they haven't any other hope." She continued to stare out across to Hythe ignoring the ships and boats. "Some had limbs missing, other's blind or partially blind, they had injuries hard to describe but ultimately they all hoped to marry one day and have a wife and children." She went quiet again. Daniel tried to absorb what she was saying. "And then there were the married ones who would ask the same question and tried to laugh knowing they had a woman at home. When we brought them back on the ships we tried to keep their hopes up. Before they fell to sleep we knew that what tormented them most was they would have to explain why they might have a limb or two missing, lungs badly damaged or being blind. For many, their working life was over and obtaining any income practically impossible. Their marriages will fail because of the hideous injuries inflicted upon them. The luckier ones who had opulent upbringings would probably become involved in their family businesses," she held her hand over her mouth, "believe me Corporal Godwin you are one of the fortunate ones," she struggled to express her words, "so far." Nurse Mahoney fully understood that the current war was just the beginning of a long and bloody conflict.

"Why do you think that?" he asked her.

"Because you'll survive your injuries and return to your regiment." She dabbed her eyes with a handkerchief. "You are young Daniel and you might not have another injury, but that is not the case for hundreds of thousands of others. They'll be rendered useless by this awful war. When we go to nursing college a part of our teachings are about the welfare of these men after any conflict. Some nurses will develop that skill and specialise in helping them."

Daniel didn't broach the subject but thought about Rob and the hostel in Bath. "Miss Mahoney please believe me you have been through a very bad time." He stretched over, took her hand and squeezed gently. The pain in his side he ignored. "Please tell me what is your first name? I enjoy talking to you but we're much too formal. Please tell me, what is your name?"

She told him her name was Fionna. "Come on, I have to take you back now or we'll be late." She stood up behind him and kicked off the brake. As they trundled back to the entrance she occasionally stopped to blow her nose. Daniel felt awkward with his back to her, but there was little he could do.

Daniel woke the next day very early. The mid-June morning light was more than a match for the flimsy unlined curtains. He waited patiently for the nurses to swap shifts so he could have a change of bottle in which to urinate. He was obsessed with leaving the hospital but had been told when his urine was clear of blood he would have a good chance. His side ached from his shattered ribs but healing is fast among the young, and he yearned to leave his bed and walk the 'corridors of hope' alone. He threw back the flimsy blanket and slowly stretched his tired legs over the side of the bed. Far from being a standard bunk, the hospital bed, offered a long drop to the floor.

"Don't! stay in bed and call the nurse," came a loud whisper.

He looked around and waved his hand at his bed bound advisor, urging him to be quiet with a finger over his lips. As his feet took his weight the pain struck his side like a lance. He held his breath for a few seconds and after donning his dressing gown Daniel limped out of the ward towards the toilet with his almost full jar of nightly urinary discharge.

Daniel returned. No-one had seen him except his fellow ward mates most of whom were not in any condition to say a word. He eased himself back onto the bed and the nurses were none the wiser.

Three days later after a visit from the surgeon he was told he could get up and move around but only with assistance at first. In no time he was out of bed. The pain had eased and he barely passed any blood although the staff continued to take a daily urine test. Quickly he became independent and was limping around the ward talking with his fellow patients and offering encouragement. They exchanged stories of what had happened to themselves and where their futures lay. Some were undoubtedly not going back to war unless the war came to them, but none imagined the Germans crossing the English Channel, even though the Luftwaffe's activities were incessant and increasing.

"Daniel. You have a visitor." The matron made a point of telling him herself. "He's outside."

The time was mid-morning and the message took him by surprise. She hadn't elaborated as to who the caller might be.

Daniel was taken aback when he saw Lieutenant Colonel Bradshaw of his own battalion. They saluted each other. "Are you alright to have a walk?" he asked Daniel.

"Most certainly sir." Daniel told him warily. He couldn't understand why he had paid him a visit.

As they made their way to the main entrance they talked about the hospital in general. Colonel Bradshaw ominously suggested the building would be having a lot of use over the next few years.

"I understand you are improving by the day. Is that so?" he inquired.

"Yes sir. I can't wait to leave here and get back with the regiment," he answered, appearing to sound enthusiastic.

"Good, but don't bank on returning into action too quickly. The matron seems to think in a couple of days time you will be sent to another ward where they prepare the men to be sent home. Chaps like yourself are not so much a problem. However, you will not be there long and you will be three or four weeks back home and then a return to the regiment for light duties, mostly desk duties until you are fully fit."

Daniel briefly thought about what he would do if he spent a month at home. The respite seemed a long time.

"What I want to ask you about is your experiences during the last two weeks in France. How did you become separated from the rest of the battalion?" The Lt. Colonel's brow puckered quizzically.

"We were asked to take and hold the Messines ridge. To our left were the Cameronian's and Irish Fusiliers. As you probably know sir our platoon were the most northerly of our battalion. The fighting became harder and harder and I think what happened was that the Germans penetrated the line to our south. We were pushed back for a while but later regained the ground we had lost. The skirmishing went on for two or three days but we had no food and little water. We were losing radio contact and Sergeant Myers went to try and find out what was happening. When he returned I remember him telling me that the enemy were between us and the rest of the battalion. He decided to stay and fight alongside the rest of the division which we did until the Bedford's came and relieved us. We stayed at Poperinge for some while directing the traffic through the town, but when we finally retreated back to Dunkerque we were told that rest of the battalion had already been evacuated." He stopped and thought for a while. "Is that how Sergeant Myer described our position sir?"

The Lieutenant Colonel was quiet and then he said, "I don't know. I am afraid Sergeant Myer died on the way back to England."

The news shocked Daniel. For a while he said nothing, taking in the devastating news. "He was a good soldier sir, a very good soldier." he said meekly.

"The other lads who were with you basically gave me the same report. Your lads keep asking after you, but at least now I have something to write down on paper."

Daniel looked at him, "please tell them I look forward to meeting up again and hopefully I won't be long."

"One other thing before I go. Your performances on the field of battle didn't go unnoticed especially from a captain in the Irish Fusiliers. When you return to barracks you will be taking over Sergeant Myer's job and be holding his same rank. Congratulations," he shook Daniel's hand, "that should give you an even bigger incentive to return to the fold. Well! I can't stay long as I have another meeting later. I'll let you find your own way back." They saluted and he turned away leaving Daniel standing at the foot of the hospital steps. Daniel's tears gently run down his cheeks. He'd lost a good friend and colleague. 'But this is war', he told himself.

Daniel climbed the steps back into the reception area of the ground floor in a muddled state of euphoria and melancholy. Having been promoted was a worthy feeling, but at the expense of Willie Myer's life made his extra stripe hard to bear. Willie had been a wonderful man and soldier. All who knew him would suffer a great loss, especially his wife and children.

Just inside the door was another wooden bench dedicated to one particular nurse from the 'Great War'. There were many such seats scattered around the hospital. He sat down upon the particular one in the foyer, and pondered over his future. All things entered his mind but Sergeant Myer came to him most. He remembered the last moments when he saw him alive floating in the water with blood pouring from his wound. Perhaps he should have dragged him back to the beach and took him to the queue for the hospital ship. He could vividly visualise his face when they were under gunfire as he barked his orders. Daniel kept mulling over that fateful day in his mind. Gone was another great friend and mentor. He held his head back and closed his eyes. 'This is war' he told himself once again. Now he had to fill Willie Myer's boots.

The matron came to thank Daniel for his help on her ward before he left the Royal Victoria for home. Fionna took him to the station where they exchanged addresses. There was nothing physical between them except a small embrace, and he thanked her for her company. She watched the train pull away and just before he was out of sight waved resignedly as if she would never see him again. He waved back.

The journey was almost the same, but in reverse from when he left home more than six months previously. He'd bought a paper to read and scrutinised the front page. The government had asked the journals to play down the severity of the war to buoy up the general public feeling. Only snippets of information were filtered back from France. The evacuation was headlined as a resounding success. That may have been so, but the evacuation was an eventuality after a massive military defeat.

Having persuaded Helen and Robert not to jump all over him because of his injury their elder brother walked through the door of the cottage only to have his mother do exactly the same. James followed carrying his son's baggage. George was quietly pleased to see him enter the cottage. He was sitting in his chair having recovered miraculously from his winter pneumonia. 'As hill farmers go, George must be one of the toughest', thought Daniel.

With permission to drink beer only, they spent the evening talking, and eventually Daniel retired to bed in a rearranged sitting room. He slept well except for the occasional excursion into the yard to relieve himself.

The next day he read the letters which his mother had kept for him.

Every morning after listening to the wireless he borrowed the car to go and collect a paper. Daniel was eager to hear or read about the news. He felt much better and wanted to return to his regiment but he had only been home a week. His local doctor kept a wary eye on him, persuading him to take his time as there was no imminent invasion and he wouldn't be needed.

One afternoon the phone rang as he was writing a letter to Mark. George was asleep. James and his mother were milking.

Daniel answered the call. "Hello. Eastrip Farm."

On the other end there was silence and then the phone rang off. Shortly afterwards the phone rang again. He picked up the receiver and listened but didn't answer. There was a pause and as he was about to put the phone down a woman spoke. "Daniel is that you?" The lady's voice was meek and barely discernible, foreign perhaps.

"Yes. Why?" He was unsure who he was talking to.

"Mrs. Sinclair would like to speak to you," she told him.

Daniel immediately held the phone to his chest and stared up at the ceiling. Her words were the last things he wanted to hear. "Alright put her on." There was a pause.

"Daniel. Have you heard?" Stella was distressed.

"Heard what Stella?" He was very coy.

"The Highlanders have been captured. Stuart was amongst them. Please Daniel come down and see me! Please. I need to talk to you." Stella was very upset.

Over the months he had tried to eliminate her from his mind but her omnipresence followed him everywhere. Willie Myer had listened to him and advised him to get on with the war in the hope that something else would crop up and now indeed Stella had reappeared, not what he had hoped for. "Alright I'll come and see you tomorrow." He mentioned nothing else, not even a time of arrival.

Daniel spent the rest of the day writing his letters, one in particular was a reply to Mark Campbell. Mark sounded bored with his new life. He was desperate to see some fighting instead of just guard duties and wished he could be in Europe. Being stationed in Nairobi helped somewhat. Daniel wondered what he was actually aware of so far away in Africa, and whether he had heard of the Dunkerque fiasco. He explained everything in his letter.

The walk up to the post office did him some good because at least he had some form of exercise. He stopped occasionally to talk to people he knew, but mentally, life had become austere. He felt the whole atmosphere in the village had changed. Everyone now seemed to be doing at least something for the war effort. Every spare piece of ground was being used to grow vegetables or somebody was knitting gloves. The railings around the memorial had been removed to be melted down for the steel. The biggest change was the noise from the aerodrome and the influx of airmen and construction workers, although the pubs were doing a very good trade from their presence.

Inside the dingy little post office, seated behind a perspex screen, was ancient Mrs. Totton. She was dealing with another old local woman and at the same time making disparaging remark's about some of the young women's behaviour now that the construction of the aerodrome was well underway. They both dreaded to think what was going to happen when the Royal Air Force men arrived permanently. A population explosion was unimaginable, although the postmistress didn't mention their presence would be good for business overall. Daniel smiled and couldn't help wondering if they were jealous and how they would have behaved had they been at the right age.

He enjoyed the walk back home abiding his time to appreciate the views on a splendid summer day. In his current condition there was too much risk to visit the woodlands where he had played with his friends, not so many years before. None of them ever thought in those days that there would be another war after a mere two decades. They were then all innocent. Few knew anything about the first terrible conflict.

The bullocks were up in the top field and they stared over the wall at him. Flies buzzed around their fluffy white faces, brought to life by the heat of the day and the attraction of the smell of cattle and their pats. Far away a cuckoo sounded his familiar call, whilst in the brambles next to the lane an angry wren could be heard, 'zeck!' 'zeck!' 'zeck!' so loud for such a tiny bird.

His side ached, probably from lack of exercise. He took the short cut to the parlour to find his father, avoiding his mother who was down at the cottage. "James can I borrow the car tomorrow please? I need to go to Bath." He sensed his father would know for what he wanted the vehicle.

"Daniel when you were away in France during the so called 'phoney war' and you had time off, did you go into town drinking and searching for desirable women? Especially on pay days and weekends."

"I went drinking but not to find a woman. Some did. Most of the women hanging around were whorish. I think the decent girls were probably kept at home by their overbearing religious parents." Daniel smiled awkwardly. He didn't understand why his father asked such a question.

"Where are you going in the car? To see a friend?" James knew why he needed the Austin but wanted a truthful answer from Daniel.

He was honest and straight to the point. "To see Stella. There is a problem with Stuart. She seems to think he has been taken as a prisoner of war. From what I read in a paper on the way back here that could well be true. He was with the 51st. Highlanders at St. Valery en Caux. The ones that survived the battle were captured."

"That's unfortunate Daniel, but how can you help? She's not your wife Daniel, she's Stuart's wife"

"She needs a friend to talk to. I don't know what's going through her mind," he held his hands up. "Well! may I borrow the car or not?"

"Yes but just be careful about what you are letting yourself in for." He went to finish cleaning but turned to him again. "Don't tell your mother where you are going tomorrow. Say it's down to Tidworth or something. I am warning you now she knows about you and Stella."

Daniel was about to ask him who told her but before he could get his words out James retorted. "Don't even ask! Oh! And by the way if the police stop you in the car tell them you're a farmer. We're exempt from petrol rationing but your journey has to be credible. Say that you have been delivering eggs or something."

Stella hardly appeared to be a grieving woman when she opened the door to Daniel. Dressed in a blue patterned dress and wearing stiletto's and fish net stockings. Her hair had been prepared that morning. Expensive perfume and jewellery adorned her body. She somehow lived beyond a staff sergeant's wage. Inside there were two bottles of corked red wine on the table with two glasses at the ready. She was not the most beautiful woman in the world but was sexually attractive and many soldier's dream. She was intelligent and seemed to know what she wanted out of life.

"I'm so pleased to see you Daniel. Here have a glass of wine," Stella poured one and handed the glass to him, "your mother told me you had been hurt. How is the injury? Healing properly I hope." She gazed at him almost mournfully.

Daniel was taken aback, 'his mother had had contact with Stella'. The consequences flashed through his mind. He half imagined his mother pushing a baby in a perambulator through the city believing the grandchild was hers.

"Yes the wound is coming on fine. Three weeks and I return to the regiment. Not long now." He emphasised the fact that the healing process would be no longer than the timescale he predicted. "Tell me Stella, what is the situation with Stuart? Has he really been taken prisoner?"

She sat back down on the edge of a chair and placed a hand over her mouth as if she were about to cry. "A friend of his rang me initially fearing the worst but then I had a letter from his regiment confirming that the remnants of 152nd. Brigade had been captured. Stuart was definitely amongst them. What I don't know is where they have taken him or whether he is still alive. The final battle had raged for two or three days and there were many killed. Hopefully he is a prisoner of war and the Germans might treat them all decently."

"I'll go and find Rob. His contacts in the army are always reliable. He'll be able to tell us." Daniel needed an excuse to leave.

"No! Don't go yet. I have some lunch prepared. Or we can go out, into town perhaps."

To Daniel, in town seemed a better idea. He would be out of her house. "Where is Caronwyn?"

"She is with the nanny today. She'll be fine. Why? Do you want to see her?" she asked.

Daniel was caught out for an answer and quickly suggested they go into the city centre.

They had lunch at a tiny restaurant buried deep in the city walls. They talked of everything that had happened since they last saw each other during the Christmas before. Afterwards he had no options but to drive her back to Shakespeare Avenue where after ten minutes of gentle arguing she lured him into the house. His morality had failed him again. He was beginning to love her.

Daniel, incapable of strenuous exercise, let Stella bring them both to their ultimate orgasms.

Stuart's name was not on the captured lists sent by the Germans. He was missing presumed dead.

Chapter 27
The Purge

"Karina. Here is some money and an address for you to go to. Have at the ready a suitcase with your clothes and everything you might need. Go now please and prepare. I will walk you to the station." Dr. Koster sounded anxious, his position in Holland was tenuous. Being a German his own people had invaded his adoptive country. Their house to house inquiries were now the talk of Enkhuizen. Any Dutchman trying to save his own skin would mention his place of birth, Berlin. Dr. Koster would be high on the wanted list. His association with the communists and then his sudden disappearance would bring him under extreme scrutiny. He waited nervously for his daughter.

Karina came down the stairs, awkwardly trailing her belongings in a large leather suitcase. Her father studied Karina up and down knowing he would probably never see her again. Proudly he held her tightly in her arms.

"Pappie let me stay here please! Everything will be alright. Please!" she pleaded with him.

"I am sorry my little one, for your own good you must leave. I do not want you to be found with me. Now listen, take out from your case everything which has your name sewn on. You are no longer Karina Koster. The address I have given you is that of Dr. Nieuweboer and his wife. He is retired but still has connections at the Saint Elizabeth Hospital in Arnhem. If you still wish to become a nurse, as your mother was, then he can help you, but for now on he is your grandfather. I no longer exist. Dr. Nieuweboer is your immediate family and will explain all you need to know. When you leave Enkhuizen do not speak the German language, deny your German identity. He is Dutch and you have to be Dutch as well. Believe me Karina, for your own safety, please believe me." He took out his fob watch. "We'll have to leave in fifteen minutes. Remember, take nothing with you which relates you to me. Absolutely nothing! Dr. Nieuweboer is taking a massive risk for you and he is a wonderful friend. Please do not let him down." He kissed her and left her to rummage through her belongings.

Dr. Koster carried his daughter's suitcase down to the station at the same time holding her hand and trying hard to hold back his tears. The train was at the end of the line and waiting to return to Amsterdam. Steam chugged out from the locomotive's undersides. As the 'iron beast' left the station he stood and watched while Karina frantically waved goodbye. He stood passively as tears poured down his cheeks and waved as his daughter finally went out of sight around a bend in the track.

The doctor carried on with his practice. His normally talkative patients said very little to him as if they knew his outcome. As always he was very professional. One evening German soldiers turned up, questioned him briefly and then took him away. He was told he wouldn't need his briefcase anymore.

Chapter 28
Devizes

The desk sergeant was filing some papers when Daniel walked through the large oak double doors. He heard someone entering but didn't turn around as he rummaged through the draw on the back wall but called out, "new recruit? Just take a seat. I'll be with you in a minute."

"No Sarge. Corporal Godwin reporting back to duty with orders to report to the desk sergeant, who I assume is you." Daniel felt a little apprehensive on his first day back.

The sergeant tried to look over his shoulder and fiddle with the paperwork at the same time. "Sorry give me a minute and I'll be right with you. Just take a seat."

Daniel chose to pace up and down in the expansive entrance hall. His leather soled boots clunked on the unkempt floor. He studied the paintings on the wall. They were of famous bygone regimental battles which had been drummed into his head during past history lessons. He wondered who were the artists, their signatures in the bottom corners being indiscernible. On hearing a draw slam he turned back to the desk.

"Right corporal, sorry to keep you waiting. What did you say your name was again?"

"Corporal Daniel Godwin sir. I was ordered to report here at eight o'clock this morning, prompt sir." He spoke formally.

"Just relax son we're not on parade now." There were several sheets of paper in front of him, mostly for new recruits and conscripted men. He browsed through them thinking he should have put them in alphabetical order earlier. There was no time now because soon he would be inundated with nervous young men, all wondering where to go next.

"You said Corporal Daniel Godwin. Well I have written down here 'Sergeant'. There must be a mistake. Just wait a minute and I'll..........." He went to go to the back office but Daniel stopped him.

"No that is probably correct but I wasn't expecting my promotion so soon. I've been off convalescing from injury and haven't really been in touch." Daniel was not vainglorious.

"Well! Congratulations then. You've done well for such a young bloke. I was in my thirties when I received my third stripe. Alright then. Also written here is that you are to meet with Lieutenant Colonel Bradshaw along with Second Lieutenant Cory. The battalion commander must have something up his sleeve for you to have an audience with him. I'll ring his office and tell him you are here." He picked up the black receiver and dialled three numbers and informed the commanders' secretary of Daniel's presence.

Shortly afterwards a young officer entered the hall. By this time there were several other men being dealt with by the jovial desk sergeant. He understood their nervousness and tried to relieve their tension with his amiable personality.

The officer recognised the experienced soldier in Daniel, approached him and introduced himself. "Sergeant Godwin?" he asked, "I am Second Lieutenant Cory."

"Yes sir." They formally saluted and shook hands. The others in the hall began to realise what they were up against. Most had never spoken the word 'discipline', let alone put it into practise.

"Come on let's go and have a chat in my office. There's not much there but I can make tea."

Before leaving to meet the Lieutenant Colonel they informally chatted for a half an hour about each others' backgrounds, more so about Daniel's experience in northern France. They agreed to talk on first name terms except in the company of their own men. 2nd. Lieutenant Paul Cory briefed Daniel on what he believed the Lt. Colonel was going to tell them.

"Gentlemen sit down please," the Lt. Colonel told them politely.

Paul and Daniel both obliged and waited silently as he browsed through the paperwork neatly laid out in front of him. He had read the notes previously but did so again to convince himself he had made the correct choice. Having done so he looked up.

"Flight Lieutenant Cory! Welcome to the British Army," he smiled at him with an air of personal success.

Daniel stole a glance towards Paul wondering what the battalion commander meant.

"I am afraid the rank of Second Lieutenant is below that which you held in the Royal Air Force but you must consider that our system differs. The choice was yours to join us but I am sure you will make headway soon enough and reach similar status. Your service record is exemplary." He put aside one set of notes and took up another. Very briefly he glanced up at Daniel.

Paul fidgeted whilst Daniel sat stock still.

The Lt. Colonel took out a brown paper envelope from the drawer of his desk. He peeped inside. "Sergeant Godwin these are for you." He handed the envelope over to Daniel who also took a quick look. "I hope they taught you how to sew in the Army Cadets." They were his new stripes.

Paul offered his hand and they shook, congratulatory, but silently. The Lt. Colonel was glad the formalities were over.

"You both may have noticed this morning the new recruits turning up. Conscription is again underway. Our battalion lost a few men in France, not many, but we need to come back up to full strength, and as soon as possible. I can tell you now the bulk of our regiment are already stationed in Liverpool on fire watch, our intelligence had been expecting an attack for some time. Two days ago the Luftwaffe began bombing the city during the night and the centre has been hit badly, especially from incendiary devices, indeed there were over a hundred and fifty fatalities from one bomb on an air raid shelter in Durning Street. We have been issued a task to assist the fire brigades which we will undertake to possibly Christmas and well into the new year. Please believe me, I cannot divulge where in Liverpool the regiment is stationed, purely for security reasons because the Germans will not think twice about bombing us out of existence." He sat back in his chair and pondered about the two men sat before him. "I believe that because of our different work requirement, meaning firewatch, we need a larger amount of smaller companies within our battalion comprising of no more than sixty or seventy men each, and within those companies possibly four or five platoons. In Liverpool itself we are already reducing the infantry system to smaller companies and they will be allocated across the city. Lieutenant, from a mixture of regular soldiers and new conscripts, I want you to form your own company in preparation for your forthcoming assignment. You have an excellent young sergeant alongside you who I am sure wants to return to his own men, and become an integral part of the battalion. I have commandeered an exceptional drill sergeant who will hammer your men into shape in no time. He may be a little old but believe me he is no slouch. Godwin I am giving you six weeks to come up to full fitness otherwise there will be a complete review regarding your expectancy on the battlefield. That concern I will leave up to you, but I am sure your determination will see you through."

Daniel was taken aback by the Lt. Colonel's sudden change in attitude. He felt he had been given the ultimatum 'do or die' but nevertheless nodded in agreement, with the Colonel.

"From you both I expect to receive an excellent company of soldiers, if not the best, fighting fit, subordinate, but above all, proud of their regiment. You have six weeks to prepare them basically, which will then be the middle of October. You will then join up with the rest of the regiment in Liverpool, spend some time integrating and then you'll all be off across the city, sent into action. It is not actually hand to hand combat but I can assure you the assignment is quite a tough one, as you'll eventually find out. I cannot say anymore than that. If you find staff sergeant Thackery at the quartermaster stores he will assist you in the allocation of your new recruits. I will be in touch. Thank you men and good luck." The meeting was surprisingly brief.

Staff sergeant Thackery was acting as the quartermaster. Near the end of his army career himself he had been lucky not to have been involved in the 'Great War' and now too old for active service in the current conflict, which probably exacerbated his cheerfulness. He had no reason to pull rank and over the last seven years had maintained his role on a comfortable seat behind a well worn wooden desk biding his time until de-mobilisation. Perched on the corner of the desk was a stocky built, moustachioed sergeant. His beret was neatly folded under his lapel and he carried a short nut stick which he rhythmically slapped into his opposite palm. Patience was not his virtue. Both stood as Paul and Daniel entered the dowdy office.

Paul politely introduced themselves. "Second Lieutenant Cory and Sergeant Godwin. We have been asked to find you sir with reference to acquiring approximately fifty or sixty new recruits."

The staff sergeant and the sergeant glanced at each other and found, in the circumstances, trying hard not to snigger was difficult. They saw a typical young 'ex-university' officer and an even younger sergeant who presumably hadn't had time to change his stripes and least of all his pants.

"They are at the back of the stores being kitted out. Would you like me to introduce them to you personally?" The sergeant asked sarcastically.

Paul Cory stood his ground. He first stared at the sergeant. "From now on you stand to attention while I am in the room." He almost shouted, but pulled rank. He drew his attention to the shocked staff sergeant. "You are one of the lucky ones. Old, not that experienced but ideal for home assignments. I appreciate your service to the Crown and Empire but now I am asking you to put your arse into gear in one final effort. Those so called recruits whoever they may be or where they are need our help to stay alive. We are here on a training programme."

Paul Cory looked back at the supposed drill sergeant. "Go and find them right now and bring them to the front of the headquarters."

"Yes sir! "The sergeant saluted and duly dismissed himself, suddenly glad to get out of the of the way.

Paul Cory relaxed a little." When I'm here, but hopefully not for long, I want co-operation. My men will expect the best from me and their immediate seniors, which includes you," he pointed his finger at Thackery, "do you understand me?"

"Don't try to tell me what to do!" Thackeray leant across his desk towards Cory. His knuckles whitened on it's hard surface. "I have more experience in my little finger than you'll ever have."

"I will never tell you what to do but believe me I will tell everyone what you don't do." Cory wasn't having anything from him. A second later he knew he had the upper hand. He turned to Daniel. "Godwin!

Come on! We have a duty to perform." They both saluted the bemused staff sergeant and left.

"Do you think he'll live that down?" asked Daniel as they walked away.

"I don't know. If something is mentioned I'll just blame discipline on my Royal Air Force upbringing," he laughed, "we'll only be here six weeks anyway and then we'll be off."

"How long were you in the Air Force and why did you want to switch across." Daniel was inquisitive. Being ex-RAF seemed odd to him that anyone with the chance to fly would want to transfer to an infantry regiment.

"Ten years. Work became boring. I was an airframe fitter by trade and managed to break through into the hierarchy but everything was all aircraft repair and not much action. I spent a lot of time trying to persuade them to let me transfer but in the end, when I told them I wanted to join the newly formed parachute regiment they changed their minds. Coming here is just a stepping stone. I have to gain some army experience and with my inside knowledge of how the Air Force works everything then seemed to them a logical thing to do. 'Parachutes and planes go together'. So here I am." Paul seemed happy that he'd achieved what he wanted. "What about yourself? You seem remarkably young to be a sergeant already."

"I was made up to corporal in Palestine and when we returned, as I told you earlier, we were sent to France. My sergeant, a great man, he was killed evacuating from the beach at Dunquerke. I was wounded, but on news of his death they promoted me to take his place. More so, I think, is that they found out I speak German fluently. A language which obviously might be useful to them."

At the main block the drill sergeant had his men neatly lined up. Each had been issued with the standard kit. Paul Cory introduced himself. He and Daniel then slowly walked along the line and they were individually asked their names. He told them what they were up against in no uncertain terms. When he'd finished explaining what was going to happen to them he pulled a piece of paper from his tunic and handed the note to the drill sergeant.

"Do you know where that block is?" he asked him.

He looked down at the short note."Yes sir."

Paul looked at his watch. The time was nearly twelve o'clock. "March them down there and let them settle in. I want them on the barrack square in full uniform at two o'clock. Show them the mess and let them know the meal times. Sergeant Godwin! Go with him and he can show you the sergeant's mess at the same time and find you your quarter. He turned back to his new recruits and saluted them and then left.

The new recruits were led lightly jogging around the barrack square by a regular physical training instructor.

Paul turned to the drill sergeant and apologised for his manner when they had first met that morning. "Your name is Staff Sergeant Ivor Powell, retired, right?"

"Yes sir. I was called back because of shortages of manpower. I found difficulty finding permanent work in civvy street so I jumped at the chance.

"With a name like that you must have some Welsh connections?" he asked satirically.

"Yes sir. My grandfather left the Welsh coalfields and came to live in Urchfont and worked on a farm, claiming we would all have a healthier living."

Paul explained to his new drill sergeant and fitness instructor about Daniel's injury and that he would need special treatment and physiotherapy on his way back to fitness. He told all three what his expectations were for his men. Complete fitness, excellent discipline, he wanted them all to get along as a company so they would have to root out any rogues. He wanted them fed properly and he left Daniel to source the local greengrocers and farmers. There would be no drinking of alcohol until the course was finished and reminded them that the next few weeks were going to be tough.

Their basic training went well. Sergeant Powell was an excellent instructor and by the end of the six weeks Daniel was on song. His ultimate intention was that most of his men could not out phase him with their physical fitness. One stood out, an excellent athlete, and he received the nickname 'Jessie Owens', although he was white. Their strict regime worked. Each man was healthier by a large margin, all acne free, standing straight and not slouching. They were eager for action and seemed to have formed a brotherhood. Few could cook, iron or clean when they initially arrived and one could barely tie up his shoe laces. All were now quite adept and they all knew each other's strengths and weaknesses. On alternate weekends Paul and Daniel shared the responsibilities of their newly formed company. Sometimes regulars, occasionally brought back for specialist courses, were also a godsend with their experience, lending a hand when they had some spare time.

Daniel would travel back to Colerne on his weekends off, or more often than not, to Bath. The last weekend but one, before joining the regiment in Liverpool, Stella came down to the Bear Hotel in Devizes and stayed during Friday night. They ate and drank. Paul came in briefly with another officer and they were introduced to her. After they left she took Daniel's hand. A candle lit up her face and her sultry look stirred Daniel. "I am afraid Stuart is dead. I had a letter. Most of the 51st. Division who were captured at St. Valery have been accounted for. He is not amongst them. His name is not on the list."

Daniel looked away. He wasn't sure whether that was what he wanted to hear. His guilt complex grew evermore powerful. He turned and stared at the woman he now loved. "Where is the letter?"

Stella began to break down. "I couldn't bring it with me," she snivelled, "our nanny burnt the letter on the fire." She pulled out a handkerchief and blew her nose. "I spent all afternoon crying because I love you both but now Stuart has gone you are all I have left."

Daniel still couldn't understand how she could love two different men and have no compunction about the situation either. He drank his wine while she gathered herself together. "Come on, we had better go upstairs and talk about this," he told her.

"No! Please not yet. Let's talk here." She stole a glance at the waitress and asked for two more glasses of wine.

"Are you convinced he is dead?" he asked, staring at her with a dead pan expression.

"Yes. The remainder of his battalion have been taken to a prisoner of war camp in Poland, Torun, called Stalag XX-A. Under the rules of warfare each side has to let the other know who are captured or not. Stuart's name hasn't come up anywhere. He has been listed as 'missing presumed dead'.

Daniel set his eyes on an ancient map of Wiltshire attached to the wall behind Stella's head and tried to understand what she had just told him. His attention was redirected at the arrival of the wine. He didn't want to drink alcohol but drank laboriously, if only to keep his illicit lover happy.

Later, in the bedroom, after passionate love making they both stared at the candles flickering on the mantelpeice. She nestled under his arm and stroked the few short hairs on his muscular chest. After a while she stretched up and kissed him on the cheek. Tempting him by sucking his earlobe she whispered, "I'm pregnant again."

Daniel lay for a few seconds and tried to take in what he had just heard. Suddenly he drew back the blankets and stepped out of the bed. He looked down at her. "Not again surely! Who is the father?"

"Yours! Whose do you think the child is?. What do you take me for?" she asked him, smiling. "Come on! Get back into bed. Where are you going looking like that?"

Laying entwined together side by side they made love again.

The morning light penetrated through the gap in the curtains. Daniel contemplated his future with a woman to whom he wasn't married and with his child on the way. If the first child wasn't his that wouldn't matter as he would have to take full responsibility as Caronwyn's father was dead, although he still wasn't sure.

At breakfast little was said. He drank tea whilst reading 'The Times', bought from the newsagents across the road. War stories were everywhere in print. His concentration was broken. He watched Stella over the top of the paper. "We will have to get married then," he asked out of the blue.

She smiled but didn't refuse his offer.

Chapter 29

Subterfuge

"Your job is security and Bath and Bristol has overriding importance in the west country area around the Bristol channel. We have many underground sites with an array of exceptional systems and stores which are paramount to the defence of our country, plus the docks of Portishead to the west of Bristol. The area manufactures high quality products for the military which needs to be kept totally secret. Infiltrate every locality with your most trusted men. Give them work within the communities as if they are ordinary laymen and have them listen in public houses, political clubs, farmers markets or anywhere we might find people agitating against the overthrow of our country and empire. Every man with subversive views must be sought and exposed. We are in great danger. Now we have the Royal Air Force's active bases in the area, Charmy Down and Colerne to name but two. They are in serious danger, they will almost certainly be targeted. Information we believe is already returning to the Germans. How? we do not know. Who by? is another question we need to answer and why, especially if they are British?" The interviewer watched the man in front of him very carefully. No-one in the world of espionage trusted anyone, but a system of defence had to be established in Britain, whether fighting on the front line, bullet by bullet, or merely one bullet in the back of the head to assassinate a spy in a dark country lane."

"Who am I answerable to when I arrive there and where do I stay? I need an innocent job which I am capable of performing and not having excessive hours. Have you made those arrangements." The interviewee's lips twisted in anticipation.

"No! You make your own arrangements. Bath has a medium engineering base and companies are currently employing for the war effort. Besides I have cash here for you to last financially for at least two months. Pretend to go to work. You will be paid by us and you know our contact number. Above all we want results. Someone with access to important information is operating out of Bath or possibly Bristol." He passed him an envelope out of sight from everyone around and stood up to leave. "That will keep you going for a while. If you want a reliable contact in the town, try the police Chief Constable first, he should know someone. You can trust him, in the last war he was a high ranked naval officer but I cannot divulge what he has done since those days. If you refer to the letters 'KM' he might talk to you."

Left alone, the grey haired middle aged man bent the brown envelope back and forth for a few seconds as he thought briefly about his task. He quickly realised his stupidity and squeezed the remuneration into his jacket pocket out of sight. His thoughts went back to the classic Bath architecture he had seen so many years before, but that was such a brief visit just after the 'Great War'. He remembered Bath as a beautiful stone built city with wonderfully designed buildings. A writer's dream or an artist's paradise, he mused?

He paid the bill and walked out onto the street. His early evening meeting in London was at an end. In one hour there would be an enforced black out and he walked home hurriedly. All the way he nervously kept feeling the money in his pocket and tried to envisage the assignment he had in hand, and where he should start.

Chapter 30
The Wedding

The phone rang in the cottage. Joy picked up the receiver and answered. She had just finished serving the evening meal. "Hello! Eastrip farm."

"Mum. It's Daniel. Is James there? I need to speak to him," he asked.

"Can't I help you?" she answered, rather put out that Daniel wanted to speak to his father and not his mother.

"No. I need to speak to him, please."

She handed the receiver to James who took the handpiece with a perplexed expression on his face.

"James, listen a minute please. Tomorrow evening I am back in Bath and staying at Stella's house. Before I go around there can you meet me at the Station Hotel? I need to talk to you."

James went to reply but Daniel interrupted him.

"Someone is dropping me off at six-thirty tomorrow. Tell mum I'll be up Saturday, the day after. Is that all right?" He went quiet.

"What do you want to talk about?" James asked.

"I can't tell you on the phone. Will you be there?"

"Yes, alright, I'll be there. Six-thirty." The phone went dead.

James stood for a moment staring at the receiver. "He wants me to go and see him tomorrow evening. He's staying at Stella's and will be up here Saturday." He knew he wouldn't be able to appease his wife but he could only do what Daniel asked.

At first she suggested going with him but James put his foot down and asked her to be patient until he returned that evening, then he would tell her all. Joy was not happy about Daniel's relationship with another man's wife, and with his friend's wife as well, but Joy was unaware that Stuart had been pronounced 'missing, presumed dead'.

Father and son sat in the corner as privately as they could be in the circumstances. James began. "So what is this all about?"

Daniel didn't beat about the bush. "Stella's pregnant and we are getting married."

James never moved. He just thought of the consequences and tried to imagine what his mother might say under the circumstances.

"I have until a week Monday before we all move up to Liverpool on fire watch. In the meantime, we thought getting married would be a good idea before she begins to show too much. You know what people are like? Fickle." He hoped his father would support him.

"You should have thought of that in the first place. Are you telling me you want to be married by the time you go to Liverpool. Aren't you rushing into things? Have you made any enquiries yet about where the marriage will take place and exactly when?" One moment James would have an unmarried son and the next he would be married, all inside a week.

"Stella is making the arrangements, here in Bath." Daniel seemed quite positive about the marriage.

"Is she going to remain at work? because otherwise you'll be paying for all this, and for a very long time, especially if she is with child," he asked him.

"Yes, the nanny will stay and she will keep the house and her job for the time being. We'll wait until the war is over and then decide what to do."

'Daniel thinks he is invincible' thought James. "I suppose you want *me* to tell your mother? She won't be very pleased."

"Is the pot going to call the kettle black? I don't think so somehow." Daniel stared at his father but James kept his thoughts to himself.

James rose from his seat. "Come on I'll give you a lift up to the 'Bear Flat'. While I'm in town I'd just as well go and find Herbie and Rob and have drink with them."

Later James returned to Colerne and the 'Fox and Hounds' where he parked his car. He thought a couple more beers wouldn't go amiss before he went home. He didn't look forward to telling Joy his news.

The Fox was heaving with new clientele mostly in blue grey uniforms. The streets were lined with Land Rovers and any other military vehicle which could transport the men down from the aerodrome to the village. The banter was jovial and the atmosphere amiable. The local population, an influx of travelling builders and the boy's in blue all helped towards a congenial and busy evening.

Near ten o'clock the door opened and wolf whistles and cheering echoed around the bar. With his back to the door James ignored the cacophony whilst trying to talk to a newly promoted sergeant who then kept glancing back over his shoulder towards an approaching lady. Most stood out of her way trying not to spill their beer over her low cut, knee length, body hugging dress. Realising no-one was paying attention to him anymore James spun around and there stood Joy. The bar went quiet except for a few mumblings and sniggers.

James briefly scrutinised her up and down. Joy's eyes were magnetic, but not for love. She'd spent some time dressing up. Stiletto heels, jewellery and expensive make up. Joy was the centre of attention.

"How did you come up here?" he asked, almost naively.

She glanced down to her feet. Her shoes were immaculate so she hadn't walked up the lane. "How do you think?" she asked with venom.

The whole pub now watched the sheepish expression on James' face. "I don't know," he answered.

She gazed around the bar seeking attention and then reverted back to her hapless husband. "You don't know. You don't know! she shouted, "I'll tell you how I came up here and then everyone else can hear. You go off down town to meet your friends in your lovely little car, your pride and joy, come back here for a few more beers and you leave me back at the farm so I have to drive up here on my own on the 'fucking' tractor. That's how! That's how I came up here. On the *fucking* tractor!"

The 'silence was deafening' until everyone gathered the gist of what she had said and then the cheers and laughter could be heard halfway down the street. Joy looked around, having not realised the attention she had caused when she walked in the door. The moment was all about her. One of the aircrew boys produced a ukulele and began a short dancing tune. Within no time the clientele were all jumping around the bar as if she didn't exist. Arnie, sitting at the end of the bar, signalled to his bar man to pour her a drink. She refused and dragged James outside.

"What's going on? I want to know!" She was far from happy.

James tried to sober his mind. There was one dust covered light bulb illuminating the front of the pub which was illegal under war ministry rules. "You want to talk about Daniel I assume?" he asked, trying to remain calm and collected.

"Yes! Who do you bloody well think I want to talk about?" she shouted at his silhouette.

He could just see her attractive face and stretched his body upwards to express his physical superiority. "Stella is pregnant and they are being married some time next week." James was sure he would get the blame, whatever he divulged.

There were air force boys outside smoking, with pints in hand and they could overhear them both. "Come on let's go down the 'Six Bells' and talk about his marriage there." James knew she would have to control her temper in the 'Bells' if she began an argument, but to argue there was better than in front of the children and George at home.

She offered him the keys. "You take the tractor and I'll take the car!" she said, holding her hand out.

In the 'Bells' the atmosphere was quite different. Here was the 'officer's club'. Small groups of men stood or sat around talking intelligently. They did turn their attention to Joy as she walked in the door.

She looked stunning. For a woman in her late thirties her body was everything a man would want. She also had a mature but beautiful face delicately made up.

With glasses of beer the feuding pair sat down. Everyone could feel there was an explosive atmosphere between them.

James explained to her everything Daniel had told him. The situation was quite simple. Daniel was marrying Stella because she was pregnant with his child, and he would take on responsibility for Caronwyn, whoever was her father. After the wedding he was being posted to Liverpool, some time in December.

Joy instantly calmed down. "Why didn't he want me to come with you?" she sounded disappointed.

"I'm not sure if he thinks you know everything that has gone on in the past. He just wanted to speak to me first," James shrugged his shoulders, "father to son perhaps."

"What do you mean by 'everything'?" Joy felt her husband and son were hiding something.

"Caronwyn could well be Daniel's child, I've told you that before but you obviously didn't believe me." Again James went on and repeated the possibilities of Caronwyn's conception.

Joy went quiet, she was deep in thought. They drank their drinks and courteously left for home.

Back at the cottage everything was quiet. The children were asleep and George gave them the same appearance. James and Joy struggled into bed and made love. Joy had her eyes open all through the engagement, staring at the moonlit ceiling, wondering what would happen over the coming few days and what next she might hear. She was going to be a grandmother, if she wasn't already.

The wedding went ahead on the following Thursday at twelve o'clock. The party was very scant. George declined the offer to go because of his traumas. Helen was a bridesmaid although her brother Robert declined to be a page boy. Rob Goode was a witness for Daniel and they stood resplendent in their 'best dress'. Joy witnessed on Stella's behalf whilst, surprisingly to James, she held Caronwyn in her arms, who was now growing rapidly. So much had happened in such a short time and even Daniel found the situation hard to bear.

After the short ceremony they walked leisurely through the city to the Empire Bars where they were met by other friends for an informal buffet.

Helen couldn't keep her attention away from little Caronwyn under the watchful eye of the mysterious nanny. Robert disclosed to Herbie that he too wanted to join the army and fight for Britain, but was warned not to mention anything for at least a couple of years, especially in front of his mother. Rob, as usual, tried to discuss the war and found other interested parties at the bar. As Stella flitted around having gained a new young husband, the other wives sat in the corner discussing maternal issues.

Joy had dressed down, careful not to outshine the bride. She watched her daughter-in-law and wondered why she had no relations of her own attending. She twiddled with her glass, staring at the red wine, but found it difficult to have any serious conversations with her own friends. Joy felt something wasn't quite right.

Rob approached James with his grimacing smile. He nudged him in the back with his only arm and nearly spilt his whisky in hand. "Lucky you, having a good looking daughter-in-law only half a generation younger than your wife?"

James had been watching them both and he slowly turned to Rob and joked. "She can pump my tyres up and then I can go home and ride the bike," he laughed and shrugged his shoulders, "I think we'll have to wait and see Rob. I think we'll have to wait and see," he repeated slowly.

"She's cute isn't she?" Joy asked.

They were on their way home and had been out for at least ten hours. James was tired and had had by far too much to drink. He was trying to concentrate. "Who? Please don't start talking to me now, let me concentrate! I'm driving"

"Caronwyn. You know who I mean!" Joy shouted above the sound of the engine.

On the straight along the top of Bannerdown the little Austin Seven had reached top speed of just over forty miles per hour as they approached the row of beech trees. James shook his head again asking her not to talk to him but he was too late and wobbled over the road, finally lost control and veered off to the left. Just before the three shire stones he ploughed into the ditch at the base of the mighty beech trees. The accident happened in seconds. Young Robert was thrown from the car.

For them the wedding day was over.

Three servicemen walking back from a late night in Bath noticed the Austin in the ditch by the side of the road. They investigated and found three people badly injured. In no time help had arrived and they were all pulled from the car. Helen, the least injured, kept crying and asking for 'Robert'. The police organised a torchlight search and he was found beyond the stonewall lying motionless in the field. He was dead, the impact from being thrown from the car had killed him outright.

The scenes in the hospital that night and morning were unbearable for the faint hearted.

Chapter 31
The Letter

The heat of the summer had now died away and the soldiers hung around the encampments bored with nothing much to do. A white junior officer arrived with his daily box of letters. One pre-requisite to join the King's African Rifles was to have a certain degree of ability to speak or understand English, or better still, read and write the language as well. One young man assisted many into the force by teaching and helping them during mobilisation, his name was Mark Campbell. The British army were seriously searching for genuine recruits but rejected some who only knew how to use a gun. Talented English speaking black African recruits often became platoon sergeants as long as they understood their subordinates local dialects, and could relay messages back and forth to the army hierarchy in English.

The 'postman' shouted out their names. Quite a few had no messages of encouragement at all as their family tribes spoke so many dialects and languages for which there were few written words. There were Giriama, Teita, Digo, Chuka and many more, some were from West Africa, but all had chosen to fight under one umbrella, Great Britain, the empire and her allies. The list was endless.

Some did receive a letter. Staff Sergeant Mark Campbell was one of them. In fact he received two. First of all, one from his girlfriend told him she would be returning to Nairobi within a week. He glanced at the post date and smiled, that was yesterday. The second one he stared at for some while and kept aside as he read out loud other letters sent to some of his army colleagues who failed to be able to read.

Afterwards Mark found a cool place sitting under the shade of a lone acacia tree surrounded by a low stone wall. Two old Boer war cannons, extricated from the south of Africa, lay either side. He opened the battered envelope and retrieved the message that he knew was from Daniel.

Dear Mark,   *November 1940.*

I am sorry I haven't been able to contact you. It was Rob who told me where you might be and so hopefully you may now have finally received this letter. Nairobi is probably better than being up on the border. From what I can gather at this end you'll see some real action sooner rather than later. Everyone talks about Mussolini and him being on the side of the Germans. Churchill won't have the despot next door to you in Abyssinia for much longer.

Anyway, are you well? From one of your letters delivered back home you suggested you might have a girlfriend. Is that true? If it is, good for you.

I'm afraid news from my end isn't very good. I'll start at the beginning.

Having joined the Wiltshire regiment, as you well know, I was attached to the 2nd Battalion and spent about nine months in Palestine. It was just routine peace keeping. We were brought back and joined the expedition force in France and Belgium with the 5th. Division. It was a debacle but most of us were lucky and managed to be rescued whilst others were either captured or killed. I took a glancing bullet but I am now fit again. I am afraid one of those unlucky soldiers was Stuart Sinclair. At first it was not known what happened but a large part of their division, the 51st., were captured but only after a fierce battle at a seaside village called St. Valery en Caux. Stella has since had a letter from the Seaforth's more or less stating that he is not on any prisoner of war list and that he is therefore 'missing, presumed dead'.

Mark rose from his stone seat and stared up at the sky. One thing he didn't want to read about was losing his training sergeant in the cadets because he had also become a friend. He tried to imagine what was going through Stella's mind. He would soon find out. He took some deep breaths, sat back down and continued to read the letter.

I don't know what you are going to think of me Mark but since Stuart's disappearance Stella and I have been having an affair. In fact we are already married. We are having a baby. I am afraid our wedding day ended in a tragedy.

The quality of Daniel's handwriting changed dramatically and became almost unreadable.

Dad went off the road on the way home and hit a tree. He broke his leg badly but managed to save his upper body. Mum had serious head injuries although no brain damage or skull fractures while Helen escaped with minor cuts and bruises. Robert died. He was somehow thrown from the car.

The ink on the paper had been smudged and had been dried quickly from blotting paper. Daniel hadn't been able to hold his emotions back when he had written the letter. Tears welled up in Mark's eyes when he read about the tragic story. He was almost sure Daniel would blame himself for the catastrophe. The incident had happened a few weeks before the arrival of the letter. 'What happened with the farm? Who would work the land?', Mark thought. Daniel, obviously deeply moved, signed off the letter straight away saying he would write later when his mood was better.

Mark was frustrated being so far away and not being able to do anything for his great friend. He paced up and down feeling completely useless in the circumstances, wondering what was swimming around in Daniel's mind, let alone his parents and Robert's twin sister, Helen.

He returned back to his dormitory a deeply saddened young man.

Chapter 32
Jack Cosnett

"Madam I am looking for a somewhere to let and noticed your sign in the window. May I ask please, is the room still available?"

She eyed the middle aged man up and down and screwed up her face. "Have you any employment?" she inquired caustically.

He hesitated, not expecting such a biting query, "why yes! look here, I am working for Horstman's." He produced his first pay receipt.

She took little notice of the paperwork but examined him over again. He was late forties early fifties perhaps, well dressed and spoke with an educated accent. She briefly pursed her lips. "I'll show you, but I am afraid there is nothing much in the room, a double bed and basin but I do keep the room clean. Follow me!" she demanded in a matronly manner.

He struggled up the stairs behind her large posterior, staring into the back of her fat stockinged legs. Her body odour, that of an obese middle aged woman, permeated the stair case. Jack Cosnett hoped he wouldn't have to refuse the room and then carry his suitcase back down again.

She repeated herself."You're lucky there is the double bedded room but I am afraid you cannot have any visitors. Here is the basin," she tapped her fingers on the edge, "this is the only room I have with one installed. The bathroom is across the landing and I expect you to tell me when you require a bath and I will make sure there is hot water. There is a war going on you know! we have to save everything." She smirked, any good excuse not to spend exorbitantly.

He gazed around the room and then out of the window onto the street below. Having ruffled the blankets and checked the wardrobe he asked the whereabouts of the toilet. Next to the bathroom he was told and he took a visit simply to see what condition they were in. There he would make his own judgement of her housekeeping. When he returned he accepted her rental offer and paid his deposit with one week up front and then threw his case on the bed.

Before she left him she said. "Please don't urinate in the basin during the night because my bedroom is the one below and I can hear everything." On the way out she closed the door behind him, more than content she had gained a small income in such a troubled time.

From River Street, his new address, Jack Cosnett walked down into the town towards the police station. His first task was to find out any contacts who might be useful to him. The Chief Constable happened to be out at a morning meeting and he agreed to return in an hour. Jack had told the desk sergeant that he was his brother-in-law. He then chose to wander around the streets of Bath, sightseeing.

Later, back at the police station he met with the Chief Constable in the foyer and they behaved as if they were long lost relatives. He was shown a door and they went upstairs.

In his office the atmosphere was quite different and they introduced each other formally and he was asked to take a seat. "How can I help you Mr. Cosnett?"

"I have been instructed to speak to you privately regarding certain activities in the city."

Chief Constable Adcock stopped him straight away. "Who instructed you?" he asked wryly.

"All I have been told was to mention the two letters, 'KM'."

The Chief Constable's next question was, "were you given a reference number."

"Four seven six two TL." Jack had simply memorised the number.

Mr. Adcock went over and pulled a sliding draw from a filing cabinet. He rummaged for a while and then lifted out a piece of paper.

He glanced down a list and crossed a number off, returned and sat back down. "Your real name isn't Jack Cosnett then?" He smiled enquiringly at the unknown figure sitting in front of him. "So what do you want to know? How can I help you?"

"I need to start somewhere in the city. There are a lot of people here in Bath and I appreciate that, but I need a beginning. A name or names. Maybe the criminal world, although preferably not, or anyone who might be able to help." Jack felt a little more confident.

"But who are you looking for and in connection with what? I at least need to know where even I can begin. You may be searching for a murderer or bank robber, though 'heaven forbid' I would have to step down and let you take my place." His lip curled up sarcastically. "I'll help you all I can but I'm sorry I need more information."

Jack, or so his alias suggested, was prepared to start at the bottom with the thieves, whores or anyone else who might betray information for money and disregard the nation's security.

"Someone, or more probably some people, are divulging information from this city to the Third Reich. So far the passing on of intelligence has gone unchecked." Jack could also be sarcastic. "Where they are receiving their information from is not known but bear in mind the Admiralty are well established here, just south are the Army, in force, and new defensive airfields are now cropping up everywhere. Not only that the old stone quarries commandeered by the government for various storage facilities etcetera are important. Bristol, significantly has a vital port as a link to our trade routes to the west, especially America. Apparently there is someone in your city pinpointing necessary information directly to the Germans." Jack remained quiet for a while and then continued briefly. "I just thought you might be able to let me know where to begin in this beautiful city of yours before she ends up resembling the quarries from which the stone was mined."

"How did your bosses come to this conclusion?" Mr. Adcock knew how, but he couldn't help but wonder what his own interrogator was privy too.

"Each area is divided up and the amount of complaints or sordid accusations which arrive at the desks of our offices are analysed. The complaints, which are apparently from genuinely concerned people are compared with the volume of population. The public on the street are asked odd questions when we are in a state of war and often from strangers. In Bath, even though most of the intrigue comes through your police service and is then passed on to us, there appears to be a high ratio of possible subversives operating in the city. Perhaps the people here are more patriotic and want to help, or that they are more paranoid. I've been sent here to find out." Jack sat back slightly and watched the man in front of him.

The Chief Constable twisted his lips in thought. "What are you suggesting when you say that some of the intrigue comes through us?" He carefully watched his adversary.

"Nothing really. If people need to complain or report something odd then the police are the first public service they approach. They have little other choice. Letter, telephone. No! How do they make contact or, who to? By word of mouth to the police. You are the first stepping stone to their government. The government ask them to become involved in the war and rightly so, but they generally only know one direct link, which is to go to yourselves, the police. They don't come to us. You have to pass their messages on. You are in a position of trust." Jack made his point. Now he wanted some answers.

Adcock gazed out of the window. Some bedraggled pigeons flew by. He took no notice as they were part and parcel of the city. He looked back at Jack and spoke placidly. "I do know some important people around obviously but for me and you it is imperative we are on the winning side of this war. I will need to speak to some dignitaries before I can allow you to make any contact with them. Most will be on your side but one or two may be a little indifferent or perhaps indignant. However, they don't even need to know you are in the city but I will make inquiries. I can give you a start in the meantime as there is one well respected man, but I am afraid to say he is physically struggling now, and sadly not from old age. The Chief Constable gave Jack the name of Rob Goode. Don't contact me directly anymore, speak to him first. Tell him straight away that I sent you and why you are here. If you lose his trust in the first moments then you'll be on a hiding to nothing. You might find him in the 'Edinburgh Castle' but every publican knows him. His name is Rob Goode. I will put my staff on alert but ask them to be discreet at the same time. As usual, which you have already mentioned, any useful information which comes our way, we will be in touch."

He showed Jack to the door and asked him to leave on his own. After five minutes deliberating, the Chief Constable picked up the phone and made two calls.

In the 'Edinburgh Castle' there were several people at the bar dressed in suits. They were businessmen having their liquid lunch and discussing the ailing stock exchange. Other older people sat around with their halves of bitter and smoking roll ups but saying very little.

Herbie went around and stood behind the pumps waiting for Jack Cosnett's request. Jack chose a pint of Usher's. Having paid and taken the top off his beer he kept Herbie's attention by asking after Rob. The bar went quiet. Here was a stranger asking after 'Robbie Goode'.

"Who wants him?" Herbie asked, as always a little wary towards strangers, especially those enquiring about his customers.

"My name is Jack Cosnett, we met early on during the last war. Had a bit of leave together in France. He was good fun. Thought I'd look him up. All I ever knew was he lived in Bath."

"How did you know to come here looking for him in the Edinburgh Castle?" Herbie was inquisitive.

"I asked a policemen on the street and he sent me straight here." Jack told a half truth.

Herbie glanced past Jack's shoulder. Bertie, an old Boer War veteran, thought Jack seemed genuine enough and nodded. He looked back at Jack. "He actually left here ten minutes ago and went up to the Saracen's." Herbie realised Jack didn't have a clue as to where the pub was and pencilled a map on a piece of paper for him.

Shortly afterwards Jack finished his beer, thanked him, and left.

Jack followed the instructions and found the Saracen's. He stood back and politely let someone out of the door who he asked, in passing, if a man called Rob Goode was inside. "Yes, on the left as you go in. You can't miss him." 'A strange answer', thought Jack, 'you can't miss him'.

Here was definitely a lunchtime pub for businessmen and farmers. The bar was very busy. Through the throng Jack managed to catch a barman's eye and ordered a local beer. He drank some and held the brew up to the light of the window. The beer tasted good, 'George's' bitter.

There were conversations taking place everywhere. Laughter broke out every now and again. No-one would have thought that Britain was at war. Jack slowly moved around to his left. He only knew the man he was looking for by name so why did the gentleman say 'you can't miss him'. Near the end of the saloon bar he acknowledged a jovial imbiber as he passed through towards the rear bar which looked out onto Walcot Street. The lounge bar was occupied by the ladies and their gentlemen hangers-on so he turned around to go back from whence he came. Shocked at what he saw, he suddenly realised he was probably facing Rob Goode. His left arm was amputated and he had a terribly disfigured face.

There wasn't any wonder why the chap had said he couldn't be missed. Jack approached him and spoke but Rob didn't respond until a friend warned him there was someone standing next to him.

He spun around. "I'm so sorry! I'm afraid I can't hear or see you from that side. Are you looking for me?"

Jack appreciated his problem. "Well yes I am, assuming you are Rob Goode."

"That is me. How can I help?" Rob raised his solitary eyebrow.

Jack glanced at Rob's friends. "I am looking for some help but I can't explain to you here. There are too many people close by."

Rob quickly apologised to his friends and politely ushered Jack into the lounge where they found a quiet spot. There Jack told him the basis of his visit and how the chief of police had recommended where and why he should come and find him.

Rob quickly deciphered in his mind what Jack's business was in Bath. Under the circumstances Rob decided they should meet in the evening elsewhere and Jack was more than content to agree. They arranged to meet again in the Saracen's at seven o'clock. They could then take a taxi out into the country, not too far, and perhaps have dinner somewhere quiet.

When Rob left for home he made a detour towards the police station. Chief Constable Adcock confirmed Jack Cosnett was in the city on what he described as unofficial undercover business. Rob arranged for a taxi to be at the Saracen's at seven thirty.

After one beer Rob and Jack set off by taxi to the 'Catherine Wheel' at Marshfield. The pub was situated in an old coaching village not far from Bath and Bristol but on the main route to London. Rob told him the eerie stories of times gone bye in the village. 'Here the ancient 'Mummer's' ritual was re-enacted year after year. Another was of a blue eyed, blonde haired, attractive witch who, if you ever dared to pass her door, she would try to force you to marry her dark haired, dark eyed, pretty, sinister daughter.

The pub offered good beer and food. They ate well, drank beer and then tried a glass of port, still available from some clandestine sources. Rob had chosen the perfect venue in which to discuss Jack's issues.

"So have you been given any indication as to who you are looking for Jack? Did they give you any description as to who he or she might be? British? Irish, who many of whom still hate us? Welsh or Jocks? Your employers have asked you to come to Bath and find out who keeps feeding information back to the Germans. You are not stupid Jack because you wouldn't be in the position you are now." Rob watched him. He felt he was little different than the same type of men he had met in the first world war and here was another undercover operative, so say, doing the same job all over again only twenty years further on. Who actually trusts who?

Rob relaxed and caught the attention of the waitress. He asked if they had any Calem port. The young girl went to investigate.

"So Jack your employers have sent you to Bath to break down a spy ring or something close to one but they haven't told you where to begin. Where are you going from here? Bath is quite a big city and when you take in the surrounding area you have a big job on your hands. You are surely not working alone?" Rob studied him through his one good eye.

Jack leant back and wiped his lips with the crimson napkin and had been more than content with the cuisine which had been presented to him. He took a final mouthful of beer to swill down his throat before beginning the port.

Jack smiled. "Well I've already made a start, haven't I?"

"Alright then, but where are you going from here? Surely they have given you some indication as where to start. What information has actually been passed on to the Germans." Rob only saw his problem logically.

"Let's simply say that whoever is operating around here is giving away prime defence positions or trade routes such as Bristol docks. Bath's industrial engineering works are producing military components for many of our new tanks and other projects designed to defend the country. These people drive around, find a new airfield and report its position. The Luftwaffe will come and attempt to destroy those areas. For example they could be the Admiralty offices. If disrupting them affects the trans-Atlantic trade route, even indirectly, then they will then be attacked. There are the Somerset coalfields, what's left of them, the stone mines, especially because some of the old ones are used for military storage. New airfields have been built, Charmy Down and Colerne. Everywhere is susceptible. In Bath and Bristol the belief is that the espionage begins within the factories and large businesses as they have inadvertently employed subversives, many of whom are British nationalists."

Rob interrupted him. "There are German workers employed over here."

Jack carried on. "Bristol is very important especially with the Rolls-Royce works, and as I have already mentioned the docks. The list is endless for any Nazi sympathiser to report back to Germany."

Rob intervened again. "The espionage might go deeper than that. Outwardly those places are obvious targets, but you may have subversive people operating within those facilities fully aware of the future planning, and they could have a disruptive impact on any smooth operations." Rob gazed across the room. He was concerned of how deep a spy ring could penetrate without being detected. Easily within a large corporate company. He turned back. "So, I'll ask you again, where are you going to start?"

"I was hoping you might have said '*we*'." Jack smiled.

"You couldn't afford me." Rob replied almost laughing.

"I'm sure we can come to some arrangement if you really wanted to help. I must trust you because I wouldn't be telling you what I'm here for. There is a possibility to bring in more of our own men but we are a rather overstretched in the circumstances and besides I'd sooner work alone and build up my own company of trustworthy men or women.

What are you doing work wise currently? Would you be interested in helping me? I need someone who knows the area well and is keen and willing." Except the financial arrangement, Jack's offer to Rob was on the table.

Rob suggested that they should take the drive across to Colerne for a drink and they could pass the new airfield on the way, although they probably wouldn't see much in the dark. He stood up and went to the bar where he asked to use the phone. In the meantime Jack paid for the bill.

"Hello Arnie! Rob here. Any chance that Maggie can pick up me and a friend from the 'Catherine Wheel' in Marshfield to bring us over to Colerne?"

Maggie turned up and offered them both a drink after informal introductions. She explained to Jack that Arnie, her husband, was past retiring age but they still kept the Fox and Hounds as there was little else to pre-occupy Arnies' mind except his arthritis. They had a convivial chat before setting off to Colerne. They spoke mostly about the change in the road system since the building of the new airfield. They decided to go to the Six Bells first of all.

"Don't get up!" Rob ordered James, knowing he was still suffering from his badly broken leg. The accident was six weeks previous but he was still struggling on crutches.

Jack indicated that he would buy the drinks whilst Rob sat down next to the still anguished father.

James spoke to Rob. "Joy will be here soon. She's not taking anything very well at all at the moment. Of course, I don't blame her, I was at fault and should never have driven. The problem is she has started to drink heavily and then everything goes wrong. Even George, helpless that he is, has noticed. He has tried to say something to her but when she is in that state of mind only her point of view matters. Poor little Helen doesn't know where to hide. I am afraid nothing is good at the moment. The atmosphere in the cottage is dire."

Jack came back with their beers.

Joy entered the bar. Maggie hugged her solemnly. Joy didn't seem her usual charismatic self, the airmen still took notice of her and she of them. Her eyes told a sad story which most people in the village knew. Jack offered her a drink and she politely accepted his offer. She said little and remained quiet while the three others chatted. After a while they decided that they leave for the Fox and Hounds.

Rob stood his ground. He was well aware of his friend's dilemma since the death of their beloved son but he wanted to have a private chat with Joy.

"You two walk up with James and myself and Joy will be up in a minute." He watched them carefully as they left. Shortly after, two more drinks came over.

Rob stared at Joy and then spoke. "Joy my darling, I know you must be going through a very difficult time. Everyone knows that. So is James and Helen as well, and her grandfather." He tried to talk softly to her but she didn't seem to want to listen. "You have to try and be a realist as to what has happened. Robert will not be coming back. Remember his short life was a happy one. How he died was a pure accident. No-one is to blame."

Joy stared at the unpainted wall. Her hand shook and the drink she held rippled, she was a desperately unhappy woman. The scar on her forehead had healed but was still reddened, directing people's eyes away from her real beauty.

Rob visualised her when he saw her in hospital that fateful morning. Her face had been so swollen and terribly bruised. Her dignity had been taken away. He had stayed when they told her of the death of Robert as James was badly injured himself. Had he'd gone home she would have been alone that morning when she found out about her dear son, with not even her father to support her.

"Look at me Joy," he asked. She slowly turned her head towards him. "I was a lucky one during the last war because I lived. Robert wasn't so lucky but he had his purpose in life to make you, your husband, Daniel, and Helen his twin sister happy, which I know he always did. Imagine all the families now reliving the horrors of the last war knowing what is happening this time around. You are already experienced having first lost your dear brother and now a dear son. Please don't break down. You are the family matriarch, not your sister. You are the one who still lives in the family home and they will all need your support even during your own grievance." Rob paused. "Please Joy, Robert didn't die in vain. He died to make us all stronger in the face of adversity. He'd been to his brother's wedding where he had been happy all day. Just try to remember him like that, as you last saw him."

He went quiet for a short while. There was difficulty consoling a mother who had lost a son or daughter in any circumstances. "How are you getting on with James?" he asked her softly, knowing that the slightest thing he said wrong might change her from the lovely wife she was into a screaming, reckless woman. James had told him in confidence of how the accident was affecting their marriage.

Joy stared at Rob. His one eye was full of both, sympathy and hope. She went to speak then stopped. From her handbag she took a handkerchief and blew her nose then wiped her eyes with the knuckles of her forefingers. "James is patient, although he is full of remorse and blames himself. I'm the one whose taking the accident badly. Everything has just overpowered me. Daniel being at war started everything off really, but now that horrible crash and my little Robert dead, it's just too much. I'd already lost my dear brother and then mother." She began to cry openly. Rob pulled her towards him and she lay against his chest and sobbed. He gently stroked her hair and let her vent her feelings.

The landlord quietly explained to the airmen gathered around the bar what had happened and out of common decency they kept up their conversations not wanting to appear rude by listening in on a very private discussion.

Slowly Joy calmed down. She pulled back from Rob and blew her nose once again. "Do you feel better?" he asked. She barely nodded her head and blew her nose yet again. "Go and do your make-up and we'll go and find your husband." Rob hoped he may have made a difference, however small.

In the illicit taxi driven by a Colerne man back to Bath, Rob and Jack talked of local issues. "Thank you for a pleasant evening out, that was quite a change for me. Colerne seems a lovely little village with congenial people. Very chatty. Rather sad about your friend though." Jack felt bothered but he was also content having made a breakthrough with someone he might be able to trust and perhaps rely on in the future.

Rob briefly explained the story of how James had come to Colerne and eventually met and married Joy.

Jack was very intrigued. "You couldn't write a better book, could you?" He would have laughed had the story not been so serious. They arranged to meet at the Bath Priory Hotel on the Weston Road the next day at nine. They could at least have coffee or tea and discuss a few things more seriously. They bid 'goodnight' as Jack was dropped off at his new digs in River Street.

At the hotel in the morning Rob came straight to the point. "I had some serious thought during the night. I will help you out, but you will need more than two of us in an area this size. What do you think?" Rob asked him, wondering if Jack realised the scale of the project.

The waitress interrupted them. "So you must be Jack then?" was her initial question.

Jack looked at Rob with a crumpled brow. Rob introduced her. "Jack this is Judith, my wife."

As a gentleman he stood and shook hands. "I am pleased to meet you." Jack never imagined that Rob was married having considered his disabilities. They ordered a pot of coffee between them and she went on her way.

"Going back to what you said yesterday, I know you are right but who we employ is another problem. Two or three more men perhaps. Bath and Bristol is a big area to cover." Jack admitted the size of the task ahead.

Rob again spoke of the story of James and mentioned Glen and Ed's involvement as military policemen, but referred to them as Dave and Pete for the time being. "I know Dave is retired, and I think Pete will soon be as well but whether they would like to participate in a little adventure at their age is something I'll will have to ask them both. What do you think?" Rob at this point did not want to give their real identities away.

"Sounds good to me. Get in touch with them and see what they say but be discreet. I'll have to speak to them myself before there is any decision made." Jack was mentally pleased as he felt he had already met a good right hand man in Rob, so to speak. He had the Chief Constable to thank.

The coffee arrived and between them they helped themselves. Judith stayed out of the way.

Jack explained his first intention. "What I need to do is form a dossier of everyone who has a German connection or speaks the language. Most German nationals returned home well before the Polish crisis as if they knew how the eventualities would develop. The anti-Hitler or pro-communist Germans have either remained in Britain or since emigrated here, probably for their own safety, but for that alone they cannot be trusted or even exempt. Rumour continues to come back from Germany that tens of thousands of them are being imprisoned along with many more Jews. At the moment our security services are stretched. The east side of Britain has been under constant surveillance for a long while but now the air battle is in full swing, people like myself are required inland. Their spies need to be eliminated. The task is difficult but when our own people become nonchalant or complacent it is made even harder." Jack spoke with honesty. He held his home country, Britain, to his heart.

Rob had given up a great deal of his own physical well being for the same reason during the last war.

Both men left each other with contact numbers and separated. Rob would get in touch with Glen and Ed but he was sceptical. The security services of Jack Cosnett seemed susceptible. Besides the whole parliament had sat on their hands for years, being indecisive about Hitler, and now their indecisions had arrived at the current situation, outright war.

In the 'Old Green Tree' Rob tried to formulate in his mind what would happen next.

Jack returned to his room and changed his clothing. He left his bed-sit shortly afterwards and walked to his car, parked on Lansdowne Hill. After a few attempted starts she chugged into life and he set off towards Filton in Bristol.

Chapter 33

The Liverpool Blitz

There was only one week left until Christmas. Paul Cory and Daniel Godwin had just finished the night shift and sat drinking insipid tea from stained tin mugs. They were tired. Since the blitz began in late August there had been about fifty indiscriminate attacks on Liverpool.

"You're a lucky one Dan having Christmas off. Are you staying at home?" Paul asked.

"Christmas day we're going to my mother's for dinner. I've only have three full days off and I'll be back in no time. I'm not really looking forward to the occasion. Christmas is going to be a sad time with Robert not being there." Tears welled in Daniel's eyes and he turned away. His dear brother's death still affected him badly.

Paul knew the story in full. Many times he had sat with Daniel talking about Robert's death with him, but this time he moved the subject on. "I suppose for me having the New Year at home is better. I don't really like Christmas but like you say, the time will soon be upon us, and over before we realise."

"This weekend should be quite good in the city, the last one before the festivities. I think the partying might start then." Daniel was hopeful that they could have a good time.

"Except we'll be at work, although I can't envisage the Krauts being too overactive either. They are religious as well. Lutherans or something, aren't they?"

Paul wasn't sure.

Paul and Daniel's conversation couldn't have been further from the truth. On Friday night the German's again began bombing Liverpool and the Wirral, continuing to do so for three nights. Fires raged all over the city and the main intended target, the docks. Liverpool was an important port on the west coast serving the Atlantic convoys and devastating the port was high on Hitler's list of priorities.

The second battalion of the 'Wiltshire Regiment barely slept at all during the entire weekend. They valiantly assisted the fire services in trying to extinguish the thousands of infernos, caused by the masses of incendiary bombs, spread over the entire city. Daring rescues were carried out, freeing trapped people in cellars and underground retreats. As morning broke fires still raged and the injured and dying were ferried to the hospitals. The railway arches at Bentinck Street were struck by bombs and over forty people were killed outright. Nearly four hundred people were known to have died in three nights of bombing, let alone the injured. The hospitals were overwhelmed.

There was huge danger in the docks, and nearby railway sidings where ships or carriages containing massive cargoes of bombs and ammunition were targeted. Brave men uncoupled and pushed the carriages apart in the vain hope that the fires would not spread from one to the other.

The city was in chaos and all leave within the battalion was cancelled. Daniel was quietly thankful he didn't after all have to sit at the table on Christmas day with his family, and without his younger brother.

Chapter 34
The Reunion

Ed Moses drove his brand new Ford Anglia along the A338 north towards Marlborough from the cathedral city of Salisbury. Ed cringed whilst driving whenever he saw the rain clouds bursting apart on the tops of the surrounding hills which made up a small area of the great Plain. As a proud owner of a new car he had yet to accept that one day the vehicle would have to get wet and filthy. Glen Paignton sat next to him taking in the rolling views and admiring the beautiful brick and stone built villages with their age-old churches. They were driving alongside a currently raging winterbourne, flushed from the rainfall pouring from the hillsides.

Both jokingly saluted as they passed through Tidworth barracks, owned by the British army. The smiles were soon wiped off their faces when at the far end of the village they were asked to stop and show their identification cards. After usual formalities they were then allowed through.

Soldiers were training everywhere, whether for fitness, artillery or the rifle range, the whole place was a hive of activity. Trucks, gunnery or any war machinery moved in and out of the barracks. Everything was painted British army green, except Ed's car.

Soon they were driving through the ancient Savernake forest and would finally drop into the Kennet valley which separated two sets of hills, Salisbury Plain and the Marlborough Downs. Marlborough itself was an old coaching town on the Bristol to London route.

They drove slowly along the High Street looking out for the Wellington Arms and found the ancient hostelry at the far end. Ed parked up while Glen went to investigate. He reappeared with Rob at his side who beckoned him over with his one good arm. First thing first was a beer at the bar and some reminiscing.

After settling into their rooms the three set off along the street to sample the other watering holes and all the time Rob explained what he required of them in Bath should they decide to join Jack Cosnett's small team. No-one in any pub could ascertain from the brief conversations what they were about. Both Ed and Glen agreed in principle to the offer made to them. Two things were in their favour. One was to get away from the south coast for a while, and the other was that neither had re-married and were both now retired from military duties. For Rob they didn't take much persuading to join in his little adventure. Having returned down the top end of the High Street they made their way back to the 'Wellington Arms' for dinner.

During their meal Glen mentioned the confrontation at the docks with a young soldier on a train, and described the incident in detail. He even pulled out of his wallet the piece of paper with the name he had jotted down. Rob read the scruffy well worn note and asked him to describe the soldier concerned, and having listened, agreed that the soldier was more than likely to be James Godwin's son, Daniel. He told them both of the tragic circumstances of his young brother's death. A solemn toast was held. For the time being they all agreed to keep in touch and Rob would let them know as soon as possible the outcome of his forthcoming meeting with Jack Cosnett.

Chapter 35
Inaction

Daniel stayed in Liverpool for the next five months, headquartered at Aintree racecourse. There had been plenty to do assisting the fire services and keeping his men occupied but the 'Liverpool Blitz' had died down by May 1941 as Hitler realised the futility of trying to break the 'British Lion's' back and resolved himself to crushing the communist threat in the east.

One morning Paul approached Daniel and asked him to come to his small office situated below the grandstand at the racecourse. Paul told him of their battalion's new deployment to Northern Ireland and that he himself wouldn't be going because he'd been accepted to take a course with the parachute regiment. Paul suggested that Daniel should try and join as well.

As Daniel walked back to his men he thought about what Paul had said. His revelation seemed a good idea.

Over the past few months Daniel had taken every opportunity to return home to Bath. He had been granted compassionate leave when Stella had given birth to their son. At first she wanted to call him Stuart but she relented at Daniel's insistence, and they named him George after the child's great grandfather. After recuperation she maintained her job at the school with the continued employment of her nanny. After her own schooling, Helen, his sister, often went and helped Stella with baby George and Caronwyn's care. She often stayed over for the night rather than making the trip back to Colerne each evening.

Later that May the battalion packed their equipment and began the ferry crossing to Northern Ireland and subsequent arduous road journey. Some time would pass before any of them would be allowed to travel home on leave. Soon they were settled, near a town called Caledon in County Tyrone.

The parachute training programme was curtailed and Paul was reunited with Daniel in Ireland. Disappointed although he was, he hadn't given up hope of playing a large part with the 'on hold' parachute regiments. He spoke fervently of the types and strengths of men they would need and what their roles would be in the future. He insisted that Daniel should make an application to join, telling him he would be an ideal candidate. Paul was convinced they would one day invade the European mainland and parachutists would be a key factor in any success by dropping in behind enemy lines.

Again Daniel considered what Paul had explained to him, and being a paratrooper sounded a lot more stimulating than being an infantry regiment soldier, border patrolling in Ireland. He would give the idea some serious thought.

The months went on and the pair were far from any confrontational frontline. Both yearned to see some serious action. They kept telling each other, 'time will tell, something serious would eventually happen'.

Chapter 36
Chance Visit

Rob shook his father's hand. He noticed how retirement, inactivity, eating well and possibly drinking had caused him to put on weight. His mother came into the front room with a pot of tea and laid the tray on the table. She took her best bone china cups and saucers from the sideboard and placed them alongside and left them to their conversation. The pair sat down and Mr Goode poured the tea. "Make the most of the brew," he told him, "tea is harder and harder to come by. Rationing is for the poor, you are fortunate if you're privileged."

They sat for a while and spoke about affairs in general but after a while Rob's father, as inquisitive as his son, asked why he wanted to see him, especially out of earshot from his mother."

"Did you ever have any subversives on the shop floor at Stothert's?" he asked his father.

"What do you mean by subversives? Union men?" he countered.

"No, worse than that." Rob told him.

"You can't get much worse than that when men want to bring a whole engineering works to a standstill," he retorted.

"Especially during a war Dad." Rob watched his father, wondering what he might disclose.

At first the ageing retiree remained quiet but peered out of the window obviously in deep thought. He turned back to his son. "What have you got yourself into Rob. Not something you can't handle, surely?"

He stared at his father. "I don't know yet."

"So why ask me a question like that? You must be up to something."

"No Dad, the question is quite genuine. Prior to the war, before you retired, were there any people working for Stothert's who might now have a political interest in bringing the factory to a close, or passing on business secrets?" An honest opinion was all Rob required.

"I think son you need to clearly define industrial espionage and wartime espionage. The former could be merely a trades' union dispute about poor working arrangements, but the latter, something more sinister. In any large workforce there are right and left wing supporters. I've no doubt the left wingers are now growing in strength in view of what has happened in Europe, and the right wingers will remain underground. I suppose Hitler would take a keen interest in view of what is currently being engineered at Stothert's at the moment." He pondered over his son's interest.

"Yes Dad but who are they? We really need to know who. We need names." Rob wanted a starting point and Stothert and Pitt engineering was as good a place as any.

"Whose 'we' Rob? Who have you got yourself involved with? Tell me." Knowing Rob's failing health he was becoming worried for his son's overall wellbeing.

"Please don't say anything to anyone Dad, but something is apparently going on in the city and information is getting back to Germany with, so say, unerring accuracy. Or at least that is what I'm told. There is a spy ring operating here in Bath and I am being employed to help try and track them down. For god's sake don't tell anyone. I am far from being alone though. I thought of Stothert's, and then you, and that's why I came here first. Someone I can believe in who might be able to give me any information for a start." Rob didn't want to tell his father what he was doing but in the circumstances he had little choice.

They heard a car draw up on the gravel driveway beside the house. Rob's mother put her head around the door. "Darling, Charlie McGovern has just pulled up."

"Send him in my dear. Send him in." He looked at Rob. "This is the man you need to speak to. Tell him everything you have just told me."

Rob wasn't sure he should, but if his father trusted the managing director at Stothert and Pitt, then there was no reason why he shouldn't divulge his secret to him either.

Charlie was just passing by and had popped in purely for a friendly chat. He was the man who had complete control of engineering at Stothert and Pitt. The managing director of engineering never imagined what Rob was about to tell him and he listened intently. Afterwards Rob merely asked Charlie if there was any way he could help.

"Obviously I know all the top trade unionists. Some are alright, others not. They tend to be more on the left of politics especially since the overthrow of the Czarists in Russia so I can't imagine they'll be shouting on behalf of Hitler. They always have something to complain about as if that is their duty, but generally the gripes are about niggling shop floor issues and workers' rights. There are some people who might interest you who we've employed over recent years. There were about six or seven of them but the government rounded them up to be on the safe side. Some were Germans, two of whom never returned to their homeland after the last war. Good engineers actually. Another one was here before the last war. He's getting on in age now, but still working. We have a couple of men listed with British names but there has always been doubt over their nationality. One other we employed back in about nineteen thirty six. I'm quite sure he came across from Horstmans."

Rob stopped Charlie. "Why do you have suspicions about the two with suspect names?"

"One is a machinist and the other a fitter. When they first came to us neither of them could quite grasp the British units of measurement properly, which obviously meant they must have been using the European system of metrication. They are both good craftsmen and there was no reason to sack them. Now because of the war, we suffer from a lack of enough properly trained men, apprentices basically. There is no reason to believe that they are German because they could have come from any number of countries." Charlie ceased explaining and thought about the pair of men he had in mind.

"Do you have a list of all these people somewhere? Rob asked him.

"Somewhere. Probably the wages department can help you. I don't think I could possibly go and ask them. I would need to be discreet. If I'm seen asking odd questions about people my name will be all over the factory in no time. I would need a damn good reason to take a look, similar to a secret police service." Charlie was adamant.

Rob's father chirped up. "Charlie why don't you go in after the offices are closed. Copy down what Rob needs to know and leave everything intact. No-one will suspect you are up to no good will they?"

All three fell quiet but eyes were on Charlie. He held the keys to the first move. Charlie pulled back his sleeve and glanced at his proud possession given to him by his wife, his Wilsdorf and Davis watch which adorned his wrist. He then compared the time with the clock on the sideboard. "I might be able to go in there tonight actually, as long as I'm home for seven, because we're dining out this evening." He looked at them both. "Yes, leave the espionage with me and I'll ring you as soon as I have something." He went to leave.

Rob warned him. "Please Charlie. Don't tell anyone what you are searching for. Make sure you have a good back up story if security accost you."

"They shouldn't be a problem. I am the man who employs them." He smiled at them both and left. Charlie quite liked the idea of being an undercover operative.

"Will he be alright Dad?" Rob asked.

"Of course. Anything which threatens production is in Charlie's own interests to make sure no secrets leave the factory. We both well know what they are manufacturing there?"

Jack wasn't very pleased when Rob told him about his day's work. 'The fewer people knew the safer for everyone', he thought. Rob persuaded him that the information was in secure hands. People he himself could rely on. He gave Jack a very brief idea as to who they were, one his father, of course.

"If he comes back with a reliable list of names, perhaps having someone posted in Stothert's as a cleaner or something, would be a good idea." Jack's suggestion was more than sensible. He also asked if there were any other factories in the city producing goods for the war effort.

"Horstmans, they have a production line for tank suspensions. They are precision engineers and produce quite a lot for the war office. Oddly enough the name Horstman is German but they have been operating in the city since the mid-eighteen hundreds. Originally there was a double "n" in the name but Sidney Horstman dropped one of them which he had inherited from his father, Gustav. Maybe as well we should be asking the same questions of them as of Stothert's in view of their original nationality." Rob raised his one eyebrow wondering if Jack might agree.

"Where did you learn all this information? Who lets you into all their secrets?" Jack was bewildered.

"I thought that is why you employed me. My father was the chief engineer at Stothert's and I worked for the sales department. We dealt with anyone and everyone in engineering and accrued a large list of clients, whether buying or selling. My job was to know these people and their businesses. I more or less retired at the same time as father because of my injuries but I keep in touch. Many of our former business partners at work are still great friends." Rob hoped he had satisfied the requirements of his new employer.

"This Charlie McGovern, can he fix either one of your chaps with a part time job in security?" The more Jack knew about Rob the more he felt he could trust him.

"Let me deal with that. You are better off not showing your face with too many people. I'm going to take you to two different pubs tonight. Those two chaps I mentioned the other morning, Dave and Pete, well I'll tell you now one will be Ed and the other Glen, that is their real names. I'll point them out, but won't introduce you to either of them. They will completely ignore us. When they see me they will know you instantly when I buy our drinks. If anyone else talks to us because they know me, don't forget, me and you met in the last war. We're old friends. I'll let you know where Ed and Glen are staying so you can have a private word with them if you so wish. If anything happens to me you know who you need to contact." Jack agreed with Rob entirely.

The evening went well and the clandestine rendezvous' were made. The picture in Jack's head was clear. He thought he knew who was on his side and hoped he hadn't given Rob too much free rein.

Two days later Rob visited Charlie's office on request. Charlie passed him a pencilled register of possible subversives. The list was larger than he had imagined and Charlie went through the file trying to explain who was who. Some had been interned and sent to the Isle of Man. There were actually six oddities regarding their exact nationalities who held British names and were still working on the factory floor somewhere. Three known Germans had been interred. Rob pushed the paper into an inside pocket. Before he left he asked to place Glen Paignton inside the factory as a security man. He then quickly changed his mind and asked if he could be a cleaner. His request was not denied.

Rob had arranged to meet Jack later at the Green Park Tavern but not before going home and copying out the file, one list for his own keeping.

"Glen is starting work at Stothert's on Monday". Rob took from his pocket the list of characters given to him by Charlie and passed the subterfuge possibilities across the table. "See what your boys in London can make of those chaps. Something might add up," he smiled to himself, 'or not add up', he thought.

Without scrutiny, Jack merely pocketed the piece of paper. "I'll take your information up to London first thing in the morning. We'll see if they can come up with any 'wanted' names."

"Are you driving up or going by train?" Rob asked.

"I'll take the train for simplicities sake, besides I can relax and read a newspaper. If I leave about eight then I can be back just after lunch." He gazed into his pint and then swirled the residue around and around and finished the beer off. He appeared uncomfortable as he went to the bar to buy two others. On his return to the table he excused himself and went to the toilet.

One bare bulb, surrounded by cobwebs, lit the only chipped toilet pan in the gents. There was no lid. The cold rim crushed the muscles of his buttocks. As Jack sat uncomfortably on the filthy porcelain he read through the names written in pencil on the tatty paper. He thought about some of them. Others he merely disregarded. He put the paper away and read the writings on the wall. Someone had drawn a swastika. By the side, another had drawn a hammer and sickle. Before he left his cold enclave and returned to the bar he couldn't help but think that the war was going to last much longer than people thought.

Chapter 37

The Disabled Nephew

"Henri! we cannot keep him here any longer without people knowing. If someone finds out they will surely inform the Germans, if only to save their own skins. What shall we tell them? The local people, they should know he is here." Madame LeClerc was becoming more apprehensive everyday.

In their tiny cliff top cottage Henri LeClerc sat drinking his home made Calvados by the hearth, which glowed from the burning of wood salvaged from the semi-destruction of their nearest town, St. Valery en Caux. Their windows were now boarded up, as glass was now unavailable since the German invasion and they sat in candle light. In one corner the man they were talking about rocked back and forth, clasping his cardigan at his chest with both hands. He said nothing, but merely stared blindly into the fire and dribbled saliva down his front and over his hands. One leg was tucked up underneath him on the solid wooden chair but he felt no pain because he was severely brain damaged. Madame LeClerc, with the aid of sympathetic local doctors, had kept him alive during a two and a half month coma with no hospital facilities. They force fed him through a tube and one day their patience paid off and he opened his eyes. Unfortunately he was now as well as he would ever become.

"Ma Cheri, I told you many many months ago he would be better off had he died. Now the poor man has to live for the rest of his life as an invalid." Henri was sympathetic but their own problems were now mounting. "I have thought long and hard. From now on he is our nephew, long disowned by your sister because of his war injuries, and you with your pitying mind refused to have him sent to one of those demoralising homes for the wounded and sick. His name is Jacques Royon." He looked at his wife hopefully. "Who will know his name anyway. Tomorrow we will take him to the market although we have little to sell. If our own people question us, then we explain. If the German's question us, we stick to the same story. Your sister is from the south of France. No-one will know."

Henri was right, they had little to sell. Some hardy kale plants and twenty chicken eggs. He harnessed the two wheeled cart to their dirty white pony and set off to the market. They met people who had known them for years but none asked the burning question, who was he sat awkwardly on the tailboard of the cart. After one hour the time came to leave, and as Henri was about to turn out of the Market Square an Oberleutnant approached and asked who was the man sitting on the back of the cart. Only Henri spoke. He had his own and his wife's identity but not Jacques. He explained Jacques story. The soldier nodded his head sadly and allowed them to carry on home. Henri had hoped he would have had him taken away and probably shot, but that wasn't to be so.

Chapter 38
Operation Aquae Sulis.

Rob had invited Jack around for dinner one evening but worryingly for Judith Rob rang her at work during the day telling her he wasn't well and was taking to his bed. When Jack arrived she went upstairs to wake him. Judith helped him onto his feet, he was very poorly but insisted he would be at the table in ten minutes. Whilst waiting for him Judith informed Jack about Rob's general health and how his lungs were no longer working to full capacity.

They could hear him moving around and then footsteps descending the stairs. In the dining room he apologised profusely to Jack for his ignorance but was told to think nothing of it, his ailing health was of paramount importance. They ate, drank and talked of the latest news. Afterwards, as Judith cleared up, the two men moved into the sitting room.

Rob asked the first question. "How did you get on in London the other day?"

Jack smiled at him. "I thought you might be able to tell me that."

"So you don't want to tell me?" Rob face was expressionless.

"Yes I do Rob but we now have to start believing in each other. We can't waste valuable time following each other around trying to find out whose side we're on. I have been told from good authority to have confidence in you. Your military and civilian past has been honourable and the only reason not to have you on our side, with no disrespect, is your inability to go undercover. However your knowledge of the area and local industrial relations are second to none. Who you know is also important, which gives us an inside view into most of the local engineering works, especially those involved with the war effort." He was about to carry on when Rob butted in.

"So in the larger picture, what do you want me to do?" Rob was still stony faced.

"Our Secret Intelligence Service are divided into sub-sections. We are mostly agreed that the problem in this area is to do with industry. We have a sub-section which specialises in that particular area. Section VII are an economic intelligence section specialising in subterfuge within all industries. I have been told they are currently our paymasters."

Rob cut in again. "So what do you want me to do?" Again he asked, emphasising his point.

Jack knew what he had to say but thought for a while. He pointed at the half empty wine bottle and Rob very slightly nodded his head in approval. When Jack had replenished his glass he stared at his host. "I want you to find a job similar to the one you had, and try and weed out any information you can. Even if the information is only rumour. Rumour has a beginning and in our trade that is of paramount importance. Rob you need to act as naturally as possible. You cannot just go around asking outright questions, but you do also need to be known as at least being employed."

Rob was sure Charlie McGovern would help him on that point which reminded him of the other issue. He stopped swirling his glass. "What has happened about the list?"

"The list has been taken to headquarters and each name is being studied intensely. In the near future we may, or may not, have some leads."

The two men talked on for another hour. Each had their own ideas and views. After another bottle of wine, this time enjoyed in the company of Judith, Jack finally left their home more satisfied than when he had arrived. He felt that by recruiting Rob he had gained an important member into his fledgling team.

Two days later Jack contacted Rob. He wanted to talk on an important issue and they met at the Priory Park Hotel. The meeting was brief.

"I've had a message from London that maybe three of Stothert's employees are worth interrogating. The others have good viable connections and in no way would spy on their adopted country. Evidently most of the Jewish internees will soon be released which will begin to considerably narrow down the number of suspects. We need to pay the others a visit. The only problem is they are on the Isle of Man at a camp called Knockaloe near a town called Peel. Do you fancy the trip? Perhaps you should take Ed with you. No-one will know either of you up that part of the country. What do you think?" Jack hoped he wouldn't refuse.

With his one hand Rob scratched at the damaged side of his face, giving him little satisfaction. He then looked up and simply asked, "why don't you put your own man in there, German speaking, and see what he can find out. If I went there, short of torturing them, they will just clam up and we will be none the wiser."

"We have no chance. Finding men of that calibre at the moment is remote. Most of our pure German speaking boys are employed all over Europe. We're working mainland Britain here. One accent anywhere out of place and you are sussed." Jack's ability to persuade his high command to loan him a quality German speaking agent was negligible.

Rob thought of Daniel but should he drop his name? Whether Daniel would want to go was another thing. He stood up and went over to the patterned veranda doors. He was thinking deeply. Jack observed him as the highly polished glass reflected his stricken face back into the room. Rob spun around. "You go! You speak the language." He was almost designating his boss to take up the reins.

"I can understand and speak the language but not well enough to go undetected. That's why I am now always on mainland duties. Between the wars there was a certain amount of leeway and I could have trips abroad. Now everything is entirely different." Jack was disappointed he had been thwarted by his own ineptitude but considering his upbringing and lack of schooling he had actually achieved quite a lot for himself.

"Jack before we go up there, wouldn't the first sensible move be to put someone in undercover. Give them a month at least and see what he or she can come up with. As soon as we start interrogating them they'll go quiet. We have to Jack! This surely must be our first option." Rob was resolute, and carried on. "Those three men have probably been honest about their backgrounds. You could glean more information from the shop floor at Stothert's about them, rather than travel all the way up to the Isle of Man to interview them. They've been in Bath a long time and have never denied being German. Some of those others you should be more concerned about, who are holding British names, especially when two of them apparently only arrived in nineteen thirty six. They are either vehemently against Hitler and hiding from his secret police or working wholeheartedly for the dictator."

Jack absorbed in his mind what his well informed partner told him. "Information comes back that Hitler has interred hundreds of thousands of his own people, mostly those who were politically against him. This began before the war, so there is little wonder that many have escaped and sought political asylum in the only western European country which is now free from his direct tyranny. Hitler also wants to throw out all the Jews. As I mentioned before there are many German Jews in Britain now because they decided to leave after the night of the 'Broken Glass'. We have rounded them up, but someone in London has said they can only be innocent people and not a danger to us, and they will be released probably in the new year."

"So what are we going to do Jack? Undercover or direct interrogation?" Rob wanted to know.

"Travel up there and speak to them. Just tell them that if they want to return home down here with their families then they have to tell us about any information of which they are aware. In fact Rob we might be lucky and one of them knows something but maybe is too scared to say anything. You never know." Jack shrugged his shoulders.

"I will take Ed with me. He can do the questioning. What are you going to do in the meantime?"

"I'm going to start pressing London to work as fast as they can on the others. We need to find out who issued them with identification cards, that's if they have any. They must have a life story which we can check up on. I know where to contact Glen after work." Jack stood up to leave.

"Oh! By the way. He started work at Stothert's as a cleaner. I thought at the last minute that as a security man no-one would ever want to talk to him, especially the types who we might be dealing with. At least as a cleaner he can potter around and speak to people quiet innocently." Rob thought that the idea seemed more sensible, and Jack agreed with him.

"Let me know when you are travelling up there and I'll organise the security on the gate and your access . What shall we say, you'll be staying there for two days?" Rob agreed. "You'll have to arrange your own accommodation when you arrive on the island." Jack left Rob to muse over the trip. He wondered if he was well enough to travel, although he seemed to have recovered remarkably from two days before.

After a gruelling journey taking nearly fourteen hours Rob and Ed finally made the trip to the Waldrick Hotel on the promenade at Peel. Both were very tired. Ed had driven to the Isle of Man Steam Packet terminal in Liverpool from Bath, and the journey wasn't easy. Around Liverpool itself there were various detours due to the German bombings. The weather hadn't been good and heavy squalls had made the sea crossing rough, inducing many passengers to spend the whole journey vomiting wherever possible. After a half an hour respite in Douglas they had embarked on a wooden framed bus to take them across the island to their final destination.

Both were disappointed that the hotel had no bar, only drinks with a meal at the table. Ed knew of Rob's failing health and had promised Judith to keep an eye on him. He insisted that they both had a quick bath and go somewhere for a beer. Ultimately he wanted his old friend to stay awake for as long as possible and then he might have a good night's rest. Before leaving the Waldrick they studied the menu, ordered their evening meal, and promised to be back at nine. Ed hoped they would be at rest in bed by ten-thirty at the latest.

Dialogue was difficult as a whole day's company together had burnt out any other topic of conversation. The pair of them could hardly stay awake and both decided to return to the Waldrick. The chef accommodated their early arrival as he wasn't busy and began to prepare their dinner. Ed ordered a bottle of red wine. Between the two of them the alcoholic grape juice would suffice after such a long day. The subject of wines became the talk across the table. Both admitted drinking more of the grape harvest than ever before, and agreed middle age had thwarted their ability to down pints of beer as they used to when they were young. They spoke of the fabulous French wines, Italian and then the German varieties.

Dinner was served, beginning with a smoked fish soup. They returned to the subject of wine while they waited for the main course. Ed brought up the subject of when he went to Germany in the mid nineteen twenties with a group of other military police investigating the whereabouts of British prisoners of war. He explained the fact finding tour was then a 'bit of a jolly'. He had spent two weeks in Germany, being looked after by the hosts, drinking and eating anything he wanted.

Suddenly Ed stopped talking as he tried to remember his trip nearly twenty years previously.

"Do you know what was unique about the place we visited?" he asked Rob.

"No! What?" he asked, now almost disinterested through absolute tiredness.

"It was the only region in Germany which produced red wine."

Rob's better side of his face contorted slightly. His tired mind perked up.

The main course was served and both ate wholeheartedly but shortly afterwards their long exhausting day drove them to their beds.

As tired as he was before sleeping, Rob's mind kept turning over what Ed had said that evening about his trip to Germany and the red wine.

The telephone rang for some time in the Waldrick Hotel before anyone answered. A maid spoke with an odd accent peculiar to the island. "Hello! Ed Moses speaking. I am staying at your residence. Would you be so kind as to wake my colleague, Mr. Rob Goode, and tell him I will have a car there for him in half an hour please."

"Yes sir! I will do that immediately sir!" She replaced the receiver and scurried upstairs.

Rob was difficult to rouse but eventually he heard the young girl's calls and responded. For a while he sat on the edge of the bed desperately trying to concentrate and bring his mind into order. He skimped at the basin and dressed, still unsure of himself. Downstairs he asked the young girl to straighten his clothing whilst he drank half a cup of lukewarm tea, which she had prepared some time before, because she had expected him down sooner. A car trundled up outside, painted in British army colours. He thanked the girl and went outside to his lift.

They were waved through the entrance on production of their identity cards but then stopped at a makeshift guardroom. Here Rob struggled out of the little Ford car. The driver kindly gave him a shove in the back to help him on his way, which he appreciated.

Ed came out and greeted his ailing friend. "Are you sure you feel alright? I could hear you all night, in the next room. Nightmarish! Rob you are not well." Ed cocked his head towards him and showed his concern by raising his eyebrows and shaking his head. "You really shouldn't have come."

"I'll be alright just give me a bit of time." He sounded weak and went inside the guardroom and sat down. "Have you spoken to anyone yet?" he asked.

"No! The first thing I did was to have all three men separated. They don't know we are here. Are you going to talk to them first, or do you want me to have the first bite of the cherry?" Ed was slightly impatient and wanted to get on with the job.

"Has anything occurred to you Ed?" Rob didn't even look up to him.

"What is that?" he asked curiously.

"They are almost bound to know me. I wouldn't know them by name, but I wouldn't mind betting I will know them by sight. I worked in that factory for a long time. I've hung around most of the pubs in Bath for even longer. At least one of them will know me, rest assured. A one armed man with half a face." This time Rob did look up and half smiled as only he could. "I'm not sure about Jack Cosnett either. Why send one of the most obvious cripples in Bath to question anybody about German subversion?"

Ed paced around in front of the guardroom desk. He was thinking on his feet. They had two days to extricate at least something from the three men they had in custody. He turned to Rob. "I'll do the questioning and keep you informed. For the time being you sit here and rest."

Ed sat at a rickety desk with as much information in front of him that he could glean from the camp administrators. His first internee was ushered in and asked to sit opposite, which he did, appreciatively. Ed pretended to read the paperwork. He didn't give any impression he was in a hurry.

He looked up, "Gunther Volke, is that your name?"

"Gunther Heinrich Volke actually," he answered.

Ed read the paper again and accepted his middle name. He then pushed aside what little was written about the man sat before him. "Gunther I want you to start at the very beginning please. How did you come to Britain and what made you stay?"

Gunther had no qualms about telling his story. His accent was obviously German. "Just before the last war began I started working as what you in England would describe an apprentice in the engineering trade. As soon as I finished my training I was called up in early nineteen seventeen into the army because of the shortage of military manpower. After only six months active service I became a prisoner of war and was brought here to England. Our concentration camp was somewhere out on Salisbury Plain, adjacent to an army base. I am not sure of the name because our camp was numbered but some people used to mention a place called Rollestone. However, none of us were a problem and because of the labour shortages in England we were asked if we wanted to work. We were actually paid, but only a very small amount, paying for our cigarettes and some beer. Out on the plain there was only agricultural work, but by far better than sitting around all day in the camp doing nothing. I came to work for one particular farmer who had a very large farm. There were about ten of us at any one time, along with a lot of English girls, and we all worked very well with each other. Near the end of the war our camp gates were never closed and hardly ever guarded. We knew the war was futile and coming to an end, but to try and make an escape back to Germany would be suicidal. If we did, as we thought, we would end up back on the front amongst the world's biggest mass killings, so we made the most of our captivity here. Some might call us cowards." Gunther stopped and thought of the good times he had had out on the Plain herding sheep, or cattle, and planting or digging crops, especially in the company of some very happy young girls.

"Then we heard the war was coming to an end but by that time I was having a relationship with one of those, as you call them now 'land girls', and we discussed deeply what might happen to us both when the terrible conflict was finally over. Jokingly I said to her we should get married, and surprisingly she jumped at the chance. I tried to persuade her our national identities wouldn't work, as I thought I would be sent back to Germany and our marriage would make our situation too difficult, but she was insistent. I was also very young." Gunther smiled to himself. In fact he almost laughed.

Ed asked him. "What is so funny?"

"One Saturday afternoon, the first Saturday in November which happened to be on the first day of the month the farmer asked me and another German worker Klaus, a good friend of mine, and still is, to drive two pigs over to a smallholding at a tiny hamlet called Chitterne. I can never forget this day because when we arrived there, the church was covered in regalia and the bells were ringing. The little pub, the Kings Head, was dressed up similarly. We stopped to ask directions but Klaus jumped down from the truck and asked me to follow him. We went into the pub and I thought, perhaps, just for a drink, but inside the pub was full of people, most of whom I knew. Klaus bought me a beer and then told me what was happening. I had half an hour to get ready because I was to marry Beth that afternoon. Someone pushed a suitcase of clothes into my hand and told me to go out the back and change my clothing. Klaus was my best man. We had a wonderful day. I can only just say this English tongue twister. Myself and Beth were married at the 'Chequered Church at Chitterne'." He laughed again.

"How did you end up in Bath?" Ed queried.

"We spent another two years on the farm, the feud between Britain and Germany was over, but I could earn much more money engineering and we decided to move to Bath where I easily found a job with Stothert's. Within a couple of months we started a family. We've been in Bath ever since and I would like to return there now if you don't mind. I know there is now another war against Germany but England is my home and has been for a long long time. My four children have all been to school here. Klaus, my best man, and friend, is here with me now. His family are also in Bath. Neither of us desire Hitler's intentions and we would sooner he was eliminated, democratically, I might add. We just both want to go home to Bath, and continue with our lives amid our wives, children, families and friends."

Ed felt he was telling the truth. He looked at the papers. "Do I assume your friend is Klaus Reimheimer". Gunther nodded. "Do you know anyone who might not have the same feelings as you? What about this other chap who is up here with you from Stothert's? Do you know anything about him?"

"Of course I know him but only from Stothert's. I don't know how long he has been in England. First of all, I think he worked for Horstman's in Bath, and then moved down the road to us at Stothert's. He comes from western Germany very close to the Belgian border, whereas Klaus and I are from the east and north. He's a lot younger than us but apparently he knows his stuff as an engineer. I don't know whether he has any family here. You'll have to ask him. He keeps himself to himself. He has little to do with us. We are quite a lot older. All I know is, his name is Matthaius." Gunther went quiet. He was deep in thought.

Ed's mind was thinking as well, but about border controls. He tried to envisage where the German's would have tried to get their spies across into other countries, especially France. There would be plenty of places he told himself, the border was stretched for miles.

"Do you know exactly where he comes from?" he asked Gunther.

"Somewhere around the Ahr valley. The Ahr is a small region south of the city of Koln. Why do you ask?" Gunther was puzzled.

"Have you ever been invited to join any organisations, especially since the war began?" Ed watched him intensely.

"You are obviously asking if I've ever been asked to spy for anyone. Well not directly. All conversations are carefully co-ordinated to try and find out your true beliefs, and if they think you are pro-Nazi they make a joke about joining them and then wait for your response." Gunther thought back, smiling at his inquisitor's gullibility.

"So you have been approached or so you believe?" Ed asked him.

"Probably, but I would not react in the way they wanted me to." His expression was dead pan.

"What do you mean?"

"I never went over to the quiet corner to have a clandestine chat unless I wanted to know something." Gunther's face became serious.

"Gunther is there something you want to tell me but you are afraid to speak about. Is someone pressurising you or your family? Yourself and Klaus, it's in both of our interests if that is a fact, providing you are on our side, the British." Ed began to show some disquiet for him partly in the hope he might speak up on Britain's behalf.

"I have been asked to reveal details about some of the important production lines in the factory for the war effort, but only because I had access to certain areas whereby others didn't. The people who asked the questions were British on paper, but myself and Klaus thought differently. Actually not just Klaus and myself, several people were asked. When I went to Stothert's originally I had to learn a completely different system of measurement. In Europe we were metric but not here. It wasn't long and I grasped your antiquated method. These people had the same problem' so we could tell they were not British. Good engineers, but definitely not British." He gazed at Ed soulfully. "Yes I believe here in Britain there are subversive elements within any factory or office closely involved with this war, and where I work is one prime example." He looked away at the shabbily painted wall and smiled wryly. "I'm sure the British have similar people in the factories of the Ruhr."

Ed had listened enough to Gunther and believed he was generally a pacifist. He didn't deserve to be here on the island, interred because of his nationality. Probably not Klaus either, by the sound of Gunther's incarceration.

"What would you like to drink, tea?" Ed asked.

Gunther smiled. "When in England do what the English do."

"Then tea you shall have, but I'm not sure if the Isle of Man is in England." Ed smiled back.

Outside he spoke to Rob after ordering the tea. He told him basically what he had heard. He would interview Klaus alone but in no way was he to meet Gunther before hand, or with the other internee. Ed had the impression that Gunther and Matthaius didn't get on. They had to be kept separate. Ed went back inside the claustrophobic room and they drank tea together.

"Do you know a man called Rob Goode, ex military from Bath?" Ed had an immediate reply.

"Not personally but he worked in the offices at Stothert's. Who in the city of Bath hasn't heard of him? A wonderful man. You could be any race, creed or colour in the world and he would try to help you in any circumstances. Why do you ask?" Ed's question interested Gunther.

"Well he is working on a project which is designed to protect the stability of engineering and manufacturing in the city. It's quite an important position." Ed didn't sound so convincing.

Gunther stood up and walked over to the tiny head high window which overlooked the wooden huts and tents housing the thousands of unfortunate inmates, portraying a dismal scene of decent people milling or hanging around their makeshift quarters, who, due to the war, were rendered irrelevant to society. He stood watching his fellow countrymen for some time and Ed waited, hoping for a reply from a man who might begin the end of a deadlock between the two, and more importantly start the unravelling of a conspiracy, as he believed, among the German workers in Bath. Few that they were. The decision was Gunther's.

Gunther suddenly spun around. His mind was made up. "I will not speak to Klaus. You interview him and try to understand what he is thinking as well. We have our own stories, but our beliefs are similar. If you need to break a spy ring back home in Bath then I cannot help you here on this tiny island. We will need our jobs back including that of Matthaius. To us Matthaius is aloof. If you interview him, immediately he will become suspicious. You need to have him back in the factory and find out who he is talking to out on the street because that is where your problem lies. If he or any others are copying important projects then they will not be sent directly from our factory they will be passed on elsewhere. Believe me if you want help then do as I say. I can tell you now, as soon as the information required from those factories has been handed to the Nazis, they will surely be bombed out of existence. You need to act fast."

"You just want to get home to your family, don't you?" Ed asked and woke a sleeping giant.

Gunther stood up and placed both hands, knuckles down on the ageing rickety desk. He leant almost face to face with Ed, smelling each other's breath. "Because if the bombing of Bath does start then there is a possibility that my family will be murdered by my own people, and not only that, if the Germans are after the factories, then there is a good fucking possibility I might be inside!" He sat back down. " So what do you want to do?"

For a time Ed took in what he had said and he went and spoke for some time with Rob. Both agreed that what Gunther was saying was perfectly logical but to allow them to return home would mean special dispensation. Ed interviewed Klaus who basically had the same answers, although a different war story as to how he came to England. As for Matthaius Schlutt they took Gunter's advice they left him alone, for the time being.

Rob contacted Jack who pulled strings in high places. The three ex-patriots were given permission to return home. Each would travel separately at different times and Matthaius Schlutt would be watched all the way from Liverpool to Bath train station. Each would have their jobs back, thanks to Charlie McGovern.

Chapter 39

The Parachute Regiments?

At the end of January Daniel's battalion were under orders to move back to England from Ireland. The job was a tedious affair but they finally settled into their new billets at Oxted, in some half derelict empty houses. Each man was given seven days leave, and the time soon came around for Daniel to take his own, which he tried not to waste. The first two days he spent in Bath with Stella and the children. They walked hand in hand through the city in the drab winter light, viewing the sparse selection of goods available in wartime Britain. Nothing mattered to Daniel. Just being back home with his wife and children was enough to give him fatherly pleasure making him feel relaxed and content.

The second evening they chose to dine at the Empire Bars. Although he still insisted the hotel was an officer's social location, Stella reassured him their money was equal. Besides he wore no uniform and was smartly dressed.

At first he felt uneasy but soon put his mess manners to one side. After five minutes a waiter came to their side. He courteously acknowledged Daniel and then courteously turned his attention to Stella.

"Madam, 'Spatburgunder'?" he asked her politely.

Daniel looked at them both, studying their faces one after the other. Between them there seemed to be an air of familiarity.

"Yes please, if you have any," she replied, and the waiter left their table to see what was in stock.

"What is Spatburgunder," asked Daniel.

"A particular type of wine I prefer, only I think the stocks have almost dwindled to nothing. If they have any try some, and see if the taste suits your palate. If not you choose something else." She smiled at him with her adorable eyes.

During the meal he looked across the table at Stella. "There is something I need to tell you. I wasn't going to mention anything but you might just as well know now." Daniel had already made his mind up, so there was no going back. "Since I've been back in England I have applied to join the parachute brigade. Subject to an interview and fitness test, hopefully I should succeed. My battalion commander has not objected, in fact he sees the application as a good move for me."

Stella sat back. She tried to take in what he meant. "Being a paratrooper is one of the most dangerous assignments in any army. Worse than the infantry." There was a look of shock on her face. Having already lost her first husband, the prospect of losing her second was becoming all the more likely. "Darling why don't you try for a duty of employment where you can use your language skill. Some branches in the services must desperately need people like yourself, especially in espionage. Have you heard of the Special Operations Executive, they would be much more interesting."

"That's even *more* dangerous," he told her.

"Maybe, but a lot more interesting than what you are doing now, and if it's a challenge you want they have to be the ultimate aim of any aspiring young soldier."

Their conversation went on for some while but Daniel could not be dissuaded. They finished their meal and decided to walk home.

A gentleman with a friend, both now sitting at the bar, turned his attention to the barman. "Excuse me. That couple who were sat on the table nearest us, are they from Bath?" he asked.

"I'm afraid you will have to ask the manager. I am not in any position to divulge our customers personal details sir." The barman was polite, but acting under orders.

"No, no! It's not them I am enquiring about actually, but the type of wine she asked for. As a matter of fact, do you sell that particular wine here?"

The gentleman gave the barman the impression that he may be a connoisseur of fine wines.

"We buy the wine in when available, but now, unfortunately, the grape and the final product, are becoming much more difficult to purchase because of the war. I am afraid the wine is also expensive, only asked for by specific, knowledgeable people."

"Thank you. That is all I wanted to know" he said with an appreciative smile.

Daniel and Stella arrived home around ten o'clock. Daniel went immediately to the washroom. Stella went to the phone and dialled an Oxford number. The ring tone was short and there was a cautious monosyllabic answer at the other end. "Hello."

'The Empire is running out of wine' was all she said and then quietly replaced the receiver.

Chapter 40
The Brief Visit

Joy heard an old dilapidated car spluttering down the lane, towards the farm, whom she assumed could only be Daniel's. He'd rang earlier, and warned he would be visiting in a couple of hours. She abandoned the kitchen sink, having sliced up a cockerel, and went outside wiping her blooded hands on her blue checked pinafore. George watched her leave the kitchen, and sighed with both relief and tiredness. The dog, with no name, lifted his head from its muddied paws, glanced towards the door, and then gently relaxed back into his original position.

Three geese and several foraging red hens blocked Daniel's path. He slowly herded them back towards the yard in front of the cottage at their own arrogant pace, much to the frustration of his mother. Not one bird could escape quickly, cumbersome as they were, over the grass banks with the stone walls atop. Patience was a virtue.

Outside the cottage Joy almost dragged him from the car in delight, disregarding her own condition. Daniel's mother was pregnant. He held her firmly at arms length and eyed her up and down. She would still do any young man proud and here she was carrying his baby brother or sister whom he would be more than twenty years older. Everything seemed surreal.

Little had changed inside the cottage. Everyone seemed to live in the kitchen. George was becoming weaker and weaker but still kept hanging on to life. Sometimes he spoke out loud, short brief stories which no-one seemed to understand. Daniel waited for his father before he once again repeated his own account of army life, boredom with no action. To make matters worse his mother passed him a letter to read before his father returned from the cowsheds. The message was from Mark. Daniel smiled.

My great friend Daniel,

Just a short letter to let you know what has been happening for myself.

I may have told you I have a girlfriend. At the beginning of last year we had news that we, the KAR's were going to invade Abyssinia. You must have read about the account. Before leaving I proposed to her. She is a beautiful intelligent woman and is actually a princess. Her father, the king, deliberated over our marriage for a few days leaving us in limbo, and then told us if I returned from Abyssinia in one piece then we would have his blessing.

I was more than nine months in Abyssinia with the King's and enjoyed every moment. We lost some friends but in return we kicked the Italians out of north east Africa.

I married Keola in a village ceremony which I have never seen or experienced before. She seems so happy and I have good parents-in-law. Please contact me as soon as you can at the address provided.

Mark and Keola.

Daniel smiled. His mother had been watching him with interest. He passed the letter to her. On the table he drummed his fingers. Here he was stuck in England trying to get away and Mark was involved in the action, and even marrying and enjoying himself, between times. Nothing seemed fair.

The door opened and in limped his father, James. Daniel stared down at his leg. "It's not getting any better then?" he asked him.

His faced cringed as he lowered himself into the seat. "No. They tell me now this is probably as good as life will ever be. At least I broke the same leg as your uncle shot." Joy turned away in disgust, saying nothing. Men's humour, she didn't understand.

There was genuine sympathy and worry on Daniel's face. He looked at his mother and her eyes confirmed everything. George's hands were clasped across his bulging stomach, probably caused from ascites, and he rolled his thumbs around and around each other and stared at the foot of the stairwell. The crass words had brought quiet, and the dog sensed an odd atmosphere, but without raising his head lifted a fluffy eyebrow, waiting for someone to break the ice.

James began by asking his son of his next postings. Daniel told them everything.

Joy's acceptance of her son being in the army had become more tolerable over the past months. As the war had expanded greatly over the last year, and the stories which had filtered back of battles won and battles lost, she had come to realise the size of the task and the worldwide effort just to resist the aggressors, whether they were German or Japanese. On any side, the chances of losing a loved one were increasing by the day. If Daniel chose to put his life on the line to save his country she would now be proud of him and not despairing. She had learnt from her own unpleasant experiences.

James on the other hand was open minded and more interested in talking about the strategies and stages of the war rather than Daniel's actual involvement. He had realised long ago that his son wanted a frontline job and had given up worrying about him openly, although he thought of him every day. James believed that until the sombre, hand delivered brown envelope arrived at the door from the war office, everything was alright.

That evening, back in Bath, Helen came straight from school with the intention of staying the night at Daniel's and Stella's home. The young girl persuaded Daniel to walk the children up to the park and back before darkness fell.

A strange remark by his sister caused Daniel to imagine something was amiss.

"Most evenings Stella goes out at eight o'clock when you're not here," she told him innocently.

Daniel stared straight onward but after a while, asked, "does she stay out all night?"

"Oh no! We sleep in the same bed at night and she's always there in the morning," Helen told him.

Chapter 41
The Update

Rob sat alone on a wooden bench outside the office of Sidney Horstman, the owner of the company Horstman Limited. On the wall opposite were photographs of one of the company's great achievements, the design and production of their cars at the beginning of the last war. Rob had seen them countless times before but rather than attempt to stand up and browse again, chose to save his energy and remain seated.

Shortly afterwards the polished brass handle rattled, and a middle aged man emerged, well dressed, wearing a black pin stripe suit. He carried a leather briefcase and bowler hat in the same hand. After momentary farewells with the office incumbent, he strode off down the corridor in his high quality black shoes. 'Clarkes', Rob hoped, because they were local.

"Come in Rob!" Mr Horstman shouted.

Rob obliged. The pair shook hands and both sat down.

"How is retirement suiting your father? Nothing is the same down at Stothert's without a good engineer in charge," he said smiling.

"Putting on weight, but otherwise he's fine. Mother tries to keep him occupied, but yes they are both quite happy." Rob sounded pleased with how his parents were bearing up.

"Good! Good! Well then! how can I help you Rob as you don't appear to have come here on a business errand?" he asked him.

"Yes you're right," Rob came straight to the point, "please, cast your mind back to someone you had working for you some years ago. A German named Matthaius Schlutt. He worked here for some time but then he left. Why did you sack him?"

"You'll have to forgive me Rob. His name rings a bell, but I don't normally become involved with shop floor affairs, unless the matter is serious. Hold on a minute, I'll find someone who will know." He picked up the phone and dialled a three figured number. A young lady answered. "Can you find Peter for me please and send him straight to my office. Thank you." He replaced the receiver. "He'll be able to tell you. If he can't, nobody will." Sidney smiled.

After a short chat there was a knock at the door and in walked Peter Benson, who Rob knew well. After a brief greeting Rob asked him the same question.

Peter thought back in time. "The chap you are enquiring about wasn't here for very long maybe eighteen months or two years perhaps. We didn't sack him, he chose to leave. In fact we tried to persuade him to stay because he was a damn good engineer, but no matter what we offered, he decided to change jobs."

"Did you ever find out why he wished to leave?" Rob asked.

"Not really. We thought someone in Stothert's had an influence over him and assumed he had a friend with whom he could be closer. Nothing more than that." Peter pursed his lips and shook his head slowly, there was little else he could say.

"Can you remember when he left?"

"About three and a half to four years ago. I can remember because Matthaius was always talking about Austria and the Sudentenland. Whether he came from one or the other I don't know. You'll have to ask him." Peter Benson was another avid news follower of the war.

Rob looked at both men in front of him. "He doesn't come from either of those places you mention, did you ever think he might be a subversive?"

Mr. Horstman laughed because his own father had been a highly respected German clockmaker from Westphalia. "Am I under suspicion as well. My company makes and sells parts for your British tanks and other military vehicles."

He went to carry on but Rob cut him short. "Please sir! with all due respect, I am not inquiring about yourself, only Matthaius Schlutt."

The office went quiet. Both men shook their heads not really knowing too much about the man in question. As far as they were concerned Matthaius Schlutt was a clean living, hard working, decent fellow.

Rob pressed them politely not to say anything to anyone, but should they hear anything untoward to contact him immediately. They both promised. Peter went back to the shop floor and Mr. Horstman and Rob sat chatting about factory security. After a while they parted company.

Mr. Horstman picked up the phone and rang a local number.

"Charlie McGovern speaking." Sounded the dour voice.

"Rob Goode has been around to see me."

He heard Charlie laugh down the other end. "I told you he would didn't I. Did you help him out?"

"Not much today, but I will in the future. I'll see you later in the week for a drink. Bye."

Jack met Rob and arranged a meeting in a place whereby, including Glen and Ed, all four of them would be involved but not be seen together on the streets in Bath. RAF Yatesbury was the venue, some way out of the city. They were to arrive at different times under their own steam and warned not to expect palatial surroundings because they had to stay out for one night. He mentioned a lively mess room. Jack gave Rob a set of four code numbers to memorise which all were to quote on arrival.

Rob later saw both Glen and Ed separately and asked them to bring any information in their heads and not in writing. Everything was set for an evening in late March.

Judith answered the phone. She spoke quietly and then asked the caller to wait. Rob was asleep on the sofa. He was breathing uneasily. She didn't really want to wake him, but felt if she didn't he wouldn't sleep during night. "Robbie! Rob! Wake up. Come on. Wake up. There is someone on the phone." He stirred and said something inaudible, then turned over with his ugly side facing towards her.

Judith went back to the phone. "I'm sorry it's a struggle to wake him. I'm afraid he's not that well. Can I help you?"

"It's probably better we don't speak on the phone. Believe me he knows me. I just need to tell him something. I know where you live and will be there in about fifteen minutes." The phone went dead.

"Rob! Come on, wake up! there is someone here to see you." Judith slowly brought him around from his other world. Peter Benson watched her efforts for ten minutes and in his heart knew that Rob Goode was an awfully sick man.

Rob sat upright on the edge of his sofa with his one elbow on his knee. He breathed deep and slow. He acknowledged Peter with a faint nod of the head but said nothing as he tried to regain his breath and pump oxygen into his brain. Judith gave him some water and he coughed slightly and then gently laid backwards. He stared at his visitor and tried to apologise. Peter thought of his health, 'should he have come around'. Rob faintly asked him what was the reason for the visit, what did he have to tell him?

Peter was concerned about the presence of Judith but she was Rob's eyes and ears.

"Some while before Matthaius Schlutt left Horstman's he had problems. Whether there were difficulties in his marriage or something else we don't know. He had one child. One of our men on the shop floor knew him as a happy go lucky man but over a couple of months everything changed. Our man says he didn't want to leave Horstman's. He had good wages and knew most people there, but suddenly he became introverted and said very little to anyone. One rumour was that he had had an affair and someone threatened to tell his wife. This could well be true because his wife and child disappeared suddenly. Everyone assumed she had left him because of infidelity, although no-one knew him with anyone else. She was also German and probably went back to her homeland to her family, but that was only conjecture. From around about those days she left Matthaius began to talk of leaving to work in Stothert's."

Judith spoke. "Do you think he was pressurised into going to Stothert's?"

Rob struggled forward and spilt water down his front. He spoke slowly with a throaty voice, impaired by withering lungs. "If he went to

Stothert's voluntarily then maybe there was simply a bad marriage, and he perhaps wanted a change. If he went under pressure then his family may have been intimidated. Two questions we have to ask are, why were they being threatened, but to where did his wife and child disappear? Had they not gone, then what might have happened? Spies can never settle down with families. They are too vulnerable. Maybe he decided to just move them safely out of the way."

Judith made a point. "Another question you have to ask is what has Stothert's to do with all this?"

"Both Stothert's and Horstman's produce military hardware, but we need to find a link." Judith and Peter could only just hear what Rob had said as he was wheezing badly.

On leaving, at the door, Peter turned to Judith. "Rob needs help badly Judith. He can't carry on in his condition surely."

She smiled. "In two days time he'll be as right as rain. You wait and see. Thank you for coming over Peter. I know Rob will muse over your enlightenment, and more than appreciate your efforts."

"Tell him I'll keep my ears and eyes open." Peter Benson left, quietly pleased with himself, although very worried about Rob Goode's health.

The four men met at RAF. Yatesbury. They all made their way separately so as not to arouse suspicion. Herbie dropped Rob off as he was now well enough to travel.

Jack had commandeered a run down office which they almost had to break into. He wanted to start the meeting immediately because by early evening the base would be a hive of activity. Yatesbury had become a radio training school. Hundreds of navigators and wireless operators passed through and as the lectures finished for the day the trainees would appear from their classrooms. Various types of aeroplanes were used for practise purposes which were now buzzing in the sky, but later on would all be parked up around the perimeter of the airfield. Some were in the old hangars, built in the last war for servicing, repairs or specific unexplained alterations.

Jack was forthright. "I'll start from the beginning. *'They'* have decided to divide the operation into two. Bath and Bristol. I will be remaining in charge of the Bath area, named operation 'Aquae Sulis', and someone else will be looking after the Bristol side, named operation 'Isambard'. Between the both of us we will work together and link any important information that comes out of either city." Jack glanced around the room. "I apologise, but if you happen to visit this place again in the future you will find the building considerably tidier. The office will be named after a local monument in the area or perhaps a village, and I will be sharing with a colleague who is running the Bristol area. The site was chosen because of the easy access to both cities and also back into London. Not only that, Wiltshire has a considerable amount of military outposts and so here we decided to set up office. For your information this is the first time anybody has set foot in this building for years. I literally picked up the key at the guardroom when I arrived. Before we carry on, are there any burning questions you would like to ask?"

Ed jumped in first. "Will you be staying up here, or remaining in Bath?"

"Now that is a good point which I should have mentioned. I will be moving here onto the base. I don't really want to because of the location in Bath, and access to the amenities, but for practical reasons we decided I should remain here." Jack looked at both Ed and Glen. "If either of you want a bed-sit in River street, I can easily arrange the accommodation with the landlady, so let me know."

"You say it is 'practical', but how do we keep in touch with each other, especially yourself Jack?" Rob was slightly flummoxed to think they would have to phone him more often, especially with the modern listening devices and susceptible telephone system.

"If we meet at each other's homes or watering holes all the time someone will become suspicious, or if circumstances become more sinister than that, the enemy will probably begin to follow us to find out why we are about asking questions. Here in Yatesbury everything appears as if I at least have an everyday job. Your visits to Yatesbury should be few and far between. What I don't want to happen now are too many phone calls. Finding any of you shouldn't be a problem and I will be visiting Bath more frequently than you might imagine. If however we send other operatives to talk to you they will approach by using a coded opening sentence which we will work out later. I am more than sure a system will fall into place which we'll all become accustomed with." Jack felt confident that the system would work.

Everyone accepted that the proposal was acceptable and Jack searched the desk's draws for some chalk and a black board rubber, but to no avail. He went off searching around the other rooms. Rob went with him, only to be nosy. They returned with a damp cloth and three sticks of coloured chalk. Jack cleaned the chalkboard and turned to face his team.

"What I want to do is put all the information we have together and try to see if there is a pattern forming. I appreciate this is early days but we need a start and we need one soon and I believe four heads together are better than one. We are two and a half years into this war and there is no sign of a breakthrough at all. What is happening in Bath might only be a tiny part but everything should add up to a broader picture." Jack chalked up the Roman numeral one in brackets. "Alright, who wants to start? It's probably better if you did Rob."

Rob began with the visit to the Isle of Man. There was nothing any of them didn't know about the interrogation, but a recollection might do some good. "Ed believed Gunther was telling the truth and broadly in line with what his good friend Klaus had told Ed afterwards. We decided not to interrogate Matthaius Schlutt because, between the pair of us, we believed he would immediately become suspicious. All three of them have now been reinstated at Stothert's." Rob spoke as Jack wrote a summary on the board.

Jack interrupted Rob. "Has Gunther come up with anything yet, since he has been back in Stotherts?"

"Not yet. He's working on those so-called 'English blokes'. We simply have to give him time."

"Right! before we go any further, two of them we know about." Jack took a note from his pocket and passed the paper to Rob. "We've cut the list down to six. The top two on the list are Dutch, and from the far east of Holland, on the border with Germany. They were working for us some years ago, even before Hitler became chancellor. Klaus, Gunther and Matthaius we also know about. This breaks it down to the other one. Why he was on the list you gave us Rob we don't know but we'd better check him out. He is operating under the name of Bill Williams and what concerns us is that he appeared in Bath at the end of the 'Great War' and we have no record of him before that year. His papers seem bona fide, although he has no birth certificate. He worked for

Stothert's shortly and then left." Jack kept writing the current information down with names, adjoining dates with arrows.

Rob was sceptical. "I'll check with Charlie McGovern. If any of their start dates are similar, they could be working in partnership. I need to know anyway. We will now also need to find out Bill William's real name." Rob passed the list to Glen, who then passed the short file onto Ed.

"Need to know what? What have you found out?" Jack was suddenly interested.

Rob told them of his visit to Horstman's and the subsequent house call made by Peter Benson. He painted a picture of Matthaius Schlutt being a very troubled man, who in one way or another had lost his family mysteriously. Rob looked at Glen. "Has he ever mentioned a family to you?"

"No. Not one in the past or the present," Glen answered, shaking his head slowly.

"This so-called 'Bill Williams' has appeared just after the last war and worked at Stothert's. There is a good possibility that Gunther and Klaus knew him in those days. They could well be working in collusion with each other although a theory with which I am dubious." Rob shrugged his one ailing shoulder.

"There are a couple of ideas we need to consider before going down this route. If Schlutt is an industrial spy, why pressure him to move from Horstman's to Stothert's? Also, why move another spy there when you might already have one or two operating in the factory anyway?" Ed was interested, but couldn't quite understand the reasoning.

Jack stepped in. "I think we are theorising far too early. We need a lot more information. Just remember, although these output factories are important, they are not the only military establishments in the city or surrounding area either, especially associated with the Admiralty."

Glen chirped up. "If we *knew* they were spies we couldn't just pull them in anyway until we find out who they are passing information onto. Another fact we have to reconcile, if we now have Gunther working amongst them, do you actually need me operating on the shop floor?" Glen sounded as if he was fed up with his cleaning duties.

Ed smiled at him. "I think you might be right. We need to get about and see who all these suspects are socialising with evenings and weekends. Where they live, and where they go. Two pairs of eyes are better than one." He looked over to Rob hoping for support.

Rob agreed with him and between them they decided to do surveillance work. The first people they would work on were Matthaius Schlutt and Bill Williams. He suggested Glen would have to keep well out of the way, because he knew Matthaius from Stothert's.

Jack came up with another idea. "Assuming we are trusting Gunther explicitly and we can afford to place Glen back on the street. I would suggest he went as a gracious retiree and merely mingled with all his ex workmates. I suggest we give him a free hand. Whatever he does he must not give away his past. Any military words uttered are a complete give away to the trained ear. I am more than sure new names would keep cropping up. Someone who knows Schlutt used to be this, or did that once, Gunther was a friend of so and so. One day the wrong thing will be said, or from our point of view, the right thing. We are going to be busy, all of us."

Ed and Rob looked at each other and then towards Glen. They were jealous. Seemingly Glen was going to have the best deal. Glen certainly wasn't going to argue about Jack's suggestion, for him to wander from pub to pub, or social club, merely gossiping, was a good idea from his point of view.

Jack was to have the final word. "Ed! You remain as clandestine as possible. You've already interviewed two of the suspects. We'll get you a downbeat car and put your own in storage. We'll take the vehicle off the street and keep it safe and dry. Your vehicle is too new for what you need. Rob! for the moment just go about your normal activities. Keep visiting the factories and wholesalers and try and find what the employers or employees come up with. Any tiny link you come across I need to hear about, and we maybe able to tie up with our information in London, or indeed, Bristol." He switched to Ed and Glen. "Referring back to lodgings, I think the best thing is you both move out of your hotels and find somewhere more fitting with your apparent lifestyles. We can retain my bed sit but the landlady must not know anything which will make her suspicious. It's probably better perhaps Ed went there."

Rob raised his hand. "No! There is a link between you both. They will have to find somewhere on their own and by themselves. Nothing to do with any of us."

"Fair enough, you'll both have to find your own accommodation." Jack tended to agree with him. "Is their anything else you have heard or need to know? Speak now because for the rest of this week I'll be concentrating on sorting out this mess." He shook his head as he didn't look forward to the task, but was determined the search for the industrial spies would be finalised.

Rob said little for a short while, but then he asked Jack what the coded sentence would be if he was approached by his unknown operatives. They all discussed the options. Glen came up with the final answer. " 'As the war goes on the end seems less and less likely'. 'As' meaning Aquae Sulis."

"I wonder how the Germans are recruiting their members. They must have their own verbal code. They aren't wandering around the city wearing swastikas. Some of them speak 'damned' good English." No-one spoke after Rob. Something was deep in his mind. Ed had said something to him in the past, and so had someone else but what, the old soldier could not remember. There was a positive link which he couldn't recollect. Rob's memory was deteriorating but he had his own ideas.

"What are you thinking about Rob?" Ed made him suddenly look up.

"Oh! Nothing. Nothing. I can't put my head around anything at the moment, but let me think." He would mention his thoughts to his dear wife Judith, but keep them under his hat for now, not that he had one.

For some while the four sat discussing all the issues concerning military hardware production in Bath, but as the afternoon wore on Rob began to suffer. He asked Glen for the time.

"I'm sorry Jack I can't stay tonight. As much as I'd like to spend the night here, I've arranged for Herbie to pick me up at six at the gatehouse. Far better for me I stay at home at the moment. In a day or so the illness will pass. I promise you." Rob sounded tired.

Herbie was waiting, as requested.

After a heavy night's drinking in the mess the remaining three men bid each other a good night. There was much to do in the following weeks.

Although Ed had arrived in his own car, and Glen by bus to Yatesbury, Ed offered his old colleague a lift back. Ed turned out onto the London road early the next morning heading west back to Bath. Some way down the road near Quemerford, a car, visible in Ed's rear view mirror, pulled out from a lay-by some distance behind. Ed kept his eye on the suspicious vehicle. Glen watched from the side mirror. "I can see him as well. Pull over and I'll have a piss. Let him pass by." Age hadn't decreased their vigilance.

The car, with two men on board, trundled along slowly and went off into the distance towards the town of Calne.

Ed quickly turned around and chose a long winded cross country route to Colerne, taken from a road map which he kept on the back seat.

"Who do you think that was?" Ed asked, keeping his eye on the road behind.

"I don't know, but we are better safe than sorry."

Chapter 42
Wings and War

"Rob is that you?" The voice down the line asked.

"Yes. Who's that?" he replied quizzically.

"It's only me, James. How are you feeling?" These days James was always anxious about him.

"Sorry James I didn't recognise your voice. I'm alright, feeling a lot better. Raring to go in fact. What is it you want? Going for a drink?"

James looked at the receiver and smiled. 'Rob must be on the mend', he thought, 'as he was talking quite cheerfully'. "Daniel is *now* officially a paratrooper. He has won his wings. So has his friend Paul and they're hoping to join the 1st. Parachute Brigade. He's home this Friday for nine or ten days before he goes off to Africa. On a week Saturday he wants to have a drink in Bath with us all and along with some of his old cadet pals, if they're available. What do you think? Do you fancy going for a jolly?"

"Of course! Of course! Let me write this down, otherwise I might forget." James could hear him mumbling down the line and then he came back. "A week Saturday," he fumbled with a calendar. "That is the twenty fifth of April. Saturday. In the evening I assume. Where are we going to meet?" Judith had persuaded him to write everything down because his short term memory was beginning to deteriorate.

"In the Station Hotel. Seven o'clock. We need to sort something out for a late drink though." James wanted everything to go to plan. Joy's baby was overdue already and he didn't want any double bookings.

"What about the women? Are they invited?" Rob wanted to know.

"Personally I would sooner they stayed at home but Daniel hasn't said no. It's up to you." James left the arrangement up to Rob's discretion and finally hung up. Rob would find a late night watering hole, probably Herbies, at the 'Edinburgh'.

Daniel and his father arranged to meet early. At first they went into the 'Edinburgh' after tapping on the door. Inside were half the intended entourage of the pub crawl, eager to have a drink before congregating at the 'Station'. Daniel had many pats on the back for his parachuting exploits and tried to shrug them off, as if war was just a boys adventure. He hadn't even been in action as a paratrooper. Sarah was talking seriously with Rob. Little seemed to worry her, she always appeared to be serene. Herbie was impatient to escape for the evening and drank his beer whilst tapping his fingers on the bar. When he officially opened at six, his customers began to drift away to the main rendezvous, the 'Station Hotel'.

The phone rang which the barman answered and stood looking around, and then he caught sight of Rob. He silently beckoned him over and handed the phone to him.

'Gunther and Klaus will be over the road at the 'Station' about eight this evening.' The phone went dead. Rob stared at the receiver with a strange look on his face and replaced the offending instrument. He returned to Sarah who was preparing to leave.

The pair walked arm in arm over to the 'Station Hotel'. "You didn't say much," she implied.

"What do you mean?" he tried to sound complacent.

"On the phone. You weren't expecting that call, I could tell because you looked surprised." Sarah was delving. She knew something was happening and her intellectual mind wanted to find out the truth. "Herbie's bored. He was the one who told me that you are involved with something, as he described, probably sinister, but even he doesn't know the full story. Do you need him as a driver? That perhaps might keep him out of the pub for a while. He drinks too much when he's there, especially on his own." She kept prying. "One of my clients, who lives in Colerne and has his business in Bath, keeps thinking he sees Ed Moses in the city." They reached the door of the hotel and Sarah pulled him up. "Other occurrences are that I keep having phone calls at work, from someone you know, who has decided he wants to come and live in Bath. Robbie what are you up to? Please tell me!"

Rob studied her in the fading light. He could hear a train straining as the engine pulled out of the station. Dirty pigeons flapped around, prior to settling into their resting place under the city viaduct. "I can't tell you. I need to find out quite a bit more myself." As they went to enter the hotel he asked her, "am I to assume Alfie keeps ringing you?"

Her elegant smile lit up the foyer. "I can't tell you. I need to find out a lot more myself."

There was much to talk about at the party, for old time's sake, and a few pubs to visit. The lads drifted uptown. The intention was to return to Herbie's and drink late into the night. For the older participants the sensible conversations had to take place early in the evening.

As Rob had been informed earlier on the phone, Gunther walked in the bar just after eight, Klaus followed. Although difficult to visually separate from other customers at the busy bar, eventually there soon appeared to be about six of them altogether. Rob watched shrewdly, although he almost had his back to them. The glass behind the bar and scotch advertising mirrors gave him a varied view throughout. Herbie noticed Rob was interested and scrutinising each one of them, but there were none he himself recognised personally. James was talking to Stella. She had her back to Gunther and his friends.

The door opened again and in walked a tall young stranger who immediately went to the bar and ordered a Guinness. He frowned when told the Irish stout would be bottled only. He accepted the drink reluctantly. "Can anyone help me? I am looking for Danny Godwin. He supposedly has a party here tonight."

Stella swung around. For a few seconds she was confused. "Paul! Are you Paul Cory? Don't you remember? We met briefly in Devizes."

He held up his hands in shame. "Daniel's wife, Stella. I beg your pardon that was such a long time ago." They hugged each other. "Where can I find him?"

"Paul! this is Daniel's father, James."

They shook hands. "I've heard so much about you Mr. Godwin. I am very pleased to meet you."

James exchanged comments. Stella went on and tried to explain who was who. They gave him directions to which pub the lads had probably reached and after drinking his Guinness he set off with no intention of missing out on an evening's fun.

Stella, during Paul's fleeting visit, had noticed the men drinking at the other end of the bar.

Gunther went to the water closet. Rob followed him. Considering the size of the hotel and the close proximity to the city centre there was little room in the toilets. As Gunther urinated he spoke quickly. "I need to speak to you seriously but not here. Meet me in the steel supply stores first thing Monday before anyone is around. Don't forget!" He went to leave. "Oh! By the way, who is that woman at the bar with you?"

"Which one?" Rob asked him inquiringly.

"The good looking one in the red dress," he paused, "she is drinking the red wine."

"That is Stella. Why?" Rob asked, more than interested.

"You had definitely better be there Monday." As he tried to leave he clashed with Herbie at the door and they both apologised to each other.

"Are you alright! What was that all about?" Herbie asked Rob.

"Nothing. We had a brief chat. I'll tell you some other time."

By the time they had returned to the bar Gunther and his friends had left.

They considered trying to follow the circuitous pub route, but decided between them not to follow the young men partying around the city. Instead they would return to the 'Edinburgh' later on. For the next hour or so, before leaving the 'Station', Stella continued to watch the clock and just after ten she left without saying goodbye and presumably caught a taxi home.

"I wonder what was wrong with her this evening?" Sarah asked suspiciously.

Herbie looked at his wife as she stared out of the window from behind the blackout curtains towards the station entrance. "Why? Did you notice something?"

"All night long she was edgy. A bag of nerves. Perpetually checking the clock. The later the time became the more she watched the clock, and then she suddenly left. Something wasn't right." Sarah turned back to her husband. "I think we'd better get back across the road before the lads arrive. Our staff will need help behind the bar."

"She was probably thinking of her children. Don't worry about Stella." Herbie gathered the attention of Rob and James who were talking to some old friends. "Come on we're supposed to be back over at the 'Edinburgh' before half ten." Herbie wasn't particularly worried, he normally had a reasonable contingent of police officers frequenting his pub.

They walked slowly back to the 'Edinburgh'. There was hardly a visible light. Some times a slither escaped between the cracks of some cheap curtains, but otherwise they trod carefully, by instinct.

The pub was in full swing when they arrived. Herbie went to help out and struggled to push his way through. Sarah grabbed some seats by the window and cleared the table of empty glasses and ashtrays. Herbie passed over some drinks and the three sat down as the evening was turning into a long night. Tuneless singing broke out but nobody complained. Even the oldest customers joined the choir. The recitals of a new female star were highest on the agenda, although not everyone knew the words. Two of Daniel's friends stood by a flimsy table and began, 'We'll Meet Again' and Vera Lynn was to become the favourite of the evening in her absence. The noise was deafening but not as bad as what was about to follow.

James was in the window seat and heard the familiar noise first. A wailing. He pulled back the curtain slightly and put his ear to the glass. Suddenly he stood up and shouted. "Herbie! The sirens are going." He didn't hear.

Sarah screamed at him and he turned. Immediately he went to the light switches and began to turn the lights off. Still the customers singing persisted until the last light went out and slowly the noise deceased only for the air raid sirens to become much more audible.

"Everyone! Take 'fucking' cover! Get away from the windows. If you want to, go down in the cellar." Herbie tried to gain some semblance of control. Two years previously he had had a visit from the fire brigade, police and military who explained what was expected of him in an emergency.

Intoxicated, most wouldn't believe what was happening and there was a plenty of laughing and giggling, but then in the distance the first thuds of bombs hitting their targets brought them back to reality. This was wartime Britain. The explosions came closer and closer and were more frequent. The vibrations were felt faintly through the building. Someone, somewhere was taking a pasting from the Luftwaffe.

Daniel crawled over to Paul Cory. "As soon as this dies away we *have* to go out there and assist the fire brigade and essential services. No disrespect to you Paul, but I know these lads in here and I know the city. Just let me motivate them. They are great friends of mine."

Paul was more than happy to let Daniel have his own way.

Several bombs began to fall in the close proximity. Slates were blown off the roof and plaster dislodged from the poorly maintained ceiling.

In between the mayhem there was banging at the door which Paul went to open. Three desperate policemen dived in to take cover, dragging Paul to the floor as the ominous whistling heralded the delivery of a batch of the Luftwaffe's hardware. There was no time for thought. The windows were blown in followed by debris from nearby buildings. Everything behind the bar was shattered. The top floor was destroyed, but mercifully had rested no lower than the first. The dust had hardly settled when another wave of bombs rained down, this time nearer the train station. Southgate had taken some serious hits. The attack on the centre of the city died away and only the bombs ejected by the retreating Germans could be heard in the distance. Eventually everything went ominously quiet.

Herbie's clientele began to rise from their hideouts. Daniel went down to the cellar. Everyone one there was safe. Paul was badly cut but one of the three police officers lay dead. Blood eked out of a small wound just behind his ear. He was the last one to make an apparent escape in through the door, but lost his life. Killed by a fluke piece of shrapnel. His colleagues cradled his head, trying to persuade him to wake up. They were in shock. Few on the ground floor escaped some kind of injury from flying glass or debris.

Cigarette lighters and matches at first were the only source of light. Herbie staggered around the bar trying to find a box of candles. Daniel spoke softly to his lieutenant. "Paul you'd better stay here. I'll take as many of the boys as I can and join the rescue parties." He looked over his shoulder. "Rob will know what to do."

Daniel went over to the one armed man. "Where's Dad?" he asked, worried he may have taken an accidental hit.

"There! under the table." He pointed towards James, Daniel's father.

His body was lying prostrate on the floor. Daniel's face was one of horror. "Is he dead?"

"I don't think so. The final thing he said to me and Sarah was 'in the last war there was nothing you could do if there was a direct hit, so we learnt to sleep through the artillery attacks', and then he told us to wake him up when the bombing was all over. Besides that, he's pretty drunk."

People had come out on the streets to search for the trapped, and help the injured. The only lighting was from several fires caused by the bombs. Daniel organised the digging for victims and designated his friends as medical orderlies. At first, overloaded rescue services were chaotic, but slowly some form of order began to take place. Towels and sheets were brought out to use as bandages or even to keep the casualties warm from loss of blood. Blankets were used to cover the dead. Most of Southgate was a pile of smouldering rubble. What had been several ancient Georgian streets, housing innocent residents, had become a graveyard over a matter of less than half an hour. Men, women and children screamed in agony, confused babies cried. The scene was almost impossible to imagine, but wasn't yet comparable to what damage had been done elsewhere in the city. The light of day would expose the true extent of the devastation. In the background eerie orange lights hung over various parts of the city. Smoke rose into the dark sky, lit up by the fires, re-enacting Guy Fawkes night, only no-one was celebrating. Firemen began the prolonged task to stem the flames spreading from one home to the next. Overstretched ambulance crews did their best to ferry the badly wounded into the hospitals, and quick minded local business men supported their gruesome task by supplying extra wagons, to alleviate the pressure. Rescue crews from Bristol and Chippenham began arriving. Buildings teetered and Daniel posted men close by, keeping anyone away from the danger. Every now and again a façade would crash into the street and spread stony debris across to the other side, or a roof and chimney would drop through a building and blow dust and rubble out through the windows below. The uninjured were shepherded to safety allowing the rescue teams to operate. Women wailed uncontrollably as they were asked to leave their lost children, buried under unrecognisable homes and decimated buildings.

Night began to turn into day, but now it was the turn of the buried to be rescued. On all streets complete silence was demanded so the whimpering or groaning of the injured and trapped might be heard. The system worked for the lucky ones and several were unearthed successfully, although badly injured. Some, but only a few, were miraculously brought out relatively unscathed.

Daniel had a message to attend a site near Manvers Street. On arrival he was directed to an area where two civilians were listening. He put his ear close to some stonework and waited. At first he thought he could hear a cat, but then realised there could be the sound a baby in the basement. He stood up and surveyed the precarious half demolished building. Next door had taken a direct hit and the explosion had brought down most of the neighbouring house. If there were still people alive below then they had been saved by the lower half of the party wall. The child had to be in the cellar. Someone, a local, told him where the cellar was approximately located. Daniel could begin digging through a vent in the street, or down some barely visible steps on the front of the building. Whichever way he went the rubble was packed solid. He chose the former. Daniel turned to his friends. "Go and find Paul Cory. He's at the 'Edinburgh'." The locals were dumfounded. The rest of the building was about to collapse.

Daniel spurted out his orders to everyone around. "I need carpenters and shutterers, and I need them now! Also a decent bolster and chisel. A measuring tape as well. Find as much timber as possible, three by two or four by two. The chippies will know what I mean." Three of his party were with him, all now supposedly sober. "I am going underground as if I am a coal miner. Every foot or so, I will make safe. I'll shout back the orders, please listen to me! whether I want wood or anything. You follow me in and pass back all the masonry. Do you understand?" They nodded obediently.

By the time Paul arrived Daniel was at a forty five degrees angle and heading downwards, convinced that what he had heard came from the basement. Paul weighed up the situation and turned to the onlookers.

"We need lamps as fast as possible and a supply of water." Some scurried away. He asked others, "I want you to carefully remove the rubble from above and take the weight off the tunnel. If a piece of stone dislodges another, leave the offending stone. We might arrive at a point where we, or rather Daniel, cannot carry on for fear of collapse."

After an hour Daniel had only made a distance of about twelve feet into the building. His whole body ached and was badly bruised from crawling over the broken stone. Slowly and painstakingly he progressed downward. Occasionally he stopped to take in some water, but he could no longer hear the baby. He shouted, but heard nothing. He hadn't perceived a sound for a while and he sent the message back to Paul. Everything seemed lost and possibly futile.

Paul knew there was no point in telling Daniel to give up, and soon the rubble started to exit the tunnel again. Another hour had passed and Daniel needed a lamp change as his light was fading fast. As he rested briefly he heard a shuffling noise and he asked for complete silence.

"Hello! Hello! Is there anybody there?" He shouted but there was no answer. He tried again only this time he shouted as loud as he could.

"Help we're here. Help!" The voice was feeble and Daniel couldn't work out its direction.

"Tap on the wall! We don't know where you are! Tap on the wall!"

They heard a knocking. "They're back here Danny! You've gone too far. They are on our right."

They shuffled backwards awkwardly, and with a new lease of life Daniel and his team of partygoers began the final breakthrough.

The tunnel began to disintegrate, and dust fell between the hastily made joists. Time was running out. As soon as they were through into the ancient cellar there was no time to be lost, no handshakes and no celebration. The baby, miraculously not crying, was handed out and gently as possible passed back into the open. Nurses were on hand to care for her. They made the exit larger. The tiny child's mother was unconscious and was painstakingly but carefully as possible dragged along on a piece of board, by ropes, out of her temporary tomb. Three were dead, crushed by part of the collapsing cellar. The grandfather was partially covered by heavy stone from the waist down. He was in great pain and any movement around him caused cries of anguish. First of all Daniel dug around the old man and released him. His hip and legs appeared to be shattered. Blood oozed around his shin bone which protruded through his skin. Initially he wanted to remain with his wife and son-in-law, but after being told what the risks had been to save him he reluctantly conceded and he too was painfully extricated out of the basement and into the tunnel. Only his wife's head and arm were visible and he had held her hand to the very last moment. Daniel, with a tear in his own eye, persuaded him to leave and the distraught grandfather was eventually brought to the surface in tears. As the old man was finally taken by stretcher into an ambulance past some waiting journalists, Daniel emerged from his five hour ordeal. Paul realised he was in no mood to be interviewed, and in no uncertain terms, told the journalists they should all leave immediately. From their experience working during the Liverpool blitz, the pair both understood the effects and emotions caused by random bombing. As they walked away someone was heard to ask 'what have they done with my bolster and chisel?'. The seven friends walked out of sight around the corner and headed to what was left of the 'Edinburgh Castle'.

The fires had been extinguished but the devastation was there to be seen. Other people still worked frantically trying to retrieve the last live victims of the Luftwaffe's attack amongst the tons of fragments from the broken buildings. Ambulances were on standby waiting for the last casualties. The city's defence was poor and people on demolished street corners were discussing why. An entourage of local dignitaries slowly walked around Southgate with hands held behind their backs. Their shining shoes and expensive clothes exhibited them as being entirely out of place in the circumstances. None intended to blemish their well manicured fingers. Clueless, some turned and watched as Paul, Daniel and their makeshift crew marched by, badly.

A temporary chalk sign stood against the wall of Herbie's pub. 'Danger do not enter'. Nothing deterred Daniel and his entourage, all traipsed through the blown down door. The pub seemed little worse than when they had left. Inside Herbie sat solemnly at the bar with Sarah. Rob was with them, ever dependable in dire circumstances. They had beer on the dust strewn bar, drawn directly from the unaffected cellar.

"You'll have to fetch your own. There are some clean glasses down there in a box. The beer is free, don't let anything go to waste." Herbie smiled ironically.

"Where's dad?" Daniel asked Rob.

"Oh! he woke up finally and went home. Didn't he leave the car in Widcombe? Well that's where he was last seen heading for. Your mother will probably be frantic." Rob's face was expressionless.

The beer came up always tasting better straight from the cask. One of the lad's joked that Herbie should start up a cellar bar. Nobody laughed. Everyone was tired and exhausted.

"What about Stella, Daniel? Does she know where you are?" Sarah's mind still couldn't understand her strange behaviour the evening before.

"I haven't had time to ring her, but I doubt the phones are working anyway." As he spoke the sunlight through the door frame was blocked out, and there stood the Chief Constable.

"Good morning Mr Adcock." Rob greeted him, hardly moving to face the local police chief. He stepped inside, into the dust and debris, followed by the station Sergeant and a young constable.

"Morning." He acknowledged them all with a slight nod of his head and tilt of his cap which he didn't take off. He wasn't happy. "I understand one of my constables died in here last night." Paul Cory listened intently and was in no mood for false accusations and ready to bite back. "I want to know what you were all doing in here at that time of night."

Herbie took responsibility. "These two lads were celebrating gaining their Parachute Wings and had nowhere to go for a late drink." He pointed to Paul and Daniel, particularly Daniel. "His family have been friends of ours for over twenty years so I took a chance and kept the bar open for them. If there is anyone to blame I am the one you should arrest."

Heavily bandaged, Paul stepped forward and went to say something but Herbie restrained him.

"When the bombing had began in earnest there was a loud knocking at the door and Paul bravely went to let in whoever was outside. As he unlatched the door and grabbed the first officer the other two frantically followed pushing their way in. They all hit the floor as a bomb went off across the street and that's where their injuries came from. I'm terribly sorry that one of your chaps has died."

Rob looked at the Superintendent and summed up the situation. "Had Paul not gone to the door at all, all three would have died. You can see the injuries he has taken and since then, along with all these other lads, he has just come back from being on the streets all night and morning helping out with the rescues. If Herbie and Sarah had gone to bed intoxicated and not woken they also would almost certainly have died upstairs. Weigh the situation up Mr Adcock. Who was right and who was wrong? This, I am afraid, is war."

The Chief Constable was a little uneasy. He hadn't heard his other two officers story as they were in hospital. "I'll take your word." He turned to leave but not before Paul Cory had the final say.

"Have you heard about the mother and baby rescued in Manvers street earlier, sir."

He certainly had. Paul pointed to Daniel. "Well here's the man who spent five hours risking his life digging them out, and you are with the rest of his team who backed him all the way. Now please do us all a favour, leave us to continue our wake and mourn the loss of Herbie's pub, and of course, your constable plus the many others who may have died in the city last night. Oh! and sir! one more thing. Please do not let the press know we are here."

"I won't. I sincerely thank you for your efforts gentlemen and congratulations on earning your Parachute Wings."

The party dispersed later that morning. After securing the remains of the pub Herbie and Sarah were to move in with Rob for the time being. Herbie's car was unscathed, parked along Green Park road, and not blocked in by debris. They gave Daniel and Paul a lift to the Bear Flat. Stella was ecstatic to see them. She offered them drink but they had had enough. After they had had a lukewarm bath, she put food on the table but their tiredness had gone beyond the bounds of human endurance and they settled for a well earned rest, and to bed they went.

Early that evening they managed a meal which Stella had made from the lunchtime leftovers. There were some bottles of beer with which they washed down the food. The feeling was one of euphoria. A job well done, but only now they began to register what had happened.

Suddenly life dawned on Daniel. "Where are the children?"

"Can't you remember? I told you. Nanny has taken them away for the week end. You wouldn't want them around after last night and besides, they were more than safe."

"When are they back?" He asked.

"Tomorrow now. After last night I thought for their sakes that they would probably be better off coming back tomorrow. They'll be alright." She tapped him on the back of the hand and rose from the table to clear up.

They sat drinking Stella's seemingly never ending supply of red wine and discussed ways of having some more leave in view of the circumstances during the previous night. By ten that evening they were both inebriated again and soon after were back in bed.

Bath was bombed again that evening at eleven o'clock. The Assembly rooms and five churches were destroyed that night. Neither men stirred as the whole weekend had caught up with them and they slept soundly, intoxicated by the red wine. Stella stood in the dark peering through the curtains towards the city centre. Each time the bombs went off down in the city her heart thumped. Next day she would deny hearing the second blitz.

Unknown to any of them, Daniel's mother had given birth to a baby daughter. She was named Ruby.

Chapter 43
First Blood

"Rob! Don't go to Stothert's tomorrow. Wait a couple of days, especially after what happened last night. Your German friend will not be there, surely." Herbie tried to persuade him but Rob was adamant.

"No I have to be there and even if I have to walk I'll make the trip. Herbie if you are so worried just take me there and wait. Believe me, nothing is going to happen." Rob was resolute.

Herbie agreed to drive him but was shocked when he told him at what time. "Seven o'clock!" He looked across the table at Judith and Sarah.

Sarah smiled at her husband. Herbie hadn't been up that early for years, the pub trade explained everything. She looked mockingly at Herbie. "You agreed to take him."

They drank for some while, sitting around the dining room table. All they had was a little paraffin lamp from which to view each others macabre features as the flame flickered in an unseen draught, creating dancing shadows behind all the ornaments, and the lamp shade above. The odour from the spent fuel tainted the taste of the fruit wine.

Most of the evening Herbie had tried to pry from his friend what was happening. Rob continually told him to wait and see, although he himself did not know. The whole conversation ceased when the air raid sirens began again and the first bombs of a second late evening attack struck their targets.

Little could be seen from Rob's house, just an orange sky billowing with smoke down towards the city centre. They chose to sit at the table and wait for the outcome. They wouldn't know anything from a direct hit, but few strikes came their way. The Luftwaffe pilots were well aware to off load their deadly cargo and peel away for home as soon as possible. The faster they gained altitude out of range from the air defences, the safer they would be. In less than fifteen minutes the bombing was all over and whose ever duty was to clear up the aftermath had already begun their grisly task. The two couples never imagined that Hitler would have had the audacity to strike two nights in a row.

Judith woke Herbie by shaking him gently, trying not to rouse Sarah. "He's almost ready to leave," she whispered.

Herbie reluctantly rose from the bed and performed his ablutions. Within ten minutes he was with Rob in the kitchen. Judith kissed Rob affectionately. "Be careful," she told him.

The factory was a five minute drive away. "Let's hope the buildings are still there after last night," Rob quietly remarked with an ugly smirk.

"Tell me who you are going to meet Rob. If something bad happens then at least I'll know where you went or who you met." Herbie meant what he said.

"I'll be alright Herb, believe me. I'm not in any danger. There will be hundreds of workers around. If you are so worried and something does happen to me you'll have to tell Judith. Just drop me off in the yard." Herbie pulled up. Rob told him to wait in the car park by the offices.

Rob was a little early. He wandered down to the heavy duty stores where they kept the steel deliveries. In between two giant green corrugated sheds a rail track was built into the ground to shunt the massive products around. Everything was geared for heavy engineering and now, in the middle of the war, production had been at full capacity from Monday morning to Saturday evening. Men were already turning up in their droves, earlier than normal, positioning themselves by their machines or in areas where they had to work. Many chattered incessantly about the two week-end raids by the Luftwaffe. Little did the Germans realise, judging by the conversations, their attacks upon the civilian population in Bath had only strengthened the workforce's resolve to beat the Nazi threat. Absenteeism was expected to be high that depressing Monday morning but everyone, from the highest management down to those with the most menial tasks now knew what they were up against, and fully understood the difficult tasks over the months ahead.

The metal store shed was a little quieter, but the demand would pick up during the morning as the factory tried to regain some kind of normal operation, although over the next few days there would be many lynch pins missing until the management could find some semblance of order. Rob wandered along past the expansive racking which held all sorts of steel, copper and brass in many sizes and shapes. RSJ's, angle iron, box section, plate and many others. As fast as the wagons made a delivery, their product was signed for, listed and then whisked away to some part of the factory to be milled, welded or pressed and then bolted together to produce the required article. The best of 'British' engineering.

Rob walked on and eventually came to stand waiting by the giant doors. Seven thirty had arrived. Gunther would be here soon, or so he believed.

"Robbie Goode. Well what brings you to this part of the factory? I thought you were retired."

Rob swung round, there behind him was an old Scotsman, Hamish as he was known. "Well well! Hamish I thought you were dead." They both laughed.

"No! She won't get rid of me that quick, nor the Germans for that matter," they laughed again, "what a pleasure to see you." Hamish always meant what he said. Everyone had respect for Rob Goode at Stothert's.

Rob had to think quick. "I'm supposed to meet someone here. We're looking for some steel which we might be able to use for a minor product, otherwise I'll have to order some in." Rob hated lying but needed the simplest excuse.

"Aye. I'm sure you'll find some piece of scrap in the yard somewhere for what you want." Hamish laughed again, he was renowned for his joviality.

Rob caught sight of Klaus Reimheimer approaching and made an excuse to leave. Klaus turned and walked the other way but allowed Rob to catch him up. He turned into a toilet block.

Klaus was scared. "I'll tell you as quick as possible. Saturday night we went back to the 'The Charmbury Arms' close to home. At ten thirty Gunther left for home, just five minutes' walk. Between his house and the pub there hadn't been a bomb dropped at all. Gunther hasn't been seen since. His wife is frantic. All the police can say is he might have been caught up in the blitz. There is not a body, no evidence. Gunther is missing. Believe me! I have to go. All I knew before he left the Charmbury Arms was he told me he was meeting you here this morning. Please believe me. I don't want to be seen talking to you."

Klaus, agitated, turned to leave.

"Wait a minute Klaus! Do you think he might have known something?" Rob wanted answers fast before the distraught ex-patriot left.

"Gunther was an engineer not a detective and for me a good friend. I'm afraid he began asking too many questions." Klaus left and there was little Rob could do to stop him.

Rob gave Klaus time to get to his work place so as not to be seen leaving together. He found a toilet, and sat on the latrine for a while thinking hard. 'If something has happened to Gunther then Klaus would surely be next on the list', was the thought on his mind. 'On Saturday evening why had Gunther asked who was Stella'. All manner of things were going through Rob's mind. He pulled the broken chain and walked out.

"He never even washed his hand." One of the workmen said to another.

Tuesday came after the blitz and Gunther Volke still hadn't been seen since Saturday night. Rob could wait no more. The phones had been reconnected and he rang the police headquarters and asked for the Chief Constable but was rebuffed because he was supposedly busy. "Tell him Rob Goode wants to speak with him and that he might have a murder inquiry on his hands. Also tell him Jack Cosnett is on his way." On the other end there was an eerie quiet.

After what seemed an age the desk sergeant came back to him. "You'll have to be brief sir." He connected the persistent Robbie Goode.

"Mr Adcock. I have reason to believe someone has been murdered. Providing we can find his body or prove otherwise I believe there is a strong possibility that my hunch may well be true." Rob was adamant he was right, only without a body he couldn't prove the facts.

"So how can I help you Mr. Goode?" Protocol came first with the Chief Constable on these occasions.

"I need access to the mortuary to see all the unidentified bodies killed during the blitz or have died naturally over the last weekend." Rob was straight to the point.

"Why? What makes you think there has been a murder Mr. Goode?" the Chief asked warily.

"I have an overwhelming feeling which might also lead to saving other lives. Isn't that good enough?" Rob tried not to become angry. "If you can't give me permission then I am more than sure Jack Cosnett will pull strings at a higher level and deliver my request."

Rob stunned the Chief Constable and he immediately agreed, but only with himself in attendance. They arranged to meet at the mortuary in one hour.

Outside the chamber of death, Rob explained to Jack everything he knew so far. The Chief Constable turned up with his senior detective and they went inside. A quaint man in a white coat greeted them and showed them the thirteen remaining unidentified corpses. There was little space after such a traumatic weekend and some were covered up on the floor. The estimation was that over four hundred people had died that weekend in Bath and still some people were unaccounted for. Identified bodies were being kept all over the city as the mortuary couldn't cope with the numbers. Although the room was chilled down the bodies had began to decompose and smelt badly. The ones with no names were kept at the mortuary but when identified they were placed in coffins and taken away by the local funeral directors.

The morticians assistants unveiled the unidentified bodies. Quickly they went from left to right. Half way along Rob, holding his hand over his nose and mouth shouted. "That's him!"

The Chief Constable began asking the questions. "What do we know about him?"

The paperwork was tied to his big toe. "Nothing. His wallet had gone. There was no identification or money. He had had a ring on his right digit finger which appeared to have been brutally forced off him. His cause of death was the back of his head had been crushed inward, a typical injury from a falling wall or building." The mortician shrugged his shoulders. There was little else he could say after the aftermath of the bombing.

The detective made a query. "Why isn't he straightened out like a normal corpse?"

"We received him this morning and rigor mortis had set in. He probably died during the blitz on Saturday night which is why he is twisted." The mortician read the note tied to his toe. "He was found buried under rubble in Henry Street down near the city centre."

They all looked at Rob for a possible explanation.

The Chief Constable looked at his detective and then asked, "so what have you brought us here for?"

Jack Cosnett stepped in. "His name is Gunther Heinrich Volke, a German ex-patriot. He worked at Stothert's. His wife will sadly have to confirm his identity. He was working for us, checking out fellow German workers, let's say, but not for very long. Saturday evening he was in town drinking and Rob spoke to him briefly in the Station hotel. They arranged to meet first thing Monday morning at Stothert's and he was going to give Rob some information. Klaus Reimhiemer, his best friend, turned up and said Gunther hadn't arrived home from the last pub they were in on Saturday evening. The pub was five minutes walk from Mr. Volke's house and nowhere near the blitz. Now Gunther is here, dead and in a strange shape."

The Chief Constable stopped him. "He could have been intoxicated, went back down town and became caught up in the bombing."

Rob spoke. "No! I don't think so. He was abducted and murdered near his own home and kept somewhere until they could dispose of his body. When the blitz began again on Sunday night, what better time to take him and dump his body and make his death look like he was just another victim of the war. That's why they can't straighten him out. He has probably been dead in the back of someone's car boot for probably thirty hours. Klaus Reimhiemer told me Gunther had been asking the wrong people too many questions. Klaus is scared. I think he feels he could be next on the list if he is not careful." Rob stared at Jack straight in the eyes. "I'm sorry. Gunther's death is my fault. I'm afraid this is probably first blood to the Germans."

Rob walked away and out of the cadaverous building. Herbie pulled up alongside him and he struggled into the car. Neither said a word as they drove away.

Jack asked the Chief Constable, "who is the bloke who picked Rob up?"

"Herbie. He used to be the landlord of the 'Edinburgh Castle' until the Krauts destroyed the building at the weekend. They've been great friends for years. I've no doubt he and his wife are probably staying at Rob's in the meantime."

Jack then realised Herbie was the man who had told him where to find Rob when he first arrived in Bath.

Chapter 44
Double Espionage

Yatesbury was a cold place to be at anytime of year but when the north wind blew on a clear day in early October the temperature dropped to just above freezing. Alone, a man, in his thirties, walked down towards No.8 Radio School Lecture Block. He entered the building and knocked on the unmarked door to his right. Jack Cosnett called him in and he sat down by the window and warmed his back on the cast iron radiator.

Jack was straight to the point. "Well. What did you find out?"

"Not much really. When her husband isn't there she goes out for an hour or two most evenings. She doesn't meet anyone in particular but flaunts herself and within no time there is always someone talking to her. She is after all a woman, sexually attractive I must add. There are people who know her but she only ever speaks to them briefly and more often out of earshot from anyone else," he thought for a moment, "I would say probably three or four men on an irregular basis but they always appear to be chance meetings, unplanned."

"And you've never came close enough to hear anything?"

"No. We've both tried. They become intimate as if they might be having some kind of affair. She talks openly with strangers who are just trying to chat her up." He shrugged his shoulders.

"Any signs of prostitution?"

"No never. She always goes home alone, not late, usually about nine-thirty to ten o'clock. Once she stayed out until the early morning."

"Did you find anything out about the nanny? She's been there since the first child was born." Jack desperately wanted a lead but wasn't sure if he was 'barking up the wrong tree'.

"We asked in the street. People see the old woman about with the children in the shops or sometimes up at the park but no-one has had a conversation with her. She presents the shopping list to the shopkeeper, hands him or her the money, takes her change and leaves. She keeps herself to herself."

Jack stood up and paced around. "So what happened when her husband came home on leave? Did the pattern change?"

"More so. The nanny had less to do with the children outdoors. The parents looked after them and pushed them around," 'which was only natural parenthood' he thought.

"So what then happened to the nanny? Did you still see her about?"

"Yes. She continued to do the shopping and she went up to the park everyday but only on her own. She just sits down and appears as if she is in a dream, contemplating something perhaps."

Jack suddenly looked up. His eyes first of all planted on his subordinate's face but then slowly drifted away in deep thought. He looked back "When she kept going up to the park did you ever follow her?"

"Once or twice but you asked us to keep an eye on the woman. Most of our time was taken up trying not to be recognised, especially when her husband came home."

"Did you see anything else? Anything odd?" Jack wanted to wrap up the meeting. He felt he had missed an important clue.

"A bloke went around there a couple of times. He was unmistakeable."

Jack smiled. "How do you mean unmistakeable?"

"He had one arm and half of his face missing."

"Did you get a list of all the places she visits when her husband isn't home?"

"Yes sir." He drew a piece of paper from his pocket and stretched over and gave the note to him.

Jack browsed through the list. There were some places she used regularly and others not, but he hardly recognised any of them. He only knew one person who might decipher a link between them all.

He was about to let him leave. "Oh! By the way!" Jack produced some photographs from his draw. "Do you recognise any of these?"

He handed the first photograph to him. Having studied the print he said no. The portrait was that of Ed Moses. He showed him another photograph and within a second he perked up. "Twice I've seen the woman speaking to this man but only very briefly." The portrait was of Matthaius Schlutt. Next was Gunther Volke. "No never." The fourth was a stranger even to Jack but his operative had seen him in the vicinity of a pub Stella frequented. He said the same of the next photograph which alerted Jack's mind, Klaus Reimhiemer. Last was that of Glen Paignton who he confirmed he had often spoken to in various localities.

"Did you find anything out about him?" asked Jack.

"He is a retired cleaner. I must admit I did think he sounded a bit too intelligent to be a cleaning operative. He was the bloke I mentioned who went off with the woman, to where we don't know. We watched her returning alone to her house about four in the morning."

Jack thanked him and after a few words of encouragement sent him back to London, along with his accomplice, who was waiting in an unmarked car. They were to report back to head office.

Jack lay back in his chair with his hands behind his head, deep in thought. 'What had this woman called Stella to do with all this? Married to a soldier who speaks fluent German, who happens to be the godson of Rob Goode. Why did Gunther Volke make a surprise remark about Stella to Rob Goode on the same night which he probably died? Was the answer to this espionage staring him in the face? Who was on whose side', Jack asked himself.

Chapter 45

Facing the Facts

Rob stood in the warmth of the breakfast room at the 'Priory' gazing out across the lawn. A song thrush hopped across his view in the search for nourishment but the hungry bird was far from his thoughts. He had to decide what to say to Jack when he arrived, and had to be conclusive.

The bell on the door rang and when opened he could hear voices in the foyer. The receptionist was talking to someone. Jack entered the room and mentioned the miserable weather. Rob agreed with him. Judith brought them tea and they were left entirely on their own.

"I've had a rebuke from London Rob. They are becoming impatient. Their view is that we are not making enough headway. There is one thing now on our side though." Rob raised his only eyebrow. "My colleague operating in the Bristol area seems to believe that there is a link to all of this in Oxford. Oxford University in fact. London now know this and if it's true we have to be careful. The spy ring is bigger than they thought originally, not just some localised espionage but perhaps something more national. We can't just round up the locals for fear of letting the big players escape. No-one knows how far anything has gone."

"If what you are saying is true then we could be up against some of the top brains in the country. Even if we do find out, I'm sure Downing Street would want the situation covered up. They wouldn't want the public to know that a massive spy ring was effectively working out of one of its top education establishments. They certainly wouldn't want the Americans to find out either." What Jack had told him interested

Rob a great deal. They were small fish in a big pond but now they had been catapulted into the ocean. If they brought in the top men to sort everything out no-one could ignore what was already known.

"I can't agree with you more. The thing is if there is any element of truth in the information, then this spy ring is being run by Britons who are seeking to overthrow the authorities, hoping to install fascist rule, probably with a puppet government." Jack poured himself some more tea.

"I'm afraid whether communists or fascists, you never have one without the other nowadays." Rob mused.

For a while they talked about the war in Europe. Since beating the Germans in Africa both men agreed that the allied war machine was now on the front foot. They had a powerful frontline across southern Italy and were pushing northwards everyday. The other good news was the German attack on Russia had been thwarted at an incredible cost to their manpower and morale. Hitler's armies were being stretched to the limits. Nineteen forty four was six weeks away and promised to be a vital year in Europe.

"I know it's early Jack but I'm going to have a beer. Do you fancy one?" Rob asked him.

"I'll have a glass of wine, otherwise I'll fall asleep thank you."

Judith brought the drinks and gave Rob a scornful look. He ignored her.

"So what do you think we have achieved so far? Are we making any headway?" Jack asked him.

"I'll go back to the night Gunther died. I told you that when I spoke to him he asked me if I knew who the woman was at the bar and I did, quite personally as well, her name is Stella. He also wanted to tell me something else but I had to wait until the Monday morning. We both know what happened after that. I'm positive he was going to tell me something about Matthaius Schlutt but obviously didn't get around to explaining. What intrigues me more is what has Stella to do with all this. Do you know who is her father-in-law?"

Jack looked surprised and shook his head. "Should I?"

"Do you remember James with the broken leg in Colerne? That's him."

Rob knew what Jack would ask next. "Is he old enough to be a father-in-law?"

"Indeed he is." Without going into detail Rob persuaded him to believe the facts.

"So James is Stella's husband's father." He stopped and thought about the scenario. "I would never have put two and two together. Something my operative never mentioned. He probably thought the information was irrelevant, or even more likely, had no reason to know anyway."

"What are you talking about?"

Jack looked up at him apologetically. "I'm sorry. When you told me at the mortuary that Gunther had mentioned her that night of the Blitz I had her put under surveillance for a month to see if we could come up with something. My boss was the one who made the suggestion." Jack didn't elaborate as to who that was but seemed to actually know more than he was letting on

Rob was annoyed he hadn't been told. "So I must have been seen going around there?"

"Yes once or twice. Quite innocently I hope." He smiled, raising his eyebrows.

"Only to see if she and the children were alright. Her husband *is* my godson." Rob reminded him, answering defensively. "So what did you find out? Anything interesting?"

"Nothing much more than what we already know. We think she is involved somewhere along the line but doing what, we still haven't a clue. She could be just a decoy." Jack shrugged his shoulders.

"Have you ever thought about searching the nanny's background. She rarely talks and Daniel says as long as he's lived there they have never spoken to each other." Rob watched Jack's face.

Jack had a look of disbelief wondering why Daniel never asked who she was. "We know she goes up to the park everyday with the children but she also went there when they were out with their parents. A bit strange for an old woman. We have already been watching her." Jack returned Rob's gaze.

"Going back to what you said earlier we can't afford to scare either of them off at this point, so be careful. I can only assume you think the old lady is meeting someone at the park or passing on information." Rob was trying to be helpful.

"What do you know about Stella's previous husband?" The question which made Rob smile.

"Missing in action, presumed dead." His answer was abrupt.

"You don't know anything else then?" Jack would have been surprised if he didn't.

Rob told him everything he knew about Stuart Sinclair. Jack knew nothing about Stuart's pre-military life and all Rob could tell him was what James had told himself which had originally come from Daniel. The problem was the story was either becoming watered down or on the contrary, exaggerated. Rob recommended he went and spoke to James about his daughter-in-law. One thing James could tell him was the story of her first child, Caronwyn, and who might be the father. Rob still chuckled about Daniel's embarrassment and guilt, although Stuart's death had somewhat put the boy out of his misery.

Jack swallowed the dregs of his wine. "Come on! Let's go."

Rob surveyed the bottom of his glass. Having a session on the beer seemed a good idea. "Where?"

"Colerne! Colerne to see James." Jack was adamant as he looked at his watch. "Get Ed up there. I might have a job for him. I'm sure Judith will know where to find him," he added sarcastically. "We have to get the ball rolling on our behalf before the big guns take the prizes."

Rob left the room to use the toilet.

As they went out of the door Judith took Jack by the arm and whispered in his ear. "Please don't let him drink too much."

He turned to her smiling. "I'm sorry but that's the only time I can squeeze the truth out of him."

Judith watched through the rain splattered sash windows as they left. Her face had an expression of trepidation because her husband was ill and wasn't helping himself, and nor were his so-called friends.

On the way to Colerne little conversation was had between the two until they levelled out on the top of Bannerdown and Rob asked. "Do you really believe Stella is involved in all this."

"We can't afford to leave any stone unturned Rob, you know that. We've already had one dead man and we don't know why, and we certainly don't want another. That was months ago. You were the one who mentioned Gunther and Stella when they saw each other at the bar that fateful weekend of the blitz." Jack concentrated on the road.

"If she is involved, what is her link with Germany. She has never given any indication of being a German. She doesn't speak the language, or if she does then she does so pretty damn well, but......" Rob hesitated and turned his ravished head towards his pay master.

Jack glanced across to him as he swept down around the bend towards the 'Vineyards'. "But what?" he glanced over again, "come on! but what!" He pulled into the 'Vineyards' car park, a popular restaurant. "Come on Rob tell me." The car ticked over slowly as he waited for an answer from him.

Rob wasn't sure he wanted to tell him but couldn't see any way of keeping quiet if there was to be any justification in the whole affair. "There could be a link but I very much doubt anything would add up." Rob stared up at the restaurant sign 'The Vineyards'. 'How coincidental', he thought.

"Just tell me Rob what's on your mind and you can have at least a second opinion from me." Jack wasn't in the mood to plead with him.

Rob didn't want to tell him. Jack hadn't told him about spying on Stella and besides, what was on his mind was a long shot. He turned to Jack. "I've been ill Jack. The drugs I've been administered and probably excessive alcohol have combined to distort my mind producing nightmares and crazy dreams. Judith can sometimes work out what I have been saying. Please, my twisted imagination overcomes me.

Annoyed and without concentrating Jack pulled away and nearly knocked over a motorcyclist who luckily avoided a collision. As the irate rider righted himself and went off towards Colerne his hand signals did not represent those of the highway code.

They found James on his own tinkering around with a ploughshare, repairing the machine for the springtime. He cursed at himself, whilst trying to undo rusted nuts and bolts. He looked up when Rob shouted at him. He grabbed a cloth and wiped the grease from his hands.

I didn't expect to see you here today Rob. You must want something." He climbed out over the machinery, glad to leave the plough alone for a while.

"Not me James, Jack wants a word with you. Shall we go down to the cottage and talk?" Rob made the suggestion knowing full well there would be a drink available.

James gestured towards the path gate leading down towards the cottage.

"Where's Joy?" Rob enquired.

"Gone to the hospital to see her father. He's not well again. They took him in again last night," he sounded grim.

"So what information can I divulge to you Jack?" James asked him as he placed the brown enamel kettle on the stove.

Rob interrupted, "I don't want tea James. Please just fetch some wine please if you don't mind, that will do me fine. You talk with Jack."

His words made James suddenly become distrustful. "This definitely isn't a courtesy visit then?" he asked.

Jack took over. "I need to ask you some questions about your daughter-in-law. Please, we need some very straight answers. What do you know about her?"

James threw a shrewd glance at Rob, whose face told him he had to tell the truth. At the same time another car turned up. Ed had arrived. As Rob put him in the picture, James opened a bottle of red wine which he passed onto Rob with a glass. No-one else was interested. They then recommenced their discussion.

"I only know so far back about her, basically when she met Stuart. Apparently she was a student at Oxford University. How true that is I don't know. As far as I know he met her in Warminster whilst he was on exercise. What she was doing down there, or why, I do not know either."

Ed cut him short. "Prostitution probably. An ancient profession not uncommon for female undergraduates to raise money in that fashion. At weekends a couple of nights away from their normal place of stay and nobody is suspicious. What better place to go and make money than a military town?"

Rob smiled. Ed hadn't beaten about the bush, speaking forthright about James' daughter-in-law.

"I don't believe she was a student at the university either. I spoke to the headmaster at the school where she works and she doesn't have a degree on her c.v.. She may have worked at the university, but in what capacity, I don't know. He told me she is a clever woman without a doubt, but what she is up to is very difficult to tell." Ed fell silent.

Jack turned his attention back to James. "Do you possibly know what her maiden name is?"

"No. When Stuart died, her first husband, as far as we were concerned we only knew her as Stella Sinclair." James held up his hands as if in mock surrender. "There was shock enough to find out she had been having an affair with our son."

Rob intervened. "Joy actually gets along with her probably because of the grandchildren. The best idea would be to speak to Joy."

Jack's last thought on his mind was to hear a woman's point of view, especially in the circumstances, and he added, "we know Stuart Sinclair originally enlisted in Edinburgh under a dubious state of affairs. His place of birth is registered in Edinburgh, a populous city where a man can easily become lost."

None of the three initially said a word. Rob tried to mask his pouring of another dwindling wine.

"I don't think he came from Edinburgh. I am sure he is from Sutherland. Dornoch in fact." James was positive. He had heard the facts directly from Stella.

Rob twirled his drink in his hand and as James was speaking he never looked up. Something was on his mind.

"Do you know anything else? Any strange habits she might have." Jack's question was directed at James but Ed smiled and stepped in.

"I've been in serious contact with Glen. When she goes out gallivanting, only in Daniel's absence, she always seems to meet somebody by accident and nothing ever seems to be planned."

Jack stopped him dead. "How can you keep an eye on her when she knows you?"

"I stay well out of the way. She doesn't know I'm in the city. We have other people on the ground Jack. Believe me, we can trust them. Over the last months on two occasions we apprehended your own men drinking too much and talking too loud. I doubt whether they found anything out. They have gone now but we had to keep an eye on them as well. They distracted us away from our ultimate aim of finding out what is going on. You are the one who said we shouldn't be working against each other."

Jack slowly faced each of the men at the table. "They did find out one thing."

Ed knew what was coming but asked, "and what's that?"

"Glen tried to have an affair with her. In fact both disappeared together into the night once having left a seedy pub up Lansdowne Hill. She never arrived home until about four in the morning. My men lost them but certainly watched her come home." Jack wasn't sure he should have mentioned the story in front of James.

"I've known Glen many years now and I can tell you he never fucked her. He made out he had travelled up from Southampton visiting for a couple of days. They know each other briefly from one of the annual get-togethers. What he did that night was to try and find out where her allegiances lay. They may have become pissed and jumped into bed together but I doubt the ultimate sexual contact because he hasn't had the natural impetus to fuck a woman for years. He is at work, and you of all men in the Special Intelligence Service should know what the fucking job entails."

James was glad Joy wasn't in the room, although the subject did amuse him. He was now in on the subterfuge.

Ed sparked up again. "Glen and myself have a theory but at the moment it's best kept between me and him."

Jack glanced over to Rob who didn't appear to know what Ed was talking about. He asked him, "so what is it?"

"I'm sorry James but we need to know where Stella is actually from. During our investigation you will have to remain completely silent. Don't say anything to Joy. Stella could be tied up in a conspiracy, quite deliberately, but also she may be caught up quite innocently." Ed became completely straight with Jack. "You might not want me to go but a visit to Stuart Sinclair's parents, brothers and sisters would be a good start. If she is to be eliminated from our inquiries then we believe the visit is imperative. They might just know something about her, after all she was married to their eldest wayward son."

"And is still married to my son as well," remarked James. He smiled. The subject was more comical than believable. He wondered what Daniel would think of everything. His self opinionated son could not possibly realise what was going on behind his back. "If Stuart had nothing to do with his parents for years, and Stella has never met them, don't you think the journey might be futile?"

Jack was open minded. "I doubt he didn't keep in touch with at least one of his siblings, though probably his brothers may have been called up or even volunteered. I agree with you Ed. Visiting Dornoch and asking a few questions would be a good idea. I don't suppose for one minute you still have your military identification papers." Ed shook his head. "I'll get them sorted out for you and Glen. Go as ordinary policemen. Before leaving there, make sure they don't get in touch with Stella because if a letter returns to Bath saying that the police have been asking questions our cover will be blown and that would be a serious set back. It's a pity you weren't nearer Stuart's age group and you could have said you were in the army together."

"I'm more than sure that since Stuart died she has had no connections with his family. Joy told me that. Just tell them she has moved to South Wales with someone else, they'll be none the wiser." Rob backed up James' belief.

"Alright. By the time those papers are sorted out, which will take about a week or so, and that is fast tracked, Christmas will be looming. Coincidentally we actually use a tiny airfield at Dornoch so I'll sort out a flight and a car for when you arrive. It's too far by train. You had just as well go up there in the New Year." Jack had made his mind up.

Rob needed another drink and James dutifully allowed him to carry on. The bottle was effectively his own.

Ed mentioned another thing that was happening amid their suspects and collaborators. "Since the death of Gunther Volke, his friend Klauss Reimheimer has been behaving very strangely. Glen seems to think that he has become extremely nervous. When he's out he's always looking over his shoulder. If a door slams shut he jumps like a scared cat. Something is definitely troubling him. He's better when he has his friends around him and then he seems much more relaxed."

"Is he the same at work? Or does he behave in that way only in the evenings?" Rob asked as he studied the label on the wine bottle for the umpteenth time.

"One of our contacts at Stothert's says he doesn't talk like he used to and he seems very wary of anyone around him, especially if he doesn't know them." Ed waited for the next inquiry from any one of them.

A question came from Rob again. "What does he drink when he's out, anything in particular?"

"I'd have to ask Glen that. He sees him quite a lot but I'm sure he is only a beer drinker."

"Klaus still doesn't know that Glen works for us does he?" Rob asked him as he replenished the red stained glass before him.

"Not as far as I know, unless anyone else has told him."

Jack intervened. "Where is this all going Rob? What's on your mind?"

"The Saturday night of the Baedeker raid on Bath, Gunther and Klaus came into the Station hotel with four other men. As you know Gunther briefly spoke to me in the toilets about meeting him on the following Monday morning. We need to find out who those other four men were. Think back James, I know we all got pissed that night, but think hard. I assume they came in and bought a round of beer as I wasn't really watching what they drank. Gunther spoke to me out the back and inquired about Stella. When I told him I knew her, he then made an urgent point of me not missing the meeting on Monday morning. That night Gunther probably died, although his body wasn't found until Monday morning, dubiously positioned. Gunther was with his friend Klaus that evening, but who were the four others?" Rob was convinced they were all involved in something or other.

"Come on Rob that was more than eighteen months ago. There was a piss up which also ended in the bombing of half of Bath." James couldn't remember and he had exaggerated about the bombing.

"Just try and think of anyone else you might have seen who were not with us. Anyone!" Rob needed to revitalise some memories.

Jack was becoming impatient and stood up to leave. "Look you two have a think about that night because I have to get back. Ed make sure you take Rob home. I'll let you know when I've sorted everything out. Please James, do not say anything to anyone."

Jack left knowing Rob was becoming inebriated and hoped Judith wouldn't blame himself. As he trundled along towards Chippenham the answer to the puzzle was no closer and if he failed, what the consequences would be for him he dreaded to think. The last thing he wanted was a desk job. Unemployment would be a better choice.

"Let's go Rob. I'd better take you home." Ed picked up what was left of the bottle. There must have been at least a large glass remaining in the bottom let alone what was still left in Rob's glass. He didn't want any himself and James had to go back to work.

"You're not going to let me leave here without finishing off the bottle are you James?" Rob spoke slowly but precisely and Ed knew then he would have to wait. "Tell me. Where do you get this wine from, the taste is quite beautiful?" He leant the bottle forward and tried to read the label once again. "Where from James? Where from?" As he went to place the dark red liquid back upright the bottle slipped and fell briefly side down on the table spilling a part of the remaining contents onto the old pine table. Rob apologised as Ed mopped up the spillage with the dish cloth but leaving a blood coloured stain almost in the centre of the table. "Tell me James where do you get this wine from? It's important."

Neither James or Ed could understand why he wanted to know and shrugged at each other.

"Where? Tell me where." Rob asked again.

"Stella. When she comes up, or Joy goes down to visit, she gives us a bottle of wine. There's nothing wrong in that." James was flummoxed.

"Thank you James that is all I wanted to know." Rob stood up and almost fell back but his chair saved him. "Please. Can I take the rest of the wine home with me?"

"Of course you can Robbie. Of course you can." James would be glad to see him on his way home not because of the alcohol but because of his general health. He was welcome to stay, but better off in Judith's hands. He pushed the cork back in and James handed the bottle to Ed.

Having helped his old friend into the car he watched as they pulled away, saddened by the way Rob seemed to want to drink himself to death. He turned and went back inside. The red wine stain on the refectory table would be there a long time. Shortly afterwards he returned to his repair work on the plough. He couldn't hear the phone ringing in the cottage.

"Why do you keep reverting back to the wine story Rob? What's special about that particular grape?" As Ed negotiated his way up the lane he kept glancing at the bottle between Rob's feet.

"How often do you drink a good wine in an evening at a restaurant but never remember what was on the label the next day?" he turned slightly and smiled at Ed.

"Never, but that's because I would have probably drank too much of the stuff." Ed answered.

"Well! When you get me home remind me to soak this bottle in the Belfast sink so I can peel the label off. This is a beautiful wine and I would love to purchase some of my own." Rob spoke slowly but precisely, he was quite drunk.

Ed drove on shaking his head. Ironically as he passed the 'Vineyards' Rob was asleep with the bottle rolling on the floor at his feet. Fortunately, there was little left but the cork held up.

Rob woke up on the sofa with a blanket over him. He was shivering with the cold and needed to use the toilet. Darkness now prevailed outside and he had no idea of the time. A lamp shone on the dining table and he struggled to his feet to read the time on the mantelpiece clock. His one eye strained to focus and he turned to go and relieve himself. The kitchen light was now on and the silhouette of Judith stood in front of him with her arms folded. He walked towards her to go out the back and she stepped aside. Judith was no dragon. When he returned the kettle was on and she was making a sandwich. He needed some sort of sustenance.

"James rang while you were asleep. He says there was one person in the bar that night who he remembers speaking to. You either ring him soon at about three thirty before he goes to do the milking or at ten when he's back in the cottage for breakfast," she looked at the wall clock, "you'd just as well ring him now."

Rob telephoned James. When he finished talking he slowly put the receiver down and turned to Judith. "I'll have to go and see father tomorrow, urgently." Judith went to ask him why, but he cut her short. "There is not good news at the farm. George is in a coma and not expected to survive through the next twenty four hours."

Neither of them said anything for some while as they tried to imagine what was going through Joy's mind. She must be so sad.

"Why was there an empty bottle of wine in the Belfast sink full of water earlier on." Judith asked as Rob struggled with the sandwich made from the meagre wartime bread ration.

Suddenly everything came back to him and he almost spat his mouthful out across the table. "What have you done with it?"

"Thrown out, I don't need an empty bottle."

He looked at her disbelievingly. "Where for Christ's sake? I need the label."

"Rob you've drank the contents, can't you remember." She couldn't understand why he would ever want to keep an empty wine bottle.

"So what have you done with the bottle, I want the label. That's why I soaked the bottle, the label is important." He couldn't shout at her because he was the one out of order and tried to hold himself back. Judith went into the spare room and opened up the side cupboard. She returned with exactly the same make of wine he was so concerned about. "Who gave you that?" he asked.

"Daniel. He gave this one to us ages ago. You can't remember anything can you. Believe me Robbie you have to stop drinking so much."

"Upstairs I've filled the bath for you. Don't wake me when you climb into bed." The stairs creaked as she ascended the stairs.

Rob had his bath in a very contemplative mood. Afterwards he donned his dressing gown and went back down into the sitting room. He stoked the fire up and picked the bottle up. With one arm he couldn't remove the cork with a corkscrew and he went and retrieved the wooden spoon from the kitchen. He held the bottle between his feet on the floor and pushed the cork in with the handle. Halfway through drinking the red grape wine he fell back to sleep once more upon the sofa.

Chapter 46
The Suicide

Mrs. Goode let her son and Herbie in through the front door. She offered them tea but they politely refused telling her they were not staying long.

"Where is Dad?" he asked and she told him, 'in the shed making shelves'.

Rob didn't give his father time to put his tools down. "Dad! I want you to think back to about twenty two or three years ago. More or less the same time when James worked in your drawing office. Further up the corridor was the engineer's office which you were in charge of and a youngish chap worked there. Do you remember what his name was?"

His father pondered over the question as such a long time had passed. Eventually he did recall someone.

"Don't ask me his name now, but if I remember rightly he had done his apprenticeship with us, and then went over to Horstmans. We were more involved with heavy engineering while they were more refined which was what interested him most. He was very good. Our loss their gain. I'm sorry I don't remember his name. Go down to Horstmans and ask. There are men in that office who have worked there for all time. Someone will remember him."

He could hardly finish his last words and Rob was out of the door, but not without thanking his father before he left.

The pair walked purposely along the familiar first floor corridor towards Stothert's engineering offices. Together they pushed open the double swing doors as if they were entering a saloon bar and in they strode. The first man sitting at an expansive desk with all sorts of instruments and paperwork strewn around looked up and asked what they wanted. Rob explained. He pointed out someone who Rob actually knew. After a brief discussion they had a name and were on their way to Horstman's, the same name James had given him during the night when he had also informed him about George's dilemma.

At Horstman's they asked the receptionist if there was any possibility of speaking to Pete Benson the shop floor manager. She made the request and put the phone down.

Five minutes later the door swung open behind her. "Rob! Come on up." Pete gestured to him.

"I'd rather talk out here please Pete if you don't mind," he asked him politely.

Rob's request wasn't a problem and he came around the desk and they went outside. Peter was well aware of the need for discretion.

"Pete you've had a bloke working here for you many years and I'm wondering if you can tell me anything about him. I know it's a chance in a million but I don't want him to know there are questions being asked."

"Who are we talking about then? There are quite a few who have been here for years, me included."

"A chap called Bill Williams an engineer." Rob watched Peter hoping he would know something about the fellow but all he saw at first was a stunned look on his face.

"Bill Williams is dead. He died last year. What did you want with him?" he asked.

Rob and Herbie looked at each other. Rob's suspicions were now even more aroused. "What did he die of?" he asked quietly.

"Carbon monoxide poisoning. Over near Wellow. He backed his car into a bridleway, tied a hosepipe to the exhaust, put the other end in through the window then sat inside, and sadly, went to sleep forever. Suicide." Peter had his turn to see what they would say.

"Did he seem he was that way inclined? Depressed or having family problems?"

"No not at all, he seemed perfectly happy. His wife didn't have a clue nor any of his friends. At work he was performing as good as usual, and with his job if you have something on your mind you tend to make mistakes, but not Bill." Peter shrugged his shoulders. There was little else he could say.

Rob scratched his cheek as he thought. "You remember our conversation around my house Pete. Did you suspect anything similar?"

"He was bit of a racist but I never heard him say anything maliciously, it was always made into a joke. Generally he was a decent man." Peter thought well of him. "Your best bet is to go and speak to his wife." He went inside to find her address.

When he came back out Rob asked him one other question. "Did he have any friends here he used to go drinking with?"

"Yes him and Bertie Young were often out together. He works around the back in the yard. Do you want to speak to him?"

"Not really. Just take me around to see if I recognise him. I might speak to him some other time." They walked around as Herbie stayed by the car.

When they returned they finished off their conversation. "I can't say I know him but his face is familiar. Pete, please don't say we've asked questions about him."

"Don't worry I won't. I told you, I'll let you know if I hear anything."

Herbie and Rob drove off back down to the main road.

"Where are we going now? His wife's place I suppose," asked Herbie, "are you ever going to tell me what this is all about?"

Rob didn't answer, he just directed Herbie to where the pair had to go.

On arrival they found a small, very well kept, detached cottage, thickly hedged all around. Bill's wife was a gardening enthusiast and the front of the house displayed an array of colourful flowers and plants. The door knocker was a beautiful fox's head made from highly polished brass. Herbie struck the ornate animal but no-one answered. Herbie went around the side of the building and peered over the gate which separated the front and back. The house had an extension built onto the rear making the building deceptively large. There was washing on the line and the garden went some way back. He caught sight of a woman on her knees, weeding, with a wheelbarrow by her side. The compost heap, freshly topped off with green waste was situated in the far corner. He shouted out. "Hello! Mrs. Williams! Can we have a word please?"

She looked over her shoulder, appearing at first surprised, and then annoyed at having to lift herself off the ground. At the gate she asked who he was and all Herbie could say was that Detective Inspector Rob Goode wanted a word with her. The gate opened and she stepped through and closed the slatted wood behind her. Naturally she didn't trust them. She thought the less they saw of her house the better. Herbie explained to her again as Rob joined them. "Mrs. Williams. I am very sorry but may I be straight to the point, it's about your husband's death?"

She stared at the grotesque figure who stood in front of her and then relented. "You can ask me but you had better be brief."

"Do you think your husband's death was suspicious? I mean, not suicide, but murder perhaps." Rob could see the look on the poor woman's face. He could tell the whole scenario was passing through her mind again. She had the look of sadness and there was redness in her eyes.

"What would he want kill himself for? We had no debt on our home, and there was money in the bank. He had a good social life and I never minded if he went out with his friends. There were holidays every year, sometimes abroad, except now of course because of this wretched war. A car. How many people have a car? Not many. Above all he loved his job, well paid and he enjoyed the company of the people around him." She stopped and thought, presumably about the good times. "Even our personal life was still healthy." She looked down at the path realising she should not have disclosed such a fact.

"What about his friends? Did they go to his funeral?" This time Herbie had asked the question.

"Strange you should ask that. No, not many. One or two he'd known since boyhood came along. His other more recent acquaintances haven't even been to see me since he was found dead."

"What makes you think that he didn't die by his own hand?" Rob needed a good excuse not to ask the police and she gave him one.

"Go and ask the farmer who found him that morning. He was adamant that the police report was questionable." She told him the farmer's name and address.

"This a private question Mrs. Williams. Prior to you meeting your husband did you know anything about his private life? I mean, where he was from?" Rob hardly expected the truth.

She wasn't sure what to say. "Bill's parents abandoned him when he was six years old. He was brought up in a children's home which he hated every moment. When he was about fourteen he ran away and for some time lived on the streets in London. Eventually he somehow came to Bath and was taken in by a kindly couple who helped him get on the straight and narrow. They made sure he found a good job as he was an intelligent youngster. From there he went to work for Stothert's. We met soon afterwards." She shrugged her shoulders.

"Was he by any chance German?" Rob asked coyly.

She smiled. "His father was a Londoner and his mother was German but he could only ever remember her speaking English. She had no need to speak her native tongue here."

Mrs. Williams answer seemed quite a logical explanation to Rob. "Please Mrs. Williams we are determined to find out the truth about your husband's death but we're going to have to ask you not to say anything to anyone for the time being. Is that alright?" Rob believed he'd asked too much already. A lot might depend on her staying silent. He had one other option, an indirect threat. "We believe your life might also be in danger so it is probably better that you have never seen us for now until we get back in touch with you. Do you understand me? Obviously in the current circumstances the German connection is better not known. Don't tell even your best friends or your own children and relatives. Try to be calm and relaxed when you are with them."

Innocently she appeared to agree. They thanked her and left her pondering in the side passageway. Rob and Herbie set off to the sleepy hamlet of Wellow, south of the city.

The front door of the Fox and Badger was still open and the temptation to enter was too great to miss, besides they had to find the main witness to Bill Williams's death, so what better place to start. Both the landlord and Herbie knew each other through the trade, and the night of the blitz, when the 'Edinburgh' had been destroyed, became the topical subject. After a while Herbie leant across and quietly asked about the body in the car. He claimed Bill Williams was an old friend of his and personally wished to pay some respects.

The landlord smiled at him. He knew Herbie was lying. "What's so secretive? everyone knows what went on." His Somerset accent was strong and a joy to listen to for a stranger from other parts.

"He died from exhaust fume inhalation didn't he?" Rob asked.

"Nope. There was more involved than just that. Charlie Hope who found him reckons he didn't die there, but somewhere else." The landlord was enjoying the little intrigue as was everyone else in the bar. "Charlie found him at first light last year up Twinhoe lane. He jumped off his tractor and peered through the car windscreen. He could see he was dead. The car had been backed into the bridleway, not far, just off the road. Sensible man Charlie, he didn't go any further and didn't try and break into the car. He noticed the hose pipe coming from around the back of the car, and like you suggested thought he must have committed suicide. Strangely enough there had been rain the day before but not during the night and Charlie, being half astute, noticed that there were no footprints from the back of the car to the driver's door, the side where he died. So how do you kill yourself without being able to walk on water." The old boys in the bar burst out in laughter.

"So what was the conclusion of the police." Herbie wanted to know more.

"The conclusion of the police is irrelevant. Everyone thinks Charlie Hope's theory is what counts around here. When the plods arrived Charlie had to make a statement on the spot at first, but then later down in Radstock. When he was still at the scene there were two things he overheard from the detective which said everything. One was that the dead man had no mud on his shoes." Rob stopped him.

"He could have parked on the lane, set the car up, jumped in and reversed into the bridleway."

"Why bother, if you're going to kill yourself would you worry about the mud on your shoes. Another thing there was no sign of a bottle of whisky or the likes of pills. Most suicide victims get themselves completely pissed first." The clientele agreed with their landlord.

"Tell him about the woman!" The old man who sat at the end of the bar in 'dead man's corner' had spoken.

Rob watched him intently then turned back to the landlord. "What does he mean? A woman."

"Another of Charlie's theories. He also heard the police mention the fly buttons on his trousers were completely open. Why have a piss when you are going to do that to yourself? Charlie seemed to think that he was lured to his death by a woman, and she subsequently murdered him. He was caught with her hand down his trousers." The customers tried not to laugh.

"Where does this farmer Charlie Hope live? Here in Wellow?" There were a lot of pieces of wood slotting into Rob's jig-saw. Above all the woman, or perhaps even women intrigued him.

"He's not a farmer, merely an itinerant farm labourer. Here today, gone tomorrow. He works for anyone he can earn money from. In fairness to him his knowledge of the farming industry is unique. If he's in their area many farmers and estate managers ask for his labour. He lives where he can, a haystack, barn or a caravan if he's offered one. Basically for want of better words he's a working tramp. You might not see him for two or three years and then he'll turn up. He only ever operates in Somerset, never anywhere else, and he always wears a black bowler hat which he's had for years. Nobody has seen him since the incident. But then that's Charlie Hope. Here today and gone tomorrow." The landlord could tell them no more.

"So do I assume the coroner's verdict was death by suicide and not murder?" Rob swore blind the police covered up Bill Williams' death. What he wanted to know, above all, if he *was* murdered, by what method?

A chap in the bar with his dog answered. "Yes, they said suicide, but everyone around here believes the unfortunate chap was murdered."

The subject was put aside and they all sat around by the fire discussing what the new year would bring them. Nineteen forty four might make or break the British Isles.

Rob kept gazing out of the window. Herbie had the impression he wanted to get away but the cider was moreish. Dark amber in colour, opaque and having a medium sweet apple taste. They drank two more pints and they set off back to Bath.

"What are we going to do for the rest of the day?" Herbie was in the mood for a few drinks.

"Can we go back to my place first as I need to make a couple of phone calls. I'll be five minutes. Then I suppose we can go out to Sandybanks because the landlady will be open all afternoon."

Herbie didn't argue with him.

Rob rang Alfie and asked him if he minded coming down to Bath and try to locate Charlie Hope. Alfie couldn't wait to get there. Rob then rang Jack and arranged a meeting for the next day at Yatesbury along with Herbie, and Alfie, who would call in on his way from London.

Chapter 47
The Return of the Soldier

Daniel stepped off the train at Bath into what seemed to him a hero's welcome. Helen, his sister, shouted his name as she struggled to reach him through the melee. All trains arriving from the south coast, via the garrison town of Warminster, were full of returning soldiers and at each disembarkation station their friends and relations were there to meet them, adding to the congestion on the platform.

Helen pulled him down by the neck and kissed him passionately. He clasped both hands on her shoulders and looked her up and down. "I can't believe how much you've changed!" She was now a fast maturing young lady with a beautiful beaming face.

Stella followed behind her with little George in her arms and Caronwyn holding onto her skirt. She looked radiant and they embraced as a couple who hadn't seen each other for nearly a year. He took George off her and bent down and kissed the shy little girl he had taken to be his daughter. She buried her head behind her mother.

Next came his own mother and she kissed him, almost politely, on the cheek. She was naturally glad to see him home and alive. The war was far from over but she counted down the probability of an end every day. His baby sister Ruby, lay asleep across his mother's shoulder. Her arm hung down motionless, she was oblivious to the noise and temporary celebrations underneath the steamy iron framework of Bath's railway station.

As the crowd filtered away he decided to wait and slung his pack down beside some benches and sat down. He didn't give the impression he was pleased to be home but he held his feelings deep in his mind.

There were many flash backs to the last year which he would have to carry for the rest of his life. He had many hurdles to overcome. As the train pulled out on its way to Bristol he almost relived the story his father had told about himself and his uncle Jimmy at Paddington station at the end of the last war.

Stella gently persuaded him to leave. His mind awoke to reality. Pigeons on the platform floor swept up the detritus before the stationmaster's boys cleared up the inevitable mess. Daniel's entourage followed him chirpily to the exit.

As he stood waiting for the inspection of their platform tickets he had hoped he could cross the road and have a welcoming beer in the Station Hotel, but that was not to be. The bar was closed. One by one they caught up with him and Stella ushered them all into two taxi's and they were driven back to Shakespeare Avenue. Daniel was home from North Africa.

Chapter 48
A Private Admission

Snow fell upon the small family gathering around the fresh grave of George O'Dell as the pall bearers meticulously lowered him into the ground next to his precious wife Helen. Black veiled ladies blew noses with white handkerchiefs as the men folk stood solemnly by their sides. The rector, equally adorned in black and white cloth, uttered indiscernible religious verses and then consolable words to anyone who listened. Together they muttered the 'Lord's Prayer' and then threw almost frozen soil on top of his coffin.

James recollected the last months of the previous war in his mind, and compared the burials of his comrades, including hundreds of thousands of others he never knew who had died before them, to the honour now being bestowed upon George O'Dell. He gently shook the dirt through his fingers in fear of waking the dead but the dead had already awoken. What happened between himself and George many years ago was now firmly laid to rest. He took some deep breaths and his eyes welled up. James stared up into the sky and he visualised Captain O'Dell, George's dear son, dying in his arms, dying because he himself had failed to heed the orders of a superior officer, one who had made him a friend, Daniel O'Dell himself. Blood had frothed from Daniel O'Dell's mouth as his ruptured lungs filled and James had tried desperately to wipe away the haemorrhaging but he had quickly entered his death throes, and there in a shallow trench somewhere in northern France he had passed away in James' arms. The shouting and screaming of the injured and other dying soldiers, persistent machine gun fire and shells landing all around flashed through what was a very young and inexperienced mind. Men groaning, lying in the trench having gone no further than being shot at the treacherous edge, he could visualise them all, as clear as the day the incident had happened. His sharp brain rendered the necessity of a photograph album obsolete. The blue unseeing eyes of Second Lieutenant McLaren, who had only joined the Londons' six weeks previously, seconded from the Norfolks, stared ghost like towards him, an effigy firmly and permanently planted in his thoughts.

"Come on Dad." A gentle voice brought him out of his private nightmare. Daniel stood beside him. Everyone else had left James to his own devices, Joy had sensibly sensed his sombre mood.

Father and son walked down through the churchyard, out of the bottom gate into the lane and then on towards the village common. Neither of them said a word to each other but waited for one of the cars to trundle by and offer them a lift. The view was one of a white winter and the valley below was obscure, the weather was worsening by the minute.

Andrew and his wife picked them up in their Jaguar car. Nothing was said during the short journey, even though Andrew's concern was returning to London that very same day. He knew the situation at Eastrip farm with the possibility of being stranded for days, and had made his mind up some time before not to dwell too long at his father's funeral. He would make haste back to the A4 and the subsequent safety of the capital.

Food was laid out on the table and Joy quickly removed the cheesecloth coverings. James, quiet and mournful, poured the drinks. Still little was said. Under Helen's supervision the children knelt in the window seat excitedly watching the snow come down.

Elizabeth raised her glass and proposed a toast to her father. They all followed suit in sombre fashion. Afterwards there was little that could be said which hadn't been broached before the funeral. Andrew kept glancing out of the window as the snow built up. He had to return to London that night.

Joy suddenly gathered everyone's attention. "James has something to tell you and I want you to listen carefully."

All eyes settled on the new, beleaguered, man of the household. He sat down at the end of the table and nervously twiddled his glass wondering where to start. He looked up at Andrew who was now head of the family. "A few years ago Joy wanted to go and visit the grave of your brother, Daniel." Joy came and sat next to him and took his hand. "I had to tell her something which might have changed her attitude towards me forever. I hadn't been able to say anything before and had hoped in all these years that the situation would never arise whereby I had to disclose some truths." He looked visibly distraught and wasn't sure of himself. Joy prompted him again.

James felt ashamed. "Joy wanted to go and see where her brother Daniel was buried. At first I tried to put her off but she insisted, and the time had come for me to tell her the truth. All those years ago when I told George that I had taken Lieutenant McLaren's dog tag and put it around Daniel's neck simply wasn't true. I should never have brought Daniel's dog tag home. That was wrong of me but seemed the right thing to do at the time. I was young and naive. Had we went to visit the Epehy Wood Farm Cemetery then she *would* have been standing in front of Mr. McLaren's grave and not that of her brother, Daniel. I left Second Lieutenant McLaren's dog tag alone. Captain Daniel O'Dell I can only assume is buried somewhere as an unknown soldier or unless the pioneers recognised him and he has a grave somewhere else." James went quiet.

Joy spoke. "I told Dad what had happened not long ago. He told me if I was happy with James then to him that was all that mattered and I had made a good choice by marrying him. That was the first time Father had ever said anything about us for years and years, or at least to me."

Andrew tapped him on the shoulder. "James please don't fret. Wherever Daniel is buried he will always be in our hearts. He's not missing, he's with his friends and fellow soldiers."

Elizabeth kissed poor James, whose tears ran slowly down his flushed cheeks. "We've seen everything James, we've seen this all before and now we're reliving the story all over again. The horrors of war. Please don't let the incident get you down." She held his head in her bosom and stroked his hair as he sobbed away his memories.

James went upstairs. After half an hour he hadn't come down. Young Daniel went and found his father sitting on the edge of the bed staring out of the tiny cottage window. He sat next to him and put his arm around his shoulder. "It's all my fault your uncle is dead. Had I not been so impetuous he would still be alive. He was a good man and he died trying to save my life. Not a day goes by when I don't think of him when I cradled him in my arms. His last words haunt me. Second Lieutenant McLaren's eyes, wide open, still watch me to this day. I closed his eyes for the last time that morning but they have plagued my mind ever since. What I did was wrong and rightly so I am being punished. I am guilty."

Daniel held his father tightly. "Dad you are not. You are absolutely not guilty of anything at all."

Chapter 49
Dornoch

A savage east wind blowing off the North Sea severely buffeted the Airspeed AS. 6 Envoy as the flimsy plane attempted to land for a second time on an unkempt grass runway at the edge of Dornoch Firth. The wind speed was easily judged by an accompanying, almost horizontal, freezing rain and sleet.

During the flight up from Charmy Down near Bath and a refuelling stop at an obscure aerodrome somewhere in Lincolnshire, the pilot had spoken passionately of his time as an observer with the Royal Flying Corps throughout the 'Great' world war before he had become a pilot himself. He had already unnerved Ed by telling him about the two times he had crash landed, once in peace time killing his co-pilot. Glen lay in the back asleep oblivious to what was happening. To make matters worse for Ed as they made their second approach a fire engine and ambulance could now be seen on standby next to the tiny granite built control tower, 'surely a pre-requisite on such a storm hit day', thought the despondent ex-military policeman.

The intrepid aviator struggled to control the plane in the crosswind and flew in at an oblique angle to the runway. Immediately he touched down the tiny passenger craft bounced back into the air from the force of the uplift only to come down again with another violent thump throwing Glen from one side of the cabin to the other. The plane skewed from left to right but eventually settled with the engine ticking over, and they taxied towards their final resting place close to the passenger lounge, built below the control tower. The airfield was south of the county town of Sutherland, Dornoch, and firmly controlled by the Royal Air Force. Already Ed was planning in his mind a visit to the railway station to book a seat on the train home, avoiding anymore trials and tribulations of modern flight.

A Nissen hut sufficed for the new arrivals, by-passing the waiting lounge, which was another hut linked by a short passage way. They entered via the back door from the airfield, briefly went through formalities at reception, and were immediately ushered through the front door where a car was waiting parked outside on the shingle. The key had been left in the ignition. A very polite RAF corporal gave them brief directions to where they were staying, saluted and turned back into the warmth, leaving the pair quite bemused.

Soon, windswept and shivering cold, they were in the foyer of the Dornoch Castle Hotel, and in no time, after booking in, were sitting at the bar having a traditional Scottish dram to warm their hearts and settle Ed's nerves.

Impressive paintings of Scottish scenes and portraits were everywhere, in the main bar, the reception and on the walls up the intricately carved wooden staircase. A red deer stag's head with imposing antlers adorned the top of the fireplace. Glass cased grouse and a solitary ptarmigan hung on the oak panelled walls amid the candelabra. The serving lass kept herself busy with repetitive imaginary jobs, polishing whisky bottles, cleaning already clean ashtrays or wiping the bar top.

The two semi-retirees went and bathed in their sumptuous rooms and returned downstairs after a while. They had just two nights to find out some truths about an enigmatic woman who lived some six hundred miles away.

"Excuse me." Glen attracted the attention of the young lady who was now filling her time serving other newly arrived customers, some she knew, others were strangers.

"Yes sir, how can I help you?" Her lilt was beautiful. Perfect English with a mere taint of Sutherland dialect. Many people suggested they spoke better English than the English.

"Do you know a family here by the name of Sinclair?" Glen held his eyebrows high in hope.

She glanced innocently at them both. "Which Sinclair family do you want?"

"How many are there?" Ed asked, equally surprised.

"At least two." She excused herself momentarily and went to the kitchen returning with the head chef.

"Exactly who are you are looking for?" he asked with a surly voice.

'Probably a Glaswegian', thought Glen, eyeing the chef up and down.

Glen was quick in the mind. "A few years ago I had a young recruit with me called Stuart Sinclair, but as much as we didn't see eye to eye at first we eventually became friends. Before we went our separate ways he had always said come and visit Dornoch one day. Myself and my friend came up here for a couple of games of golf and thought we'd look him out or, if we can't find him, his family."

The obese chef kept wiping his hands on his filthy apron. "There is more than one Sinclair family around here, but there is a Hughie Sinclair who drinks in the Dornoch Inn just down the road." Without uttering another word to Glen and Ed he turned and left. 'Definitely a Glaswegian', Glen concluded.

Hughie Sinclair was at least six foot six and was a placid man in his early forties but he drank his shillings worth, so to speak. He was a difficult man to understand as his poor education and stronger Scottish accent made easy conversation problematical. With the help of some fellow drinkers Ed and Glen managed to extract the whereabouts of Stuart Sinclair's parents who apparently lived in a street called Cnoc an Lobht. Stuart's father worked on the golf course as a green keeper and both were strict church attendees. Stuart was a young cousin of Hughie's and had had a close relationship with him when he was just a boy. After gleaning as many facts as they could Ed bought them all a drink and thanked them for their help and information.

Both men hadn't envisaged the weather in the far north of Scotland and were poorly dressed, 'even a Russian greatcoat wouldn't keep them warm in the bitter wind', they joked.

The street of Cnoc an Lobht ran from east to west and the houses offered no protection or respite from the January onslaught. What made matters worse was the complete lack of street lighting but they had been warned and given directions by following such and such a building or church. Importantly the tiny pauper's cottage they were searching for had a Christian cross as a polished brass door knocker only just visible in the dark on north side of the street. A light barely escaped through the thickly lined curtains. Glen and Ed huddled together on the meagre doorstep of Mr and Mrs. Sinclair and rapped on the door.

A tiny lady creaked the door open and peeped at the two strangers. "My husband is not in he's at the cathedral."

"Mrs. Sinclair we are friends of Stuart, your son. Can you talk to us please?" Glen still enacted the role of Stuart's mentor.

At first she was reluctant but her church upbringing told her to be good to all mankind and she allowed them into the simple hallway, off the windswept street.

One candle lit the bottom of the stairs and another the top. "How is he?" she asked, desperate to know.

Neither men could believe that she wouldn't have known her eldest son was probably dead.

Ed and Glen glanced sympathetically towards each other. "That is why we are here Mrs. Sinclair. Can we come in and sit down? We have something to tell you."

She placed her hand over her mouth expecting some shocking news. With no words she ushered them into the sitting room. Two armchairs before the fire and a tiny table with chairs to place cups of tea on were all they had. The walls were bedecked with cheap religious artefacts. A miniature clock told the time. 'Life here was frugal', both men thought.

"Where is Stuart? We haven't heard anything from him for years." She was distressed naturally, as any mother would be.

"Mrs. Sinclair when is your husband coming home? Perhaps if he were here you could both listen to what we have to say. Better for you both." Ed raised his eyebrows in anticipation, hoping he could tell them any truths about their son.

The clock told the little lady he would be back soon and although frustrated she went to make tea.

Sure enough two disgruntled men, having heard there were men in Dornoch asking questions of their family, stumbled anxiously through the front door, kicked off their boots and hung up their coats in the hallway.

Before the elder of the two had even entered the sitting room he was already angrily muttering questions. "Whose inquiring about my son?" He stopped dead after entering the sitting room when he saw who he was confronting. A younger son peered from behind him. The father belligerently asked, "get out of my house! You've been drinking! Nobody smells of alcohol in a house which supports our Lord!"

Glen smiled at him. "Not even at communion sir?" he asked calmly.

"Get out! Go on! Get out! This is not your house and you have no right to ask my wife questions when I am not here!" He was obviously livid.

"Then we'll take you both down to the police station sir, and ask our questions there." Ed produced his newly acquired identity card.

Mr. Sinclair went completely quiet. He turned to his son but, flummoxed himself, gave his father no support. The last thing Mr. Sinclair needed was to be seen taken to the police station. He relented. "So what is this all about?"

They waited for Mrs. Sinclair to return from the kitchen.

Glen then took over. "We are not sure if you both know. Something your wife asked us a couple of minutes ago," he hesitated, "Stuart, your son, presumably died whilst attempting to evacuate his platoon from France in the early part of the war. He is registered as being 'missing presumed dead'. I am sorry to be the one who has to tell you. Sometimes the bureaucracy from the defence ministry is very uncertain, if not slow." Glen was solemn and waited for either of them to say anything, although appreciating they might be in a state of shock.

Mrs. Sinclair spoke first. She stared at her husband whilst blowing her nose. "Tell them the truth. Go on!" She looked scathingly at her husband. Ed and Glen had entered into a very sensitive family situation. "He's our child but you won't admit it," she told her husband, and turned back to her visitors. "When I fell pregnant we married straight away. Ever since, he denied the child was his and hated him. Most of the town know Stuart was our child. So he was conceived out of wedlock, but who really cared, he was born within wedlock. Only the likes of his father worry about their own personal ambitions before the hierarchy of the church. If the Lord wants to take revenge then so be it, but the Lord never hated his own son whatever the circumstances of his birth. He always had forgiveness as he does for all mankind. Something *you* couldn't have for our dear son." She stared vehemently at her husband then turned back to Ed and Glen. "Stuart became wayward. Driven out by his father who had disowned him, he took to earning money by any means possible, by hard work, rustling sheep, poaching deer and even theft to keep the rest of us in food. Money we couldn't refuse because of austerity and looming destitution. One day he simply left Dornoch. He was in Edinburgh the last we knew but still kept helping us out for some time and then the extra income just stopped." She pointed at her husband. "He wouldn't accept what Stuart was up to, keeping the rest of the family from destitution but was more than happy to accept the extra income and turn a blind eye. Who *was* the thief in the Lord's eye? Stuart was a lovely boy. He cared about people and his own family. His father drove him away." She pointed at her husband again. "Years later letters then began to arrive from a city called Bath in the south of England. They were not written by him but a woman who said she was his wife." Mrs Sinclair was heavy hearted. She looked down at her hands clasped between her knees and then looked up again. "I had a daughter-in-law whom I have never seen or spoken with."

"Did you ever reply to her letters?" Glen asked softly.

"No, she never ever wrote an address on any of her letters. I don't know where they lived except that it was in Bath or at least the postmarks were from Bath."

"Did she ever mention in her letters where she came from?"

She shook her head "No. Most of the letters were about her trying to persuade Stuart to come home and visit his family. That never happened and I suppose now never will."

Ed was curious. "Did she ever disclose anything about a child? A girl."

She quickly glanced at them both. "No. Why?"

"We know she has two children and one of them is Stuart's. The elder one is a girl and probably about three or four years old now. She has since remarried and has a little boy as well. I'm surprised she didn't tell you about the little girl."

Mrs. Sinclair rose from her seat and went upstairs. She returned with a small cardboard box. "I've kept the letters in here. They are all in chronological order. The last one was about three or four years ago, maybe the child wasn't born then. Can you tell me why you are asking these questions? What has she supposed to have done?"

Ed was quick on the uptake. "Nothing, but we have been fed some information which suggests her life might be in danger. When we started to investigate we found out that no-one knows who she really is or where she comes from and at the moment, before asking her outright, we don't want to arouse any suspicions."

Glen browsed through the box. "Mrs Sinclair do you mind if we take these with us? We'll get them back to you first thing in the morning. We are staying at the Castle hotel if you think of anything else and wish to tell us. We will be here for a couple of days. Please don't hesitate to contact us if you feel there is something we might need to know," Glen looked at her husband, "and you sir, any information would be important, however trivial."

Mrs. Sinclair raised her eyebrows at them. "Everything I know about her are in those letters. They don't actually tell you much but if it's for her and the children's safety then you are more than welcome to read them."

As Mrs Sinclair had ushered them in off the street, Mr Sinclair happily ushered them back onto the street and the pair headed back to their hotel.

During a meal of venison stew and boiled kale Ed and Glen leafed through the letters. The correspondence itself told no real story about Stella, but an excited glint appeared in Ed's eyes. He suddenly pulled out his wallet and sifted through the folded leather for a phone number. "I think I might have sussed out where she is probably from. I'm going to make a phone call. Get some whisky on the table. 'Only the best'." They were actually spoilt for choice, and despite his roots, Glen was no connoisseur on the world's most famous alcoholic beverage.

When he returned his face was glum. "I spoke to Judith. Rob's in hospital. He's not well at all, semi-conscious evidently."

Glen pursed his lips. "We can't afford anything to happen to him because he knows too much, but the trouble is he never tells you what is going through his mind."

"Funny you should say that but he once told me that Jack could speak German and that's why I rang. Judith's going to try and contact him and ask him to ring here. Glen, there is something in those letters which might be blindingly obvious. It's the biggest clue we've had so far. Let's hope he rings back tonight and can confirm what I am thinking. Then tomorrow we can get as pissed as farts and play golf all day."

"Not in this weather I'm not." Glen wasn't keen on golf at all, even though he was born in Scotland.

The phone rang and their eyes went to the door leading to the foyer and reception. The doorman showed his head and waved Ed over and handed him the receiver.

"Jack! Is that you?"

"Yes. What is it you want?" he sounded tired and irate.

"Rob told me that you could speak the German language to a reasonable degree. Is that true?"

"Yes but not enough for a German not to know I was foreigner."

Ed was trying to stay calm. "What about grammar and punctuation marks, do you understand them?"

"I'm not too bad, why?"

"What are those two little dots they put above their vowels? The ones we don't use in the English language."

The phone went quiet as Jack tried to remember what they were called. "I know what you mean but I can't think of the name. Why?"

"In our possession we have about nine hand written letters sent from Stella Sinclair to her ex mother- in-law and in the letters she uses them. Has anyone ever seen her write them down before."

"Daniel, her husband is a fluent German speaker as you know. He would surely have known." Jack wasn't entirely convinced.

Ed went quiet. 'Unless Daniel does know something' he thought.

"Get back down here and we'll talk about them then. Bring the letters with you. By the way we might have had another breakthrough. I'll tell you about it when you are back here." The phone went dead. Jack hadn't seemed over excited.

"She's a German Glen, I'll swear by it." He went on to explain what he had told Jack.

Glen mused for a while. "Alright. Let's assume she is German. We have to be rational. Stella appears all over the city. She flaunts herself, even when her husband is away at war. Remember that's how I first met her at the bar in the Station Hotel. If she is spying for her home country it's now becoming a little late. What can she tell them now they don't already know. Our allied forces are now one third of the way through Italy, possibly further. So why, if she is a German spy, would you keep operating knowing that all might be lost. You would go quiet, underground, and wait and see what is the outcome."

Ed went to say something but Glen held his hands up. "Please don't stop my train of thought. Let us now assume she is English. She could be anti-communist and would rather see a right wing government here but even more so a national socialist government or if not what is she up to? Daniel must surely know her nationality. If she is German then she is very clever at hiding her origins, but not that clever judging by these letters. It's a slip up but a give away. I am positive she is German or at least European."

"Maybe she thought that no-one would put two and two together this far north and just wrote them casually." Ed merely made the suggestion.

"We need to get back to Bath and find out what her real name is and we can to talk to Rob before something happens to him. He's almost bound to have information which he's been keeping back. Something important like a seed growing in the back of his mind which is about to germinate." Glen was determined there was a simple answer to the whole story. "So now we have a spare day what are we going to do tomorrow?"

"Fancy a round of golf?" Ed asked him.

"Fuck off! I wouldn't play if I was in the Caribbean." Glen went quiet in thought and then looked up. "I'll tell you what we should do tomorrow."

"What!" Ed envisaged his round of golf as just a dream, a golden opportunity to play in Scotland, the home of golf.

"We should copy out those letters word for word and punctuation for punctuation and give the originals back to Mrs. Sinclair. That should only take a couple of hours and we can sit here and sample the whole top shelf whilst we are writing them out."

Ed tried to imagine the scenario of either of them walking around to the Sinclair household under the influence of 'god knows' how many whiskies and Mr Sinclair answering the door.

Chapter 50
Rob Goode

"He's very weak and on oxygen. I can't let you stay long the doctor's have told me he needs complete rest." Judith was unsurprisingly very concerned about Rob's health.

He was in fact healthier than both Ed or Glen imagined. He was slow with his questions and took some time gathering his breath between sentences. "So what did you find out? Anything we didn't already know?" he asked weakly.

They showed him one of the letters and explained the German grammar. "That adds up with what I have been thinking for months. They are known as 'umlauts'. It's to do with how you pronounce the vowels in words of most Germanic languages," he struggled and took some deep breaths. "Stella always drinks red wine and preferably German red wine. The wine she drinks is rare, especially now, but they still sell the same produce in the Empire bar. We have had no trade with Germany for years now, so where does the wine keep coming from? Someone somewhere has a cellar full of that particular wine. That is a question which must be answered. I think she knew Gunther Volke, who is now dead, and also Bill Williams. He was also an engineer and has since died, apparently suicide, but I have some reservations as to how he lost his life." He stopped and wheezed but then carried on. "When myself and Herbie went asking questions there appeared to be a cover up. The main witness, Charlie Hope, the man who found Bill in his car, had since gone missing but now an unrecognisable body has turned up. All the local people swear that Bill's death wasn't a suicide as the coroner concluded. Alfie had been out searching for Charlie Hope, making enquiries here and there. Now he's come up with a body but in a very degenerative state of decomposition. The body was actually found by some walkers. What I don't want is the Somerset police involved especially if it *is* a cover up. His body was found in Wiltshire, which is odd in itself because he only ever worked in Somerset. We'll let the Wiltshire force deal with the discovery for the time being. The body is being kept at Trowbridge and has been there for many months. I am quite sure the coroner will conclude he died from natural causes. Alfie is staying at my house at the moment. Speak to him but the three of you be careful, this intrigue could be simply localised or maybe bigger than we think. Jack I feel is definitely on our side but doesn't know who he is up against. Gunther and Bill Williams were eliminated and if my feelings are right, sadly Charlie Hope died only because he was a witness. I have a theory about the wine but for now leave that with Judith. She's a woman, and they like wine. There are probably more people involved but I don't yet know who, possibly scapegoats for people with a lot of power. We don't know where this conspiracy is going to end, if conspiracy is the right word to use, perhaps there will be a surprise."

A nurse entered the ward. "Beware the matron is coming!" Rob closed his eyes and she escorted Ed and Glen away from the bed with a view that Rob was too weak to carry on.

Judith sat waiting in the corridor. She asked how he was, her face forlorn. They helped her to her feet. "He'll be alright he's just a bit overtired. Come on let's go for a glass of wine down at the Empire bars before they close." Ed made the suggestion as he and Glen's eyes met.

Matthaius Schlutt was standing at the bar when they walked in. Glen went over to him and asked how he was. "I've never been so tired in my life. We're working seven days a week, now mostly for the war effort. Something big is going to happen that is the talk around the factory and at Horstman's as well. Most of us will be glad to get back to normality."

"Can I get you a drink?" Glen asked him

He viewed the remainder in his glass. "No thank you. I only popped in for one just to see somebody." He glanced at the clock.

Glen went across and sat down with Ed and Judith. Ed kept his back to the bar. Almost simultaneously in walked Stella. She didn't notice them.

"Glen, does she know we are staying in town?" Ed asked trying not to be recognised.

Glen watched her. He remembered the night he had spent with her trying to pry but felt she was doing exactly the same thing to him. "I don't know. If she asks what we are doing here, then we've come to visit Rob. It's the excuse I used last time, only this time it's true."

Stella walked up to Matthaius Schlutt and the barman poured her a glass of red wine without question. Matthaius put his hand in his pocket and paid. She handed him a note which he briefly read and then slipped the paper away along with his change. In two gulps he finished his beer and promptly left. Only then did she notice the threesome sitting drinking in the corner and she went over to greet them.

They appeared surprised but pleased to see her. She asked the two men the obvious question, "what are you doing up here in Bath?"

"Judith rang us about Rob's illness so we came up to visit him in hospital. He is very ill, but hopefully he'll be alright. We're driving back in a minute when we've drank these." There were two whisky's sat next to their empty pints.

The two women began talking about Rob and then the children, and so for good reason the men decided to leave. They toasted Rob's health. After embracing and false kisses Glen and Ed went, leaving Stella and Judith together.

"That was fucking close. Do you think she suspected anything, or more to the point what about Matthaius Schlutt. They obviously know each other. Let's hope he didn't see her make a beeline for us as he was leaving. I wonder if either of them have put two and two together." In the darkness of the street outside the 'Empire' Glen was shaking his head in the hope that he and Ed hadn't been recognised together for anything more than visiting Rob. A bad mistake he kept telling himself. The blackout was still in force and the pair walked quickly and quietly, then separated and disappeared into the night. No-one appeared to follow them.

Ed had other things on his mind.

Chapter 51
The Old Spotted Cow 1944

"Lieutenant Cory please take a seat. Oh! and by the way, congratulations on your promotion." The Colonel shifted around to the front of his desk, but still standing, he leant back on the edge, folded his arms and crossed his legs as if relaxed. "I cannot tell you what is about to happen over the next few months as you well know the discreet procedures of secrecy, but to keep your men occupied for the time being there is a task I wish you to undertake." The Colonel was doddery, near retirement and serving out his final posting. He had served his time in South Africa and the last war. Paul merely wanted to hear his orders and leave. "We are all well aware of your past participation with the Air Force and believe you are the ideal man to lead your group on this particular home based mission. We have two small airfields under construction, practically complete, near a town called Cricklade in Wiltshire. They have to be ready for full operational use by late April or early May at the latest so I have been informed. These airfields are two of many around England, and in all probability each will be used for airborne assaults on targets of which even I don't know the whereabouts, but not even a genius could work out mainland Europe is the priority. We need them up and running, initially for training purposes, but ultimately thousands of paratroopers will be passing through and they have to be extraordinarily well organised."

Paul sat hoping for just an inkling of information. An offensive which he and his colleagues had a vague idea was eventually going to happen on a large scale, but when and where none of them knew.

"I want you to take your lads, divide them up, and create two tented villages on each base. You will also have the use of several Nissen huts but these will be for the use of stores, offices and general military equipment. On a three day basis expect about five or six hundred men on each base exercising and training for a large scale invasion, but working hand in hand with the Air Force. When our men eventually move for the real event, each should know where their exact point of departure is and be familiar with the bases as a whole should anything go wrong. They will need to be comfortable, well fed, fit and ready to move at little notice. You will be in charge of security and all arrangements to defend those bases in the event of enemy attack, but there will also be Air Force defence systems in place. On the ground you will be subordinate to the Royal Air Force aerodrome commander but ultimately, I am your overall superior officer in the army. Any problems! let me know, and I will liaise between them and yourself. We have chosen you and your platoon because of the good reports which have come back from actions abroad in Africa. Please believe me I am sure you and your men will be back amongst the real action in the not too distant future. Good luck. You know where to contact me." Both men stood and saluted each other. Paul, reluctantly but militaristically, turned and marched out of the door.

Paul and Daniel headed away from Salisbury Plain in an army green Austin Seven. They had to meet the camp commander who sought their advice on two projects in North Wiltshire, RAF Blakehill and RAF Down Ampney. Paul had studied the map. "In between the two bases is a small town called Cricklade with several pubs and shops so we won't be entirely out in the middle of nowhere. This deployment could be an eye opener for the real thing. I think probably an invasion of Europe, and more than likely France."

Daniel eyed Paul with a smile. "Do you mean the opening of the second front? The one we're allowed to know about but not talk about," he almost laughed, "it must be the third front if we take into account the Russians. The snippets of information that filter through suggest the Krauts are suffering badly in the east but holding out in Italy."

"Whatever happens in the near future I have a deep feeling that we won't be involved. That's why they are sending us here for now, merely to keep us occupied. I suppose we will be able to take in the ambience of the area." Paul's reply was one of disappointment and sarcasm.

The atmosphere Paul spoke about was apparent as soon as they approached the industrial town of Swindon, where they were now producing the Supermarine Spitfires en masse, amongst many other industrial and commercial productions. Certain areas were impassable unless the required 'confidentiality papers' were in legitimate possession. Most military police waved them through, rightly or wrongly, in their army coloured car. The town was a hive of activity and as with all the other industrial areas of Britain the chimneys blew out lung bursting gasses and smoke in its attempt to put Hitler to rest once and for all. Towards the north and west lay the Cotswold hills, sleepy and beautiful? Not as Paul and Daniel had imagined. Beautiful, but definitely not sleepy.

Passing through Cricklade was abominable. Every car, wagon and pedestrian was checked thoroughly. The queues were extensive, made worse by break downs and forgetful people with no identification. Not just the town itself, but the whole area was under complete surveillance. Once inside the cordon everything became easier to manoeuvre but individual access into Blakehill farm, their final destination, was made difficult by the construction works which prevailed over most things. It was impossible not to find a place of employment in Britain in early nineteen forty four.

A temporary construction served as a gatehouse, likewise so did the guardroom which the two men were directed towards. Paul asked to speak to Squadron Leader Phelps. The corporal made an internal phone call, such was the progress of the infrastructure, and was told he would be with them in less than five minutes. They stood outside and gazed across the new airfield. Already nine Douglas Dakota's sat on the freshly laid tarmac, being tinkered with by the ground force engineers in front of the hastily arranged 'Blister' hangars. Building works were going on all around. Nissen huts were being erected or anti-aircraft gun emplacements installed. The whole area buzzed with industrial and military endeavour.

A Land Rover screamed around the building, braked hard, and out jumped a high ranked Air Force officer. The vehicle sped off. "Phelps my name. I take it you are Cory." Paul went to salute. Phelps pulled his arm down. "We haven't time for that. Every second counts now. Call me Phelpsie. Good! Come on! Is this your car?" They nodded. "Let's get in, I'll show you around." The Squadron Leader chose to sit in the back and he conducted a tour of the airfield with his head pushed between Paul and Daniel's shoulders, both highly embarrassed by the eccentric officer. He described every new building and its use. They stopped and a ground crew member gave them a guided tour around a Dakota while the Squadron Leader went and discussed any forthcoming implications with the flight engineer. Both Paul and Daniel were impressed. 'Phelpsie' came back and took them to a part of the airfield which backed onto the Cricklade to Malmesbury road. They clambered out.

"Someone has come up with the idea that something might go wrong and we will need to house the chaps temporarily, maybe overnight. These small airbases, and there are many, will have a massive amount of troops going though them." He briefly ceased talking. "You probably have imagined where their destination is but feel you cannot discuss the situation." He smiled ironically. "Many tents are turning up and we want you to make these men as comfortable as possible if there is a hold up. They may only have to stay one night or at the most two. They are your men, army chaps. Many won't be coming back alive and the ones that do will need a lot of hospitalisation which is being arranged here at Blakehill. Here, and at the village of Down Ampney, will be transit camps for soldiers travelling into Europe. I cannot beat about the bush with you both but there you have the information. This war is heating up. The sooner the bloody fighting is over the better. Those workmen over there are laying a telephone line so you will have a contact number. Six Nissen huts are to be built as soon as possible, but bear in mind other huts are needed elsewhere. Use them for an office, toilets and stores etcetera. Come on! I'll quickly show you Down Ampney aerodrome and you can perceive the requirements with your own eyes. Your responsibility will be to accommodate these soldiers and make sure they have everything they might need. Make them comfortable and feed them well. The less I have to do the better at the moment, and if you can take this load of my mind you will be much appreciated." They jumped into the car and set off to Down Ampney.

The similarities of the two airfields were striking. Comparable control towers and buildings let alone the regulatory Nissen huts and Blister hangars.

Afterwards Phelpsie took them to a local pub where they could stay for two nights. The 'Old Spotted Cow' at Marston Meysey. Anna, the landlady, was very welcoming.

Chapter 52
Another Murder

Herbie and Sarah walked back through the city streets having had a business meeting with a view of taking over the 'Old Green Tree'. The time was mid afternoon and Herbie stopped off at the newspaper vendor's to buy a copy of the Evening Chronicle. There was a vague reference to the war on the front cover, but the headline was about a local Bath builder being found dead in his car in a lay-by. His name was Ian Brierly, and the police described the incident as a suspected murder. Herbie read the details and then set off in pursuit of his wife.

As they reached the car he handed her the paper. "Read the headline, that might interest you," he told her.

After browsing over the front page of the local journal Sarah asked why he thought the story was interesting.

"There must be a serial killer about. Between the wars in Bath I can't hardly remember one murder. Now we've possibly had three, plus another body in Wiltshire, which all look suspiciously like homicide, although unproven. I'll drop you off at home and go around to Rob's. I shouldn't say this because there is another man dead, but it's what we want, another lead. There's a missing link somewhere to all this."

"Whatever you do, don't let Rob drink alcohol, he's on medication," she warned him.

Two days later Ed and Glen visited Rob at his house. He was alone as Alfie had returned to London. Rob now appeared to be a lot healthier. "Well what did they say?" Rob asked them, wheezing and coughing.

"Ian Brierly died from a small puncture wound to the heart. The weapon used was something like a stiletto, perhaps a professional hit with only one wound." Ed couldn't tell him anymore.

"That was how the coroner thought Charlie Hope had died but was unproven because of the state of his body. Animals had had a feast of him, plus the decomposition made him hardly recognisable. In fact the only way they identified him was his bowler hat which was thrown down by his side." Rob paused for thought. "Did you go and see where they found Ian Brierly?"

"Yes. At the top of Tog hill there is a lay-by with bushes on the road side. If there is a car parked there anyone driving past wouldn't be able to see anything. Ideal for lovers. Whoever done him in might well have had an accomplice unless he was meeting a lover and she, or perhaps he, then drove off. That would mean they had two cars." Glen was puzzled.

"Gentlemen please do not discount the fact there might be a homosexual contact involved." Rob smiled. "But anyway why murder your lover? Unless he *or* she was going to spill the beans. As far as I can gather Ian Brierly was married, so that would mean his lover probably might have been as well. Herbie will be here soon. He's gone to ask a few questions about him."

The three men sat discussing the issue whilst waiting for Herbie to turn up. As always Stella's name cropped up.

Rob mused over the subject of Stella. Searching out information about her was difficult. Short of asking Daniel outright she was an extremely elusive woman. They thought her and Stuart had married in Warminster, but apparently that wasn't so, and there were no records of them marrying in Wiltshire or Somerset. They had arrived at another dead end.

Herbie walked in. First of all they congratulated him when he told them that in two weeks time he and Sarah would acquire the 'Old Green Tree' pub as tenants.

Once he had settled down he told them of his findings. "Ian Brierly was not a well thought of man. He employed about ten men, having a variety of trades. I found one of his sites and his men were more concerned about how they were going to be paid under the circumstances of his death. What they did say was that he paid the best builder's wages in the city and that's why they stayed with him. He was cantankerous, highly critical, and generally nasty towards them. He was married but hasn't lived with his wife for some years." The three in front of him all looked up at each other. Herbie didn't question why and carried on. "One of the lad's wife is friendly with Brierly's wife and describes him as I have just told you, basically disliked, but his wife believed that Brierly was an out and out racist. That is one of the reasons why Brierly's wife left him."

"Not that what you have just revealed seems likely, but did you find out if he had any friends?" Rob asked him.

Herbie searched his pocket and found a piece of paper on which he had written down two names and handed the note to Rob.

Rob peered at the paper. He read the names of Peter Thompson and Bert Young. "I don't know a Peter Thompson but that Bert Young I'm sure works at Horstmans. I am more than positive that Pete Benson pointed him out to me."

"One other thing then which might link them all together. I thought of this when I was driving up here. When we were at Mrs. Williams house you probably didn't notice but she has a relatively new extension on the back of her house. I wondered, just by chance, if Ian Brierly's company were involved in the construction. That would link her husband, Bill Williams, with him who you think was out drinking with Gunther Volke on the night of the Baedeker raid in Bath. Charlie Hope has died in similar circumstances as Ian Brierly. Sadly it seems Charlie was probably in the wrong place at the wrong time and knew too much. "Herbie held his arms up, he had his own opinions.

Rob was glad that one night he and Herbie had sat up at his kitchen table and he had told him about everything that was happening or what had gone on in the past. He had become an asset.

"If Brierly did build the extension, I wonder what Mrs. Williams is thinking now. Her husband being dead as well. She probably doesn't know anything about poor Charlie Hope." Rob had his thinking cap on. "Herbie! First find out who built her extension. If he did, then at least we know all these people are being persecuted by the same person or group of people. Ask his workforce but whatever, don't ask her, she may start putting two and two together, and we don't know yet whose side she is on. So far, as for the dead, there has been a domiciled German engineer, an English cum German engineer, now a builder who no-one appears to like because of his racist attitudes, and a vagrant farm labourer who I still sincerely believe has nothing to do with what has happened." Rob's head was swimming with ideas. "Glen you go to Martin Schlutt's house or flat when he is at work. Ask after him and try and find out what the neighbours know. We know he is German but where did his young family disappear back in nineteen thirty six. We think there is a wife and child or perhaps even two children. Ed we have to nail this nanny of Stella's. Stage a hand bag robbery or something but don't become involved yourself. Pay someone off. A youngster perhaps. There are plenty of them around looking for a quick wage. Daniel's sister, Helen, she stays there once or twice a week to help with the children but she has never spoken to the old lady in all the years Daniel and Stella have been married, which is quite some time. Even Daniel has hardly ever spoken to her, if ever! She just shuns him but his attitude is if Stella's happy for her to care for the children then so be it. Daniel is an out and out soldier and as far as he goes that's the way he's staying. I am afraid war and the sound of guns blasting off is music in his ears. Talking of Daniel, the other factor we need to sort out is his German school teacher. James, his father, has met him. Odd that he had been incarcerated by the Germans in the past. He could be a bitter man, but we don't know." Rob thought about the man and his influence over Daniel. "No! Forget him. Leave him to me and James and concentrate on what I've already told you."

They left Rob alone and then shortly afterwards Judith came home. She made dinner for her ailing husband, carefully cooked with all she could procure during restricted times, but Rob was uncomplaining. To him his hunger was irrelevant against his desire to find out what was happening in his home city. With the meagre rations she made 'Humble Pie' with kale and turnip. Frail as he was, he managed to eat only half of what she offered to him, as he so desperately wanted an alcoholic drink as an accompaniment. He asked her pleadingly and Judith went to her shopping bag in the kitchen.

Back at the table she placed a red German wine in front of him. "Is this what you have been searching for?" she asked mockingly.

He read the label. His interest in the bottle perked up. "Where did you get this from?"

Judith knew something her husband didn't. "A place where you and your friends are never invited. A tiny uninspiring restaurant right here in Bath. You can buy the wine there and in the Empire bars."

Judith went to the kitchen and brought back the corkscrew. "One glass only Robbie Goode or I won't tell you the whole story."

He agreed to listen to his sweet wife. The wine would be a later argument.

Chapter 53
The Flying Nightingales

A heavily panting private knocked on the door of Lieutenant Cory's Nissen hut office and was asked to come in. He stood to attention but never saluted. "Jimmy Anderson has fallen off the back of the Albion truck sir and we think he's broken both of his arms."

"What the hell was he playing at? Where is he now?" Paul was not amused.

"They've taken him over to the medical centre sir." The messenger had calmed down and was breathing easier.

Paul took his hat from the makeshift coat rack and the pair of them set off in the Austin Utility to find their wounded soldier.

Paul dismissed the young man asking him to return to his work party. He sprang up the steps of the gleaming white washed building with a large red cross painted on the outside. The military hospital's operational heart was completed but there was still construction works being finished at the rear, mostly wards. A young WAAF approached him. "Can I help you sir?" she asked quietly with good manners.

His eyes redirected from the corridor onto the girl and he smiled. "I understand you have a member of my platoon here. Jimmy Anderson," he let slip, "sorry! Lance Corporal Anderson."

From a side office, the Flight Sergeant had overheard the conversation.

"Is there any chance I might be able to speak to him?" Paul simply wished to see that he would be taken care of, and be made as comfortable as possible.

"He is with the Station Medical Officer who will undoubtedly send him for an x-ray sir. If you would like to take a seat sir I will ask him to come and speak to you when he is available." She showed no signs of panic in her eyes, only patience. Paul sat down and run his cherished cap through his hands as an expectant father might do waiting for the birth of his child.

He didn't realise, but from the confines her office the Flight Sergeant occasionally cast eyes upon him.

"Lieutenant." Paul was taken by surprise. "Lieutenant, sorry to keep you waiting. Your chap, silly fool, could have been worse. Might have broken his neck had he not put out his arms to save himself. He'll survive though, for now," he added. "We'll set his arms and he can have a couple of months at home. Lucky fellow, knowing what is going to happen. He's out of the fray for the time being."

"Where is he now?" Paul asked.

"The boys are just straightening him up and putting him in plaster. Good practise for them. He's the worst case we've had here so far," he laughed. "Wait and see what happens when the assault begins. We won't know what will hit us."

He took him down to see his man. Jimmy was shaken but not deterred. He was adamant he didn't want to be sent home. He'd joined the army to escape from his family and a congested back street life. The problem Paul had was his corporal's personal hygiene. Effectively for some weeks Jimmy would have no use of his arms and he would be better off at home.

"Let him stay on the base if that is what he wants. I'll make sure the girls look after him." Appearing from behind, the Flight Sergeant, a lady, in charge of the nursing corps spoke softly but surely. "Him being here will benefit my girls to learn a little bit at a time, rather than let them try and imagine what they have let themselves in for." The elegant, uniformed lady stood by the door.

"Ah! May I leave you both to decide the future of Lance Corporal Anderson together, because I have other things to attend to." The

Medical Officer grinned. "Cuts and bruises probably." He spun around on his heels and went, his white coat tails flailing behind him.

Between them, Paul and the Flight Sergeant concluded Jimmy Anderson's fate. He was to stay at Blakehill until his recovery was complete. The parachute brigade were to accommodate him but he was to report to RAF Wroughton medical centre as required.

"You care about your men don't you," the Flight Sergeant asked admiringly.

"Of course I do. They are better off alive than dead. One day, when this ghastly mess is over, we'll all have a drink together," he went eerily quiet, "hopefully," he added deep in thought.

"Come on I'll show you around the Medical Centre." Paul willingly followed her.

"When the injured lads return off the planes they'll first come through here. The most serious ones will be assessed by our nurses on the flights back, and without delay sent straight to Wroughton. We will help the less injured and try to move them back near their home for the time being. The walking wounded for example. If this was ten weeks in the future then your Lance Corporal would be on his way home in no time, but at the moment we can accommodate him here." She smiled at Paul.

There were numerous wards and newly delivered beds were being erected as soon as being unpacked. Mattresses and sheets followed. An operating theatre with four tables was almost fully equipped and impeccably clean. Paul was informed of the need to eliminate infection. Young nurses busily patrolled the corridors as if an invasion was imminent. Everyone knew their place. To the rear of the building, ambulances were backed onto the car park waiting to ferry the injured away. Everyday exercises and practises took place to ensure the procedure would run smoothly at the crucial time.

"You don't seem old enough to be a flight sergeant in these circumstances. Where did you learn your trade, if that is the right word?" Paul became interested in the woman. She was intelligent, not necessarily beautiful but challenging to talk with.

"Disillusioned with a country girl's life in Norfolk I left home and went to live with an aunt in London. She was good for me and put me on the right track where I started at the Royal London Hospital in

Whitechapel. To cut a long story short, I ended up working for one of the country's top trauma surgeons and became extremely adept in theatre operation procedures. He had learnt his profession during the first world war but everyone knew he was one of the best. He was a lot older than me but we had an affair and, as with all relationships of the same kind, they end in tears. Andrew was his name but in fairness to him, when we separated, he knew people in high places and recommended me to the military where I then embarked on a career in the Women's Auxiliary Air Force at the start of the war. So here I am." It was a chapter in her life that appeared not to worry her and she smiled at Paul, expecting another personal query.

"And who is the new man in your life?"

"No-one. To begin a new relationship then find the man you have begun to love goes to war and doesn't return, is not for me at the moment. Maybe one will and be none the worse for his experiences, but on the other hand he may come back crippled for life. I might be cynical but I will wait until the end of this current sickening conflict. At the moment I am more than prepared to help the wounded return home, nurse them back to health and help readjust them back into normal life." She was philosophical in her outlook.

Paul glanced at his watch. "I have to get back. Thank you for your guided tour, an eye opener I can assure you." Paul turned to leave but hesitated. "I'm sorry. What is your name again? he asked.

"I never told you but if you must know I am Flight Sergeant Andrea Morrison. And you?"

"Lieutenant Paul Cory." He went to leave again but turned towards her. "What are the chances I might be able to take you out for a drink or a meal one evening," he asked sheepishly.

She had him on a string and went into her office and browsed her diary. "I'm afraid that I am not available until next week at the earliest. Probably Wednesday, in the evening possibly. Would that be alright with yourself?"

He thought about the time and date. "I'm sure I can come to some arrangement. I'll send over a confirmation for you in the meantime."

Paul was pleased with himself as he drove back to his office. He had felt he'd made a good impression on her. She definitely affected him. He was almost thankful that Jimmy had broken his arms.

Chapter 54

The Pincer Movement

"What did you find out Herbie? Anything interesting." Rob quizzed his friend hoping for a new lead.

"I found two other tradesmen working on a bomb damaged detached house, one of whom divulged that Brierly part owned the building with someone else, although he refused to name the partner. They were repairing some walls and a section of the roof. He also told me they had worked on Bill Williams' extension about five years ago and that Brierly and Williams were closely associated with each other. Brierly's estranged wife and Mrs. Williams are still good friends. That was all he could tell me. We began talking about the night the German's came and the bomb damage that had been caused. His mate overheard us talking and slyly remarked that Brierly thought '*they* were on his side', I assumed he meant the Germans were on his side. The bloke guffawed but when I asked what he meant he refused to elaborate, saying that he'd made the remark as a joke and turned away."

Rob's face went dead pan when Herbie told him. What Judith had told him the day before offered a clue but he was still far from finding out the truth. He would wait until Ed and Glen came back to him.

Glen knocked on the door of Matthaius Schlutt's terraced home knowing he wasn't in. He tried time and time again only to attract the attention of Matthaius' neighbours. To his left he saw the curtain gently move and decided to try there instead. At first there was no response but then the door opened just a little, and an old woman cautiously peered out from behind.

"Ma'am, Mr. Schlutt has had a minor accident at work and I am trying to find his wife to tell her what has happened and where he has been hospitalised. Might you know where I can find her?" Glen asked trying to be as convincing as possible.

"As far as I know he has no wife. He has lived alone for years," she answered meekly, pointing across the road, "ask the woman in number forty five." She then closed the door in his face.

Before he even reached the pavement on the other side a woman in her thirties had obviously watched the old lady gesticulating. She stood waiting on the threshold wondering what Glen wanted. She said much the same. "Nobody else but him has lived there for probably about eight years now. When he first came there was a woman and child, a little girl about two or three years old at the time. She herself was in her late teens or maybe early twenties. She didn't stay that long, approximately a year, eighteen months perhaps and then she disappeared. Where to, I don't know."

"They were married though?" Glen asked her.

"No. Definitely not. I think you'll find she was his sister. We very occasionally talk with each other but he never ever mentions anything about them. In fact he rarely talks of his past." She described the woman to Glen.

"Did you know he was a German?" Glen asked.

She hesitated. "We thought he might be because he always plays German composers' music on his gramophone player, especially Mendelssohn. In the summer when the windows are open we can all hear the classical music. None of us know what his surname is, we only know him as Matthew. He speaks good English and never does us any harm." She couldn't elaborate anymore.

Glen went off back to Rob's with his tiny piece of information, but where was Matthaius Schlutt's sister and nine or ten year old daughter now?

At first Ed faired a little better. Afraid of being seen robbing little ladies' handbags he first of all chose to ask questions instead. "At the shop on the 'Bear Flat' I went to buy a newspaper where Stella's nanny apparently visited daily. Aside of the fact that the old lady was a regular customer, one assistant suggested she might be 'Hungarian, or something'. I decided to watch her movements using a different ruse, or car each day. At the park there was the same routine with the children, although one of them, I thought, must now have been old enough to attend school. The old lady sat on the same bench everyday as the children ran around, but she only ever called their names out if they strayed too far away. They were always very obedient. One very early morning there was a lucky break. Maybe two hours before Stella usually left the house to go to work, a man emerged and eyed the street both ways before getting into an old Humber Pullman parked further down the street, a black and badly kept car, dented and covered in mud. One tyre was nearly flat. I had to keep my head low as the ailing vehicle trundled past. I waited and watched the car turn left at the bottom of the road and then set off in pursuit. I knew little of the roads outside Bath but they finally came to the village of Peasedown St. John where my suspect finally arrived at a cottage and stopped. Cautiously I drove on past and parked off a small side street and vigilantly waited. In my rear view mirror I watched the road behind. Soon after the Humber passed by I went to ask some questions. At the back of the post office the mail was being sorted, and I asked the postmen the question, who lived at the 'Red Rose' cottage, close to the Wagon and Horses? Busy as they were, they looked up at each other. The older one glanced over his shoulder, and then replied, a bloke by the name of Peter Adcock. They all carried on sorting out the morning mail, and I simply left."

Rob mulled over in his mind what the revelations had brought, and decided to leave his conclusions until after Herbie's take over of 'The Old Green Tree'.

"So what are you going to do with the pub then Herb?" Glen asked the question. Everyone wanted to know the answer about the improvements of the 'Old Green Tree'.

"There's not a lot of room for improvement." Jibed one of his customers, about Bath's smallest pub.

Cheers went up when Judith walked in with her ailing husband. As much as Rob put on a convivial face, deep down he was seriously ill but refused to cease drinking. He forever referred back to the previous war and repeated that 'I was one of the lucky ones'. People always smiled at him wryly.

Herbie's first night in his new pub was at least going to be jovial.

Shortly afterwards the phone rang and Sarah took the call. She spoke briefly and at the same time glanced over to Rob. Barely visible she made a slight indication to Glen and he disappeared out of the door. Rob was watching, and smiled in hope.

Shortly afterwards James, Joy and Stella walked in but against all beliefs, Daniel followed them. With him was Paul Cory and his new woman, Andrea.

Everyone had to stand. There was little room to sit down. Drinks were held close to the chest. Smoke permeated everyone's lungs and clothes, as alcohol spilt down women's dresses and men's corduroys. Conversations were shouted out with no particular themes. The evening moved on and the 'opening night' party went well.

Ed stood back on the pavement. Little light was shed along the street. Glen tried quietly to open the door made from the replica of young Helen Godwin's key. The key was not well worn and awkward but finally he gained entry. Ed followed and pushed the door backwards leaving it slightly ajar. He went upstairs, found, gagged and blindfolded the nanny then tied her to the bed. At first she tried to struggle, but old and weak as she was, soon gave up.

The intrusive pair searched the house quickly to find anything they could to implicate Stella Godwin in the supposed murders. When they left, some items were taken and drawers and cupboards ransacked to make their intrusion seem like a burglary. Unknown to Glen, the nanny was apparently sleeping like a baby.

Ed sped out of the city. In the dark interior of the car Glen wondered what he was up to. "Where are we going for Christ's sake?"

"To a pub where no-one knows us. If we're not there soon they will be closed. I've got something to tell you." He drove recklessly onwards.

The Wagon and Horses were unused to strangers but Ed was in no mood to be intimidated by anyone's attitude. He bought two beers and they sat down out of earshot. Within no time he had drank his and then ordered two more. Glen was mystified by his behaviour and asked what was wrong.

"I think the old woman is dead. I put my hand over her mouth then gagged her and tied her up but she just went limp. At first I thought she had given up in fear, and after searching her bedroom I went and checked to see if she was alright. She was dead. I hadn't done anything else but try to keep her quiet and immobilise her." Ed was shaking his head in disbelief.

Glen peered over his shoulder to see if the other incumbents at the bar might have heard what Ed had just told him. "Did you tell anyone what we were going to do tonight?" he asked him.

"Definitely not." Ed didn't sound convincing but covered his old friend. "If anything is revealed Glen I will tell them I was there on my own. You will never be implicated." He was well into his second pint and Glens' turn came as the bell rang for last orders. He willingly obliged.

Ed tapped his fingers down the outside of his glass deep in thought, not even acknowledging Glen when he sat back down.

"What's the matter? What are you thinking about?" Glen needed to know as their situation had become dire.

He came out of his trance like state. "I found nothing really in her bedroom but on the top of her dresser was what appeared to be an old family photograph in an ornate frame. There were children sitting on the ground in the front or between the legs of the older members who sat on chairs. Behind them were the younger family members from teenagers to middle aged men and women. Two babies, one a girl and the other a boy were held in the arms of a man and woman. Most of the men were wearing beards, even the younger ones and they were all well attired and wore unusual hats." Ed went back into his deep train of thought.

The landlord was easy on the time and Glen bought two more beers to keep Ed's mind lubricated because he knew he would come up with something. When he returned to the table he asked him outright. "So what was the photograph of then? A celebration? A Christening perhaps?"

Ed shook his head slowly. Everything was beginning to add up. He stared at Glen and smiled.

"No. Rob has always been infatuated about the wine. The wine is something which has bugged him for months, probably since we came to help out." He then began nodding his head slowly. "He's no fool Rob. No fool at all."

Glen couldn't agree more. "So what is on your mind? Come on tell me!"

The landlord shouted over and asked if they wanted another beer. He annoyed Glen as he desperately wanted to hear Ed explain his storyline. Ed went to the bar knowing Glen's frustration. Both men now had more than enough beer with which they could contend with in such a short space of time.

"I think it was a harvest festival," he told Glen. Despite the demise of the nanny previously that evening Ed was pleased with himself. His police instincts began to kick in. If the old lady had colluded in the murders she has had her come-uppance he thought.

"What do you mean a bloody harvest festival," Glen asked him irately.

"In the photograph they were sitting in a vineyard. Behind them were vines of black grapes. They were probably celebrating a successful harvest and the whole family were involved. Stella has always drank red wine. Her family are perhaps viticulturists or basically they own a vineyard somewhere."

Glen contemplated the facts whilst struggling to drink the excess beer on the table. The landlord gave them grace and told them not to rush. "Listen to this then Ed. Although I didn't pick it up, I just left it there, but on the sideboard there was an eight inch long paper knife. A vicious weapon in the wrong hands."

"I agree but we've walked ourselves into a corner. We can't tell anyone about the photograph or the knife because they will know we've been in the house. However important those two pieces of evidence are, the old lady is dead and we would get the blame. Anybody could have a paper knife but the photograph is a give away." Ed shrugged and pulled a face. "Another thing is that Stella and the nanny must be related."

"Unless we trust Rob explicitly we'll have to wait until the outcome. 'Old lady found dead in bed after burglary goes wrong'. The story will be all over the papers. We will have to wait and see." Glen seemed to accept her death as one of the trials and tribulations of the job.

Ed drove carefully back to Bath. Nothing was said between them, although the gravity of their actions could well be taken up by forces they knew nothing about. A powerful blame culture existed between various governmental departments and they could quite easily be on the receiving end of something quite sinister. Time would tell.

Ed dropped Glen off and went home himself for a disturbed night's sleep.

After catching a taxi home Daniel and Stella were held up. Shakespeare Avenue was almost cut off and they were dropped off at the bottom of the hill. People were unusually out on the street, the time being two in the morning and as they made their way up through crowd, all the indications were that an incident involved their own home.

A police sergeant confronted them and asked for their identity. They confirmed to him who they were. He told them a neighbour had rang them and warned of some strangers entering their house.

Stella became frantic. "Where are my babies? Where are my babies?" She tried to push past. Daniel held her back.

"Ma'am your children are perfectly safe but I am afraid your grandmother appears to have died of natural causes." He was profound but honest. "There appears to have been a burglary gone wrong."

Daniel was perturbed. "Where are the children?" he asked impatiently.

"In the house sir, but they are still asleep. We felt it better that they remained that way. Another ten minutes and we will have finished our investigations upstairs. Believe me they are perfectly alright." The sergeant could not say anymore until the detectives had done their searches.

Stella cried. Daniel held her close and she kept asking to see Caronwyn and George. She then mentioned one word which Daniel interpreted as grandmother. He was taken aback and couldn't believe she had used the word *'Grosmutter'*. He said nothing else but held her tightly and awaited the outcome of the police investigation.

Two medical men carried the covered body of Stella's nanny out through the door and into the rear of their waiting ambulance. Stella became hysterical and Daniel had to restrain her before she hurt herself.

"Had she been attacked?" Daniel asked.

"No not at all. In fact she may have already been dead before the house was burgled. It's difficult to say. Her bedroom where we found her seems to have been untouched."

A detective came out of the house and introduced himself. "You'll have to let me know what has been taken. We'll have to check your fingerprints with those which we have found but whoever did this crime seemed very professional. They appear as if they were looking for something in particular. Strange. There has been a burglary and a coincidental death." He gave them a telephone number to contact him later that day. "We'll leave a constable on guard here for the rest of the night." He then hastily left.

The next morning when Daniel and Stella left, the house was besieged by reporters. They took the children up to Colerne to stay with their grandmother, then returned to Bath to pay their nanny respects at the morgue.

Afterwards back at home they couldn't think of anything which might have been missing. The police took a statement. When asked who the nanny's next of kin were Stella didn't think she had any. She gave the old woman's full name as Miss Agnes Margaret Hopkinson.

Daniel remained quiet. Something was more than odd. He felt sure she had relations who had been mentioned in the past. He only had himself to blame. He should have asked questions about her long ago, but in all the time she had stayed with them the old woman had remained completely aloof. All along the situation had been very strange. He was unaware his wife was being investigated by some of his closest friends.

The burglary and her untimely death were headline news in the evening paper. The Evening Chronicle stated that 'she was found dead at the scene but no foul play was suspected. There was all the appearance of a coincidence, but the police were making great efforts to locate the intruders'.

"Glen I'll pick you up at six o'clock. I'll have Rob with me and we'll go somewhere where we can talk." Ed was worried. Glen could hear the nervousness in his voice and agreed to be ready when he arrived.

They chose Sandybanks and sat in the corner. Rob sensed there was something wrong. "What's the matter? What has happened?"

Glen let Ed do the talking. "Have you read the front of the evening newspaper?"

Rob nodded at them both. "Yes. Obviously things didn't go as you imagined last night. James rang me, he is not very happy. I managed to calm him down. Fortunately he is still on our side but we have to remember his family is involved one way or the other.

"Listen Rob. Something else is going on. The report says she died of natural causes and her death was just a coincidence but there is no mention that she was bound and gagged. That's how I left her. Why would the police want to hide something like that? Her death is serious enough, let alone hiding the true facts." Ed was agitated because he felt more than sure the police would make every effort to catch the burglars. They would be next to turn up dead in a country lane somewhere.

"Well now the deed is done did you find anything else out while you were there?" Rob asked them.

Glen mentioned the paper knife and Ed told him about the photograph. The evidence more than convinced him she wasn't British, but he also had no real proof that she was of German descent either. Then Ed dropped the bombshell and told him about the bloke he followed from Stella's house to Peasedown. When he mentioned the name Peter Adcock something began to add up. Rob became excited by the news.

"He is the Chief Constable's son. A known communist, raging anti-fascist, and a waster. He does work now, but didn't do for years. His parents kept him, but when they finally booted him out of the family home he had to find an income. Now I'll tell you something else which might interest you now you've mentioned his name. If he is living in Peasedown then it's only a couple of miles from where Bill Williams was found." Rob watched his fellow counterparts.

"So Stella and this Adcock bloke know each other so they must both have leanings towards the communists. There were a lot of German communists before Hitler came to power. Afterwards many fought in the Spanish civil war, men and women. I can't imagine Hitler welcoming those back home." Glen was trying to picture in his mind who a German communist might resemble.

Rob reminded them both. "There are also many British communists."

"What if Adcock's son is involved with these murders. Do you think his father is covering up for his son. Hence the lack of information coming from the crime scenes." Ed was going off on a tangent.

"And does his son know something about his father which needs to be kept quiet." Rob hadn't quite worked out what the intrigue was. "A police chief never normally attends the crime scene initially. He lets his dogs in there first. Unless the whole station knows, to cover him, there must be a crony who arrives at the scene first who keeps everyone at bay and makes the preliminary report. He then allows the forensics in, having covered everyone's tracks. So! If what you say is true about last night, who was the first man from the Bath police force in that building after you left? We need to find out don't we?" Rob began muttering to himself about the vineyard photograph and then asked Ed. "Do you think the old lady was in that particular picture or perhaps Stella or maybe even both of them?"

"Rob we didn't allow ourselves much time and the photograph was quite old. If Stella was one of the babies then the photograph must be nearly thirty years old or more. There were young boys and girls as well so the photograph might not be as old as we think. If we had the frame in hand now we might be able to tell, but I couldn't hazard a guess." Ed was perturbed and rightly so.

Rob changed the subject which surprised both of them. "Jack has been taken off the case. There is no more money in this intrigue for us. No more money funding the investigation. Up the top end their finances are far more importantly spent on what happens after the invasion which we aren't suppose to know about, but Jack did tell me invading the European mainland is pretty imminent. The inquiry here is being left in the local police hands which is worrying, especially after what you have told me this evening. The original investigation began as military and industrial espionage but now only seems to be some form of feud or vendetta, but between who, no-one is quite sure. There is much confidence that the war will not last much longer and the expenditure in our security system will be directed into Europe. I am afraid gentlemen there will be no more brown envelopes coming our way unless the Bath police would prefer our services to their own."

Glen rose wearily to his feet and went to the tiny bar where the buxom barmaid served him more beer. Ed stared out across the valley watching the wood pigeons settling for the evening as the sun had done so behind the hills one hour before. Each took turns to go to the gentlemen's.

After some while Ed spoke first. "I've come too far to let this go. Money or no money. There is a murderer out there and your local police are not doing their business or they could well be the instigators." Glen agreed and went along with him. "I'm carrying on regardless." The two old sleuths had little else to do.

"First of all we have to bring Daniel into the picture and tell him what we think. It is about time he knew. His children will have to be protected, but Stella mustn't know what is happening for now. Leave him with me and I'll let you know. Ed! Keep trying to find out information on the Adcock's and who is the main detective the Chief uses on these cases. Glen, there is a strange name which comes to mind about communists infiltrating and trying to upset our British labour force. Go and see my father because he will remember. I am sure the man was a German but I cannot fully picture his name in my head. The name began with 'K'. He pondered over the name but couldn't think clearly. We'll let the furore of last night die down and I'll arrange to meet Daniel but I'll have his father with me at the same time. We're going to have to make Daniel see sense over this."

"Three days later Rob met James and his son in the Old Green Tree at opening time when there few people around. James had warned Daniel of what he was about to hear and asked him to stay calm. Rob explained everything he knew to date, his suspicions about the murders, and doubts as well.

"Did you ever suspect Stella might be German by birth?" Rob's first question seemed to shock Daniel.

"The first time was the night of the burglary when she cried out 'grosmutter' which is grandmother in German. I know she's partial to red German wine but I thought that was just a personal choice," he sat back and shrugged his shoulders. "Don't forget since the war began I have hardly been here."

James asked him about the wine. "Where does she keep acquiring the stuff from? That's what we want to know."

"You can buy that wine in the Empire bars. Or you could the last time I was there." Daniel was becoming annoyed. He was being made to look a fool.

"Maybe, but you wouldn't buy the wine at retail price and stock your shelf, you would at least purchase the product at wholesale or cost price. In either case who is selling them the wine anyway? Europe has been under siege since nineteen thirty nine. Besides that, why is German red wine still available?" James had his business head on.

Angrily, Daniel answered. "Have you thought about asking the owners of the Empire bar?"

Rob interrupted them and changed the subject slightly. "You are right. Maybe we should ask them. About the photograph at the vineyard, you say you have never ever seen the picture frame."

"Never. I had never been in her room. I had no reasons to go in there and I was certainly not invited to go there. That was the nanny's domain." Daniel was even more angry.

Rob calmly asked him. "Can you do something for me please. I know Stella is your wife but she could easily be in a lot of trouble. Find the photograph because we need to take a look for ourselves. Also if you have a photograph of Stella when she was a bit younger then I'd like to borrow that as well, just for a day."

Daniel stared strangely at Rob and then turned his attention to his father. "Don't you have a set of wedding photographs?"

"Yes. Yes of course we do but they are kept out of the way. They remind us too much of your brother. I'll look one out Rob. Leave that with me." James turned his head away and pursed his lips. His guilt from that fateful day would never leave his already tormented mind.

"Go back to your school years Daniel. Did anyone ever mention someone named Peter Adcock?" Rob didn't expect him to know as the man in question attended King Edward's some ten years before him.

Daniel hesitated. "I've heard of the name but can't say I actually know him. Why do you ask?"

"Your German teacher, Mr Hayman, did he influence you to join the army and fight against the rise of Nazism and national socialism? Apparently he certainly put the seeds of communism into Peter Adcock's head, and your close allegiance with Mr. Hayman points in the same direction."

Daniel smiled ironically. "Rob if you think I have anything to do with these murders then you are mistaken. I actually enjoyed modern history at school which taught me to listen to everyone's opinions and formulate my own personal views. I joined the army because there was a great chance to see much of the world as a young man, and then one day settle down in life. This conflict was another entity. As the old adage states 'war is a wonderful experience, providing you survive'. Your own involvements have taught you both respect and humility. Now listen to mine. To me, Stella has never shown any signs of being associated to any political persuasion. I agree how we came together was untoward but that is now in the past. There are two children to worry about. If this chap Adcock has been influenced by Mr. Hayman then so be it. Hayman came across to me as being highly political as a communist but not a Stalinist, more so a Trotskyist. Trotsky hated Stalin and has since been assassinated in Mexico. Hitler is another psychopath, but on the far right, and has to be eliminated. Either side in control, extreme left or right, are both as bad as each other. Two days after the nanny's funeral I have to return to my brigade. I will do anything you ask, but believe me don't make any mistakes because you'll suffer my wrath. If Stella is involved then I have been a fool but there must be a deeper reason which you haven't even touched upon, but politics are definitely out of the question." As he stood abruptly to leave he banged his glass down on the table. "I'll tell you what! I will keep my mouth shut. You carry on with your dirty investigations. I'm going back to Down Ampney after the nanny's funeral and carrying on with the war." He turned to leave, highly irate.

He was thwarted at the door. "A little selfish I would say coming from a so-called warrior. When the pressures up get away from the cooker. Is that the answer?" Sarah asked him. She had been listening.

"What's that supposed to mean?" Daniel asked with his hand on the door handle.

"Your wife is in danger and you are not helping. I want you to stay calm and think. First of all your children are important. Nobody knows what is causing this strife, but whatever the problem is, the situation needs to be resolved. The children are in the firing line. Someone is going to shoot back. Whoever killed those men have done so for a reason, although none of us believe there were sexual gains involved. Politically motivated perhaps, but many things point towards Stella. Married twice to soldiers, and promiscuous. She is a temptress, not a whore, a mere temptress. Peter Adcock was seen leaving your house recently, although I have to say, your sister Helen was staying there that evening. There could be other associates, but so far the connections do not add up. With our help, Rob is still working on them. Daniel your war might be in Europe, but you also have one on your doorstep. Say nothing please when you go home, but try and find out what might be happening without upsetting the apple cart at the moment."

As he went to leave Rob warned him. "At the funeral you might see Ed and Glen floating around outside the gates, possibly disguised. Please! Whatever you do don't acknowledge them or point Stella in their direction. I'm expecting a stranger to turn up.

Chapter 55
The Road to Arnhem

Paul Cory's platoon were called back to rejoin their brigade days after the invasion of the French mainland, their job was complete. Jealously they had assisted the Sixth Airborne Division to participate in the invasion of France. The previous weeks' build up at Blakehill and Down Ampney were frenetic. Training flights in the Douglas Dakota's had been trebled. Everyone had to know their assignment so as to make the task in hand operate as smoothly as possible, hence avoiding excessive loss of life. As described what would happen by Flight Sergeant Morrison in earlier days, the 'flying nightingales' worked tirelessly as planned tending horribly injured young men who passed through the doors of the Medical Centre. They came in dribs and drabs at first, but when the allies established themselves on captured airfields more and more returned by air. Many tears were quietly shed over cups of tea in the back rooms by the medical ground staff before returning to the wards to nurse the unfortunate young soldiers. The worst victims were ferried straight to Wroughton, the unlucky ones to the mortuaries. The efforts of the nurses, doctors and ambulance men were barely recognised as the papers and journals concentrated on the battle front opening up in Normandy. The screams of pain and agony of the wounded soldiers in the hospital wards back at home were hidden from the general public by the media, but the progress of the assault on the French mainland by the allied forces was highlighted day by day.

Having been kept in reserve, the 1st. Parachute Brigade along with their parent, the 1st. Airborne Division were disappointed not to have been included in the initial landings. Fit and healthy as they were, everyone wanted to be part of the action. Paul Cory's platoon were no different and seventeen times they trained for special assignments which were aborted at the last minute. Such was the allied progress on the ground there seemed little need for airborne troops and frustration often crept into the young men's minds. The division was given the dubious nickname, the '1st. Stillbornes'.

The summer began to fade towards the autumn and the brigades of the 1st Airborne took turns to practise their drops from the airfields around the eastern Cotswolds. The engine noise from the workhorse Dakota's was perpetual, but the local population knew only too well the importance of what was happening in Europe. Unhitched Horsa gliders were often seen floating through the air delivering troops, vehicles and guns to designated spots in preparation for another undisclosed assault. They had been successfully used in Sicily, on D-Day and in southern France during the Anvil landings.

The atmosphere around the towns of Fairford and Cricklade was one of great expectations, nervousness and constrained jubilation as the great German war machine, the 'Wehrmacht', began to slowly disintegrate.

In early September the 1st. Airborne Division began mustering in and around RAF Blakehill. Paul and Daniel worked their platoon everyday if only to keep their minds off an approaching battle. They soon learned of their target and drop zones. Each brigade commander summoned his battalion officers and lay a picture before them emphasising the pitfalls of such a dangerous operation. Some had doubts of the strategy to drop so many men behind enemy lines in view of the rapidity of the allied advance, but were silenced by talk and hope of the European war being over by Christmas, should they succeed.

A charismatic Irishman had joined Paul's platoon who happened to be a semi-professional footballer. Corporal Gerry Kelly always smiled but deep down he was a very serious soldier. He understood the need to produce the best from any man was for that individual to have a healthy diet, and maintain his body in the finest condition as possible. In the early evenings he arranged six-a-side football tournaments to keep the lad's minds occupied. In the pub later on he would recite stories of the matches he had played on the municipal parks around his native town of Liverpool. Although Daniel wasn't particularly keen on Gerry's preferred sport, they had become good friends.

"Gerry. I'm sorry but no more football from now on. We cannot afford any stupid injuries. We're going in this weekend, alright." Daniel stared at him sympathetically.

"Where are we going exactly?" he asked with interest.

"So I'm told, we're off to central Holland," he reflected on the information he had received, "in behind enemy lines."

Gerry smiled. "Good! I'll arrange a match with the Dutch boys when we get there."

"We have to beat the Germans first before we reach the final." Daniel countered. They both laughed aloud.

"Can you tell the lads to write their letters home in the next forty eight hours. Tonight is the last night down the pub so tell them to enjoy themselves while they can, which means no fighting. I want to inspect them at six o'clock prompt tomorrow morning." Now was Daniel's turn to smile. He would soon find out how his platoon fared from their last night out before their own D-Day.

Paul dated Andrea that evening at the Old Spotted Cow. Their friendship was purely mutual. Any intimate question he asked her and she would politely remind him to wait until the war was over. As they parted that night on the aerodrome she told him not to return from Europe to England through the medical centre doors. Walking back to the dormitory she brushed away tears from her face. Paul had watched her disappear into the night, then turned and left. He had a job to do and he wanted to perform well for his men.

Daniel wrote several letters. Above them all was to his wife and children. As far as he was concerned Stella was a good mother and lover. Whatever she was involved in, he was none the wiser and opted to keep it that way.

More importantly there was a war on and his participation couldn't have come sooner. He laid down his pen at midnight, licked and folded the envelopes methodically, and stuck on his last remaining postage stamps. He rubbed over the portrait of the man on whose behalf he would soon be fighting, King George VI. His final letter was addressed to his good friend Mark Campbell but sent to his parent's home in Bristol. The only inclination he had of Mark's whereabouts was that the King's African Rifles were operating in Burma. He went to bed in anticipation of an early roll call.

The Army Postal Service arrived on Thursday afternoon. They delivered the last letters prior to the airborne assault in Holland. Many of the soldiers would take these precious last words with them in their breast pockets. Some, sadly, received nothing at all, and looked on forlornly as their fellow soldiers read their own messages, perhaps their last.

Daniel was standing near Gerry Kelly as one letter was handed to him. The hand writing was Stella's. He opened the white envelope. The letter was brief and took him seconds to read. He muttered some indiscernible words and walked away, screwing the paper in his hand. Shaking his head he walked across towards the perimeter fence stopped and read the letter again. He placed both of his hands on the top his head in disbelief still shaking his head.

Gerry caught up with him knowing something was seriously wrong. "Sarge! What's the matter? Are you alright Sarge?"

Daniel flattened the letter out and put it in his pocket. "Nothing. It doesn't matter. Please! Just leave me alone." 'Just leave me alone' was all he kept saying.

Daniel hardly spoke to anyone personally in the next two days, except for operational purposes. Paul tried to coax out of him who the letter was from and what was the actual implications of the message. He refused to say anything and asked him politely to mind his own business. Whatever was in the message conveyed to him had changed Daniel drastically. Paul even considered preventing him from participating in the operation but his better judgement and dependence on one of his best men persuaded him to put the thought to one side.

Sunday morning 17th. September 1944 at Blakehill and many other aerodromes throughout England, the roar of the Dakota's engines began their routine warm up. The 1st Airborne Division began their immense foray into Nazi occupied Holland.

Each aeroplane was laden with either nervous soldiers or a variety of vehicles, guns and mortars. Others towed the Horsa's piloted by the army's Glider Pilot Regiment and had equal adaptability to carry troops or logistic supplies. They would be unhitched approximately one mile from the drop zones to be left alone, totally dependent on the skill and bravery of their pilots to fly them, powerless, to the designated drop zones.

Before take off Lieutenant Cory had explained to his platoon the task set before them. They were a part of the 1st. Battalion and as soon as the landing was made they were to hold a brief reconnoitre and then follow the railway line, the 'Leopard' route', into the town of Arnhem and capture the bridge which crossed the lower Rhine. They were to maintain their position for as long as possible before they could be relieved by XXX Corps attacking by land from the south. He warned them of the dangers of the two hour flight and wished them the very best of luck.

His platoon were divided onto two aircraft, himself on one and Daniel the other. Corporal Kelly went with Daniel as Paul was still concerned about his mental state, and was unsure how he would react. The last thing Paul wanted was a carefree suicidal sergeant in charge of a squad of well thought of young soldiers. Fortunately Gerry Kelly had a sobering influence on Daniel.

During the flight any conversation was impossible to hold although, fraught with nervous energy, few had anything to say. Daniel sat motionless deep in thought. Their time to leave the Horsa came and they hitched themselves up in readiness to jump. The door was opened by the crew who would usher them out as soon as they received the signal from the cockpit. They didn't have to wait long and soon they were floating over the flat monotonous Dutch countryside, with their hearts palpitating off the normal scale.

Each man had to concentrate fully on landing as they carried heavy packs and broken legs were not uncommon, even in training. By two o'clock in the afternoon the first phase of 'Operation Market Garden' was complete. Inevitably there had been mishaps and mistakes.

Except the injured everyone had found their muster points. The 1st. Airlanding Brigade had been designated to secure the drop zones in readiness for the second airlift on Monday. The Ist., 2nd. and 3rd. battalions of the Parachute Brigade prepared themselves for the march into Arnhem.

Daniel seemed much happier pre-occupying himself with checking each individual in the platoon. So far the training had paid off as they had no injuries amongst them. At three o'clock Major-General Urquhart, pleased so far how the operation had begun, gave the order to proceed into the town.

There had previously been questions about the distance of the drop zones from the bridge itself but intelligence reports suggested the German army were actually weak in the area. The first serious problem they encountered was not the Germans themselves but their own hand held radio sets which were practically useless, rendering impossible contact between the battalions and Urquhart's makeshift headquarters.

They were running a half an hour late as they had experienced problems unloading the jeeps from the Horsa's, and unknown to the Brigade, this gave the German's time to form a blocking formation.

Soon this was apparent, the 3rd. Battalion had encountered heavy resistance as the sound of gunfire became incessant from the direction of their forward position. The 1st. Battalion under Lieutenant-Colonel Dobie were given a change of orders and told to take the higher ground north of Arnhem. He considered that due to increased resistance they were encountering they would never reach their newly designated position, and decided to press on towards the bridge to assist Lieutenant-Colonel Frost's 2nd. Battalion who were fighting their way through the town.

Progress was slow and they continued on through the night sometimes pushing their vehicles so as not to attract attention. They intermittently met resistance and the battalion gradually fragmented due to small skirmishes in the side streets. They began to lose men, not only killed or injured but lost in the dark. Many died by unknowingly walking up to isolated machine gun fire or the odd sniper with excellent night scopes. The pockets of lost men were easily captured. In the morning only half the battalion were accounted for. Daniel had ten men alongside him, including Gerry Kelly, and his party were one of the misplaced.

As a part of 'T' Company they had initially made good progress but now, as the sun began to rise, Daniel could see they were definitely separated. He believed he was ahead of the rest of his battalion. What appeared to be the railway station loomed in front which made him decide to take its general direction and make the building their objective. If they could seize the station, and hold the building for any length of time, the rest of the battalion might be able to catch up.

He and his men crept forward. A German motorcyclist and side car with an occupant swept from a side street in front of them and their lives were swiftly ended with bursts of machine gun fire. Unbeknown to Daniel, the 2nd. Battalion had already passed through and were holding the far side of the bridge but were now almost cut off by the German army advancing southward. They would be cut off themselves if help did not arrive.

Daniel's men jumped a fence and followed the track at the rear of some houses and industrial buildings. The platforms at the rear of the station were deserted on both sides of the track. He told his men to stay low, and he alone went to investigate.

Most of the windows were shattered and he could hear voices. Two Germans were holding about five or six British soldiers prisoners probably awaiting transport to take them away. He beckoned Gerry Kelly over but signalled to the others to stay where they were.

He whispered. "I'll call them out by pretending to have been injured. One will almost certainly come to the door. There are five or six of our men in there. You have one burst to kill the other Kraut outright. Don't shoot until I do." He raised his eyebrows. Gerry agreed.

Daniel stood back from the door out of sight near the edge of the platform and shouted out to the German soldiers. Not expecting to hear one of their own speaking, an inquisitive soldier peered out of the window. Two short bursts and the attack went according to plan, much to the relief of the captured boys inside.

Gerry signalled for his platoon to join them. Daniel's plan was to hold the station until the rest of his battalion arrived and then rejoin the overall attack but the rescued Lieutenant tried to outrank him. The Lieutenant, knowing the battle situation between the station and the bridge believed they would be better to pull back and rejoin the oncoming battalions.

"No way! We fought our way this far and we're not going to fight our way backwards only to try and take this place again. My lads are gunned up, have two Browning machine guns and now two German guns in our possession. We also have a number of grenades left and a part time sniper. There are now fifteen of us including yourselves, and if you don't want to stay then piss off, but don't relieve us of our weapons." He showed him the back door. Everything went very quiet inside the station. "You have a better chance of staying alive here than trying to make it back down that street I can assure you." He turned to Gerry. "Corporal, set up a defence, front and back please. I don't think the Lieutenant's going anywhere right now."

"Sir! Sir! They're across the concourse hiding up the backstreet."

"Keep down out of sight. They must have heard our gun fire. Gerry! can you see them?!"

"Yes Sarge. There are quite a few of them."

Daniel turned to his sniper boy. "Now's your chance Patrick. Find yourself a safe spot and keep them pinned down." He turned back to the Lieutenant. "I'm afraid we are all in the same boat here sir and will just have to defend our position until help arrives." He took his pack off and stooped down to find a small Union Jack which he handed to him. Can you ask one of your chaps to hang this flag up somewhere quickly so that we don't get blown to smithereens by our own men?" Daniel asked the lieutenant sarcastically.

Shortly afterwards a gunshot was heard from close range and Patrick Donaghue had injured one of the enemy. Cheers resonated from the building.

An Oberleutnant from a small section of Battalion Krafft reviewed the situation. He desperately needed to retake the station along with the concourse in front and made a woeful decision to attack, assuming there were only five men inside. He ordered a full scale machine gun attack. They then attempted to charge across the concourse with the intent of delivering grenades through the front of the building but were mercilessly mown down by the defenders. The game of 'cat and mouse' went on for some while.

"Sir we think there are Brits holed up in the railway station. We can see dead Germans lying around but our flag is flying from the building." The reconnaissance man watched the man in charge solemnly. Both men seemed to realise the situation was becoming more dire by the hour.

Lieutenant-Colonel Dobie assessed the situation. The Germans were now coming in from all sides and he didn't want to become trapped and cut off from behind. He still only had sporadic radio contact which was now made worse by the buildings along the Utrechtsche Weg. He needed to neutralise the area between the Amsterdamseweg and Onderlang which ran alongside the river.

Having little choice if they were to progress he ordered the attack. The battalion pressed forward assuming their men were under siege. Street by street they took out the defenders and the assault from the station greatly helped their cause as the Germans were pinned down on the other side. After an hour of intense fighting the German 'Battalion Krafft' eventually withdrew and Dobie's men had progressed further than they had all morning.

Daniel's men suffered only a few cuts from flying glass. His sniper had taken two lives and injured some others but the battle of Arnhem railway station was over for the time being. His temporarily attached 1st. Battalion members thanked him and went to find new orders. Paul Cory was still missing with perhaps five or six others from the platoon. Dobie left Daniel in charge of his own men and any stragglers who wished to join, ordering him to take a break.

The battle for Arnhem Bridge was far from over.

Other operational disasters had occurred. The second drop had run into trouble and tons of supplies fell directly into German hands. One Dakota full of paratroopers landed almost on top of a machine gun nest. 4th Parachute Brigade effectively dropped onto a battlefield believing all the drop zones were safe and secure, which was far from the case. Several men died and many were wounded, including Brigadier John Hackett, after being strafed by the unexpected arrival of Messchersmitts.

The 2nd Battalion under Lieutenant Colonel John Frost were now completely cut off at the north end of the bridge and were taking refuge in the surrounding buildings.

With little rest Daniel took his men and rejoined his Battalion. Dobie tried a different route through to give at least some relief to Frost's men but were driven back. They were joined by the remnants of the 3rd. Battalion in retreat who agreed to protect their rear in another attempt of a breakthrough during the night by following the river bank, but that was also all in vain. At first light there were only about forty fighting men left and Dobie, realising the futility of the attack, ordered the rest to take refuge in the neighbouring buildings and houses or to retreat back to Oosterbeek. Most of his men had actually been captured or wounded. Soon afterwards Dobie himself was both, wounded and captured.

The 3rd. Battalion had suffered just as badly. After attempting to break through, their commanding officer Lieutenant-Colonel Fitch ordered a withdrawal, an action during which he was killed by a mortar bomb.

All manner of attempts were made to advance by different groups but Urquhart realised Frost would have to remain alone with his brave men until XXX Corp arrived from the south.

Of Daniel's ten men at the Station only seven remained fully fit. Two were injured of whom which only one could walk. Gerry Kelly had a bullet wound in the thigh which bled profusely. One had died instantly from a bullet to the head, an act from a German sniper. Daniel decided to try and retreat back to Oosterbeek. They followed the railway line for a while but then took the road. Rumours emanated from Oosterbeek that the British forces were trying to create a defensive perimeter down to the river bank and await rescue. What they saw as they began their way back was alarming. Bodies were lying everywhere. Mostly British.

"Come on!" Daniel tried to hurry them knowing they were exhausted. "If we stay alive until nightfall and the Krauts haven't caught us then we have a chance." They had little choice but to keep moving, even though what really lay in store for them was absolute uncertainty.

Eventually he chose to rest for an hour until darkness fell by which time their group had grown in number. Some were members of their own Brigade, and some South Staffordshire's. They were tired, hungry and completely despondent, many had some sort of wound. Back up on their feet Daniel urged them all on. Gerry needed carrying and he passed on his gun and Daniel took him on his back. He could feel him slowly losing consciousness through loss of blood and stopped to apply the tightest tourniquet he could above the wound. The others had carried on except his other two fit men, both determined not to leave them behind. They watched for any enemy action at their rear.

Mortars began to rain down in the dark but they simply took their chances and carried on to get out of their range. One exploded nearby and a metal shard sliced into Patrick's neck. He screamed and dropped like a stone. Jimmy Anderson went to see and then came running back to Daniel. "He's dead sir. Little Patrick's dead."

"Come on keep going! There's nothing we can do." Soon they walked out of mortar range. 'Thankfully', Daniel said to himself, 'some other poor bastards are holding up the Krauts'.

Tears cascaded down Daniel's face as he staggered the last mile back into Oosterbeek . 'Why them and not me' he kept asking himself. 'Each man or lad he knew so well but how many were left. Little Patrick the sharpshooter was now dead, where was Paul Cory, Gerry was probably by now a corpse on his back taking a free ride to the morgue. Everyone from the platoon had gone except, strangely enough, young Jimmy Anderson. Maybe he wasn't accident prone after all'. Daniel, with his mind in turmoil, staggered on to apparent safety.

He heard shouts, and lights were directed his way. Two men ran towards him with a stretcher and carefully lifted Gerry off his aching back. The battle was now in the background. He lay on the grass and every muscle ached, every nerve twanged but every thought screwed his mind up even more. 'Who had planned this ludicrous attack', was what he wanted to know.

Lance Corporal Anderson helped him up off the floor. "Sarge, someone is here who wants to speak to you."

Tired and sharp tongued he asked. "Who! for fuck's sake?" Suddenly he calmed down. "Sorry Jimmy I'm not getting at you." Daniel apologised to his young subordinate.

"Sergeant, come with me over to the Hartenstein Hotel. It is the 1st. Airborne Division Headqurters. Have a good clean up and meet me in the foyer as soon as possible. We need to debrief you." Brigadier Hicks spoke as if he was at a 'ball' with his wife, not in the middle of a major battle, but realised only too well how tempers frayed when men had been in the thick of the fighting.

"What about my men?" Daniel asked, "they come first!"

"Sergeant, the Brigade has taken rather a pounding but the chaps we have here will be well cared for in the circumstances. Please follow me." He remained quite calm.

Reluctantly Daniel obeyed his senior commander and followed.

"Can you tell us anything about the front line in the town. I know there is a complete communication breakdown but those mistakes were not made here, they were made at home, back in 'Blighty'. We need to hear from any sensible soldier who has been up at the front." He waited calmly for Daniel to evaluate what he had been through.

There were many things Daniel didn't know about the strategy. He told Hicks as he had seen the action. First of all he explained how they had reached the railway station and then held off the Germans until the rest of the 1st. Battalion arrived and how they rejoined the fighting.

Then the retreat and the apparent death of Fitch and capture of Dobie, or so he had heard. He explained the trek back to Oosterbeek with the rest of the stragglers.

Hicks supported his chin by clasping his hands together with his elbows on the shining hotel table. He showed no emotion.

"Basically sir, as I see the situation now, this operation was a disaster waiting to happen but I am talking in hindsight. I cannot imagine what else has gone wrong. The best thing General Urquhart can do to prevent any further unnecessary loss of life on both sides, mainly ours and the allies, is to withdraw back here to Oosterbeek and form a citadel and hope someone comes to our rescue. Most of my brigade, I think, are dead, wounded or captured. 2nd Battalion are probably surrounded but you probably wouldn't tell me if they were. The South Staff's are trying to retreat and the General is still trying to think of ways around by sending in more troops. I wouldn't mind betting the whole of the 1st Airborne Division are completely surrounded and cut off from all of our allies in the south. What was the idea? Jump in behind what was one of the best armies in the world and hope to put an immediate stop to Hitler's shenanigans. No chance! Never confront a wounded tiger with just a knife. I can guarantee you that most of the German people want this war put to rest, but its despot rulers are determined to see the conflict through to the bitter end. If any individual challenges the ruling party even now they are assassinated as traitors. *Fear* sir!" Daniel emphasised the word fear. "They are controlled by fear! If you think the Nazis are overwhelming then wait to you see what comes from the communists in the east. This ridiculous exercise has been designed as a propaganda stunt to raise the hearts of the British and its European allies at a tremendous cost of lives, our lives! This defeat will now undoubtedly put the race to Berlin on hold on the Western front. Unless something happens in the next two days in our favour, this simple exercise, planned miles away in London, will be a complete failure. Unfortunately for many of those brave men who fought down those streets of Arnhem, their voices will never be heard again. For their parents, wives, children or girlfriends they will be just distant memories, slaughtered in the name of impetuosity." Daniel went quiet and then looked up. "May I go now sir?" he asked.

"I could arrest you for insubordination do you know that?" Hicks hadn't actually tired of Daniel, and actually found him quite interesting.

"Tie me up sir. Another soldier lost. When I'm up against the wall please make sure you are watching and take a look at the men's faces who are firing the bullets. You can summons me for insubordination but I cannot summons you for incompetence." He challenged the Brigadier.

"Why are you so bitter?" he asked Daniel.

Daniel glanced at the Brigadier's lapels. "I'm not, but after the war people of your rank will disappear back into a social world none of my men will ever be able to enter, although many will have given up their lives to protect. You will return to your large rural houses with gardens tended by the very men, the lucky survivors, you sent onto the battlefield, paying them a pittance to survive. I cannot deny you are on the battlefield now, but so far you are not consistently facing the bullets and mortars. I appreciate the best intellectuals must be in charge but this particular operation hasn't been thought out correctly at all, probably from England. Now I feel it is too late. Let us start pulling our boys back out of harm's way." He stood up and made a lackadaisical salute and turned to go.

"Sergeant Godwin I haven't finished with you yet! Sit back down!"

Daniel turned on him and in German diatribe ranted at the Brigadier whilst pointing his finger into his face. Two guards came in swiftly and held him. The Brigadier was shocked. "What was that you said?"

Daniel shook his head from side to side. "You are not listening. What I said was 'In the next two or three days, or maybe a week, you are going to need me to go out there and talk peace, or for want of better words, 'fucking surrender'. One fact is I am not going back to England. Here is where I might die and so I had just as well stay here and fight to the bitter end'."

The Brigadier relented. What Daniel had said was basically true. The cause was lost and a retreat inevitable. He asked him quietly. "Sergeant Godwin, find somewhere to set up an independent headquarters for the remainder of your brigade and try to ascertain whose left. If you know of any definite deaths or prisoners of war then list them and let me know. I will have an officer in charge as soon as possible." The Brigadier stood up and ordered his guards to take him away and make sure he was fed and made comfortable for the time being. He sat back down wondering what kind of man he had been up against. Most of everything Sergeant Daniel Godwin had said was true but what would Urquhart think of his opinions or, indeed, what action would he take.

"Come on it is time to go now" The Dutchman was apprehensive as he spoke to Paul Cory in faltering English.

With their boots heavily wrapped in rags Paul and two others, who were all that remained of his part of the platoon, set off along Beekstraat in the dark. The Dutchman was to lead them out of the town to an open area between Arnhem and Oosterbeek. From there onwards they would be on their own but there was a good chance they would make the short journey back and rejoin other British forces in the area.

At the first corner they stopped, weighed up the situation and then turned into Broerenstraat. They walked briskly. Behind them, back towards the station, there was a lot of activity. Gunfire and shelling could be heard all over the town as the 1st. Airborne troops slowly fought whilst retreating in the hope of returning to Oosterbeek safely. Jaap van Reimer specifically told them to avoid the Utrectsche Weg as the street was continually being bombed. He would lead them down to the river where they could follow the footpath easily and make their way back and rejoin their own troops.

The guns they carried were devoid of ammunition so there was no possibility of defending themselves. The choice was stark if they happened to be confronted by the enemy, surrender or die. After twenty minutes they were on the Rijnkade and here their Dutch saviour shook hands with them and pointed them in the right direction. He then disappeared back into the dark of the night.

The river's edge was soft and they removed the rags from their boots and began the hike back to apparent safety.

Disinterested in having something to eat Daniel asked where the wounded were taken and was told they were in the basement below the 'Hartenstein'. Before he set off to find Gerry he asked Jimmy Anderson to try and find any remnants of the 1st. Battalion, and afterwards report back to the hotel.

"How do I get downstairs?" Daniel asked a member of the staff.

"Go around the back of the building and you'll see some stone steps leading down to an oak door. I'm not sure they'll let you in though, it's terribly crowded down there. Not only that, the smell is bloody awful." Daniel shrugged his shoulders and walked away.

The door was wedged open and when he entered, the reason why he might not be allowed in was apparent. As he had been warned the air was fetid from drying blood and festering flesh wounds. He put his hand over his nose and mouth.

"You will get used to the smell after a while. Who are you are looking for?" The nurse who spoke to him was not English but her command of the language qualified her enough to work with the British wounded. She also understood most medical terms.

He politely removed his hand from his mouth and smiled at her meekly. "I am sorry I should not be so disrespectful. I'm looking for Corporal Gerald Kelly. He is with the 1st Parachute Brigade."

"Wait here I will fetch the patients' list." She turned and went away. Daniel watched her as she walked, 'attractive, slight in build, and intelligent'.

The dimly lit basement was completely full of injured men lying almost shoulder to shoulder. They were eerily quiet, too proud to cry out in pain, or full of morphine. None knew what their fate would be trapped so far behind enemy lines with no possible chance of an airlift back to safety. Some were too ill to care. Two medics were attending one particularly badly injured man who appeared to have had both legs amputated whose life was on the line. Others had similar injuries but not quite so bad. The horrific facial injuries reminded Daniel of Robbie Goode and how the medical facilities should have advanced so much in thirty years. The planners of this campaign never envisaged that the ten thousand or so men of the 1st Airborne would be completely cut off from the allied forces in western Europe. Daniel, deep down, seethed once more. The battle for Arnhem Bridge was proving to be a chaotic disaster and was still far from over.

"Sir. Sir!" The nurse aroused him from his mental judgements. "He is probably upstairs if he has not regained consciousness or I am afraid there might be worse news. I have to go up there myself. I will show you the way."

She led him off up the steps. He was deluding himself. "That is an awful place, that cellar."

"Maybe you should stay away from there for you own sake. We have too many problems here now, and are running out of everything. There is no blood and very little treatments for infections. We now only keep the morphine for the worst cases. The last supplies fell into the hands of the Germans and there are very few dressings and bandages left. There is also the fear of the water supply being cut off by all the bombing." She told him to wait and went to find who he was inquiring after. Shortly the nurse came back and asked him to follow her.

Gerry was laid out on some tables still unconscious. A medical officer came quickly to explain his condition. "The wound would not be a problem but he has contracted an infection. He has lost a lot of blood, of a type we no longer have. We'll clean his wound as often as possible but I'm afraid you will have to wait and see whether he improves or not. That's all I can say at the moment. You'll have to excuse me but I'm rather busy at the moment. Karina can you come with me please?" he asked the nurse politely.

Daniel now at least knew the name of the young nurse.

Sympathetically Karina looked at him with doleful eyes. "I am sorry about your friend but I will try to keep an eye on him," she said apologetically, and followed the medical officer out through the door.

Daniel stared down at his corporal lying prostrate on the table. He whispered in Gerry's ear,"come on Gerry! you didn't come all this way to die of a fucking infection! Only you can get yourself out of the situation." His tears welled up once more and he turned away and went off to find Jimmy and try and contact any others of his Brigade who might still be alive.

Daniel hung around the headquarters for some time in the hope Jimmy Anderson would return. His impatience had the better of him and he went off to commandeer a suitable establishment in which to evoke some pride back into his men. Daniel thought hard about where his headquarters should be and configured that most retreating soldiers would attempt to return close to the river at the south east of the small Dutch village. More importantly if there was to be a rescue that could only come from across the Rijn where there would be an easy access. He came across a road called Benedendorpsweg which he found hard to pronounce, and followed it in the direction of Arnhem. Here he found a disused church. 'Not necessarily disused', he thought, 'but temporarily evacuated perhaps'. Besides, who now believed in God'.

Outside a few graves existed but none were recent. The doors were locked but he had found what he wanted and headed back to the Hartenstein Hotel.

Jimmy was waiting for him and he apologised. "Did you find anyone?" he asked.

"Not many sir, but everyone are digging in to defend the village." Jimmy wasn't sure himself of what was actually happening.

"Go and find something with which we can blow open some solid oak doors and be back here as soon as possible." Jimmy ran off.

Back at the hotel there was no change with Gerry and he went to find Karina. He was straight to the point with her." I need a nurse. Probably from tomorrow onwards. Can you help?"

"I just cannot leave these men, they need someone with them all the time." She wanted to help but was committed to the Hotel.

"Karina you have too many injured men here now. I have found a place near the river which could well be an excellent evacuation point for the wounded. We can create a second temporary hospital which will alleviate the pressure off this place. It is only sensible. Please! do not hesitate. Say yes for me! Please!" Daniel desperately pleaded with her.

The poor girl looked around and viewed the dire situation where they were. Too many injured in such a small space. "Tell me where. I will speak to the chief medical officer and if he agrees then I will arrange to meet you there tomorrow."

Daniel smacked a large kiss on her forehead. "Thank you!" He left almost immediately, a changed man. He now had hope he could begin evacuating the wounded.

He went to find Brigadier Hick.

Karina was moved by his care of his comrades and she couldn't forget the kiss he had given her.

"Come in!" The Brigadier was doing nothing in particular because of the circumstances.

Daniel told him of his plans to take over the church and create the south eastern perimeter fence close to its vicinity and down to the Rhine. The church would be the headquarters for the remnants of his brigade and they would be able to hospitalise some of the wounded thus alleviating the congestion away from the hotel. Daniel waited for his response as the Brigadier gazed at a map on the wall.

"What makes you think we are going to set up a stronghold Sergeant?" he asked first of all.

"We are running out of supplies sir. We are running out of men sir. The ratio of injured men against men left to fight tells me we cannot win, and the list of injured men is growing by the hour. We have to retract, stop expending our resources and dig in until someone comes to our rescue. If we don't, then we will be overrun entirely. Dead, or prisoners of war."

Daniel didn't know his plan was already in action. General Urquhart had realised the mission intended, the taking of the bridge at Arnhem, was untenable and his officers were already drawing up plans to save as much of the division as possible. None would ever admit to a mere Sergeant in his mid-twenties that he was absolutely right.

"Sergeant Godwin, carry on. Damned good idea! Any extra chaps you might need let me know but you obviously realise fit soldiers are hard to come by. Sadly, at the moment, we have returned to the days of trench digging but only to create our first line of defence."

Hick had conceded they had to build a solid perimeter defence as soon as possible.

Daniel and Jimmy went back down to the church and blew open the doors with some explosives, and found a temporary home and hospital for the time being.

There was little peace in the church that night as mortar shells began to achieve their range within the supposed British enclave of Oosterbeek. Fortunately for them the German's target was the Hartenstein Hotel.

The very next day stragglers from the Brigade began turning up and some were allocated to go and collect their injured from wherever they could find them. Evacuating them from the hotel to the church took tremendous pressure off the medics at the Hartenstein hotel. The rest were given the dubious task of digging trenches in preparation to defend the Oosterbeek perimeter. Mortar fire was now continuous, gunfire could be heard all across the town and was slowly approaching Oosterbeek. The noise became louder and louder and more and more stragglers entered the confines of the makeshift perimeter. Oosterbeek would soon be under complete siege and all wondered where and when the Germans would finally break through.

As all this was taking place the badly injured Major 'Dickie' Lonsdale, now in command of the 11th. Battalion summoned all his men to the outside of the church and gave a rousing speech which he ended by saying to them, 'we've fought the Germans in North Africa, Sicily and Italy. They weren't good enough for us then! They're bloody well not good enough for us now!'. As the senior surviving officer of the battalion, he gained command of the whole section, which also included the last of the South Staffordshire's.

Tired and hungry as they all were, and becoming dangerously short of ammunition, the soldiers of the 'Lonsdale Force', as they were now known, created a line of defence to thwart any German onslaught. Supporting them were the guns of the Light Regiment Royal Artillery.

By night fall the south eastern perimeter was as secure as could be in the circumstances, indeed the whole perimeter was much the same with the 1st Borderer's defending much of the western edge.

Daniel worked tirelessly alongside the Brigade's medics, and with the help of Karina, whose company he enjoyed. When he realised she was German by birth they spoke in her indigenous language which annoyed some of the walking wounded.

Half way through that evening Karina called Daniel over. She was standing by Gerry Kelly's bed, made from two church pews face to face. Gerry was ranting as if he was having a nightmare. Sweat was pouring off him and she continuously wiped his brow.

"Gerry. Gerry wake up, it's me Daniel. Gerry! Come on wake up." If he could bring him around there was a good chance he would survive. Karina cooled him with a damp towel.

Gerry was talking out loud and almost sounded like he was at a football match. Daniel gently slapped his face hoping to shock him. It worked. He went quiet but he then slowly opened his eyes. He stared up at the timber structure which formed the inside of the church roof. For perhaps two minutes he lay there wondering where he was.

"Gerry can you hear me? It's Daniel." He moved his head and the first person he saw in two days was Karina. He turned his eyes back to the church surroundings and then returned his gaze to her and said weakly. "Fuck me! I must be in heaven." He said nothing else and fell back to sleep.

Daniel smiled. He at least had one other close friend who was still alive. Karina watched the relief in his face and the tear which rolled down his cheek. Here she saw a man with a hard exterior, but one that cared so much deep down.

Later that night aside of the siege, news improved for the better again. Major Lonsdale entered the church-cum -dressing station with two men carrying a wounded soldier on a stretcher. Daniel recognised him straight away.

"I'm afraid he was hit by friendly fire. Our chaps thought they were Krauts." Major Dickie Lonsdale told him. "The lads' nerves are on edge."

"Who were the others?" Daniel almost asked desperately. He eagerly wanted to know who else was with one of the remnants of his platoon.

He didn't have to wait long to find out. In walked Paul Cory. After a quick robust handshake he took him over to see Gerry Kelly and explained his condition. The day couldn't have worked out any better for Daniel. The fighting had died down, the Germans were probably taking stock of the situation.

He spent the rest of the night talking quietly to Karina about both their own lives, even though they were still lacking in years. Their attitudes to the war were akin, ideological failures causing the deaths of millions of innocent people. He told her about his wife and children and how their relationship had come about.

Eventually he mentioned the letter he had received shortly before he came to Arnhem, whom Karina was the only person he had explained the wording. Eventually he drifted off into a much needed sleep.

Daniel had a rude awakening that early morning, and rejoined the battle.

A major offensive by the Germans began at first light and the squeeze on the perimeter began. Shells and mortar bombs fell all around. Gunfire was continuous and casualties again mounted up. Ominously the church began to fill with more emaciated bodies. The ground between the east and west perimeter at the river began to shrink considerably. If there was to be an escape route with the aid of the slowly advancing XXX Corps from the south then they could not afford to lose access to the river. All ways around, the Airborne division fought gallantly but were taking hundreds of casualties. The fighting force was being whittled down, but extraordinarily they hung on. Officer participation became negligible as one by one they were killed or wounded, but after four or five hours strangely the Germans pulled back and concentrated their efforts on the north of the town.

In the west the Borderers had also suffered considerably, but for their brave efforts hadn't conceded much ground. They ended that day with a successful hand to hand skirmish which threw the enemy onto the back foot and changed the battle plan for the next couple of days.

Between the British slit trenches and the German line of attack lay many enemy dead and dying. As the battle raged more so in the north, Daniel called across no-man's land at the German's own position. He waved a white flag of temporary truce and slowly stood up. Opposite, the German command was given, do not shoot. Major Lonsdale, Daniel's commanding officer understood and reciprocated. Daniel climbed out of the slit trench. He lay his gun down in front of everyone to see. On his side a tired and irate soldier shouted out 'coward' but was soon berated for his stupidity by Major Lonsdale.

Daniel approached the middle ground where several German soldiers lay dead or dying. He turned one over but he was dead. The whole battleground was silent except for the noise in the north of Oosterbeek. He found another dead, and then one struggling to breath. He stood up and gestured for the German's to bring over their stretcher bearers. An Obersleutnant stepped forward and waved two men through to rescue the injured man.

Daniel and the Obersleutnant approached each other and between them the two factions saluted.

Daniel spoke first, in immaculate German. "You have several brave men out here injured or dying. Please! You are welcome to take them off the battleground."

"Is that all you want? For us to take our men to safety," he replied politely.

"No, not really. Bandages, anti-infection drugs and morphine would be helpful." Daniel nearly asked for more ammunition, but thought he'd better not.

The Obersleutnant spun backwards and shouted instructions.

"I also have four of your own men badly injured here in the church and they would be better off if you could take them back and be treated by your own people. Our medical supplies are now dangerously low." Daniel was taking chances. "Your men will be perfectly safe to come and collect them I can assure you."

As the German stretcher bearers began to take their wounded off the field one soldier brought a knapsack. "Here this is for you. I hope your men do not suffer too much." He held out the pain relieving drugs.

After one hour the German wounded were removed and the severely injured British were evacuated to the Saint Elizabeth Hospital in Arnhem. Both men exchanged names.

Obersleutnant Petr Bakker asked. "Why did you do this?"

Daniel could only reply. "Neither of us wanted this stupid debilitating war did we?"

"No you are perfectly right. You have my respects. One day, when it is all over, perhaps we will meet again."

They shook hands and then saluted each other.

'Dickie' Lonsdale wasn't fuming but wanted to know why Daniel had taken such action without permission. Daniel eyed him up and down. Dickie Lonsdale's head was bandaged, arm in a sling and had a bloodied wound in his thigh. He held the bag up. "Morphine sir! Anti-infection drugs sir! Might you need any! Because if you don't I am going to take this across to the church where the poor bastards are desperate to be put out of their misery and then I will be back on duty to defend our lines." He went to walk away but hesitated. "Oh! one other thing Sir." He dipped his hand into the knapsack. "A bottle of brandy from the Obersleutnant to help you sleep in peace tonight."

Daniel walked away leaving Dickie Lonsdale flabbergasted. He turned on a sergeant. "Go and find Lieutenant Cory. I want to see him straight away.

A little later both Lonsdale and Cory met. "Who the fucking hell is this insubordinate Sergeant of yours."

Paul was reluctant to vilify Daniel for what he had done. "Do I take it you mean Sergeant Godwin sir."

Dickie Lonsdale didn't even know Daniel's full name and stuttered.

"Sir! With all due respect, he tends to ignore people who never bother to learn their own soldier's names properly, and his attitude is if you don't care about him, why should he listen to, or care about you." Paul watched Lonsdale's eyes widen and then added. "His father was an under age soldier in the trenches at the latter end of the last war and there is an interesting story of how he came about. Daniel Godwin speaks immaculate German and is far from being stupid. He should be officer class but seems to have no inkling to pursue his rank much further. He genuinely wants to preserve his own men in battle. He'll fight for you until the end, and I believe he could well be the last man standing here. However much persuasion sir, Sergeant Daniel Godwin does not intend to go home from this war. Shortly before we left the Cotswolds he received a letter and Daniel changed completely. We don't know what the letter read but he was quiet and unapproachable. Even I wasn't allowed into his personal mental domain and I know him very well. Besides all that, he has been a damn good soldier throughout this campaign." Paul spun away then turned back. "Please don't take him out of the line sir because of his insubordination, he is a classic professional soldier who cares deeply about his men and they think the world of him. If you do sir, you will lose the respect of many of the Brigade who know him," Paul hesitated, "the ones that are left sir."

The Germans, as well as the British, had taken a beating but hadn't gained very much ground. They changed their tactics and resorted to incessant artillery fire and mortar bombs. For three days they tried to break the Ist. Airborne's resolve but they had refused to give in knowing the Polish Parachute Brigade was trying to find any means to cross the river. Rumour was also abound that sections of the XXX Corps were within sight of Oosterbeek. The perimeter took a massive pounding and all the men could do was to dig in even deeper and hope they would not take a direct hit.

Casualties were mounting up again and within Oosterbeek itself the estimation was that there were well over a thousand men, British and German, out of action. Suddenly the German guns began to cease firing and everything went quiet. Orders down the line were for the Airborne troops to stop retaliating. The belief was that the British high command had finally given up and would surrender after eight days of fighting.

The Germans' Senior Medical Officer, Major Egon Skalka, had realised the growing problem of the casualties and to his opposite number, Colonel Warrack, offered a ceasefire to evacuate soldiers of both sides to the safety of Saint Elizabeth hospital in Arnhem. The age of chivalry in war was far from dead and again, that particular afternoon, most of the badly injured on stretchers, and many of the walking wounded were escorted to the hospital. Brigadier Hackett was taken by Red Cross Land Rover personally driven by the Germans themselves, although they never knew his full rank. For the British injured their war was over and they reluctantly became prisoners.

General Urquhart more than welcomed the uninterrupted rest for his beleaguered Division. After salutes and handshakes from both sides of the high commands, hostilities resumed that evening.

Contact with XXX Corps was regular and the message everyone didn't want to hear was that a decision had been made that an attempted crossing from them would be futile. General Urquhart was left to decide what was best for the remaining men and his fresh casualties. After two hours of deliberations and realising the Germans were attempting to cut off their only means of retreat across the river in the south east of the sector, he made the decision to retreat that night after nine days of being battered almost into submission.

The organisation of the evacuation began that afternoon and was decided that the 1st Parachute Brigade would be first in line due to the great sacrifices they had made during the ineffective campaign.

Daniel told Paul he was going to remain with the men and help out with the medical corps.

"Sergeant Godwin I am ordering you to be one of the first back across that river!"

"Sir! I refuse. There is nothing you are going to do to make me go. I speak German, which would be better for the injured men's sakes that I stay here." He was adamant that going home was not an option for him.

Paul went and asked the advice of Major Lonsdale who decided to speak to Daniel himself.

"So why are you are so determined to remain here. I am told you are a damn good soldier, well respected and the army needs people like you to help finish off this war as soon as possible. If it's a personal problem there are always ways around that in the army. Postings abroad, out of the way, et cetera. Tell me what is eating at you and I might consider your request, otherwise we'll have you bound and gagged and carried across the Rijn." Dickie Lonsdale could only be honest with him.

"I'll tell you but as long as you tell no-one else. Promise me!" Daniel was on the verge of having his way, or so he hoped.

"I promise with all my heart I will not tell anyone but you'd better have a damned good reason. Please go ahead. Tell me."

Twenty minutes later Sergeant Daniel Godwin walked out of Major Lonsdale's makeshift office with a red cross band on his arm. Paul said very little to him as he then realised he was going to lose his good friend after all they had been through. The future was still uncertain.

As darkness came and the rain swept in, the German guns fell silent. Except for sporadic British fire to deceive them into thinking that they had no intention of surrendering just yet, the remains of the 1st Airborne silently set in motion their exodus down to the river and began the crossings. With the help of XXX Corps and the Polish contingent, the escape put an end to the worst British defeat of the war. Much less than two thousand men from more than ten thousand escaped across the river that night. One hundred or so drowned or were gunned down and another five hundred or so were left to find their own way home, aided by brave Dutch partisans. Perhaps two hundred of them found their way back to the allied lines. The unfortunates became prisoners of war. Except the soldiers who were taken prisoner or were left behind wounded, the rest had died.

The bridge at Arnhem was still in German hands.

Chapter 56
Daniel, Prisoner of War

Although relieved, the German command were taken completely by surprise on the Tuesday morning to find the remaining fit British fighting men had evacuated Oosterbeek. They had stealthily disappeared during the night by crossing the Rijn. The Germans were left with the residual casualties and the entire 1st. Airborne medical staff which included Colonel Warrack.

They worked tirelessly to make those seriously injured more comfortable before transporting them to Saint Elizabeth's Hospital in Arnhem.

A decision was then made that a Dutch Army barracks near Apeldoorn would be commandeered to create a temporary medical centre and house the rest of the British victims from the battle. This move would relieve the Arnhem hospital from the burden of overcrowding and return the Saint Elizabeth to public duties only.

Within two days Oosterbeek was devoid of casualties. Because of his command of the German language Daniel became Colonel Warrack's right hand man. Together they had organised a peaceful transfer of their remaining troops, albeit to the prison hospital. Karina along with several local volunteers would join them at Apeldoorn. Before leaving, Daniel and Karina were allowed to spend some time together with kind permission of some sympathetic German officers.

The village itself was completely wrecked and many inhabitants who had been trapped in the debris themselves, had died or were badly wounded. For some time afterwards the remaining villagers dug amongst the rubble hoping to find living relatives or friends. The dead however were only afforded a swift burial in a makeshift cemetery. In just ten days the celebrations of their liberation from the Nazi yoke was in complete reverse and a sombre air hung over the once proud Dutch community. Some of the menfolk and a few women were taken away by the Germans, presumably for collaborating with the enemy. Daniel watched solemnly as the accused were tied up and dragged away to an inevitable death. Helpless to do anything, he knew these were the scenes which would never be reported in the British papers, another hidden side to the great unnecessary debacle, organised by the military hierarchy and incompetent politicians back home in their comfortable chairs in London. Deep down Daniel's thoughts smouldered away.

Little time had been given to the military dead, most of whom lay around the battlefield. Body parts were strewn everywhere. Daniel organised their burials. Each identifiable soldier was tagged for future reference and then buried in shallow graves or the slit trenches in which they had sought shelter during the bombardment. Some were unrecognisable. Sombre Dutch people and even German soldiers assisted in the macabre task.

During his time there, whilst out searching for the dead, Daniel came across the Obersleutnant, Petr Bakker, whom he had confronted on the battlefield. He arranged to take Daniel on a tour of the area before being sent to Apeldoorn.

After a week Oosterbeek was cleared and the living villagers themselves were left with the job of rebuilding their homes and shattered lives. The pessimists amongst them believed the Germans were there to stay and began the restorations, but the optimists hoped the allies would be back and chose to wait and see, in case the village became a battlefield again.

Petr Bakker would show Daniel what he had been fighting for and then take him to Apeldoorn. They were to meet at the church.

Before leaving, inside the church, Daniel had put everything back in order and he sat quietly alongside several villagers. One in particular was the 'Angel of Arnhem' Kate ter Horst. They prayed, but in doing so she made him feel uncomfortable. He heard a car pull up outside and excused himself.

It was Petr. "You have been here long enough Daniel, I will now take you to see the bridge. Jump into the Kubelwagen."

They drove steadily out of Oosterbeek and towards Arnhem. The damage to the houses and churches was immense. It would be safe to say that not any windows were intact. Many buildings were completely destroyed but much of the rubble which had spread into the road had been cleared away, enough to allow single file traffic through. Bomb craters had been temporarily filled. The railway station, as Daniel remembered, was now almost unrecognisable. Surprisingly the tattered remnants of the Union Jack still fluttered from the front of the building. No-one was brave enough to remove the offending flag from the teetering brickwork. Daniel smiled inwardly. The 4th Parachute Brigade had made a brave stand in its vicinity after he and his boys had withdrawn back to Oosterbeek.

Along Weerdjesstr the top of the bridge came into view through the broken houses. Further on, at Oranjewachts Straat, the bridge loomed in full view.

Petr stopped and allowed Daniel out of the car. He stood next to him. "This is what your mission was, to gain control of this bridge. I am afraid your efforts did not work in your favour. Your comrades were very brave, but we had them surrounded, and eventually they began to run out of supplies." Daniel's emotions ran high once again. "Come I will take you to the end of the bridge."

Daniel could see where the battle had raged. Single file traffic was now allowed across under control of the Wehrmacht police.

"I am afraid many of your 2nd. Battalion died here. Bravely, I must add." Petr was almost apologetic.

Daniel turned to him. "What have you done with the dead?"

"I can assure Daniel they have been taken care of and properly accounted for. We, like yourselves are professional soldiers." Petr held his cap in his hand in respect of the dead from both sides.

Daniel looked back at the bridge and stared for some while, turning over in his mind what his fellow countrymen had been through, but above all, what for? He went down on his knees and held his hands over his face and sobbed uncontrollably. Petr moved closer and placed his hand on his shoulder. Tears rolled down his own cheeks. Dutch women gathered around to see the strange spectacle. One stepped forward and pulled Daniel to his feet and offered her handkerchief.

"Come on Daniel I think we may have seen enough in these last weeks. We'd better go." The women and children stood around the Kubelwagen talking raucously wondering what was going on as the unlikely pair set off in the general direction of Apeldoorn.

Neither men said a word. The noise of the wagen didn't help. Petr pulled off the main road and drove into the village of Zutphen. At the Stationsplein he parked the car outside the Restaurant Lekker. Other German military vehicles were parked in the vicinity.

"This will be your last day of freedom for a while, let us go and have some enjoyment." Petr showed him the door and they stepped inside.

The restaurant went quiet as a British soldier appeared. Two Dutchmen at the bar cheered, but then went sheepishly quiet as Petr followed him in. Other German soldiers acknowledged them.

"Twee bier bedankje?" Petr politely asked the girl behind the bar.

They sat down together with other members of the German army. One ordered hand bites of food, anything which was available. The conversation was congenial and Daniel easily held his own with them. The beer was not in short supply and the young officers laughed and joked loudly. The two Dutchmen had slipped away quietly.

One of Petr's colleagues stared sternly at Daniel and asked him one question he didn't want to hear but knew the subject was always going to be brought up. "What do you think the outcome of the war is going to be Daniel?"

Daniel was absolutely blunt at first and then philosophical about the long term effects. "I am afraid you cannot win this war. Arnhem was a big setback for us and our allies, but we have a massive reserve strength. Before I left England the papers were always talking about the race to Berlin between us and the Russians. You might not want to make any bets but I think I know who you would prefer to enter your capital city first." He watched his adversary across the table and then carried on. "The division of Germany has probably already been decided. What will happen after Hitler has gone will be made plaintively clear after the war. Make your judgement now and decide whose side you wish to support. Stalin has already murdered millions of his own people and unless you are in a state of denial, so has Hitler. The stories I have heard in the short time I have been here are truly unbelievable, but I'll have to wait and see if those stories materialise. If I live that long," he added.

"We will become good again and no-one will defeat us!" Daniel's counterpart across the table couldn't imagine a defeated Germany.

Daniel watched him rather sadly. He believed he was probably a product of Hitler's youth and their perpetual propaganda machinery.

Petr stepped into the verbal affray and explained Daniel's part in the battle of Arnhem. There was genuine respect for his actions. He was asked what he would do when the war was finally over.

He squinted at them one by one. "One odd thing I have noticed is that soldiers always talk of when the war is over and what they will do afterwards. None of them believe they might die. When they are in the trenches injured, they talk about getting home out of the ugly war they are in as if they are almost indestructible. With regards to myself, I am not going home, but what happens to me, I haven't a clue."

The German officers were a little confused. Why wouldn't he want to go home? They all wanted to.

Petr Bakker drove Daniel back into captivity at the British 'Airborne' hospital at Apeldoorn. Before leaving they exchanged their names and addresses. Daniel never looked around as he entered the gates he only wanted to find, first of all Karina, and then Gerry Kelly. He wasn't disappointed.

That evening Karina and Daniel sat at the desk in a makeshift ward which housed Gerry Kelly amongst many others. He was much better. Now the anti-infection drugs were working the swelling had decreased considerably and the wound began to heal properly. He could sit up in bed and joke with some of the other inmates.

"So where are you going after the war or what are you going to do?" Karina asked him almost sympathetically. She knew he didn't intend to return to England.

"I'm not sure. I am a full time soldier. If we occupy Germany for any length of time then I will have to change my identity. Perhaps I will be able to get employment as an interpreter. If I lose my papers I wouldn't want to be caught by the Russians. From what I have gathered from people like Petr Bakker they are showing no sympathy for Germans at all in the east. They have a shoot to kill policy." Daniel sat back and mused over the coming months. No-one really knew what was going to happen he thought, but there would be a great many more lives lost before the outcome would be decided.

He eyed Karina in the fading light. She was prim and proper in her blue and white uniform. "What will you do when the war is over.?"

"I could stay in Arnhem, what is left of the town, and work in the Saint Elizabeth hospital, but Dr Nieuwbauer doesn't need me in his house anymore. I have many friends in Enkhuizen, perhaps I will go back there and work in Hoorn which is not so far away." She seemed a little sad.

"Why do you call him Dr. Nieuwbauer? Isn't he your father? You carry his surname." Daniel was puzzled.

Karina told him the whole story of her life as had been explained to her and how she had come to Arnhem. One thing she didn't know was what had happened to her father. Since she'd left Enkhuizen she, nor anyone else who knew him, had seen or heard from him. Daniel was sorry and placed his hand on hers to offer small comfort. At first she never moved but then tapped him gently on the back of his hand and suggested that they should together check their patients in the ward before putting the lights out.

They administrated painkillers according to the severity of each of the wounded. The worst cases were being kept elsewhere, and the majority of their inmates were now being described as 'walking wounded' now the healing process came into full swing in the clean environment.

Daniel stopped and chatted to Gerry for a while. Gerry smiled cheekily at him. "You're a lucky bastard! Hundreds of injured soldiers and you, fit as a fiddle, with a nurse whose fallen in love."

"What the hell are you on about?" Daniel tried to keep his voice down.

"She loves you Daniel! Karina loves you. Can't you see it?" Gerry was astonished he hadn't realised. "When we left you back down in Oosterbeek, everyday she asked about you as if we might have heard something. Everyday she asked us." He couldn't put his point over enough.

"Gerry I have enough problems at home let alone becoming involved with someone else." Daniel only repeated what Gerry already knew.

"You keep telling everyone that you're not going home, and I even think now you have told Karina why. That's why she's latching on to you." Gerry told Daniel straight, the blossoming affair was what everyone around believed.

"Come on Gerry let's forget this issue please! There's a long way to go in this war, it's far from over. Too many things might happen." Daniel wanted to put the subject out of his mind but the scenario between himself and Karina wouldn't go away. When Daniel and Karina walked back through the bunk beds together, wolf whistles were heard quietly in the background.

News came that the Apeldoorn barracks were to be evacuated and all able soldiers were to be moved to Stalag X1B at Fallingbostell, a prisoner of war camp near Hamburg. Prior to them leaving Obersleutnant Petr Bakker made an official visit at Apeldoorn. He searched out Daniel and took him aside.

"You must have heard where you are going. Fallingbostell. The prison camp is far from pleasant. Food is becoming scarce, not only for us, the soldiers, but our people as well. Feeding prisoners is obligatory but I am afraid they are at the end of the food chain," he took a deep breath, " I can have you moved from here and taken back close to your lines for your escape if you so wish. I will leave the decision entirely up to you."

"How long do you think the conflict will last now Petr?" Daniel asked him sardonically.

"The Russians in the east are being held up by lack of supplies. Otherwise they might have been on our border by now. The approach from the south is similar. After Arnhem your western allies have taken a different approach but gain ground every day. We think the war will be over before next summer. Our people are drained from the onslaught and now we only have old men and young boys left to fight."

"I am sorry we had to meet in these circumstances Petr and I do appreciate your offer. I think I will stay here for the time being to help nurse the men back to health then escort them to Fallingbostell. I am not going to leave them now." Daniel was adamant he should not return to the allies.

At first Petr remained uncommunicative. He thought he could help his fellow soldier out of a dire situation but had misunderstood Daniel's mood. Daniel, on the other hand, fancied his chances. He believed that in the coming months Petr would be the one needing serious support.

The pair exchanged few other words and briefly saluted each other. Petr was disappointed he couldn't help Daniel, who would now soon be on his way to Fallingbostell for an unknown period of time, languishing in an austere prisoner of war camp.

Methodically the Dutch army camp was emptied of invalid soldiers who were ferried to a railway siding and evacuated on cattle trucks to their new home, Fallingbostell. There was still some bargaining with the injured troops safety and comfort. Curiously before this action was taken, many of the high command in the Army Medical Services who had remained with the troops at Apeldoorn went missing. Rumours were abound about their disappearance and circumstances, but most had tried to escape and attempted to return to allied lines.

Petr Bakker was absolutely right. Stalag X1B was austere but mostly because food all over Germany was now almost unobtainable. There were no imports of any kind. They ate hard black bread, strange cheese and maybe, if they were lucky, one boiled potato a day. Sometimes they were given sauerkraut which they nicknamed 'Whispering Grass'. If they complained the answer was always repeated, 'it is the same for everyone in the homeland now'. The toilet facilities were dire and faeces piled upon faeces. Eating only sauerkraut exacerbated the problem. The men became gaunt with lack of proper nutrition and were unshaven. Sickness prevailed and some died simply from weakness or unable to pull through the most uncomplicated illnesses. Skin diseases were rife caused by lack of vitamins. The weather was freezing due to the time of year and the straw mattresses and meagre blankets were no protection from the night time cold. In the morning they would check who was still alive. The water became scarce and even failed to flow when the freeze set in. A pot bellied stove remained useless as long as there was nothing to burn. Irrepressible lice also became rife, a source of irritation which would open old wounds and infect them again. Human body warmth was a louse's saviour. Boredom set in and Daniel tried to persuade them to exercise but their energy levels were so low there was no point. Most had lost at least a quarter of their muscle weight in only two months.

Christmas came and went. The new year was heralded in by anyone who was fit enough to sing or who could remember a recital. Their

German guards even contributed to the concert, resigned to the fact the Russians were now knocking on their borders in the East. The Germans felt safer staying friendly with the western allies than to face a 'Red Army' intent on a terrible revenge. Even the guards appeared gaunt, but many asked questions as to whether the cause was hunger or excessive nervousness.

Prisoners of war from the east began arriving and told of terrible suffering and mass murders. Health wise they did seem much worse than themselves but few from the west believed in the 'Death Camp' stories of which they spoke.

An occasional plane flew over from the west and they were the called the 'Engines of Hope', but little success appeared from their forays. 'Reconnaissance' someone suggested.

One day as the winter began to mellow and the ground thawed heavy guns could be heard in the far distance. Very faint but enough to lift some desperate hearts. Jubilant prisoners suddenly found enough energy to rejoice. Others, in no uncertain terms, told them to be quiet and listen.

The noise over the next three days became louder, and optimism crept through the camp. German guards listened as intently as their inmates. The outcome of all their lives was imminent.

To spoil the party everything in the distance went silent for at least a day and no-one knew what was happening. Red Cross parcels failed to arrive and the situation was more dire than one month before. The young Germans knew their time was up.

Daniel kept in touch with the camp Commandant and reassured him of special relationships should everything go wrong, which it inevitably would. The boot was on the other foot and the commandant knew only too well what was happening on the ground. Daniel spoke to him sincerely and gave him a name to contact should anyone try to bring him to justice after the war. The Commandant accepted his offer.

"Gerry! It's going to be all over soon. You'll be going home. From what I can gather the Desert Rats are on their way." Daniel seemed mellow and relaxed.

Gerry stood away indignantly and stared at Daniel. "So you are still not coming back home then?" he asked.

"No Gerry, I'm afraid I am not. We'll meet again one day, but which one of us will be staring at the other's headstone will remain to be seen." Daniel eyed him carefully. He wanted to know how strong his feelings were.

"No way Daniel! You are coming back with us! Our boys have fought tooth and fucking nail to liberate us and you say you are staying here! No fucking way!" Gerry was livid with him.

"Calm down and save your energy Gerry. My future isn't going to happen that way." Sporadic gun fire again could be heard not far away. "I am going to stay here and that is all I can say at the moment so please get used to the idea. I simply cannot return to England. My life there is far too complicated. Please believe me." Daniel cocked his head, raised his eyebrows very slightly and smiled at his friend.

As the gunfire approached ever closer to the barbed wire compound the hearts of the men inside, however weak, lifted. Although each man waited in trepidation of the final outcome, they knew their liberation was impending.

Five guards suddenly burst into the wooden dormitory which housed Gerry Kelly demanding to know the whereabouts of Sergeant Daniel Godwin. He was quickly found and after a struggle his hands were tied behind his back. As they attempted to escort him from the louse ridden block Gerry lunged at them and was defied by a rifle butt into the face. He fell to the floor, blood pouring profusely from his nose and mouth. He stood up but Gerry was held back by his own men.

The young German stared defiantly at the other prisoners. "Have you ever considered whose side this man is on!" He turned and left. Daniel was dragged away.

Chapter 57
Rob Sums Up

"That is definite then. She recognises her from the photograph." Rob smiled. He believed he could name the murderers but wouldn't be able to prove they were at the scenes. "So Matthaius Schlutt and Stella Godwin are more than probably brother and sister."

"So the woman, Matthaius' neighbour, was adamant that the photograph of Stella is the woman who lived with Matthaius Schlutt." Glen watched Rob ponder over the information.

"We need to seriously speak to Matthaius. The trouble is if he is to do with this, he'll just clam up, and then Stella and Adcock will almost certainly go about their lives normally as if nothing has happened."

"Why don't we just tell the police what we know and let them deal with the murders." Ed felt that would now be the simple thing to do.

"We can't tell the local police. They are as much to blame for this as anyone indirectly. Perhaps if we informed them in Taunton at County Headquarters they might take action, but again, as soon as the Bath police find out they are being investigated they'll cover their own tracks. I honestly believe we should speak to Matthaius. We should pressure him by making him believe we know what has happened and why." Rob felt he had little choice left.

"We'll have to corner him in a pub somewhere. Glen could do that by inviting him out for a drink, and then we can turn up, unsuspectedly." Ed's suggestion was agreed upon by all four.

"What we will have to do is pre-arrange a fail safe. If he does confirm to us what we think is the truth then Stella and Adcock will have to be arrested almost immediately. Also, if Matthaius is involved someone needs to be in the vicinity to have the power of arrest. I think now, first of all, we should take a trip to Taunton and speak to the Chief Superintendent. I'll get my father to take me down after I arrange an appointment. In the meantime we'll have to wait and see." Rob was confident he could bring Taunton police onto their side as the issue was too serious. "Another problem is the children. They may need a new permanent home, I hope it doesn't come to that but I will speak to James."

"Something has puzzled me for a long time Rob, is how was Bill William's death covered up? If he was already dead when he was pushed into the bridleway there is no way he would have appeared as if he died from carbon monoxide poisoning." Glen had his own theories but wanted to know the truth.

Rob looked across to Herbie. "Tell him.

"That puzzled me as well Glen. I had a friend years ago who died in similar circumstances but his skin was an unusual colour. If Bill Williams' was already dead then he could not have inhaled the fumes. Myself and Rob decided to visit the city mortuary and find out what was the cause of death. Evidently he was never taken to the mortuary but straight to a seedy funeral director's in Combe Down on the edge of the city. Mrs. Williams saw the death certificate signed by a doctor. It read, 'suicide, death by carbon monoxide poisoning'. She now seems to remember that they hurried the funeral making the war an excuse, and he was cremated within four days of his death. Now, obviously, it would be impossible to tell how he really died, because this is all conjecture." Herbie put them in the picture as best he could.

Two days later Rob and his father met the Chief Superintendent of the Somerset Police in his office and explained exactly what he thought had happened and what they intended to do. He took the story all the way back to when Jack Cosnett had approached him in the 'Saracen's Head' years before.

The Superintendent was completely intrigued by Rob's whole version of events and gave him his full backing. He would have a policemen planted in the public house of his choice and a watch would be put on Stella and Adcock that same evening. He asked Rob to give him some notice before the official date of action.

Rob left Taunton quietly pleased, although there were unanswered questions prior to speaking with Matthaius Schlutt. One obvious question was whether Matthaius would go with Glen for a drink when asked, or merely become suspicious and decline.

Glen met Matthaius after work one day, apparently quite by accident, and politely suggested they have a drive out one evening to visits some pubs in the countryside. He mentioned Marshfield, Colerne and Box villages. Matthaius accepted his offer but suggested he wanted to be back in Bath by nine o'clock. They arranged to meet on a Saturday at five-thirty in the evening.

Rob thought about the scenario cleverly. Judith at short notice invited Joy, Sarah and Stella for a ladies Saturday night out at a restaurant in Bath, on the pretence her birthday was that day. The children would be safe at the farm with Helen and their grandfather James. At first Stella was reluctant to accept, but did so hesitantly when her mother-in-law rang her and said the children could stay the night at Eastrip Farm. Stella, when asked, even suggested using the 'Hole in the Wall' restaurant which, via the phone, all the women agreed. Rob rang Taunton police and told them the interview would be in the 'Bear at Box' at seven thirty in the evening of the same Saturday. Everything was set.

Having had a drink at Marshfield, and then Colerne, Glen and Matthiaus drove down into the By-Brook valley to the village of Box. Glen pulled up into the car park at the 'Bear' and nervously switched off his engine.

The landlord, an ex-rugby player and entrepreneur, was a large amiable fellow, he greeted them and they chose his best bitter. After a mouthful both men acknowledged the quality of the beer and then chose to sit at a table in the corner by a window facing the main road. They discussed the business at Stothert's.

Matthaius believed the war was coming to a conclusion because, according to him, demand at the factory had declined considerably over the last few months. Thankfully Glen added his own opinion which extended their stay at the pub. Shortly afterwards Rob walked in with Ed. The pub itself was reasonably busy and they chose to sit at the same table as Glen and Matthaius. Seeing Rob, Matthaius immediately became suspicious. Agitated he looked back and forth at all three. He felt cornered and desperately wanted to leave.

Rob leaned across the table and spoke quietly, but went straight to the point. "Your sister is having a meal with my wife this evening at the 'Hole in the Wall' restaurant."

Matthaius squinted with one eye barely open, shook his head slowly, and claimed, "I have no sister."

Rob produced a photograph and placed the proof on the table for Matthaius to see clearly. He placed a finger on one particular woman in the photograph." A householder across the road from you says, categorically, that some years ago this woman lived with you but you were not married to her. Was she your wife, or lover perhaps?" he asked sarcastically.

Glen pretended to be innocent of the proceedings. Ed remained quiet.

"You do know her though, don't you?" Rob asked.

Matthaius refused to answer.

"Why did you turn up outside of the gates at the funeral of Mrs. Agnes Margaret Hopkinson?"

"I don't know who you are talking about! Leave me alone," he shook his head violently.

Ed stepped in and made a statement which surprised all three of them. "Calm down. Calm down please Matthaius. The old lady probably has nothing to do with you, but that day of the funeral the police decided to retain her body for further investigation. She is still kept in the mortuary. The court decision was made so late that they allowed the service to go ahead but the disposing of her body never happened. Or at least not yet." Ed was lying.

Matthaius stood up spilling his drink across the table and vociferously complained that no-one could do such a terrible thing.

Ed climbed to his feet slowly and faced him across the table. "When your grandmother died during a 'so say burglary', why didn't you say anything about the incident?" The two men stood eye to eye. "Come on! answer that question. She was after all your grandmother, people would have sympathised, unless of course your are hiding something. We know you know Stella because she came into the Empire bar and chatted with you, very briefly I might add, and passed you a note. That was after Glen had spoken with you. Or can't you remember that either?" Ed pointed at Glen. "He was there as you well know, but who you didn't notice was myself and Rob's wife, Judith. Three people who can categorically say that you know Stella Godwin."

Matthaius melted down into his chair, he was beaten. He stared angrily at Glen. "So you brought me here in the name of friendship and have me questioned as if I were a criminal." He shook his head, saddened by the betrayal. His voice broke, and hints of his German accent exposed his nationality all the more.

"Please Matthaius, tell us, is Stella your sister? We think she is in great danger." Rob asked him quietly and reassuringly.

He thought for a long time. His mind dwelled back into the past. There had been good days, and then bad, and just when everything seemed to be going alright another disaster had struck. He turned his eyes to the disfigured face of Rob. "Yes! Yes she is my sister," he answered resignedly.

"Who was the old lady then, the nanny, whose funeral you went to?"

"She was our grandmother. Our *grosmutter,*" Matthaius' face was full of sadness.

"I am afraid we can almost link Stella to a series of murders, which will, of course, bring you into the frame." Rob observed his face, half expecting him to admit being involved.

"Those murders are nothing to do with me at all," he told him, adamantly.

"But you know about them obviously?" Glen asked him.

"I only put two and two together when the builder was found dead." Matthaius' hands were shaking.

"So how did you link them all up then?"

Gunther Volke, Bill Williams and Ian Brierly, together were all good friends. A long time ago my only mistake was telling Stella that there was another German working at Stothert's. His name, Gunther Volke, was a give away but had I not told her he existed she wouldn't have been any the wiser. Gunther would have probably been alive today along with the others unless she had met them in other circumstances. She began to stalk him and it was probably then that she found out about the others. Listen. Please believe me there are a lot of things you do not know about my sister. I doubt she'll ever be convicted of those crimes."

Glen stopped him. "How many murders do you know of then.?"

"The three I've just mentioned from Bath and at least one in Bristol. The one in Bristol I'm not sure about but he lived this side of the city between Bath and Bristol. Those three now deceased would meet up on a Saturday night in Bath and have a drink together. When they were all together there would be quite a few of them. I once overheard them talking one night and apparently the one from Bristol simply stopped coming over. Days later he was found dead and the newspapers reported the incident, in a snippet, as a tragic accident."

"You've never heard of Charlie Hope then?" Ed asked him.

Slowly Matthaius shook his head. "No. Not at all."

Ed mentioned that Charlie's death hadn't actually been splashed all over the newspapers.

"Tell us why you think she'll never be convicted." Rob's interest was such that he felt he was about to find out the entire truth.

"You'd better get some more beers in because this is going to be a long story." Glen obliged and they settled back down to listen to Matthaius as he began to tell them all he knew.

"We come from a wealthy family in the extreme west of Germany near the French border. Our family go back hundreds of years and have been viticulturists for all that time. Our vineyard was in the Ahr valley, a unique and beautiful region and we produced only red wines from the Spatburgunder grape. For your information the grape, centuries ago, was originally from Burgundy. 'Spat' is the German word for late, interpreted as 'late burgundy', hence the grape is the last to ripen in the winemaking season. Our family had problems in the last war because of the vicinity of the vineyard, but when that war was over we went back into full production. For years the 'Ahr' valley was the only red winemaking region in the whole of Germany.

Then the disaster struck. Hitler came to power in nineteen thirty three and having listened to his rants of the past we knew we could be in deep trouble."

"Why would you be in trouble?" Glen asked.

"We are Jewish. Not practising Jews, but Jews nonetheless." Matthaius carried on methodically as the three sleuths began to put the story together. "With Hitler's 'Youth' programme came threats to our family and all other Jewish families and businesses which culminated in the 'Kristallnacht', or in English 'The Night of the Broken Glass' as you probably well know about. Ethnic minorities began to be persecuted as well." They all nodded their heads accepting what Matthaius had told them so far could probably be true.

Matthaius took a large gulp of beer. He was nervous. He spoke slowly but forthrightly. "The nightmare began for us about four years before that particular night when Stella was caught alone in the woods nearby while she was picking flowers. She was just a young girl. A gang of youths, 'Hitler youths', beat her up and took turns to rape her. The police turned a blind eye, claiming the incident was her own fault for wearing a short skirt. Before the assault she was a wonderful fun loving child and extremely intelligent but the attack changed her completely. She became inward and rarely spoke for almost three months, and then one day, to everyone's disgust, she told my mother she thought she was pregnant. Pregnant! Imagine that! At the age of sixteen, pregnant by known rapists who were *never* taken to trial." Matthaius emphasised what she had been through. He was disgusted.

He drank some more beer and carried on. "She became an out patient at a mental clinic for months, but again Hitler's cronies had no time for those people either. Being a pregnant Jewess, still of school age and mentally ill, your chances of surviving were very slim. After the child was born, a girl we called Greta, Stella appeared to have improved but the troubles in Germany were becoming worse and my father decided we had to leave for our own safety. We hired three or four large wagons and loaded as many bottles of wine from the last harvest on board as was possible and set off to England where we have an uncle living in Oxford. At that time bribing the border guards was easy with our wine and there were plenty of bottles because no Germans would buy from any Jewish businesses. We also had important contacts in the family to guarantee us a safe journey to England. The rest of that year's wine was taken across the English channel. The harvest was the last our family ever produced. Apparently much of the wine came to England through Cherbourg but I am not sure of that. Whatever happened, most of what we had left was divided up between here and Oxford."

"What happened to the child and the rest of your family." Rob asked him sympathetically, although he couldn't prove that Matthaius was telling the truth.

"We lived in Oxford with our uncle and aunt for a while. Stella still needed treatment, and often spent weeks in a mental home on the outskirts of the city. Mentally she was a very sick young woman. First of all I found a job in Oxford in a small works. I was fully qualified as an engineering machinist. Then a better position came up here in Bath at Horstman's. The job was interesting and well paid. Our family bought the house where I still live in now." Matthaius stopped and thought deeply. No-one said a word as he recollected his past then suddenly he began again. "Strangely, for all she had been through, Stella never at any time wanted to part with the child. Then one day she turned up at my house in Bath with Greta and insisted she was moving in. She was my sister after all and I could not say no. She was my beautiful little sister. The neighbours then began to think she was my wife but that was not so." Matthaius became emotional, remembering stories of their days back in Germany in the late autumn sunshine, happily picking the grapes and playing on the slopes.

Matthaius needed little prompting. Above all, he wanted an end to all the intrigue. "She often went out in the evenings leaving me with little Greta. I didn't really mind because I had to work in the mornings but one day she asked me if I could have Greta permanently because she was going to get married. I was taken aback and asked her what I was supposed to do with the child." Matthaius paused and tried to explain. For a while he remained quiet and then he looked up at them. "Please you have to understand, Stella is not a sane woman," he shook his head sadly, "she might appear to be for much of the time but deep down she is very unstable. She is seeking retribution for what happened to her that fateful day back in Germany, but understands no guilt about what she does. She is the sole judge in this affair. Only her. She was left for dead that day she was raped but miraculously survived and believes only she can enact revenge in her own right. You have to realise she was given no justice in Germany."

"When she married, what happened to poor Greta? What did you do with her." Rob asked him compassionately.

"Stella married a soldier by the name of Stuart Sinclair, who some time afterwards left the army. He had served his time but that is all I know. She left Greta with me initially but I took the child to Oxford where she still lives with our uncle and aunt. Greta is not now a little child, she is a young girl."

"But then what happened to your parents back in Germany and all the other relations you had?"

The merciless question which he only asked himself, always haunted Matthaius. He closed his eyes and took deep breaths. They waited. This point in his life he didn't appear to want to discuss. Ed signalled to the bar and some more beer was brought over.

Ed gently placed a hand on his shoulder and asked. "You haven't heard from them since have you?"

Matthaius struggled to speak. He breathed heavily and merely shook his head from side to side as tears trickled down his cheeks. He tried to point at the photograph and explain who was who but he was too distressed even to look at the picture. "I'm sorry. Please I am sorry. Stella, her children, our uncle and aunt and some cousins who drove the wagons here are all the relatives I have left."

"Please, you don't have to be sorry to us Matthaius." Ed told him. They all knew the stories filtering back from Germany and Eastern Europe were abominable.

Matthaius gathered himself together. "While we were sent with the wine to England along with our grandmother everyone else stayed to clear up our belongings but Hitler's fledgling Gestapo found out about our family's intentions. I am more than sure I don't need to explain to you what happened next. In that photograph, except for the few who were on that convoy, none of our family have been heard of or seen since." Matthaius began to break down once again.

Rob left the table and spoke to a couple of gentlemen at the end of the bar. They were clearly not needed, but respectfully he told them he would speak to their immediate superior officer later. He returned to the table and sat back down.

He leaned forward on his one elbow. "Matthaius I know this is difficult but we need to know one more thing."

"Ask me. Nothing matters now. What ever you say or ask, I have told you our side of the story."

Rob watched the man in front of him, Matthaius Schlutt. He knew he had a tortured mind. Rob remembered his own mother when she first saw himself after returning from the Somme those many years ago. He was barely able to speak with half his upper body ripped away. Blind in one eye and completely deaf in his ear. There were months of recuperation but, above all, the tears she had shed on the landing or behind the bedroom door he could not forget, something she had told him years afterwards. He was her only son, destroyed by politician's, on all sides, foolhardy decisions and inactions.

"Matthaius tell me what is Peter Adcock's involvement with all this?"

Matthaius thought seriously about Rob's inquiry "I am not sure where or how she became involved with him. I don't actually know him but she has mentioned his name to me briefly. Possibly around the time she left my house but believe me I do not really know. Perhaps she had met him before, but she could be very aloof some days. I know he has leanings towards the communists but I know little else about him."

Glen frowned. "Did they have a sexual relationship?"

"I don't think so, but then again I don't really know." Matthaius held his hands up as if to say he was completely innocent of everything his sister was involved with.

Matthaius viewed all three casually. He was blameless as far as he was concerned but his sister needed a great deal of help and taken off the streets for her own safety and the safety of other people.

Rob came back to him. "Do you think they were both involved with the murders? Adcock and your sister."

"I am not sure if you understand what their motive was, but if you did, then everything would be plain to all those who are reasonably sensible." Matthaius began to stand his ground.

"What was their motive then?" Glen asked impatiently.

"Who would a Jew like to murder most?" Matthaius bit back as if he were sat amongst fools.

Rob answered first. "Nazi's"

"And then who would a Communist like to murder first?" he asked.

Again Rob answered. "Nazi's"

They all went quiet but then Matthaius spoke. "I am afraid as Jews we had no chance against the National Socialists and so Stella has naturally taken sides with the Communists especially after what happened to her. She became a murderer. Stella wants revenge, that is all I can assume."

Ed was livid. "There is more to this than you're letting on. What is the real reason?" he continued, "you are just as bad as she is. You are both in it together!"

Calmly Rob stepped in. "Are you saying they were all fascists, the ones who were murdered?"

"Very likely. They were definitely racist. As far as Stella is concerned she would sooner have them all dead. In fairness to her, although she has gone the wrong way about it, how many people in Europe have died because of racist dictators or for want of better words 'ethnic cleansers'. Countless." Matthaius tried to defend his sister's philosophies as if they were an eye for an eye.

Rob left the table and asked to use the phone. He spoke to a very serious minded policeman on the other end and quietly put the receiver down.

"Glen can you take Matthaius back home, or wherever he wants to go? Ed I need to get back into Bath. We're going to the 'Hole in the Wall' restaurant." Rob hurriedly swung around to leave.

Matthaius interrupted his departure. "Why are you going there?"

Rob, for the first time, turned on him. "I told you earlier that is where your sister is having dinner with my wife and two other women you probably don't know. There are two children indirectly involved here who need to be protected. One of those other women happens to be their grandmother. Do you know who their father is!?" Rob asked him exasperated.

"There are two fathers. I vaguely knew them but only because Stella told me about them. Both were British soldiers. She was very proud of them."

Glen couldn't help asking, "why would she be proud of them, because they would be both be killing Germans?"

Matthaius looked at him with a sad expression on his face and shook his tiresome head. "I am a German by birth, but now, because I am also a Jew, I have no homeland. Even here there is no place for us, so where can we go in this crazy world. You cannot imagine what is happening to our people just because of our religion." He took one look at Rob. "If you are going to arrest my little sister then *please* let me go with you."

After a short discussion Rob went back to the phone.

Judith always made a point of kissing Rob on the broken side of his face. She told him once that when she stopped kissing him there then she didn't love him anymore. She still loved him.

Deep down, after Rob had arrived in the little restaurant, 'The Hole in the Wall', Judith knew there would be tears but didn't know the full story by half. Surprised as they were, one by one, the girls made an effort and hugged him.

Rob was in no mood to beat about the bush. "I have someone with me who has come to see you Stella."

At first she looked aghast. "Who?" she asked abruptly.

"Matthaius Schlutt. I understand you know him quite well." Rob was in no physical state to fight off a raging woman should she lose her temper.

"Who? I do not know anyone by that name," she shrugged her shoulders in defiance.

Rob nodded to the waiter by the door, which he obediently opened. Matthaius walked in with Ed and Glen. Matthaius walked over to Stella, sat down beside her and whispered in her ear. "They know about you 'little sister'. I'm sorry, they know about you." He held her hand and caressed her hair. "No more killing please."

She appeared to be stunned. Her eyes were remote and stared at the flowered curtains. Her tortured imagination moved back into the past to the woodland where she was so brutally beaten and raped. She cried and laid her head into Matthaius' chest. "Where is Daniel? I want to speak with Daniel!" Stella sobbed, speaking in her native German language.

Joy shifted around the table. The scar on her forehead had reddened in the warm surroundings, but little else suggested there had been a tragic car accident. "Stella! Daniel is a prisoner of war somewhere in Germany." She held her daughter-in-law as she sobbed and Matthaius moved away. "Stella, believe me, he'll be back." Joy was as hopeful as any mother would be.

The head chef came from the rear of the restaurant. "What is going on?" he was irate, but then he saw Matthaius. "What are you doing here?"

Matthaius pointed in the direction of Stella. "I am afraid the news is not good Heinrich." Matthaius told him what his sister had been doing over the last years.

Rob and Judith exchanged glances. She nodded at her husband.

Rob turned his attention to the chef. "Do I understand you are both related?" he asked politely.

Matthaius and Heinrich nodded in agreement. "We are cousins. Heinrich was one of the drivers in the convoy. We brought a lot of money with us to England and this little restaurant is an investment." Matthaius answered.

"So this is also the other source of the German red wine, Spatsburgunder?" Rob suggested, although he already knew.

"I am afraid there isn't any left. The stocks we had have finally run dry." Heinrich sounded deeply saddened. "The vineyard has disappeared along with the rest of our family into the hands of the Third Reich. This restaurant, Stella's house, Matthaius' house and a home in Oxford is all our family have left. We also manage the Empire bar. Not much after four hundred years work do you not think? But we are the lucky ones. Many have absolutely nothing left, not even their own lives. The name Schlutt will hopefully live on."

The Taunton police arrived and took a desperate looking Stella away. Matthaius, a protective brother, chose to go with her. Glen took Joy around to Stella's house and they moved the children's clothing back to Colerne. The others solemnly walked back down through the city.

Glen returned to Bath and they all met in the 'Old Green Tree'.

Rob took the chair. "I am afraid this evening has been a sad event. Tomorrow I will be visiting Bath Police station and demand a meeting with Chief Constable Adcock. He has some questions to answer."

"He won't turn up on a Sunday." Judith was sceptical about the Chief Constable.

"I am afraid he is going to have to. He is culpable in all of this. The situation should never have been allowed to get this far." Rob could see an end to it all but some things had to be tidied up. "Glen, Ed, tomorrow go and find Klaus Reimheimer. Bring him here at opening time. Do not give him any choice. He has to be here. There is one final thing I need to know."

The next day Sarah went with Rob to Bath Police station. After several minutes of hammering on the door a constable, supposedly manning the desk, answered, bleary eyed. They pushed their way in, taking the young man by surprise.

"Get hold of the Chief Constable please, and tell him to be here as soon as possible," Rob demanded.

"It's Sunday, he isn't back until tomorrow morning. I'm afraid you will have to wait until then." He took up the diary and was about to ask what the appointment was in connection with when Sarah, using her expert sultry litigable voice, told him in no uncertain terms that at least four people had been murdered, and it would be best if he could come back to work and begin a serious investigation.

The young police officer asked them to wait, and made a phone call. Shortly afterwards the telephone rang back. The nervous young policeman answered and handed the receiver over to Rob. Rob said few words and sat back down to wait. Sarah took his hand and told him to calm down. She kissed her ailing friend who she had first met a quarter of a century earlier, and quietly smiled at his determination and resilience.

The Chief Constable turned up, extraordinarily, with his wife. He immediately ushered them all upstairs out of earshot from anyone.

He sat, arrogantly, at an angle and gazed at Rob almost across his shoulder with his fingers intertwined. He had a supercilious air as if he felt he was impregnable thought Sarah. His wife seemed the opposite, timid and unassuming.

"What do you want to know from me at this ungodly hour? We were going to church," he asked irately.

Rob stood up to leave. "Then go. Don't let us stop you. Just remember to pray for your conscience. Come on Sarah I am sure the newspapers will tell all tomorrow."

"Sit down Robbie I don't think the Chief Constable will be going to church just yet." Sarah, as calm as ever took control of an embarrassing situation. "Sir," she glanced at his wife, "or madam, both of you perhaps, can you please tell us what your son Peter has to do with Stella Godwin."

The Chief Constable thought hard about what he had to say. He realised that Robbie Goode had sussed out what had been happening, and with Sarah at his side, had an intelligent friend as company whereby he couldn't stop Robbie dead in his tracks.

The Chief Constable's wife took his hand, more or less willing him to tell the truth and he chose to speak. "Peter was a perfectly normal child but at the age of eight he had an accident falling from a horse. He fractured his skull and was kept in Frenchay hospital for some time. Eventually he was deemed fit enough to come home. Everything seemed, at first, to be alright but his moods and tantrums became worse as he became older. We assumed the accident was the cause. He attended King Edward's school for heaven's sake! He was far from dim. One day on the advice of a good friend we paid for him to attend a clinic in Oxford for the mentally ill if only for a professional assessment, maybe to calm him down which would lead him to a more stable life. Few people, I am afraid to say, want to be known to have odd relatives, but he had become so bitter and twisted. There they declared he was a very intelligent young man but had an icy and very dour view on the world, especially its political landscape."

"So that is where he must have met Stella perhaps. In a clinic for the mentally ill." Sarah watched Rob fidgeting as he may have put something finally into place. He asked the Chief Constable. "Your son went to King Edward's, but did he ever learn German?"

"No. He was never any good at languages. In fact he hated the German teacher there." The Chief Constable was adamant. His wife peered at him with a different opinion in mind but remained quiet. "Can I ask you a question? Why am I the one being interviewed?"

Rob stared at the man who he believed had covered up his own son's crimes. "You knew about Gunther Volke's death. Also Bill Williams' and Brierly the builder. Charlie Hope's murder was investigated by you and subsequently covered up. Your son and Stella Godwin murdered all of them, including someone in Bristol who I know little or nothing about. You have a lot to answer for Mr. Adcock." Rob remained passive.

"You will never be able to prove this, do you know that?" Adcock looked at him arrogantly.

Rob watched the couple for a short while, he had probably made the connection between Stella and Adcock's son but nothing would matter in a mental institution. "No! You are perfectly right. Case unproven. But you did have an affair with Stella Godwin didn't you? She said last night she enjoyed having sex with you."

Adcock's wife's face was overcome with shock and dismay. She stared at her husband in disbelief, trying to come to terms that her husband could do such a thing. Then she suddenly rose from her chair and left the room.

Rob peered with his one good eye at the Chief Constable and said mockingly, "I believe your son was arrested by the Taunton police late last night but obviously no-one has informed you yet, I wonder why. I look forward to reading tomorrow's evening newspaper. Goodbye." Rob and Sarah left the man in a disconsolate mood.

As they walked away from the Police Station Sarah couldn't believe Rob had mentioned the affair in front of his wife. He smiled at her. "Sarah if can't prove he had any involvement with the murders then I can't let him get away with everything scot-free. Besides that, I didn't know he was having an affair with Stella, but whose going to believe Stella anyway."

Sarah shook her head disbelievingly. As they walked up towards the 'Old Green Tree' Rob coughed up some rotten blood and phlegm from his chest and spat it into the gutter. Sarah turned her head away in disgust.

"Klaus Reimheimer! Come in and sit down." Rob tried to make the ex-patriot feel comfortable but Klaus was far from calm.

"Why have you asked me to come here when this a day of rest?" Klaus was annoyed that anyone might spoil his Sunday lunchtime.

Rob grinned as only he could. Grimacing was a better description. "You chose the wrong option didn't you?"

"I don't know what you mean," he quickly shook his head.

Rob coughed into his handkerchief and then apologised. "You chose to go with the wrong party Klaus. Telling everyone what your mistake was which led to Gunther's death. A fool's choice I believe? Had you remained stoic and pro-British, Gunther would be still alive today, your great friend. Now tell everyone what you chose to do."

Klaus tried to explain but he knew he had to concede. "Before this new war began we were more than happy to be part of the British Isles and its people. As you well know our children were born here. We always said this, myself and Gunther. However, between us there was always discussions about Germany and Hitler. We tried to imagine the scenario if Hitler had invaded Britain and won. We were genuinely scared. Had Germany succeeded, as soon as the Gestapo found out we were Germans living in England we would have been shot as traitors. We took an option, which now seems ludicrous as we didn't envisage the outcome of the war correctly, and we became members of the British Union of Fascists. Foolishly Gunther and I really believed that the Germans would successfully invade Britain."

"Did you believe that Gunther died because of the bombing that night?" Ed asked him.

"We'd all been drinking together that night and the pub we were in at the end of the night was the nearest to his house. Where he was found down in the town didn't make sense at all. When Bill Williams was found dead we then knew something sinister was going on. We could hardly go to the police and tell them a group of British fascists were being murdered one by one."

"Does the name Peter Adcock mean anything to you?" Rob was still searching for a viable excuse to prosecute.

Klaus shook his head. "No. Not at all."

"What about Stella Godwin?"

"I know only one woman called Stella but I don't know her second name. She used to be a bit of a flirt when she was around, promiscuous perhaps." there was nothing else Klaus could say about her. Glen showed him her photograph. "Yes that is her. Why do you ask?"

"Because those two are the people who instigated the killing of your friends, the woman in the photograph and the man we have just mentioned."

Klaus looked shocked. "I think Ian Brierly was having an affair with her. I'm not entirely positive, but that was only the gossip amongst us when he wasn't around."

"Well Klaus I would consider that you are one of the lucky ones not to have ended up the same way as your friend Gunther. That night he died, had you left the 'Charmbury Arm's' first of all at the end of the evening I am sure you would have been the 'dead man'." Rob gave him time to think.

Klaus contemplated his luck at the expense of his friend. Except for making the mistake of becoming a member of the British Union of Fascists, he was innocent of anything. They allowed him to leave.

James joined the tiny entourage. They hoped soon he would have his son home, but who was going to explain about Stella's circumstances to Daniel. He didn't know. They all sat around drinking and chatting about events. There was an air of euphoria in 'The Old Green Tree' as the mystery had been solved, and an air of euphoria around the country as the end of the war was imminent

The next day the Bath evening paper printed all across the front page about the shock resignation of Chief Constable Adcock and one of his detectives. The reason given was vague and was under investigation from Somerset police. A prosecution was imminent. His wife would subsequently file for divorce.

Rob found out that the murder victim from Bristol was a barman from the 'Gin Palace' in Old Market. His death was of similar circumstances. One fatal stab wound to the heart from a thin bladed knife. Rob never concluded what the connection with his and the other deaths were.

Peter Adcock was committed for trial for murder. Stella was sectioned under the mental health act and was sent to Stoke Park Mental Institution in Bristol. Her children, Joy's grandchildren, were to stay on the farm at Eastrip.

Chapter 58
Daniel's Disappearance

The European war between Britain and her allies against Germany ended in early May 1945. The atrocities, hostile towards the Jews and ethnic minorities, began to become evermore clear. Millions had died at the hands of the Nazi's. Continental Europe was divided up between the Communists in the east under Russian rule, and the west under Western powers. The decision as to who controlled what and where, was dubiously made in early February of that same year.

The prisoner of war camps were slowly cleared and the inmates returned to their native countries. Many Polish people drew the short straw, and for whatever reasons they had fought for, to free their country at the beginning of the war, found themselves under an equally oppressive regime.

Gerry Kelly was herded onto a bus along with many of his fellow inmates. They were all drastically underweight, most needing medical attention. He had no idea what had happened to Daniel and the general view was that he had been taken away and shot. Daniel's unerring ability to speak German had cost him his life, probably one of the last nefarious acts of the Gestapo or SS during the final days of the war. Gerry was taken back to England aboard a similarly reliable Dakota which had dropped him near Arnhem eight months before, only this time he didn't have to bale out.

After recuperation, celebration, many telephone calls and letters he decided, with ample leave, to return to Cricklade and visit a young woman he had met whilst stationed at Blakehill. He wasn't disappointed. A love had blossomed before the Arnhem debacle and hadn't waned. Soon he was engaged, a couples act which became a phenomena all over Britain as the troops returned from the war, back to the male starved women.

They decided to go and visit the aerodrome which was still active, bringing back the remnant prisoners of war, and sick or badly injured men. There was little security and they walked hand in hand amongst the buildings. The medical centre was still operating, and purely out of curiosity, Gerry went inside and asked for the Flight Sergeant.

Andrea Morrison was still in charge. She half recognised Gerry but excused herself by virtue of the fact that so many men had passed through the doors. He explained who he was and who he had been attached to during the latter part of the war.

She beckoned the couple into her office, partially closed the door and made a phone call.

Someone answered. "Paul. It's Andrea. I have someone here who you might like to speak to." She handed the phone to Gerry.

"Hello! It's Corporal Gerry Kelly sir. Freshly back from P.O.W. camp." Gerry laughed. He was alive and the camp was an experience he would never forget.

A few words were exchanged and then an arrangement made. "I'll be up on Friday. Meet us both at the "Old Spotted Cow' in the evening. I look forward to seeing and talking to you Gerry. There will be a lot of questions. You'll have to excuse me but I have an audience at the moment. I'll see you Friday." Paul was over the moon that Gerry was well and he couldn't wait for the weekend to come around.

Friday evening was one of mixed emotions. Both men had witnessed a horrific battle where many men were lost and some of them were personal friends. Along with many others Paul so desperately wanted to know what had happened to Daniel. The two women left them to their anxieties, went outside to sit and discuss their own futures.

"What happened then Gerry? Was he always just as determined not to come home?"

"At Fallingbostell he had a great deal of influence. Our blokes depended on him as did the Germans because of his command of both languages. Not only that, we both know he is far from stupid. The

Germans had a lot of respect for him as well. One day we could hear the guns in the background, maybe twenty miles away. The distance was difficult to ascertain. The next day they were definitely closer. We were ecstatic and all felt liberation was coming our way. The German guards were treating us better but we were still starving, although by this time they were hungry as well. Nobody really tried to escape, probably because we were so weak. The guards became our friends, almost."

Paul stopped him. "I think you will find out in due course that they would have sooner fell into our hands as prisoners than into the Russians hands." He waved and asked him to carry on.

"One morning some guards stormed in demanding frantically to know where Daniel was. He didn't put up a fight for fear of other people becoming involved. I tried to stop them from taking him away and received a rifle butt in the face. In poor English one of them suggested he was a spy. Of course he did speak both languages but the question asked amongst us all was who might have he been spying for, us, them, meaning the Germans, or the Russians. The accusation seemed rather odd. Anyway he was taken away and I am afraid we never saw him again." There was nothing else Gerry could tell him. Both knew Daniel didn't intend to go home, but Paul knew Major Lonsdale had given him an option not to by giving him the medical orderly armband.

The real question in Paul's mind was why didn't he want to return home. Neither he nor Gerry knew much about the complexities of his previous life. There was always something he would not tell them.

Paul knew the story about Stella and told Gerry but the timing did not add up. Some time even before Rob Goode had almost unveiled what she had been doing, Daniel had made up his mind not to return home. Whatever happened lay in the letter sent to him after D-Day and shortly before he dropped into Arnhem. Between them they dearly needed to find out.

When they visited Daniel's father James, he told them what the authorities had said, that he had been taken by the Germans and hadn't been seen since. Joy, James' dear wife, had lost her mother, father, youngest son and her eldest son in not much more than eight years. Let alone her brother in the 'Great War'.

Chapter 59
The Nairobi Connection

Red tape letters in brown envelopes from the Secretary of State for Commonwealth Relations fell onto the desk of Mark Campbell. He first of all observed all the stamp dates and compared them to delivery times, and always smiled when some of the brown envelopes arrived a week late from London. A white envelope, had 'personal' written on the top left corner, one, which he opened up last. The letter was from his dear mother and father, dated 11th. October 1954.

His mother, as mothers do, asked after him, his wife and children. Mark had a respectable job in the Kenyan civil service and he sat with his feet up reading about his parents private business. Then she mentioned a small letter which she had inserted into the envelope and told him that it was important. Having initially gone unnoticed Mark slid the short note from the envelope and perused the contents of the words. The English was not particularly discernible. The message was obvious. Nine and a half years after the war had finished a small piece of writing paper had turned up, on which was what appeared to be a disguised message. He stood up, read the message again and subconsciously rubbed his forehead with his fingers. Mark wasn't sure what to make of the note. 'How did one small piece of paper turn up in his mother's possession? Posted? Delivered by hand?' He was bemused and rang his wife.

A Bristol Britannia flew into London airport after a long and interrupted flight from Nairobi. Having stopped off at Aden and Nicosia a very tired Mark Campbell disembarked and headed for the terminus. Outside he was ushered into a waiting government car and taken into the city centre. The Foreign Office took charge of his welfare from there on. He was housed comfortably for two days and would go about his civil service business but had no intentions of remaining in his accommodation. Private business was the primary reason for his trip to England, secondary, was his role in the Kenyan civil service. His objective was first to travel to Bristol and visit his parents, and then onto Bath to meet some old acquaintances. Importantly his first act after settling into his room was to ring his parents, warning them of his impending visit. Also there was something he needed to know. Reliable information he needed badly because of a seed firmly planted in his mind, a seed which he desperately needed to flower.

The dialling tone rang for what seemed an age. Mark tapped an imaginary tune on the desktop with his fingers. Suddenly a meek female voice came on the line. "Hello! Who is it?" she asked, not giving her own name away.

"Mother it's me Mark. I am in London." They went through the normal greetings before Mark told her he would be down in Bristol before lunch the next day. "Mother that letter with the note inside you sent me, where did the note come from? I need to know."

His mother hesitated and then spoke. "You had better speak to your father. Here he is."

Obviously his father was standing beside his mother listening. "Hello son. What's the matter?"

Mark repeated his question.

"We had a bit of an accident with some coffee and the postmark was practically obliterated. The envelope is still here though."

"Please tell me, is there anything decipherable. Anything you can tell me." Mark was impetuous.

There was silence for more than a minute but then his father came back on the line. "The stamp is definitely Dutch."

Mark and his father concluded little from the conversation but accepted they would meet the next day.

In a car loaned to him from the Foreign Office he travelled to Bristol and spent two enjoyable days with his mother and father but soon became impatient and badly wanted to find out what had happened to his old friend Daniel and perhaps visit his gravestone, wherever that might lay. 'Hopefully', he thought, 'a gravestone wouldn't be the final scenario'.

In Bath he made his way to the 'Old Green Tree' where he found, as pre-arranged, Daniel's father and Herbie. They welcomed each other, having not met for probably well over a decade, appearances had changed. Age and maturity had crept up on all three of them.

Settled in a nook, James, Daniel's father, explained to Mark the whole story as he had been told and had tried to understand from Daniel's associates and colleagues. James concluded, as he had done time and time before, that close to the end of the war the Germans took Daniel away, accused him of being a spy, and presumably shot him. He also disclosed the complete, bizarre, but very sad tale, of Daniel's wife Stella. Mark had known little about Stella such was his isolation in Kenya but now heard her story in such detail. Any information he had came from years before, prior to Daniel leaving for Arnhem. Mark at least now knew what had happened to Stuart Sinclair. After hearing the story from start to finish he suggested someone should write it down on paper.

The other sad news they gave him was the state of Rob's health. He had, at the most, a month to live. He had been suffering from emphysema for the last few years which now had developed into lung cancer. The fact he had lasted so long was considered a miracle by all who knew him.

Before Mark left, James mentioned Gerry Kelly, who was living in Cricklade, and told him that he was the man with Daniel right up to the time he was taken away from the prisoner of war camp. He explained the location of the pub in Ashton Keynes which he frequented, the 'Horse and Jockey'.

Mark never commented on the note he had received in Nairobi for fear he might be on a fool's errand and he did not want to give anyone false hopes. He never suggested at all that he was in Europe for the sole intention of finding out what had happened to Daniel. James assumed he was taking time off to go visiting friends and relations. Mark had three weeks leave and one of those had almost passed by.

Before Mark left the city he visited the hospital to see Rob who he found was terribly emaciated and very weak. His breathing was permanently supplemented with oxygen. Judith was at his side and between them the couple were trying to compile prayers and songs for his own funeral service which Mark felt was quite strange in the circumstances. They spoke together for some while and then Mark brought up the subject of the note he had received from his mother. Rob tried to smile and then asked him where his journey was leading him next. First of all, Mark told him, he was going to try and find Gerry Kelly, afterwards he wasn't sure. Everything now depended on Gerry Kelly's revelations.

As he left through the swing doors tears rolled down Mark's cheeks. He was almost certain he would never see the 'great man' alive again but he would do his best to find the whereabouts of Daniel and try and pass a message back to him before his inevitable death.

In the meantime Judith and Rob agreed on the final song at his own funeral. Immobile that he was, between drug induced sleep, Rob's mind still ticked over.

Within two hours Mark was at the Horse and Jockey in Ashton Keynes where the landlord was about to close for the afternoon.

"I wonder if you might be able to help me. I'm looking for a chap called Gerry Kelly. Do you know where I might be able to find him?" he inquired.

The landlord eyed Mark up and down. Seeing someone of West Indian descent in Ashton Keynes was extremely rare. "Gerry works on the Eisey estate. Unless he has an accident I can assure you he'll be here on the dot at opening time this evening. Six o'clock, and I can almost guarantee you his company."

Mark glanced at the clock. "Where can I go for three hours? Is there somewhere I can stay for the night?"

"Cirencester. It's a pleasant little town with two or three hotels." The landlord gave him directions and politely closed the door behind him.

Mark set off and found a pleasant place to stay in the centre of the old Roman town, the 'Fleece' hotel. He settled in, had a bath, and then wandered around the quaint streets before returning to Ashton Keynes.

As the door opened dead on the hour the old wall clock finished its chime and Gerry Kelly was waiting outside. "Somebody's been looking for you. Tall black bloke. Well dressed and spoke the queen's English. I forgot to ask who he was or what he really wanted. I think he will be back though. He gave me the impression he was determined to find you."

Gerry scratched his head. Did he know anyone of that description? A black bloke? Then he thought of Daniel's friend. Someone Daniel had mentioned in conversation.

A flash of sunlight reflected from a car windscreen through the pub, catching the landlord's eye, and he peered out of the window. "Here he is now."

Mark drew up in the car park, climbed out and entered the pub. He introduced himself and went straight to the point of his visit. "Can I assume you are Gerry Kelly?" Gerry nodded, rather taken aback. "Daniel Godwin! His father, James, told me you were one of the last people to see him alive. Please! what can you tell me about him?"

"Ah! so you are his good friend who Daniel often spoke about." They shook hands. "I am pleased to meet you, and I mean that quite sincerely,"

Mark introduced himself. "Mark Campbell. Daniel and I were in the cadets together, that's where we met."

"Myself and Daniel were very close colleagues, both of us were in the Parachute Brigade during the war, Ist. Airbornes actually. We were taken prisoner after the battle of Oosterbeek and ended up at Stalag X1B near Hamburg, Fallingbostell to be precise. We were there for a few months when we began to hear in the distance the fighting. Artillery, tanks and machine gun fire. Slowly but surely the noise came closer and closer. About a week before we were liberated the Krauts came and took Daniel away, asking us whether we knew whose side he was on. I tried to help but they smashed me in the face with a rifle butt. I'm afraid that was the last any of us saw of him. We assumed he was taken away and shot for spying or something. Whatever they done to him was a pretty callous act so close to the end of the war." There was little else Gerry could tell him.

"My parents received a letter a while back which simply said *'I know the whereabouts of Daniel Godwin's grave'*. The stamp is from the Netherlands but the postmark has been damaged. From the first three letters I can only assume it is a town called Enkhuizen. Did he ever mention the place?"

Gerry had never heard of the town mentioned. "He was very friendly with one of the nurses when we were trapped in Holland, Oosterbeek actually, but we last saw her when they put us on the prison train to Fallingbostell. I am more than sure though that she wasn't Dutch, I am positive she was German. They always spoke to each other in German."

"Do you know her name by any chance?"

"Karina. We would never forget her because she saved so many lives. She cared for me as well, in fact she saved my life. I'm afraid I don't know her surname. There were other nurses just as good. Dedicated, all of them." The moment was poignant for Gerry to think that he should be talking about the beautiful young lady after so many years.

"I can tell you now in the next couple of days I will be travelling to Holland to try and locate her. I can only imagine that somebody like herself sent the letter. Someone Daniel knew." The stratagem excited Mark.

"If Karina did send the letter, how has she found his grave. She was last seen in Apeldoorn, miles from Fallingbostell in northern Germany. The Germans would never have murdered him and sent his body back to Holland, especially by which time the Allies had retaken the country. That's what puzzles me. The Commonwealth War Graves Commission would surely know and would of informed his parents or next of kin. As far as I know that has never happened." Gerry was sceptical, nothing added up.

"He would have at least been registered as 'missing presumed dead', or missing in action, presumed dead, bearing in mind he was removed from the prison camp." Mark suggested.

"Before you go to Holland there is someone else I know who'll be more than interested in Daniel's fate. Someone who now lives close by." Gerry asked to use the phone and rang Paul Cory. All three arranged to meet at Mark's hotel in Cirencester later that evening.

At the 'Fleece' all three men debated the legitimacy of the the tiny note, which was now laid out on the table, having been sent to Mark's parents, who then posted it onward to Mark in Nairobi.

"My mother and father have lived at that same house for a long time. Daniel might have known the address and possibly kept it in his possession all this time, which can only mean he is still alive. Who else could possibly know my parents address? Only Karina." Mark wasn't really sure what to believe.

"Why then didn't she or he send the note directly to Daniel's parents. That would have been much more simple." Paul Cory couldn't fully understand the circumstances.

Gerry piped up. "No! If they posted the letter to Daniel's parents they might never had it forwarded. By posting it to Mark's parents the letter would almost guaranteed to be sent on, which obviously is what happened. Mark, whoever is the compiler of that note wanted you to be the recipient. As I understand from this note we have here, whoever put their hand to paper, never came back to England with any of Daniel's close colleagues, which is backed up by the fact, the envelope came from Holland. Whoever sent this little intrigue must have known him intimately, man or woman. One we have spoken of, and we all believed while we were in Oosterbeek that she was madly in love with him, Karina! I would honestly say that Karina could well be the one who sent the note with an extremely tempting unexplained message. Simple, nothing elaborate but 'tempting' none the less." Gerry stopped and thought, holding up his forefinger as if he had more to add. His eyes were screwed up as he thought back to those grim days. He began again. "He was also friendly with a German soldier, an Obersleutnant. He met him in the middle of the battle field and they swapped injured soldiers for drugs. When Daniel did eventually arrive at Fallingbostell he spoke about him quite a lot. Although he probably mentioned his name I don't remember what he was called, but then I never actually knew him, only in conversation. There is a possibility that he may have sent the letter. The fact that it reads 'I know the whereabouts of Daniel Godwin's grave' points more in the direction of the German. The Germans took him away and supposedly shot him so *they* would know where his body is." This was just another snippet of information from Gerry, however trivial.

Paul remembered seeing the Obersleutnant but only from a distance across the battlefield. He wasn't privy to his name either.

"Don't forget one thing Paul, we have discussed this time and time again, he always said he was never going home. From the day he received that letter at Blakehill, and we didn't even know who sent that particular letter or were privy as to what was inside, he was always adamant, 'I can't go back'. He always insisted he couldn't go back home."

Mark asked them. "Might his reason have been possibly to do with what Stella had done."

Paul and Gerry disagreed to a point. Gerry was very sceptical. "If Daniel knew what she was up to then he had every excuse to stay away. The problem is she wasn't arrested until a long time after Daniel flew into Arnhem. He wouldn't have known about her behaviour. Whatever he read in that letter was a shock to him and affected him for several days, but quite some time before the revelations of her past life. No. He wouldn't have known."

Paul had no particular theory but one person knew what had gone on in Daniel's head. "There was someone who perhaps knew what was on Daniel's mind, Major 'Dickie' Lonsdale. First of all, when the time came to leave, he demanded that Daniel evacuated himself from Oosterbeek, but after they had had a private meeting together Dickie appeared to have changed his mind and Daniel emerged with a Red Cross arm band. He'd suddenly joined the Medical Corps and Dickie Lonsdale allowed him to remain with the wounded men. Brave but foolish?"

Mark couldn't believe what he'd just heard. "Did you just mention an officer called 'Dickie' Lonsdale, who would have obviously been something to do with the parachute regiments?"

"Yes. Why?" Paul answered.

Mark pondered. "Are you saying Daniel actually knew him?"

"Not intimately, but well enough."

"What a co-incidence! I knew him as well. Some time after the war he came to Africa as a part of the King's African Rifles. I'd left the army by then but if we were invited to some of the sumptuous government balls, occasionally we would meet. Because our allegiance was with the same regiment 'Dickie' would always make a point and come over for a quick chat. He was a good man, a very good man who led by example, well respected. His record in the army is exemplary. How strange is that? Both me and Daniel knew the great man." Mark slowly shook his head deep in thought.

Gerry brought him around. " What are we going to do then?".

Mark could listen to the theories all evening. "I'm staying here tomorrow night but then I will be off to Holland. Enkhuizen is my destination. My intention is to get to the bottom of this before returning to Nairobi, and unless I can wangle something or find a damn good excuse to stay longer then my time is running out."

"Do you mind if I come with you?" Paul suggested. Mark needed some company and agreed.

"If I can get some compassionate leave do you mind if I tag along as well?" asked Gerry.

"Of course not. You might be the leading witness if and when we meet the elusive Karina. Three heads are always better than one." Mark, so he thought, was getting somewhere, although he had little time.

They spent the rest of the evening discussing Daniel's plight but all the time they merely talked round and round in circles. They needed more positive leads but would have to wait.

The three men flew into Amsterdam airport and caught a train into the city centre where they spent the night touring the notorious central 'Waal' district. Prior to leaving their hotel Mark organised accommodation for the following night in Enkhuizen at the 'Hotel het Wapen'.

The next day on their arrival in Enkhuizen between them a strategy was formed. Each would go their separate ways and ask of the woman known as Karina, possibly a nurse. They would refrain from mentioning that she was a German by birth because none of them knew how sensitive the subject of the war still lingered. The Centrum Bar in Westerstraat was to be their headquarters, a good drinking hole. Each would take on a certain district within the town and ask all businesses, shops and bars about Karina the nurse or a German and English speaking man known as Daniel. Every now and again they would return to the 'Centrum Bar' and discuss what they had found out or any scraps of information they had discovered.

Gerry specifically concentrated on the medical centres, dentists and opticians. He came up first with a possible lead. A woman receptionist remembered, before the war, a young girl with possibly the same forename but had disappeared mysteriously shortly before the hostilities had begun. Rumour and speculation had been that she left to become a nurse. The woman mentioned the girl's father being a doctor but never broached that his abduction was equally as mysterious. Her description of the girl matched that which Gerry held in his memory although he only knew Karina as being in her early twenties, probably even younger. All she could say was that if she was now still in the area then the main district hospital was in Hoorn, a town fifteen kilometres away. Gerry left and returned to the 'Centrum Bar' with hope in his heart. Even if Daniel was dead, to meet the woman Karina, who had so graciously saved his own life, would be a wonderful honour for himself. Paul and Mark's day had been futile but both had the feeling that the townsfolk were hiding something and saying nothing. The Dutch people were still very wary from the war and their past associations with the German regime.

The next morning Gerry went off alone by train to the hospital in Hoorn and made some personal enquiries. He casually mentioned the names of the two people he was searching for, but had no response and left disappointed. He had told the girl at the main reception that should she hear something he was staying at the Hotel het Wapen in Enkhuizen. Rather than waste the trip he continued his search within the town. Little did he know that as soon as he had left the hospital the receptionist made a private phone call.

Back at the 'Centrum' Mark came up with a surname, 'Koster'. At the beginning of the occupation a young girl and her father disappeared from the town. The wizened old woman who had told him was in her eighties. She remembered many Germans coming to West Friesland to escape Hitler for whatever reasons, they may have been Jews, communists or criminals. The father of the young child was a doctor. A very good one and very well thought of. The old lady remembered little else.

Whatever the old lady had divulged, to a small degree her story was similar to Gerry's findings the day before.

That evening in the 'Wapen' as the English three were eating, several people were sitting at the bar drinking. One lonely gentleman, possibly about forty years old nervously glanced over to them. No-one spoke to him and he never tried to engage in any conversation. He then left, but returned a half an hour later. He bought one small Amstel beer which he drank immediately and then walked across to their table. He placed a note in front of Mark, and with no explanation briskly left the hotel. On the note was a telephone number. The number meant nothing to Mark and he passed piece of paper across the table. He beckoned over the waitress and asked her if she knew who had given them the simple message. She went away and came back with an answer. "Mr. Bakker. He is a German." She could tell them nothing else.

Gerry thought for a while, something deep down stirred in his mind.

"What's bugging you Gerry? Something is suddenly on your mind." Paul asked him, intrigued.

"I'm sure I've heard the name mentioned before but from whom I don't know. Perhaps Daniel has spoken of him, bearing in mind everyone in the town must now know who we are searching for. Let's be honest if I have heard the name before it would have only been in Holland or Germany, not England. In Oosterbeek I spent most of my time either unconscious or semi-conscious." Gerry looked up at Paul. "I think we are onto something serious."

Paul and Gerry immediately prompted Mark to ring the number. Mark went upstairs to his room and picked up the phone and dialled. His conversation was concise and to the point.

Shortly afterwards Mark returned to the table. He was agitated, looked around and then sat back down. "That was this Karina woman we have been speaking of, the nurse. Karina Koster is her full name." He stared solemnly at Gerry. "If she is genuine, then Karina Koster is certainly still alive. In two days time we are to meet her inside the Arnhem -Oosterbeek War Cemetery at ten o'clock. I didn't have a chance to ask exactly where in the cemetery she would be, or what she might be wearing. Her message was brief and the phone went dead."

Gerry was very sceptical. "How could Daniel have ended up in there? The last he was seen was in Fallingbostell. I told you before, the War Graves Commission would have notified his parents or his wife. You should have asked her to come here because I would have recognised her. She was standing by me when I woke up from days in a coma. I knew her well. If Daniel and her were not shagging each other at the time then I still am a dead man. I'm sorry Mark the circumstances do not add up to me. Someone is having us on surely."

Paul nudged him gently. "Calm down Gerry. Why would they pull our legs. At least we have a lead. The staff here have already confirmed that Mr. Bakker delivered the telephone number. We have to go and find out. We can always come back here and continue searching."

They decided that they should travel down to Arnhem but still spent the next day asking questions. Their zeal for the job was considerably dampened by anticipation.

The winds had switched now, blowing in from the north-east. The early November day was freezing cold as Mark, Paul and Gerry walked up the gravelled path to the entrance gates of a very poignant war cemetery. Trees had been planted, leafless but standing tall and straight, lining their route, as saluting despondent soldiers might when their comrade passed by in a resplendently draped coffin. The three men tilted their heads towards a veiled woman dressed in black, sitting on a bench apparently reading a bible. They had deliberately arrived early and solemnly wandered around the place of solitude where few wild birds ventured. Perhaps though, an odd cheeky sparrow flitted onto a head stone.

Snow flecked the air but barely settled. No flowers bloomed, but the colour of the occasional wreaths and bouquets enhanced the sombre winter greyness.

Like a ghost from a terrible past the woman in black had risen from her feet and watched the saddened men inspecting each grave one by one. They read out loud the ages of the deceased lives, destroyed so young. Many were fatherless virgins who had set out on an adventure to create a better world. She tried to imagine what might be passing through the three men's minds after such a terrible event which ended a mere decade ago. Softly she approached them as the snow grew thicker, blown down from the arctic.

"Mr Campbell?" she asked quietly. At first he didn't hear as he was so engrossed in each individual name on the gravestones and she asked again, a little louder.

Woken from his private thoughts he turned and acknowledged the veiled woman with the Bible nestling in her gloved hands. Gerry and Paul stood watching their solemn encounter.

"Come! I'll show you a grave. There are at least one and a half thousand here, but there is one I want to show you in particular." She gestured for his friends to follow.

The four of them stood in front of a headstone. The woman watched them contemplating the engraving. Mark asked her if she had sent the letter to his parents. "Why have you dragged us all this way. This isn't Daniel's grave."

Paul and Gerry stared hard at the epitaph. 1st Parachute Brigade Patrick G. Donaghue. Born 1924. Died September 21st. 1944 between Arnhem and Oosterbeek. Their eyes met and both remembered 'Little Patrick'.

"Keep walking to your right," she asked them.

Each gravestone they read, Paul and Gerry knew the names of their former platoon members. Only about seven had ever made the journey back home. They began to salute each dead soldier.

Mark scrutinised the woman in black. He questioned her motives. "Why have you done this? Why bring us here? You must have sent that note to my parents, but what is this all about? Please tell me!"

She took him by the hand and approached Gerry and Paul. She pointed a finger. "Do you see that tree over there in the middle of the cemetery which has the seat underneath with a gentleman sitting down reading a book. He comes here once a week without fail and helps to tend these particular graves. He claims he knows everyone in this row."

All three looked back along the neat line of graves and then towards the seated gentleman.

She stared at them. "He also claims to know who are not here and assumes they are alive or are missing presumed dead. I think you had better go and speak to him."

As the three men began to walk towards the tree, the solitary man closed his book and stood up. He wasn't reading but watching them all, soberly. He never moved and waited as they approached him. The woman in black silently watched them through her veil and the worsening snow storm.

Before them stood Daniel Godwin. They behaved as if there was a mental barrier between them, as like poles on two magnets. Each had believed Daniel was dead but here he was alive and well. Equally, Daniel had not known what had happened to the men standing before him. Here they were, unapproachable after so many years with so much to say but rendered speechless by war, a lost decade and locked in memories. The woman came and stood by Daniel's side and took his hand. She unveiled herself. Her eye make up had ran haphazardly down her cheeks from tears of mixed emotions. Gerry smiled at the woman who, so many years before, had worked so tirelessly to save him and all the other soldiers trapped in the siege of Oosterbeek. She was his nurse, Karina.

They still kept apart but Mark's eloquence broke the deadlock. "Why didn't you come home Daniel. I know you had problems but there was no reason not to come back to your family, or at least you could have sent a letter."

Karina nudged his elbow prompting Daniel to tell the truth.

Daniel remorsefully set eyes on Mark. "I had a brief affair with Stella when Stuart was away, "he stared at the ground beneath his feet and shook his head in shame, he then very slowly looked up, "Stella became pregnant. I was so embarrassed that I had crossed Stuart in his absence, and my terrible mistake sent me crazy. Everyday felt as if my mind had an infection which couldn't be rid of. Then, when we were kicked out of Europe by the Germans, Stella told me Stuart had been killed in action and what I'd done didn't seem to matter so much, although that was far from an excuse for my behaviour. Stella became pregnant again and we decided to marry which we did, but even then what I had done haunted me. Stuart was an anvil tied around my neck and I couldn't forget him. There has always been questions about who is Caronwyn's father, Stuart or me. Believe me Mark, I cannot forgive myself for what I did behind Stuart's back. I am so ashamed."

"Is that the only reason why you wouldn't come home?" Gerry asked him, rather curious.

Paul then asked him "So what was in that letter that made you decide never to come home? The one you received just before we left for Arnhem."

"All Stella said was that some time after the D-Day landings Stuart had been found alive. She didn't elaborate. She just told me he was alive." Daniel watched them all, fearing that something was wrong.

Mark stole a glance. "I spoke to your father only this last week. Stuart was found alive but I am afraid what you don't know, or Stella hadn't told you in the letter, was that he suffered major head injuries and now recognises no-one. Most of his brigade died or were captured but he was kept alive by a French couple. He sits rocking back and forth perpetually. Stuart needs full time care and he now lives with his mother back in Dornoch in the north of Scotland, and ironically with his father who, so I have been told, always hated him. Apparently Stuart wouldn't know you if he saw you. I am afraid he is effectively almost brain dead. Great man though he was, I am sorry to be the one to tell you, but that is the truth. He is effectively a living vegetable."

"Where was he all that time?" Daniel asked him.

"I have just told you, the French woman and her husband had taken him in and looked after him until the end of the German occupation. She claimed he was her nephew. The German's didn't know any different because he couldn't speak as he had been rendered utterly useless by an artillery shell." Mark could only tell him what James, Daniel's father, had told him.

Daniel glanced at Karina who clung firmly onto his arm. "So what happened to Stella and the children?"

Mark stared up at the white sky then looked back at his old friend. "I am afraid it is a long story. It is best we went somewhere warm and I'll tell you there. Come here Daniel you've been a fool. But I still love you!"

Karina stood back and watched four grown men embracing each other unable to speak because of their floods of tears. War, she had concluded long before, was a crying game brought on by unnecessary deaths and injuries because of decisions by inept politicians and despot dictators. Everyone became affected, men, women and children, old and young. She fully understood these men's emotions as she had seen what they had been through. Although caught up as a neutral, she had witnessed with her own eyes one of the most devastating and irrelevant battles of the second world war. Some of the brave men, herself and her colleagues had managed to save, but many now lay dead, clinically laid out in neat rows and marked by marbled white headstones before her. Each was a lost soul. A deceased son, brother, father, uncle or perhaps even a grandfather. As the snow swirled downwards and began to settle Karina scanned the whole cemetery and tried, as she had tried so many times before, to contemplate the reasons for such an unnecessary loss of young life.

Before the four men left the cemetery together they gave a solemn salute in honour of those who had given their lives in the fight against tyranny. Karina followed. Her own life had also been blighted by the war.

Time was running out for Mark as he had to return to Nairobi. He made several phone calls from the hotel. One was particularly disturbing. He went to the 'Centrum Bar' and found Daniel, Paul and Gerry. He told Daniel what he had heard. His words were simple, Rob Goode, Daniel's godfather had passed away.

Having finally persuaded Daniel to return home, however temporary, Mark booked their flights back to London and arranged for a limousine to meet them on arrival at the airport. Karina would travel with them. Mark was a very privileged man in the Kenyan civil service, but the costs he would pay for himself.

On the plane the tension in Daniel's mind was apparent. As the flight came closer to London, the more he wrung his hands. Karina tried to hold them but he squeezed her own until she could bear the pain no longer. Paul and Gerry broached past subjects in an attempt to keep his mind off the inevitable reunion with his family and friends. Politics became the topic of conversation rather than the war, which was nearly ten years in the past, although, in awe, nuclear weaponry was mentioned.

As they approached the City of Bath along the London Road, Daniel grew ever more nervous. Butterflies disturbed his stomach. Just outside the small town of Corsham he asked to stop the car. He climbed out and stood by the stonewall, coughing. He tried to heave up the acid in his fraught stomach. Karina patted him heavily on the back and slowly he recovered from his attack. Daniel pointed across the valley some two miles away towards the village upon the hill and its prominent church. "Colerne," he said wistfully, "Colerne. There is where my heart lies Karina. Maybe that is where I can find my children." He turned towards her and kissed her. She held his hand evermore tightly. Daniel was so close to home, within sight but not quite there.

Black Mark prompted them to get back into the car as time was running out.

The chauffer pulled up as near to the Abbey as possible where hundreds of people had gathered and were slowly making their way inside. The situation became clear that not everyone would be able to have a seat. The ten bells were peeling. The atmosphere was far from complete solemnity. Few wore black. Judith had asked the funeral attendance to respect Rob's dying wishes. Mark left the Bentley and approached the verger who was quietly and politely ushering the congregation inside. They spoke briefly and Mark decided to wait and returned to sit patiently in the car.

Soon after he saw someone he knew. "Daniel! Look!" Mark pointed to a small entourage of people who had gathered amongst the crowd. "Come on let's go. It is your mother and father."

Daniel was still unsure of himself and he grabbed Mark by the shoulder. "Please no! This is not the time. This is Robbie Goode's funeral. Not a family reunion. Please Mark, with all due respect, wait until later."

Mark obliged him and waited until most of the mourners had passed through the doors of the beautiful Bath Abbey.

They abandoned their car and walked across the road and eventually entered the Abbey. Each politely made room for themselves, shuffling into position amongst the other mourners and standing at the very back only just inside the nave. Daniel could see the privileged friends of Rob Goode sitting near the front. He had difficulty recognising them. Karina studied his face and then tried to see who he was trying to scrutinise. They had their backs to him but he recognised his mother whose own hair was now grey and she sat next to his father, James, whilst leaning on his ailing shoulder. The young woman with them he could only presume was his sister Helen, and perhaps her husband at her side. There were two adolescent girls sitting between them, maybe older, one, Ruby he thought, his youngest sister who he hardly knew. Next to her was a young boy. Herbie was next to the forever beautiful Sarah, his wife, who would probably console Rob's ageing parent's when they came to sit down in the front row. Two older men sat behind them. He presumed they were his uncles, Andrew, his mother's brother, and Jim his father's brother. Daniel wasn't sure, they had their backs to him. With them were possibly his aunts Jennifer and Elizabeth, both with their partners. Daniel found difficulty in recognising them all after so many years of absence.

A sparrow flitted around from window to window searching for a way out, having been trapped in the dour proceedings. The long candles at the altar flickered occasionally caused by the influx of external air. The choir sat solemnly awaiting the arrival of the coffin of the deceased, Rob Goode. The murmurs ceased when the organist struck up a more positive note and the seated congregation rose from their pews. Never before had the Abbey been so full at a funeral for many years.

The great oak doors were slowly opened and the pallbearers carried in the coffin of Robert Henry Goode. Daniel and Mark touched the wooden box gently with respect as they slowly passed by. With help from Judith, Rob's aged parents followed and then his immediate family. Sadness prevailed even more so, as no-one ever wishes to attend their own son or daughter's funeral, however old.

The congregation settled down.

The reverend spoke some short but reassuring words about the life of Robert Henry Goode. He made a numerical reference to the hymn book. The recital of 'Amazing Grace' followed.

> Amazing grace! How sweet the sound
> That saved a wretch like me!
> I once was lost but now am found;
> Was blind, but now I see
> 'T was grace that taught my heart to fear,
> And grace my fears relieved,
> How precious did that grace appear
> The hour I first believed.
>
> Through many dangers, toils and snares,
> I had already come,
> 'Tis grace has brought me thus far,
> And grace will lead me home.
>
> The Lord has promised good to me,
> His word my hope secures,
> He will my shield and portion be,
> As long as life endures.
> Yea, when this flesh and heart should fail,
> And mortal life shall cease,
> I shall possess within the veil,
> A life of joy and peace.
> When we've been here ten thousand years,
> Bright shining as the sun,
> We've no less days to sing God's praise,
> Than when we first begun.
> Amazing grace, how sweet the sound,

That served a wretch like me.
I once was lost but now am found,
Was blind, but now I see.

Afterwards he then mentioned Rob's selfless life and the work he had put in for so many years at the hostel for the injured and crippled ex-soldiers of the first world war. He read a prayer and then asked a young man to come forth and read a poem.

"George, please take the lectern," he asked politely.

Nervously George rose from his seat, edged along the pew in front of his grandparent's and stepped into the aisle. He held a piece of paper to his chest and climbed the few steps up to the lectern. He placed his paper onto the opened Bible and sombrely glanced up toward the inner roof of the abbey. The young man took a deep breath.

Strangely the captive sparrow briefly landed on Rob's coffin, hopped around as if searching for food and then made a dash for freedom through the open abbey doors, outside of which, a large crowd had gathered.

George smiled. Young as he was he looked sympathetically towards his assembly. "Some years ago Mr. Robbie Goode told me a simple story which I will never forget." He paused in thought and briefly looked upwards. "I am stood here in God's house, embarrassed to tell you what he said to me." George paused again. "Robbie told me there were only three God's. Firstly, the sun, without which we cannot exist. Secondly, the moon, whose gravitational pull gives us our tidal systems which affects two thirds of our globe. Robbie Goode then told me that the third God was our Earth itself, the Earth which upon we stand. Never abuse any of them he told me. Treat all people the same with equal kindness and also the plants and animals which thrive from the influence of our Sun, Moon and Earth." George remained quiet for which seemed a long time. He then continued. "Judith, Rob's wife, came to me four days ago and asked if I would read this poem written by Major John McRae in the first world war. It was Rob's choice." George perused the notepaper he had before him. There was nothing written down. He had promised himself he would recite from memory. George viewed his audience and caught sight of the tall dark skinned man standing at the back of the abbey. He then glanced at the man standing next to the stranger and felt sure he recognised them both, if only from a photograph. He made eye contact with his grandmother and nodded to the rear of the congregation. Joy had wondered what was stalling her grandson from reading the poem. She quickly looked over her shoulder and caught sight of her eldest son, Daniel. She stood up and held her face in her hands and began to cry. James pulled her back down but she was inconsolable. George began the poem. At first he stuttered but was resolved to complete its oratory;

> In Flanders fields the poppies blow
> Between the crosses, row by row,
> That mark our place; and in the sky
> The larks, still bravely singing, fly
> Scarce heard amid the guns below.
> We are the dead. Short days ago
> We lived, felt dawn, saw sunset glow,
> Loved and were loved, and now we lie
> In Flanders Fields
> Take up your quarrel with the foe:
> To you from failing hands we throw
> The torch: be yours to hold it high.
> If ye break faith with us who die
> We shall not sleep, though poppies grow
> In Flanders fields.

Throughout his recital 'Little George' kept his eyes on the man whom he believed could well be his father. He stepped down and returned to sit by his grandmother. He whispered in her ear, asking about the man standing at the back. His grandmother was not listening. He squeezed her hand. His grandfather, James, had come to realise who was amongst the congregation behind them, but tried to remain calm and patient. Rob Goode's funeral procedure was the priority. Prayers were read and another hymn was recited. 'I Will Sing the Wondrous song'.

Afterwards Herbie, with great difficulty, stood on the pulpit and told stories of his great friend and how he had designed his own funeral template with the help of his forever loving wife, Judith. Judith now knew herself that Daniel was in the Abbey. She realised now how her husband had designed his own funeral service. Robbie had seen so much sadness and had always told her that when he goes to his grave to make sure everyone was cheerful. Coincidentally, and shortly before Rob had died, Mark Campbell had turned up, searching for his best friend Daniel after so many years. Judith smiled. Her darling husband had made his choice of the final song. The jig-saw was finally in place.

Herbie couldn't help continually glancing towards the standing congregation. He hesitated with his own words and stared down at James, Joy, little George, as he was commonly known, Helen and Ruby, none of whom were now preoccupied with the funeral service. Before he stepped down he asked the congregation to listen or sing along with one of the finest young female choral singers in Bath. He gestured toward a young lady. "May I introduce you to Caronwyn Sinclair."

In the pulpit the young woman faced the congregation. The organist remained silent. Unaccompanied she began to sing. Nobody attempted to sing along with her. The whole congregation stood in appreciation as the body of Robert Henry Goode was slowly and respectfully removed from the Abbey and taken to his burial ground. The incredibly beautiful voice of Caronwyn Sinclair resonated between the abbey walls. Robert Henry Goode had his last dying wish. Childless himself, Daniel his godson, had returned home. Judith, his devoted wife, dampened her reddened eyes.

>Oh Danny boy the pipes, the pipes were calling
>From glen to glen, and down the mountain sides
>The summer's gone and all the roses are fading
>'Tis you, tis you must bide and I must go
>But come ye back when summer's in the meadow
>Or when the valley's hushed and white with snow
>'Tis I'll be here in sunshine or in shadow
>Oh Danny boy, oh Danny boy I love you so.
>But if you come, when all the flowers are dying
>And I am dead, as dead I well may be
>You'll come and find the place where I am lying
>And kneel and say an 'Ave' there for me.
>But I shall hear, tho' soft you tread above me
>And then my grave will warm and sweeter be
>For ye shall bend and tell me that you love me
>I'll simply sleep in peace until you come to me.
>I'll simply sleep in peace until you come to me.

The End